STARGÅTE
SG·1·ATLÅNTIS ™

FAR HORIZONS

Volume One of The Travelers' Tales

SALLY MALCOLM (EDITOR)

FANDEMONIUM BOOKS

An original publication of Fandemonium Ltd, produced under license from MGM Consumer Products.

Fandemonium Books
United Kingdom
Visit our website: www.stargatenovels.com

STARGÅTE
SG•1•ATLÅNTIS
TM

Print ISBN: 978-1-905586-67-7 Ebook ISBN: 978-1-80070-057-4

CONTENTS

Editor's Foreword

This year marks Fandemonium Books' tenth birthday. To celebrate, we've commissioned ten original Stargate short stories from ten fantastic authors.

We think there's something in this anthology for everyone, with tales that capture all the adventure, humor and comradery that make STARGATE SG-1 and STARGATE ATLANTIS two of the most beloved sci-fi TV shows of all time.

The last ten years have been an amazing journey for Fandemonium Books, but we couldn't have done it without our wonderful authors. Their talent and genuine passion for the shows, and for the characters we all love, have allowed us bring to life almost fifty new Stargate adventures in the past decade. We're hugely grateful to them all.

But, most importantly, we couldn't have done any of this without you, our readers. Thank you so much for your enthusiasm and loyalty, and for sharing with us your love of the Stargate universe. With your help, we'll keep the gate open for another ten years of fun and adventure…

Sally Malcolm
Commissioning Editor
October 2014

STARGATE SG-1
Draw Down the Moon

Suzanne Wood

"It is not amusing, O'Neill."

"Oh, c'mon, T. How can you not find that funny? One of the all-time best jokes. You gotta laugh."

"I do not."

Jack O'Neill heaved out an exasperated sigh. He looked around the empty stretch of beach and appealed to the rest of his team. "It's *funny*."

"Perhaps it's your delivery, sir."

Carter hopped off the mostly buried Stargate platform and picked her way over sand drifts to check on the DHD.

Daniel averted his eyes, but Jack could see a grin trying to sneak out.

"Daniel thinks it's funny," he said, a little too desperately.

"Actually, I was picturing you and Teal'c doing a stand-up routine. He's the perfect straight man."

Daniel scuttled off up the beach before he could offer any more opinions about his leader's comic abilities. Wise move.

"Okay. Well, here we are." Jack eyed the surf crashing onto the empty beach, the shining white sand that stretched for a couple of kilometers along a crescent bay. "Guess we'd better make our presence known, then."

As planets went, this was one of the nicer ones. SG-1 had, for once, had a win when they drew P3X-228 in the mission rota. After a string of missions that had proved less than successful, if not downright death-defying, they had pulled this one. Three months earlier, they had spent an uneventful two days here in the sun, surf and sand. And weren't Coburn and the other team leaders just a little bit envious when he'd told them, in intricate detail, about this island chain where the most dangerous thing SG-1 had encountered was mild sunburn and not being physically able to sample all the local cuisine. Jack fully intended to catch up this time on the dishes he'd missed.

The locals, a cheery bunch of humans led by a lady called Rosal, had invited them to return for some big ceremony; something to do with the moon. That, of course, had been shelved as unimportant to the SGC, until Coburn and his team, trading for information during another mission, had come up with the gem that the good folk of P3X-228 possessed some kind of protective shield on their planet. A return trip was bumped up the rota, and here they were. Privately, Jack didn't believe they'd missed a shield on their first trip, but, hey, stranger things had happened. And they could certainly do with a little R&R.

Teal'c took point and headed along the beach. Jack ambled along in the rear. To their right, a tumble of rocks rose out of the sand. SG-1 skirted the pile of boulders that stood a couple of hundred meters high to form the backbone of this island. It was the first in the group of three islands and held the small settlement his team had originally visited.

Barely halfway along the beach, Teal'c raised his staff and pointed to a group of people who had rounded the furthest end of the rocks and were jogging toward them.

"Nice lookout system they've got."

Jack searched the rocks but could not pick the spot that hid whomever had spied their arrival. Friendly folk or not, things like that made him jumpy.

The two groups came together rapidly; the islanders skipped and trotted along the sand, waving happily as they neared. Children darted in and out of the waves while the adults chatted and called out to their visitors. Bright, delicate sarong-like skirts fluttered on men and women alike. Jack felt over-dressed in his desert camo t-shirt and tac vest.

"Ayehoy! Ayehoy!"

Jack recognized Rosal, the mature lady who was the local equivalent of a town mayor. Behind her were Piday and Honet who had given over their home to SG-1 on the previous visit.

"Rosal, ayehoy to you," Daniel said. He got the pronunciation perfect, as Jack knew he would. "You recall Teal'c, Sam and Jack? We have returned for the moon festival."

Rosal stepped forward and dispensed a floral-scented hug to each of them. "We are so pleased you have come to share our Triad festival. You honor our people and our blessed one. Welcome. Welcome."

Daniel flashed a glance at Jack and turned back to Rosal. "We thought the festival marked the confluence of the moons."

"It does, dear guest." Rosal beamed at them. She ran her hands through her long sun-bleached hair, freeing strands and woven ribbons to flutter in the wind. "You are fortunate. This festival falls on the day of our blessed one, so there is to be a double celebration!"

"Blessed one?" Funny how such innocuous words could send a chill down a guy's back. One of the reasons Jack had been happy to return was the lack of local deities.

Rosal laughed and beckoned them to follow along the beach.

"It is an old name from the times of our mother's mothers," she said. "The ancestors would lay out shells and dried fish in baskets made from the reeds that grow along the tidal river. They would leave them when the moon was full and she would bless the people with full bellies and true hearts."

"And does the deity have a name?" Daniel strode alongside Rosal, their conversation floated clearly back to his team mates.

"Oh, she was known by many names — Lady of the Road, Birth Mother, Moon Witch — just about every family has a different name for her."

"I see."

Daniel's expression lightened and he gave a surreptitious nod to Jack. He dropped back to pace alongside.

"Are we about to have a problem here?" Jack muttered.

"I don't think so. It sounds more like local beliefs, passed down through the generations, than a Goa'uld imposing a belief system on them. We didn't see anything here last time that made me suspect a Goa'uld presence."

Jack grunted. "Keep your eyes and ears open, just in case."

The beach trek turned inland along a path paved with slabs cut from the slate-like rocks, through sand dunes capped with grass and wind-stunted bushes. People were scattered all along the sand and up in the rocks; many waved and called out as the group passed. The roar of the surf diminished as they entered the settlement. A cluster of thirty houses hunkered amongst the rock formations, their wood and stone facades faced a wide spit of sand that had been submerged by the sea on the team's previous visit. Now exposed, the spit ran for over two kilometers to the second island in the group. This island was a post-volcanic mountain, its steep sides blanketed in lush forests. Another tiny town lay in the folds of a valley. By design or chance it looked back toward the first settlement across the spit.

"Wow, this is quite a change from our last visit."

Carter stood on top of a boulder to get a better view of the bustling roads. What had been two isolated islands were now joined by an exposed causeway. The sea had retreated a considerable distance under the convergent moons' influence. People now moved freely from one town to the other.

"There is much rejoicing when the moon-way opens for us," Rosal said. "Families are reunited, food and wares traded, tales are told. It is a good time. See there… ?" She pointed out a young couple heading for the causeway. They pulled a wooden cart loaded with furnishings. "Ellene and Jante have betrothed and leave to begin their joined lives on Second Island."

"And what of those who live on that island?"

Teal'c indicated another island across a wide stretch of brilliant aqua-colored water. It was relatively flat and sported another small settlement that gazed from the closest shore back at its sisters.

"The Third Islanders must come to us in their *doccies* at all times, except for tonight and the next night." Rosal's teenage son, Curti, bounced up to them.

"And what makes these nights so special?" Jack found the young man's excitement infectious.

"Moon Witch brings her two sisters together and draws back the sea. We are able to walk across to Third Island and bring their harvest to the other islands. We must be fast, though, because the Three Sisters will separate and let the water come between us again."

"That would be the conjunction of the moons, sir." Carter was scanning the afternoon sky. "Our own moon has been known to generate huge tidal events back on Earth."

"We invite you all to join our people and celebrate," Rosal said.

"Thank you, we are honored to share this time with you." Daniel had his camera out, already capturing the bustle of folk around the houses and crossing the causeway.

"Carter, why don't you and Daniel get to know the folks here? Teal'c, feel like taking a walk?"

Teal'c followed his glance to the causeway beyond. "I do, O'Neill. I find the sea air most invigorating."

Curti plucked at Jack's sleeve. "May I guide you, Colonel Jack? I know where the biggest sand claws can be found."

"I like a man with a plan. Lead on."

Daniel watched Jack and Teal'c follow the teenager down the road and on to the now exposed causeway.

Rosal excused herself and most of the locals had already returned to their work. The smell of baked food drifted from the houses. Baskets filled with woven blankets, finely made clothes, and other goods ready for trade were being assembled beneath a tall lamp post at the edge of what amounted to a village green.

"I need to look for those power signatures I picked up last time," Sam said.

He was going to say, 'Sure, where do you want to try?' Instead he blurted, "Do you hear that, Sam?"

A weird soughing moan caught his attention. Then another, a key higher and longer held than the first. Curious, they couldn't see the source of the noise. None of the locals paid it any notice, either.

"How about we go around the shoreline," Sam said. "We spent most of the last visit climbing through the rocks and I didn't find anything there."

He let her lead the way down the main path toward the water. As he reached the lamp post and its accumulation of baggage, Daniel paused. Another path intersected theirs, the two paved in stone for a short distance reaching away from the lamp.

"Something interesting?"

"Oh, no, well… a little. This is a crossroad — of sorts."

"That happens when two paths meet."

"Yes, but these have been paved and the edges are well kept." He looked around at the shaggy coastal grass that grew all over, none of which had been cropped like that edging the paths. The rest of the pathways were beaten earth and followed the contours of the land.

Sam studied the crossing paths and the tall, stone lamp post in the center.

"Significant?"

"Maybe. Or, sometimes a crossroad is just a crossroad."

They moved on, turning away from the causeway Jack and Teal'c were embarking upon. The path they followed wound down to the sandy beach, noticeably narrower on this side of the island. The noise and chatter of the islanders quickly faded, replaced by the rustle of long grass lining sand dunes and the high, piercing cries of sea birds.

Sam tucked her hair under a boonie and chose a trail along the top of the dunes. Daniel looked edgily at the water, more than glad to keep a nice distance from it.

"All this water —" Sam waved her hand at the brilliant

expanse between the islands. "Brings back memories."

"Yeah, ones I'm still fuzzy on. Not that I'm not okay with that." He still got flashes of drifting through the living water of the world connected to the Russian Stargate.

"You don't want to know who or what that water was?" She slowed to walk next to him.

"I do, yes. It's an incredible life form, but it's the whole drowning/not drowning thing I'm having trouble with. We don't know what happened to us after we were pulled from the sub."

"I know. Wish we could go back."

"One day. Maybe. When we can speak 'water'."

Sam laughed. "That will be another first for you."

"I can wait."

The curiosity that had made him push his hand into the sentient water was well and truly buried by a desire not to drown any time soon.

"Hey, Daniel. There's that sound again."

The unharmonious moan was coming from further up the shore. They jogged along the track for ten minutes, drawn on by the sound that teased their senses; one moment they were certain it was close by, the next it was faint and far away. A small headland drew them around a corner to a small inlet. Emerald-hued waves crashed onto a rocky shore. Here, the sound was much clearer and louder.

"Sounds like an organ… played really badly."

Daniel frowned. He searched for the source of the sounds.

"There — what's that?"

He hopped across rocks to a flat-topped boulder. Set in the top of the rock was an intricately worked metal grill. He knelt down for a better look. A blast of sound and warm salty air hit him in the face.

"Whoa!"

He reeled back, slid off the boulder and slithered to a stop several rocks down the beach.

"Found it!"

Sam took his place on the flat-topped rock. Holding her hand over the grill, she smiled as a soft gush of air flowed out, accompanied by a low-toned musical note.

"I think I know what this is. Daniel, can you look down on the waterline — is there another grill like this one?"

He scrambled over the fall of rocks down to the line of waves lapping the shore. Sure enough, he quickly located another metal grill molded into the face of the rock. He dug behind it and discovered the rock was actually the mouth of a pipe tunneled under the rocks and presumably leading up to the vent where Sam stood. As Daniel watched, a wave rolled in, covered the grill and seconds later an oddly sweet moan emanated from the top.

"Huh. Well, they must be connected. What is it?"

"I think it's a tide organ," Sam called down. "The waves displace the air in the pipe, creating the sound. Just like an organ."

Another wave reached the end of its journey and set off a rolling chorus of tunes all across the inlet.

Intrigued, Daniel splashed through the waves and foamy detritus, looking for more pipes. He found another as Sam located the corresponding outlet above him.

The tide was starting to come in now with greater vigor and soon the pipes produced a non-stop parping. Sound filled Daniel's ears. As more pipes were brushed by the waves, the music melded together and began to sound harmonious. Entranced, he waved up to Sam. She waved back, then called down to him on the radio.

"Daniel, I'm picking up an energy reading. Could be that shield."

"Can you locate it?"

"No. It's fluctuating all over the place."

"Think the tide organ is related to the shield?"

"Possibly… maybe… It's gone. Completely dropped of the scale."

By contrast, the tide organ was showing no sign of diminishing. As the incoming tide pushed up the beach, the odd song increased until all the pipes were in action.

Sam slipped and slithered over the unstable sand on top of the dunes, sometimes crawling on all fours to discover the grilled outlet for the next tidal organ pipe. It was a remarkably simple but effective piece of engineering. Now that she was getting used to the sounds it produced, she found the atonal notes soothing, even mesmerizing.

Fourteen pipes located, none the same distance from each other. She sat back on her heels for a moment. From this height, she could see Third Island, its fields a patchwork in shades of green and brown surrounded by a white rim of surf and the emerald water. The wider ocean was a deeper blue-green, unbroken by other land masses. Whoever had chosen these islands for a Stargate had certainly chosen well.

"The water holds its beauty and mystery in equal measure."

Sam started and whipped around. A woman approached, elegantly mastering the shifting sands. She was dressed the same as the islanders, her long red sarong fluttered behind her like fairy wings.

"Oh. Hello, there."

The woman nodded. She stopped on the crest of the dune, gazing in turn at the magnificent vista before them, and at Daniel pottering around the shore. She folded her hands over her belly, which, Sam realized, was a near-term pregnancy.

"I'm Sam. Samantha Carter, one of the visitors. We found your tide organ. I hope its okay to study it. We're looking for the source of some power readings."

"The music belongs to the air and the sea. I do not believe they will deny you."

"That's — very — er, thanks."

"You seek power other than that which resides within you?"

"I... don't have any powers," Sam replied, thinking for some reason that the woman was talking about superpowers.

Although, sensing Goa'uld could be called a superpower. Being a successful woman in a man's air force was one too.

"You have the power to create with your body. Is that not a power?"

"Yes, of course." She glanced at the baby bump with a certain amount of envy.

"The ability to destroy must always be tempered with creation, do you not agree?"

"Destroy? I don't…" Blow stuff up? Well, yeah, but usually in a good cause. Guess saving others' lives could be called creation. *Why are we talking about this?* "Um, what are you going to call the baby?"

"Her name is Diana."

"That's nice. Well, I'd better get back to what I was doing. Day's nearly ended."

"Yes, the moons approach."

The woman gazed out to sea for a long moment, then turned and continued on her way. Sam watched her go until Daniel's call from the beach jolted her back to business.

"It's getting late," he said. *"We'd better head back, see if Jack and Teal'c have found anything."*

Dinner that evening was a merry affair. The night air was still warm and the team sat amidst the villagers and visitors from Second Island. Food piled everyone's plates in an endless and wonderful variety. Jokes and stories circulated the tables set up in the open green space and had everyone laughing.

Jack sat at a table to one side of the roasting fire in the middle of the gathering, relaxed and replete. From his seat he could see Carter and Daniel laughing at a tale told by newly-wed Jante. Across the square, Teal'c sat listening politely, eyes watchful and not missing a movement. They traded glances. Nothing awry. All is well.

He and Teal'c had walked the causeway and met a nice bunch of fisher-folk who swiftly offered an invitation to join a boating event planned for the next day. He'd accepted, not just because it sounded like a heap of fun. His kids were finally getting a chance to unwind. After a string of trying missions with dubious successes, topped off with an unexpected sky dive, and a deep-sea dive for Daniel and Carter — they could all use a break for a couple of days.

A clanging bell broke him out of his reverie. Immediately, people began to rise from their tables. Rosal walked into the center of the gathering with raised hands.

"Kin and friends and our honored guests, the sea retreats and the way is open to Third Island. Come!"

Jack rose and meandered through the crowd to Carter, Daniel and Teal'c.

"Have enough for dinner?"

"Way more than enough." Daniel patted his stomach and repressed a burp.

"These islands provide an impressive bounty," Teal'c declared, still clutching a warm fish cake in one hand.

Jack grinned. "How about we join these good people and work it off?"

They merged into the flow of people heading down to the causeway. As they passed the lamp post, Jack hefted a basket full of new shoes onto his shoulder.

"How often do they do this trade with the other island?"

"The tide recedes far enough only once a year." Daniel balanced a tray of baked pies in his hands. "They do cross by boat the rest of the year but these extreme tides come at the end of their harvest season, so it's a good opportunity to walk over and trade goods and grain."

"And generally party."

"That too."

"Sweet. Carter, keep your doohickey on. We need to pin down the location of this power reading… signal… thing."

"Doohickey at the ready, sir."

She snapped a salute at him and picked up a basket of turnipy-looking vegetables. He narrowed his eyes at her back as they moved down to the shore. She was really starting to refine that attitude-as-an-art-form routine.

He felt so proud.

In the gray-toned light of two risen moons, the exposed sea floor sparkled. Tiny rock pools still filled with water lay between patches of sand and rock. The island folk scattered across a wide area as they made their way to Third Island. From the shore of that island Jack could see a flock of people making their way toward them.

His boot slid off a piece of weed and into a pool, soaking his foot. A creature, long, white and scaly, flashed out of the pool's shadow and snapped an impressive array of sharp teeth at his leg.

"Damn."

He jerked his leg out of reach. Cold water absorbed into his sock. He sighed and placed his burden on the sea floor. If there was one thing he hated, it was walking with wet feet. You could almost hear the tinea growing. He undid his boot and pulled it off. As he balanced on one leg, wringing the sock out, he became aware somebody had halted next to him.

"Don't say it, Daniel."

"I am not Daniel, therefore I cannot say what it is he would have said."

Jack glanced up, overbalanced, and put his foot in the pool again.

"Aht!"

"May I assist?"

A hand steadied him. Jack looked up at a striking woman, tall, white hair falling free around a face that had seen many years. The strength in her grip was at odds with her apparent age. Her lean body spoke of a life well lived. She carried a carved stool, one of the goods for trade, which she placed on the rock in front of him.

"Why, thank you, ma'am."

He plopped his butt on the stool and fished in his pockets for his emergency socks. "Name's Jack O'Neill. I don't think we've met before."

"We have not."

The lady crouched by the pool and trailed her fingers across the surface.

"Careful, there's a thing in there with lots of teeth: sharp teeth."

"Yes, they live in the shadows. The departure of the water disturbs them."

The ghostly creature showed its head above the water. Intrigued, Jack watched the woman stroke its scales. It nuzzled her hand for a moment, then slid back into its hidey-hole.

"You have a knack with, er, those things."

"All creatures have goodness in their nature. One needs only to treat them with kindness for it to be returned to you."

He pulled his boot back on over a dry sock. "Wise words."

"Wisdom comes to all, whether the passage of time be short or long."

Jack looked her over carefully as she rose unhindered by creaky joints or old bones. He stood and concealed a scowl at the twinge from his left knee. "Didn't catch your name."

"I am called Diana by many."

He handed her the stool. "Thanks for the helping hand."

"Fair journey to you, Jack O'Neill."

She walked on toward the island, long hair swinging with her stride.

"Sir?"

Carter was walking back to him.

"Yeah, coming. Just… paddling my toes."

"Oh. Well, I just got a massive spike on the readout." She waved the doohickey in a circle, then glowered at it. "But now it's gone again."

"Seems to happen a lot here."

"Mmhmm."

She shook her head and retraced her steps. Jack picked up his basket of shoes and followed, giving the rock pools his close observation and a wide berth.

Third Island turned out to be quite ordinary. Beyond the tall trees along the shore that provided a wind break inland, there were large fields filled with grain, vegetable, and foliage crops. There was no town as such, just a communal hall that faced across the strait in view of the other two islands. Fields defined by meandering rock walls stretched from one side of the island to another, with little blue and yellow painted houses tucked into a corner of each field.

Jack dropped his basket in the pile growing beneath a stone lamp post that matched the one on First Island. Daniel was staring up at the lamp.

"You have that look."

"What look?"

"That look you get when something doesn't add up."

"I have a look that says that?"

Daniel dipped his head, peered over his glasses and raised his eyebrows: his classic *I don't believe Jack* look.

"Forget it. What's so curious about a lamp post?"

"Nothing, *per se*. It's just a mix of things: a monument standing at a crossroad, a lamp as a monument…"

"That's a crossroad?" Jack scuffed his boot in the dirt track at the foot of Daniel's 'monument'. He could barely make out the other track, more an impression in the ground, which intersected it.

"Well," Daniel waved an uncertain hand. "Crossroads are a significant symbol in many cultures."

"I repeat my question. You think the lamp has anything to do with this shield that's supposed to be here?"

"Uh, ye — er, well, no. Sam said it's not giving off any power readings, same as the one on First Island."

"Some times a lamp is just a lamp."

"Yeah."

He patted Daniel's shoulder.

"How long do we have here?"

"Come, everybody, come gather up our goods. The tide returns soon as we must also return to our homes."

Rosal bustled past, directing people to stacks of grain bags and small hand carts filled with vegetables.

"Not long, apparently."

Daniel quirked a smile at him and went to load up for the return trip. Jack caught sight of Teal'c and Carter in the throng of people. Carter shook her head — nothing new to point the way to this supposed shield. He was going to have a chat with Coburn about wild goose chases when they got home.

Next morning brought a day vibrant with sunshine. Teal'c stood on the bank of the causeway, his break-of-day exercises finished, the blood in his veins singing, his body primed with strength and hungering for the coming activities. He fished out the sunglasses O'Neill had given him before embarkation. Although he had no need for them — his symbiote shielded his eyes from sun damage — he had tried them on in the gear-up room and was forced to admit O'Neill was correct: they looked cool.

He slid the glasses on and struck a pose designed to show all, including his team leader, that he was a man not to be challenged. Also, that he looked pretty cool.

"Oh, Teal'c!"

O'Neill ambled down from their village.

"Good morning, O'Neill."

"Yah, morning."

Despite — many — assertions to the contrary, O'Neill was, as ever, ready to face a day of unknown challenges.

"Are you prepared to undertake Jante's ordeal by water, O'Neill?"

"It's called rafting, T. Should be fun."

O'Neill gave him one of those looks that invariably left Teal'c feeling as if he'd been stripped and searched. "Are you okay with it?"

"I have fallen to earth from one of your airplanes and survived. I believe I shall survive floating over the sea with Jante and his friends."

"It's not something you have to endure. It's supposed to be fun. You'll enjoy it!"

How difficult it was to partake in an activity purely for the purpose of enjoyment. Decades spent in the service of Apophis had brought no enjoyment, merely reward for victory. Nonetheless, he was a part of SG-1 now and, particularly in O'Neill's team, enjoyment was factored into one's daily life.

"Indeed."

A short time later Teal'c stood on the thin beach of Second Island and stared dubiously at the craft he was to use for this enjoyment expedition. He doubted he would actually fit in it, let alone float across the water. Carved from the wood of the trees that covered this island, the *doccy* was barely five feet long, a squat, bulbous wooden blob to which he was supposed to entrust his life.

O'Neill was already floating a few inches offshore, testing the propelling device he'd called a paddle. Daniel Jackson and Major Carter had taken one look at these craft and declared they would spend the day walking in the woods. He could see their pale uniforms etched against the dark trees and ruthlessly quelled the urge to join them.

Entering the vessel was not the most dignified moment of his life.

Teal'c glared at the water sloshing over his legs, which were tucked underneath his body and uncomfortably soaked. He dug the paddle into the water, aiming to follow O'Neill and show his leader that his guffaws — an apt word he had learned from Daniel Jackson — were neither appropriate, nor required.

Oddly, the more he applied the paddle, the more the craft

veered around in a circle.

"Teal'c, may I show you?" Jante powered his vessel alongside with admirable dexterity. "One stroke this side, one stroke the other. That will move you in a straight line."

Teal'c complied, and his course immediately straightened. Confidence filled him and he floated quickly across the water, gaining on O'Neill whose wandering course had taken him halfway across the bay.

"Hey, there he is! Way to go, T. Knew you'd get the hang of it."

"Once one knows the mechanics of the steerage implement it is easy to master."

"Told you."

O'Neill gave his paddle a flick and increased his pace. Teal'c swiftly overtook him. They raced over the brightly colored water, the local women and men surrounded them, engaged in their own private races. The discomfort of wet clothing and potential embarrassment faded. He found that the physical effort, mastery of a new skill and the challenge of overtaking O'Neill, combined with the warmth of the sun and the splash of water, did indeed combine to produce enjoyment. He would not, however, mention this to O'Neill.

They spent a couple of hours paddling across the calm waters of the bay, even halting to partake of refreshments some of their companions had stowed in their craft.

"Do you feel skilled enough to challenge the devil's gap?" Jante asked them.

"And what would that be?" O'Neill's caution was disguised by the smile he liked to consider polite.

Jante pointed to a high cliff at the end of the bay closest to them. Thickly covered with vegetation, it dropped abruptly to the green water, then rose again in a series of steep rock outcrops that jutted out into the deep ocean.

"When the moons join, the tide pulls the water through the devil's gap with great force. It is most exhilarating to ride through."

Teal'c felt a stir of unease, or perhaps it was his symbiote.

"How fast would you say that water goes?" O'Neill's eyes sparkled with interest.

"Faster than the great mountain birds can fly when hunting."

"Pretty fast, then. Teal'c, what do you say?"

O'Neill was eager for this challenge. Teal'c could understand his companion's wish to test himself against a foe that was not actively seeking to kill him or his team mates, particularly after the three months confined to the SGC in the time loop. Golf lessons aside, Teal'c had also found the confinement hard to endure.

"I believe this would be a suitable test of my new ability to traverse over water."

"Let's do it!"

The locals cheered with approval and moved with much splashing toward the rocky gap. As they neared, he could see the water rushing through the opening with great speed. Swirls and eddies marked the surface which was otherwise unbroken. Rocky sides of the cliffs were smoothed by centuries of tidal action.

"How deep is it?" O'Neill called across.

"The bottom has never been seen, even in the lowest tide," said Ellene. "We believe its depth is great."

O'Neill held his craft steady, a not inconsiderable effort as Teal'c too felt the water pulling them toward the gap with increasing strength.

"Allow us to demonstrate."

Ellene lined her little *doccy* a few feet off the center of the flow heading into the gap. She back-paddled energetically, then when the rounded front of her craft was pointed dead on, she let out a whoop and plunged her paddle forward. The little *doccy* shot into the channel and was pulled along with alarming speed.

Ellene deftly guided her passage with one, two strokes, then she was between the cliffs and sucked through to the other side. A joyful whistle floated back to them.

Several more locals rode the water before O'Neill took his turn. He held position for long moments then launched with a hefty stroke of the paddle and a very loud 'Yihaa!'.

Teal'c watched, impressed, as O'Neill sped over the water and disappeared into the bay beyond. Soon only Jante and Teal'c remained.

"Please proceed, Jante. I shall follow."

"Remember, if you get close to the rocks, don't connect with them, it could overbalance the *doccy*."

Jante paddled off enthusiastically. Teal'c was left on his own to contemplate his new-found need for enjoyment.

Well, he could not leave all the 'fun' to O'Neill.

He took aim on the center of the race of water. It did appear higher against the cliff walls now than when Ellene had first embarked.

The moment had come. Teal'c released his *doccy* to the tide's grip. It surged ahead, quicker than expected. He could do little against the power of the water other than adjust his course with a nudge of the paddle. The cliffs loomed overhead. In a flash he was between them, ears assaulted by echoes of gurgling water. An eddy swirled in front of him, slewed him sideways. He dug into the water with the paddle, but his strength was insufficient. The nose of the *doccy* went down. Water flooded the hole in which he sat. Teal'c had time enough to gasp in one lungful of air then the *doccy* was sucked into a dizzying spiral and the water closed over his head.

Teal'c kicked free from the sinking *doccy*, grateful O'Neill had advised him to remove his boots before embarking on this ill-advised adventure. The clarity of the water was remarkable. He clearly saw the protruding rock seconds before his shoulders impacted it. Symbiote-enhanced reflexes allowed him to grab it and stop his body spinning down into the depths.

Resisting the urge to breathe, Teal'c instead forced the symbiote to provide his blood with oxygen. Peering up through the rushing sea, he spied several more rocks offering hand holds.

He reached up and began to climb.

Teal'c had not been long under the sea, but the first breath of air when he broke the surface was delightful. Cautiously, he hauled himself clear of the water, each shift of hand hold threatened to dump him back into the surge below.

"Teal'c!"

O'Neill — paddling furiously but ineffectively against the tide race — bobbed some distance away, frantically calling for him.

Teal'c reached the base of the first tree growing on the side of the cliff. He tested its grip on the rocks, then pulled himself up and straddled the trunk. He relished a deep breath.

"Teal'c! Teal'c!" O'Neill was becoming desperate.

Teal'c stood, clambered further up into the trees and waved down at his friend and hosts. "O'Neill, I am here."

"Oh, for the love of Mike. You okay?"

"I will be fine."

"You wanna jump? We'll pull you in."

Teal'c felt his eyebrows rise. "I do not. I have had enough enjoyment for one day. I shall walk back to the village."

"What if you get lost?"

He opened his mouth. Reconsidered his words and opted for, "I will not."

Once he had climbed to the top of the cliff, Teal'c was pleased to find his clothes drying in the midday sun. Picking a careful path through the forest, he headed around the cliff top, back to the bay — and his boots.

When he finally had his boots back on, Teal'c sat in the sand and allowed himself to relax. He was never comfortable without footwear. One never knew when circumstances would dictate when engagement with an enemy would occur. Even on this apparently friendly world, he would not wish to be at a disadvantage for long.

He replenished his body with some of the food left by the

boating party. With the warm sun and sweet breezes coming off the water, Teal'c found it difficult to deny the impulse for sleep.

A shadow crossed his face. He jolted awake. A young girl stood next to him, bare toes curled in the sand, dark hair twisting loose in the wind.

"Are you lost?"

Teal'c blinked at her. "I am not. Are you?"

"I could never be lost here. This is my home."

"Indeed? It is a most attractive island."

"Yes." Her face dimpled in a smile. The light dress she wore fluttered over the thin body beneath. She was young, barely into her first years as a woman.

"I am Teal'c of the Tau'ri."

"I am Diana. You are very old, aren't you?"

"That I am."

Curious. Not many outside the Jaffa could recognize his unnaturally extended age.

"Many years bring wisdom, does they not?"

"Only if one is open to the accumulation of knowledge." He'd known many senior Jaffa gone to their graves firmly believing Apophis had been a true god.

"The goddess will send her wisdom under the moons' next eve. Will you partake of what is offered?"

"How does your goddess deliver this wisdom?"

"When the moons shine down as one, those who wish can draw inside themselves the goddess's spirit. It is a very special experience."

Teal'c found himself lost for words. Was she describing what he thought? Could this be anything other than a Goa'uld entering a host? Were the potential hosts offering themselves up willingly, or were they being duped into this?

"I do not believe I will take part in this ceremony."

She smiled at him with the ingenuousness of youth. "Perhaps you will change your mind. Farewell."

Teal'c watched the girl until she had vanished into the trees at the far end of the bay. More than a little disturbed, he gathered up his vest and radio.

"SG-1 niner, this is Teal'c. Please respond."

Daniel had enjoyed his day in the forest with Sam. They had followed several trails, now and then picking up those same strange energy signals but each time they dissipated before they could be tracked to a source. He was beginning to believe there was no protective shield to be found. None of the locals had any knowledge of one. There weren't even any tales in their mythology that spoke of a shield that had existed in the past.

"How's it going, Sam?"

He peered up through the branches of one of the tallest trees. Here on the highest part of the island she'd decided to climb up to try for a clearer reading.

"Great, these trees are really easy to climb."

He sidestepped a shower of bark as she settled into a forked branch.

"Hey, I can see Teal'c and the colonel out in the bay. Okay, I'll take some readings now."

Daniel looked around while he waited. The forest was a busy place, humming with insects, birds and small animals. He stilled as a fat ground bird appeared from behind a bush. It paused, then waddled out, leading a troop of chicks. He grinned at them. They walked right past him and disappeared beneath another bush… right next to a pair of bare, sandaled, human feet.

He flinched, looked up, took in a woman clad in a green tunic that perfectly blended with the forest. Her auburn hair was coiled around her head and shone in the sun.

"Hello…" He resisted the urge to look up and give away Sam's presence. The woman studied him. There was a lot of confidence in her hazel eyes. He got an impression that this was a woman who had traveled far and experienced much.

"I'm Daniel."

"I am known as Diana."

"Do you live here — on this island?"

"At times."

"Oh. That's nice. Uh —"

"You are one of the visitors?"

"Yes. We are from a land called Earth."

She nodded. She appeared pleasant, but her sharp gaze was taking in every aspect of him.

"You will not bring harm to those who live on these islands." It was not a question.

"No, not at all. We seek to make friends, trade information. Perhaps we have something that is useful to the people here; maybe they have something here we could trade for, medicines or such."

"Your companion." She glanced up Sam's tree. "She seeks these medicines in the trees?"

"I'm sorry, I hope we haven't broken any taboos in going into the trees. She, uh, actually, we were trying to locate a substance that is giving off power signals. We just wanted to know what caused them."

Diana cocked her head to one side and considered him. "Do you seek this power for your own use?"

"Not — solely, no. If it's something the islanders would benefit from, we would be happy to help them harvest and use it."

"And if they do not wish it harvested?"

"Then we will leave and not disturb them further."

That might require some fudging of mission reports, but that was nothing new to the team.

"Will you attend the festival tonight?"

"Yes, we have been invited." He paused. "Will you be there, Diana?"

"I always attend the Drawing Down of the Moon."

Daniel seized the chance; several times he'd asked the locals what it involved, but gotten only vague descriptions that ranged from a block party to a religious experience. "Can you tell me — what happens in this festival?"

"The three sisters — Virbius, Egeria and Diana — rise as one and stand united in the sky. The people witness their joining and draw the moons' blessings down into their souls. It is a most moving and beautiful experience."

He held himself carefully, trying not to show the unease making gooseflesh on his skin. "They draw the moons' blessings inside?"

"They do."

"And you're named after one of those moons?"

"I have that honor."

"Then what happens?"

"Those who are open to accepting the blessing are given rich and rewarding lives." She smiled, an innocent and genuine smile.

"Daniel?" Sam called down, interrupting his next question. "Who are you talking to?"

"Sam —"

He looked up. She was making her way back down the tree. He turned back to the woman… who had vanished. He spun around, but she was not to be seen.

Sam jumped the last few feet. "What's going on?"

Daniel frowned. "I think I just met a Goa'uld."

"*A Goa'uld?*"

Funny how Jack could shout while maintaining a whisper.

They were all back in the guest hut. Jack still had sea salt crusted on his face. Daniel and Sam had arrived minutes after Jack, and Daniel wasted no time filling the others in.

"Well, possibly. She wasn't your normal bow-down-or-I'll-melt-your-brain kind of Goa'uld, but after the way she described tonight's ceremony… I think it's something we have to consider."

"This Goa'uld have a name?" Jack was on edge, pacing back and forth in the cramped living area.

"Yes, Diana. I've been thinking about that; it's possible she's based herself on the Roman goddess Diana. She was sometimes known as the Lady of the Lamp, and was worshipped at crossroads. We've seen one of those on each of the islands… What?"

Sam, Teal'c and Jack were all staring at him.

"I met a woman, last night crossing to Second Island," Jack said. "Old bird, but canny. Called herself Diana."

"Yesterday, when we were at the tide organ, I met a woman up in the dunes." Sam looked bewildered. "Sir, was the woman you met pregnant?"

"Ah, no. Think I would have noticed that."

"Mine was. Near to term. She was young, though — mid-twenties. Said her baby was going to be called Diana."

"Well the woman in the forest was young-ish," Daniel said, "but she wasn't pregnant."

"I too engaged in a disturbing encounter with a woman calling herself Diana." Teal'c's deep voice cut into the argument Jack was about to raise. "She was, however, barely a woman. No more than thirteen years of age. Certainly not with child."

"So there's lots of gals called Diana around here?"

"Or it's just the one and she can shape-shift." Daniel screwed up his face at the disbelieving looks that earned. "It's one factor of the mythology. I'm not saying she actually… Unless she's another species of some kind…" He wasn't really certain about anything now. "Regardless of who or what she is, the ceremony sounds like it could be a cover for a host selection."

"The child I spoke to said one drew the spirit of the goddess within. Perhaps a description for the possession of a host by Goa'uld?" Teal'c was on his feet and looking like he wanted to join Jack in the pacing.

"I knew it," Jack growled. "No matter where we go there's a snake waiting to spoil the fun."

Sam held up a hand. "But how do your explain Teal'c and I not sensing any Goa'uld? We were both close to these women. We didn't feel anything suspicious."

"Perhaps the elusive power source negates the naquada we sense in a Goa'uld," Teal'c said.

"It doesn't matter." Jack reached for his P90 and began to check it for sand damage. "We need a plan. We're gonna bag this snake before she can take any of those nice people as hosts."

While the others scoped out the grotto where the ceremony would take place, Daniel sought out Rosal.

"I'm serious. We think there is an alien calling herself Diana. She's going to use the ceremony to enslave you as a host for her species."

That just made her laugh even harder.

"We've seen it happen, many times. Even to people we know."

"Oh, my pardon, Daniel." Rosal sobered, but still had a twinkle of mirth in her eyes. "Your concern for our welfare is very generous. If these villains have caused such harm, then I appreciate your warning. But we have conducted the ceremony of Drawing Down The Moon every Triad for generations. Nothing evil has ever happened. Nor will it tonight. It is a time of peace for the soul, of renewal, affirmation of one's life path. You have no cause for fear."

"Rosal —" Daniel clenched his fists in frustration. "Yes, previous ceremonies have brought no harm, but believe me, there is someone in this village planning to do great harm tonight."

"A woman you call Diana?"

"Yes."

"But we have no woman in any of the islands called Diana."

"Exactly!"

Rosal shook her head and turned away, hand raised to cover renewed laughter. "I have pies baking. I will see you later, Daniel."

Defeated, he activated his radio. "Daniel to Jack — you there?"

"Read you, Daniel. Any luck?"

"Negative. Rosal thinks I'm nuts. She's more worried about her pies than soul-sucking aliens."

"Roger that. Get down here and give us a hand. We've got a trap to set."

The grotto was a semi-circular cave carved into the rocky cliffs facing Third Island. The deep overhang above made it feel confined despite being open to the sea. A row of jagged rocks lay in the waves: fang-like teeth that barred passage into the grotto from the sea. Access was limited to two narrow paths cut into the soil by the passage of many feet, over many years, which led from the top right down to sea level.

All afternoon villagers from Second Island had walked the length of the causeway to greet family and friends on First Island. The Third Islanders had already arrived at midday when the tide had pulled back long enough for them to cross the sea floor. Presents were shared and casks of home brew were tapped and sampled with enthusiasm.

"They're half tanked already," Jack grumbled to Daniel.

"Nobody will listen to reason."

Daniel could feel his stomach knotting with anxiety. He took a deep breath, tried to channel the emotion into energy to use in the coming battle. "I've tried half a dozen people, they all reacted like Rosal." Her laughter still burned his ears.

"Here comes Teal'c."

Their friend's surly expression foreshadowed his lack of success.

"I have tried to convince Ellene and others from our water expedition of the danger they face, but none would heed my words." His tone suggested they may deserve their fate.

"Teal'c, we can't give up. If the islanders won't accept the danger—" Daniel broke off as an elderly pair of women reunited with a particularly loud 'Ayehoy!'

"—they're in, then it's up to us to protect them," he hissed.

"I concur, Daniel Jackson." He faced Jack. "Are you considering laying in wait for the Goa'uld to show itself, O'Neill?"

"Yeah. We haven't seen any sign of Jaffa yet, but they could be up there," Jack jerked his gun's muzzle skyward, "waiting to pounce."

"It could be this Diana is a lone Goa'uld, trying to assemble a fighting force," Sam added.

"Or she takes people by stealth and leaves the rest to breed more hosts for the next cull." Daniel grimaced at his own words.

"Whatever the intent, we're gonna stop her." Jack gave the grotto another careful consideration. "Teal'c, you take the north end of the bay, I'll take the southern end. Carter, Daniel, find a place to hide near the ends of each path. We'll wait till this Goa'uld shows itself and then take it out."

"What about the civilians?" Daniel felt that knot in his stomach clench even harder.

Jack patted the telescopic sight on his weapon. "If it turns up alone, no one else will know about it till it's all over. If it shows up with a squad of Jaffa, you and Carter get the locals out of the way, ASAP. Teal'c and I will see to the Jaffa."

"Maybe we should call in reinforcements."

"There's not enough time, Daniel." Sam pointed to the first moon, already risen over the sea. A glimmer of light on the darkening horizon announced the imminent arrival of the second moon.

A burst of laughter and chattering voices above them heralded the first of the villagers.

"Let's do this, quickly and quietly," Jack ordered.

They split up, each secreting themselves behind rocks. The rapid onset of night helped conceal them from the islanders who began to make their way down the two paths.

Daniel wedged himself uncomfortably in a small gap between clusters of boulders. He watched as the trickle of people became a steady flow, winding down the paths, their figures outlined by flaming torches they carried. Shadows leapt grotesquely on the walls of the grotto.

Within half an hour, in the now full dark of night, every inhabitant of the three islands was milling on the sand, their cheerful voices blended into a buzz that echoed loudly around them.

He peered closely at every woman and girl but could not see any resembling the woman he had spoken to in the forest, nor could he see the girl, old lady or pregnant woman the others had described.

Time dragged by with aching slowness. His feet were going numb in this awkward crouch. He carefully resettled, first kneeling, eventually sliding down to sit on the sand when his knees cramped. The moons rose, all three shining in blue-white brilliance that illuminated the growing party in the grotto. Moonlight shone on the water, a silvery path leading the eye to the three moons that soared in a perfect line up into the indigo sky.

After an hour, Jack's voice came over his earpiece. *"Anyone see anything yet?"*

"Clear, Colonel."

"I have seen no suspicious persons, O'Neill."

"Nothing, Jack." Daniel suppressed a sigh. "Maybe we jumped the gun here?"

"How many times have we found Goa'uld lurking on planets, trying to take people over? No, this time we're ready for them. Hold tight and stay sharp."

Stay sharp. Easier said than done when another hour crawled by and brought SG-1 nothing but the sense they were missing a really good party.

The moons were coming together now. Daniel couldn't hear the surf anymore. The tide was being pulled well out into the bay by gravitational forces as the conjunction of the moons reached its climax. He looked up at the sky and caught his breath in admiration. Lined up in order of size, the three moons hung in the sky, one beneath the other, their light combining in a dazzling illumination. He could clearly see the people in the grotto, just as clearly see the cliff top and paths that were completely devoid of movement.

The party noised hushed. As quiet rippled through the crowd, the islanders arrayed themselves to face out to sea and the triad of moons. Rosal stood at the front, lifted her arms, hands outstretched in a welcoming, embracing gesture. Behind her, the women, men and children matched her gesture, a forest of hands reached up to the moonlight.

Someone began to sing, a sweet soulful melody. Another picked up the song and soon they were all singing, their voices melding, tenors, baritones and many ranges between merged into a beautiful harmony.

Now? Surely the Goa'uld would pounce now, when everyone was so occupied? Nothing untoward stirred. The rocks, the exposed beach, the cliff: everywhere around the grotto remained empty, peaceful.

Gradually the song dwindled to a few voices. Daniel could see the faces of many people; they gazed into the moonlight or closed their eyes, happy to be bathed in light.

Happy. That's what he was seeing: happiness, pleasure, contentment on every islander. They were experiencing bliss in the purest, simplest form.

The singing faded to just one voice. A young boy, standing on a rock by the northern end of the grotto, near Teal'c's hiding place. His clear, heartbreakingly beautiful voice rang out over the gathering. No words were used, none were needed. Just a song from the soul that reached into the heart of everyone present, bound them together and lifted them all.

The final note echoed in the sparkling night. Daniel sagged, gun slack in his hand, blinking rapidly. For long moments nobody moved. Above, the moons began to separate, resuming their individual journeys through the cold darkness of space.

Gradually, people began to leave, many holding hands and linking arms. Daniel stared at his gun, then jammed it back in its holster. He stood and picked his way through the people to meet Sam. She looked stunned; her eyelashes glinted in the moonlight. Wordless, he gathered her up in a hug that she returned whole heartedly.

Rosal passed them with a pleased smile. Soon it was just the four of them standing together on the beach, in moon-cast shadows. Teal'c looked… sated was the word that came to mind. Jack looked like he was confused, suspicious and a little shaken. Daniel gave him a hug and Teal'c too, for good measure.

"So…" Jack finally got a word out, then stalled.

"That was beautiful." Sam blew her nose, fiddling with her vest to avoid eye contact.

"Indeed it was."

"No Goa'uld?" Jack kept looking around like he actually wanted one to show up.

"No Goa'uld," Daniel echoed. "Sometimes a spiritual experience is just a spiritual experience."

"I need a drink."

The sun was way, way too bright.

Jack winced and pulled his cap further down over his eyes. He'd only had the one cup of home brew last night but, boy, did it pack a wallop.

He found his team in a similar post non-battle party mode, scattered in the shade of the village square.

Already, the other islanders had departed for their homes, returning to their lives that — thankfully — had not been cut short by some egomaniacal snake in a skirt. The party had gone on until dawn and now it was all over.

His team had nothing to show for this mission but a good serving of egg on their faces, and, Jack reflected, he was okay with that.

The anomalous power readings remained undefined, unlocated, unknown… He could hear the tide organ's weird noise floating over from across the island. Turned out it just made music. Who knew?

He looked his kids over. Teal'c was kel'no'reeming his heart out — looked like a big bronze Buddha that could go on someone's mantle, if they had a big mantle. Carter was sitting cross-legged, sea grass in her hair, a happy smile on her face as she watched a group of kids playing down in the surf. Daniel was sprawled asleep in the sun in a bonelessly relaxed way Jack hadn't seen in a long time.

Now, this was what he called a successful mission.

STARGATE ATLANTIS
BONE MUSIC

Peter J. Evans

IT WAS cold, up on the hill, and the wind was strong enough to lift sea spray high into the sharp grey air, dropping it back onto John Sheppard's head in a fine drizzle.

He scowled at the chill. There was no cover here, no respite from the wind and spray. Only a few stone slabs reared around him, heaped up amid the tough, tangled grass; too tall to be natural, too rotted to identify. Dwellings, maybe, or monuments, it was impossible to tell. Time and the slow corrosion of wind and salt water had eaten away all their certainties.

Only the broad faceted ring of the Stargate remained recognizable, and that was tilted, its dais stained and slick with moss. To Sheppard, the glossy, rippling mirror at its heart looked utterly out of place. Nothing so new, he thought, nothing so perfect should exist in this forlorn, abandoned landscape.

This was a dead place. Whoever raised these stones was long gone. And if it hadn't been for the sky, Sheppard wouldn't be here either.

The information that had brought him here was itself as old and degraded by time as the stones. A fragment of a reference in the Ancient database, brought to light several weeks earlier by Rodney McKay's translation programs, had matched a similar rumor unearthed by a previous sweep. Two wisps of data that meant almost nothing in isolation, but together told of a world where some quirk of atmospheric physics adversely affected bioelectronic sensors. A place where the Wraith would not go, or could not see.

This, Samantha Carter had decided, was of interest.

A gate address was locked down, and a survey team sent through. They returned blinking and stumbling, grim-faced. The sky over M3T-211, they reported, was vile. It did things to the eye. Little wonder that the only hints of habitation there were dripping ruins.

Despite this, the sensor-blocking properties of M3T-211's atmosphere were too potentially valuable to ignore. A scientific expedition was required. Which meant sending Rodney McKay to see if the effect could be replicated, Jennifer Keller to determine if it was harmful, and John Sheppard to make sure neither of them fell into the ocean.

While Sheppard was making sure the gate site was safe, McKay had been unpacking the test equipment he had brought with him. There seemed to be a lot of it, enough to make Sheppard uneasy about how long the mission was going to last. "Did you have to bring all your toys?" he grumbled.

McKay glanced up at him, and then quickly down again. "You want me to do this properly, or miss something so we all have to make another trip?"

He was kneeling by the dais, surrounded by open hardshell cases, while the fourth member of the team, a marine lieutenant called Wright, glared at him from some distance away. It was Wright who had carried the lion's share of equipment onto M3T-211, McKay loading the unfortunate woman like a pack mule, and it was clear from her body language that she wasn't going to forgive him anytime soon.

"So I'm guessing maybe a particulate layer," McKay muttered. "Self-sustaining, if it's been here long enough to show up on the Ancient database."

"Artificial?"

"Maybe. Pretty high — what do you think, mesospheric?"

Sheppard shrugged. "Give me a jumper and I'll go find out."

"I'll need a few hours to pin down the ground-level effects first, then we'll grab one and rig up a capture scoop."

"And hope your particles don't screw with Ancient flight systems." Sheppard raised an eyebrow at Wright. "You okay?"

"Yeah, I'm good," McKay replied, before the marine could reply. He made a dismissive waving gesture, his attention already back on the cases. "Go help Keller pick flowers."

Keller was already some distance away, off the ragged crown of the hill, among the jumble of broken ground that flanked it on all sides. Sheppard began making his way down to her, trying to keep his eyes low. He had taken a good look up when he had first arrived, through the broken, scudding clouds to what lay beyond, and that had been enough for him.

There was no blue up there, no visible sun. Instead there was just a distant roil, a slow, churning sprawl where the sky should have been. It was faint, but unending, a pallid shimmer like grease on filthy water, and the color of it, a sickly lavender-yellow, made Sheppard think of old bruises. Or the shades that dead skin can turn.

It was oppressive, claustrophobic. It bleached the world.

Keller was crouched next to a boulder, carefully scraping something mossy from its windward surface. In addition to her medical kit she had brought a large carryall, filled with padded racks of specimen containers, and Sheppard had the nasty feeling she was intending to fill every one.

He watched her tip gray-green residue into a plastic tube and screw it shut. "Anything I can do?" he asked when she was done. "At all?"

She grinned. "Bored already, huh?"

"Should have brought a book."

"I hate to tell you, but we're going to be here a while." She nodded at the carryall. "The bio team need as broad a spectrum of samples as possible. Plants, insects, microbial life. Blood from higher mammals, if there are any. How's Rodney?"

"He's got a scientific mystery to explore and three boxes of shiny things that go 'bleep'. I've never seen him happier."

He watched her start to clamber around the boulder, edging through the gap between it and a crumbling heap of slabs. Sheppard followed warily. "Where are you heading?"

"Downslope. It's too exposed here, everything has to grow like crazy just to survive. I want to get some samples that have been around for a while, so the bio guys can check for toxin build-up."

"Just try to keep to the path. These rocks are a maze."

"Path?" She glanced down. "Huh. I hadn't spotted that."

"Easy to miss." They were moving between taller stones, now, more regular fragments, some even joined at right-angles where wall had once met wall. "No-one's lived here for a long time."

As he spoke, the wind dipped. And John Sheppard stopped in his tracks.

Impossibly, he could hear music.

Keller had halted too, turned back to him, her mouth open to speak. He held up a hand to still her, tilting his head slightly, straining to hear.

The sound had ceased. Sheppard listened for a few moments, growing increasingly convinced that his imagination was playing tricks. He was about to discount it entirely when it began again; a reedy piping, thin and eerie, playing out the same halting, breathy cadence as before.

He reached up to trigger his headset. "Wright? Heads up. We might not be on our own here after all."

"Understood, sir. Want me to dial home?"

"Stand by." The music halted, started again. The same series of notes, this time slightly faster, with a little more confidence. Louder too, enough for him to pin down its source. The piper was a couple of dozen meters downhill and to his right, past a ragged jut of wall slabs.

He raised his P90, slipped past Keller and down the ancient path, boots sure and silent on rotted cobble.

As he rounded the walls, the music stopped dead. The player was staring right at him.

It was a girl, very young, perched on top of a tilted slab, her face pale and small under a shapeless woolen cap. She was dressed for the cold, layer upon layer of rough, flat fabric, dark and unadorned, and her gloved hands gripped what looked like a short white flute.

Sheppard lowered the gun. He was facing a child. "Hi."

"Please." The girl was shaking her head, her face a blank mask of terror. "Please. We're not ready."

"What?" He took a step towards her. "Ah, I think you've got me mixed up with —"

He was talking to air, to a tumbling flute and a blank space above the slab. The girl had launched herself away from him. He could hear her footfalls, light and panicky-fast, skittering over the path as she fled.

She got maybe five yards before fear and the slickness underfoot brought her down. Sheppard heard it clearly: a high yelp, a scuffle as she lost balance. An impact of flesh on stone.

He scrambled up and over the slab. On the far side, further down the path, a motionless bundle of dark fabric lay slumped among the rocks.

Sheppard ran to her, dropped to his knees. "Doc! Get down here!"

The child's eyes were closed. There was a nasty-looking abrasion close to her left temple, already welling with dark blood. She had fallen badly in her rush to escape him, and her skull had connected with one of the hill's myriad stones.

Keller was right behind him. He got up and stepped away as she reached under the girl's collar, past gingery curls, feeling for the carotid pulse.

In Sheppard's experience, most people who were knocked unconscious tended to stay that way for just a few seconds. Anything longer was usually the result of serious injury; concussion, spinal damage, bleeding in the brain. Head trauma, despite what tended to happen in the movies, could be horribly dangerous.

Thankfully, the girl was already blinking awake. She would be confused for a time, though, and unlikely to remember the fall. Maybe not even running away.

Her eyes focused on Keller, and widened in panic.

"It's okay. No-one's going to hurt you." Keller smiled comfortingly. "My name's Jennifer," she said. "And this is John. I'm sorry if we startled you, we really didn't mean to."

The child shook her head, and then the pain of her injury must have hit her. She winced. "Ah. My head hurts."

"You fell over, but I can help with that." Keller was opening her medical kit. "What's your name?"

"Ceana."

"Do you know where you are?"

"Among the Old Stones," the girl replied. Her initial terror seemed to have faded. She was still deeply unsettled, but didn't seem to be on the verge of trying to escape again. "Who are you? Are you ghosts?"

"No," Sheppard replied. He'd been called worse. "Just tourists."

"I'm a doctor," Keller told her. She had a wad of antiseptic gauze in one hand. "This is going to sting a little, sorry."

Sheppard gave Ceana what he hoped was a reassuring smile, acutely aware that he was holding a gun. Then McKay's voice crackled in his headset. "*Will somebody talk to me? What the hell's going on down there?*"

He moved away to answer, unwilling to unsettle the girl further, and explained the situation as concisely as he could. "Doesn't look like trouble at the moment, but I'll be having serious words with the survey team when we get back."

"*Want us to come down?*"

Two new faces had already spooked the girl. More could destroy the fragile rapport Keller was building with her. "Best stay put for now."

"*You never let me have any fun.*"

As he cut the connection Sheppard heard a shout from Keller, a startled yelp of warning. He whirled.

A great dark shape was hammering towards him out of the rain.

Something lashed out from it, hissing through the grey air, long and brutally fast. A staff, maybe, or a spear. He dodged back, trying not to slip on the wet ground, saw the weapon whirl around and back at his head. He feinted left, brought the P90 up to block the blow, felt wood slam into metal hard enough for the shock to echo painfully up his arms. The impact staggered him, just for a moment, but that in turn gave him enough space to bring the gun up. He snapped off the safety.

"Stop!"

It was the girl's voice, high and sharp, almost commanding. Sheppard saw his adversary freeze, turn his hooded head towards her. "Ceana?"

"Put the bloody stick down, Ferrick." She was on her feet, holding the gauze to her forehead. "They don't mean us ill."

Ferrick was a big man, a head taller than Sheppard and clad in a brutal variation of the girl's winter clothing. He slapped the end of the staff hard down into the path. "There's blood on your scalp that says different, child."

"I slipped and fell, is all. Jennifer is a healer, she's tending me."

Ferrick nodded at Sheppard. "And him?"

"He's a two-wrist. I think it means warrior."

Sheppard took a deep breath and lowered the P90. "Close enough."

"Bloody Mainlanders," muttered Ferrick. "Knew you'd come crawling back one day. Where are you moored?"

"We're not—"

"Because there's a fog coming in, bad one. Tarry much longer here and you'll never see coast again."

Ceana made an exasperated sound. "In the name of the Folk, Ferrick, look at them. They're no more Mainlanders than we are." She beamed up at Keller. "You're portal people, aren't you?"

"Portal people?" The big man barked a laugh. "Don't be daft, lass."

"Sorry pal, but I think the kid's right." Sheppard grinned at her. "We certainly didn't get here by boat."

Ferrick gave a wordless snort, obviously far from convinced. "Whatever you say, two-wrist. Ceana, it's almost time."

"Time for what?" Keller asked.

"For the festival," said Ceana. "I have to play for the Sea King. It's my first time, that's why I was up here practicing…" Her face fell, abruptly, and she began patting at her clothes. "Wait. Where's my pipe?"

"Oh, I'm sorry." Keller reached into her jacket and took the instrument out, handed it to Ceana. "You dropped it when you —"

At that moment, a change came over Jennifer Keller. Sheppard saw her freeze, for the briefest of seconds, shiver and tense up. She was staring not at the girl, but at the flute, probably the first time she had seen it in detail. And something about it had drained the blood from her face.

The moment passed. He saw her smile return, all attention back on the child as she passed the pipe over. "Here. Say, this festival sounds like fun."

"I just hope I'll play well."

Ferrick rapped his staff again. "Ceana…"

"Sorry, Ferrick." The girl smiled shyly at Keller. "Thank you for tending me, Jennifer. We'll be away now."

Keller picked up her carryall. "Is it far? We can walk back with you."

"No." Ceana's smile vanished. "I mean, I'm fine, you don't have to walk all that way."

"You've hit your head, what we call a cranial trauma and LOC." She reached out and tapped the girl's forehead, very gently. "I can't let you out of my sight until I know there's nothing bad happening in there, can I?"

Sheppard frowned, irritated but unsurprised. Keller was a

physician: there was little chance of her allowing an injured child out of her sight unless she was certain there would be no lasting damage. However, he could sense another motive behind her words, so he kept his silence.

"Might be for the best, lass" Ferrick rumbled. "Besides, Sul Dughan needs to be told."

"Who?"

"Our Elder," said Ceana. She chewed her lip for a moment. Then: "All right. But just to the gates, Ferrick."

"Aye." The big man nodded to her, then stalked away down the path. Ceana turned to follow him.

Sheppard drew close to Keller. "Everything okay, doc?"

"I think so. Probably nothing more than a graze, but I want to be sure. Besides, if there's a village here, maybe we can see if they're affected by the sky."

"That's not what I meant."

A darkness crossed her face, then.

"That flute," she breathed. "I thought it was wood, but then I got a closer look at it. John, it was made of bone."

"Don't tell me it was human."

"I wish. It's Wraith."

Sheppard dawdled slightly on the way down, staying just far enough back to contact McKay without drawing attention. It was quickly decided that McKay should remain close to the Stargate and continue his tests. Sheppard's instincts told him that he and Keller were not walking into immediate danger, but if things went south it made sense to have half the team able to head back to Atlantis at a moment's notice, and if necessary return with a puddle jumper full of reinforcements.

Ceana's village hugged the coast as if sheltering there, a ragged cluster of stone houses nestling around a rocky cove, ringed by a high wall. The far edge of the cove rose into a sheer face of jagged gray granite a hundred feet high, the churning sea at its base studded with broken boulders. The cliff was terrifying, splintered and saw-edged, but it gave the cove some respite from the wind. Sheppard could see boats down there, drawn up onto the narrow beach.

Looking at them made him shiver: they looked too small, too frail to brave the angry black ocean beyond.

The gates Ceana had mentioned were tall, solidly built and firmly shut. Ferrick lifted his staff and rapped them hard, three times, then turned back to Sheppard. "You'll wait here."

Ceana glared at him. "Ferrick…"

"It's for the Elder to decide, lass."

Heavy thudding sounds were issuing from the gate, bars being withdrawn. "I guess you don't get many visitors," said Sheppard.

"No," Ferrick replied, almost proudly. "We don't."

The gates swung open. Past them Sheppard saw a knot of figures, dark-clad and hunched against the weather. A few turned to stare at him, eyes and mouths wide, and then the gates were hinging closed again.

Just before they shut, he saw Ceana walking away through the crowd. The figures around her were stepping aside, dipping their heads in something close to reverence.

"Atlantis." Sul Dughan shook his head slowly. "Can't say I've ever heard of such a place."

Sheppard edged a little closer to the hearth. "Yeah, well. It's not on this planet, so I guess if you've never met anyone from off-world before…"

"Walking from world to world…" The Elder rubbed his chin, fingers rasping audibly. "And here I was, all these years, thinking that was just an old stone ring on a hill."

Plainly, Dughan's curiosity had won out over Ceana's concerns. The gates had been opened again after only a few minutes. Ferrick had led Sheppard and Keller to the Elder's lodge, a long, low structure close to the point where the cove sprawled upwards into cliffside. There they had been welcomed with wooden cups of what appeared to be fish soup, and given seats next to the hearth while Dughan, a slender, stubbled man in his fifties, tried to make sense of them.

"You must have had some off-world contact in the past." Sheppard's soup appeared to contain every part of a fish he could imagine, and a few he didn't want to think about, but if he closed his eyes while he drank it the taste was far from unpleasant. "Ceana called us portal people."

Dughan shook his head. "Children's tales. Portal people use shadows like doors, step through to steal noisy babies away. There's a song, but I'll do you a kindness and not sing it."

"A lot of old stories have elements of truth to them," said Keller quietly. "And Ferrick, what did he call us? Mainlanders?"

"There are no Mainlanders, lass. Not any more."

"Any more?" Keller glanced across at Sheppard, then back to the old man. In the strange smoky light her skin looked colorless, like marble. "What do you mean?"

"They left us, left the village, a long time ago. Ten families, maybe more. Headed for the largest island to make a new start." The Elder frowned. "Never came back."

"What do you think happened?"

"Starvation, maybe. Disease, madness… Life here is hard, lass. This is midsummer." Dughan picked a clod of what looked like dried peat from a pile, dropped it into the hearth. "It's not unknown for men to just… Go. Walk into the sea. So we forget the painful truths and keep our stories. Like Sea Folk and the portal people. And we mark our days by the festival."

"Ceana said that was today," said Sheppard.

"We hold it whenever the moons align." The Elder smiled. "It's just a tradition, there's nothing to it. We give thanks to the Sea King, ask him to keep the storms away and drive the fish to our boats. Probably sounds foolish to such as you, but it brings a little cheer to the village. Lets us think of something other than mending nets and keeping warm." He shrugged. "And if someone out there really is listening, and sends a good catch or two our way, where's the harm?"

"Mister Dughan?" Keller set her soup down. "Would it be okay if we stayed around for a while? For the festival, I mean."

The Elder looked momentarily unsure. "And why would you want to do that?"

"Well, the reason we're on this planet is to study how your sky affects living things. Being here for a while would give us the chance to see how you deal with it." She held up her medical kit. "And if any of your people have minor injuries that I can treat while I'm here, I'll be happy to do what I can."

"Unless," said Sheppard carefully, "there's a reason you wouldn't want us around?"

"No, lad, not at all." Dughan blinked. "Your offer's a fair trade, and I don't see the harm in it."

"Thank you."

"Until nightfall, of course. I hope you'll not be offended if we ask you to take your leave by then."

"No problem," said Sheppard. "What happens after it gets dark?"

"There's a fog coming in," Dughan told him, his voice perfectly level. "A bad one."

The villagers were already gathered for the festival when Sheppard and Keller left the lodge. Maybe two hundred huddled figures clustering on the hard stony beach; quiet, watchful groups among the boats and the ropes, and lined up along either side of what looked like a narrow wooden jetty.

Sheppard had checked in with Wright and McKay after leaving the lodge, letting them know that he and Keller wouldn't back until nightfall. When he mentioned the festival he had been forced to cut McKay off before the tinny echo of his protests could be heard leaking from the headset. The villagers had their secrets, he was already certain of it. Only fair that he should keep a few of his own.

They found a place to stand. Dughan had loaned them coats,

thick constructions of pressed wool which made the shore's chill more bearable. Sheppard hoped that the clothing would lessen the villagers' shock at seeing off-worlders in their midst for the first time. Besides, the P90 was still hanging snug against his chest, and the coat hid that too.

Abruptly, any conversation among the villagers ceased, replaced by a hushed expectancy. Sheppard looked about, trying to see what was going on, and saw a familiar figure. He tapped Keller's shoulder, nodded wordlessly at the new arrival.

Ceana was walking towards the jetty.

The villagers parted for her, smiling and nodding encouragement as she passed. Sul Dughan walked with her, and there was another man on her far side, bare-headed, his rough, blocky face topped by a tangle of reddish curls. Ceana's hat was off too, exposing identical hair.

Runs in the family, thought Sheppard.

The two men stopped at the end of the jetty. Ceana hesitated for a moment, then appeared to steel herself. She walked out onto the creaking wood, towards the sea, only stopping when she was within a yard of the jetty's end.

Then she lifted her bone pipe, and began to play for the Sea King.

The music was high and clear. It carried easily over the sea's muted roar, came back over the beach and the crowds, breathy and lilting and slow. It wasn't a festival tune, not to Sheppard. There was no joy there, no celebration. It was a dirge, a plea, a mourning song. A lullaby for dead children.

He looked over at Keller. She was clearly getting the same unholy shivers down her spine as he was.

A more recognizable feeling returned to the festival after Ceana had finished playing. Sheppard and Keller left the beach surrounded by villagers, many of whom seemed fascinated by their strange accents and tidy hair.

Before long, iron braziers were burning between the stone

houses, and strings of bunting, tattered and colorless in the wet air, were raised to flutter madly above the streets. Wooden bowls of rough spirit were passed around. Sheppard declined, but Keller took a sip, purely, she told him, in the interests of science. With a heroic effort she just about managed to stop herself coughing the stuff straight back up again, professing it more akin to turpentine than moonshine.

By then, word of Keller's medical prowess had gotten around, and after one man had plucked up enough courage to present her with a broken and infected toe she quickly gained a small crowd of potential patients. Sheppard helped her and a couple of the local healers set up a temporary clinic in what looked like an old storehouse, then excused himself. "Are you gonna be okay without me for a while?"

"Sure." Her borrowed coat was off, and she had rolled her sleeves up to wash her hands in a tarred basin of water. "Where are you going to be?"

"Just taking a look around."

Keller nodded. "Good idea. Just be back here before dark."

"Okay, mom."

"And John?" She leaned close, dropped her voice to a whisper. "Be careful. We're being lied to."

Outside, a very different kind of music had started up; drums and a jaunty whirring. Sheppard tugged his hood up, and set off towards its source.

He couldn't immediately tell where the music was coming from, but the players were at least a street away. He slipped through the narrow space between two houses, taking care not to catch himself on the jagged stone walls. Whatever secrets Sul Dughan might be keeping from him — and Sheppard was certain there were many — the loan of the coat had been a kindness, and he didn't want to return it damaged.

Screams greeted him as he emerged from between the houses.

His hand darted under the coat on reflex, fingers brushing the P90, but he had already seen the source of the noise; a group of children, younger than Ceana, were flinging themselves up the street, yelping and shrieking in what sounded like a mix of excitement and genuine fear.

Sheppard stepped out behind them, watching villagers shake their heads in the youngsters' wake, and then heard a wet scrape of metal on stone, a rasp of labored breath. He turned.

Something vast and ragged was clattering towards him, its face a blank, terrifying mask. Sheppard stumbled back until he hit wall, saw the thing lurch to a halt and bring its awful head slowly around to study him.

It laughed. "You're jumpy, two-wrist."

"*Ferrick?*" Sheppard stared. "What the hell are you supposed to be?"

The mask was wood, rough-carved and crudely whitewashed. Ferrick's eyes glittered down at Sheppard from behind it: the man was on stilts, supporting himself on long canes and covered in shreds of what was probably an old sail.

The costumed man's only answer was a derisive chuckle, and then he was away, stalking with surprising speed up the street and growling theatrically at those he passed.

His headset blipped. "*John, where are you?*"

"Next street along. Everything okay?"

"*I think so… Something weird just happened.*"

"You too, huh?"

"*I just had Ceana's father in here, kinda drunk. Got the feeling he wanted to talk to me, but there were too many people around.*" Keller's voice was muted. She must have stepped away in order to use her radio, and was keeping as quiet as she could. "*I tried to call him on it but he got spooked. Asked where you were and then bolted when I said I didn't know.*"

"Okay, I'll head back. Any idea which way he went?"

"*Didn't see, sorry.*"

Sheppard ducked back between the houses, poked his head out and peered left and right along the street. A couple of villagers were there, but no-one he recognized, so he crossed the cobbles, up a tiny side-path and into the winding road beyond.

For a moment or two he was convinced this street was entirely deserted, but then a bulky figure emerged from the shadows, pulled a hood up over gingery hair, and paced away. "I've got him. Stand by; I'll let you know what happens."

Sheppard cut the connection, began to follow as quickly as he could without drawing attention. He was within ten yards when another figure appeared, quickly crossing the street to intercept the red-headed man. "Marchal!"

It was Sul Dughan, the Elder. Sheppard slowed his pace, found a hiding place close to the wall.

Dughan moved up close to the other man, put a hand to his shoulder. "Where's Ceana?"

"Home." Marchal's voice was slurred. "Elder, she's terrified. She keeps talking about Ornal…"

"Oh, Marchal…" Dughan dipped his grey head. "Ornal was careless, the poor girl. Ceana won't be, not with you at her side. But you have to be strong for her."

"She shouldn't have to do this."

"None of us should." The Elder sighed. "But the King takes his due. We've no say in it."

Marchal shrugged out from under his hand. "Have we not? What about the strangers — if what they say is true, if that stone ring really is a portal to another world, can we not go there? Away from the Folk?"

"I hope so. I'd not have welcomed them otherwise. Maybe, next time, we can gather our people and return with them." Dughan's tone had changed. There was steel in it now. "But not today. We've been too long without a catch, without giving tribute. We lost Yenna last night, two of Rostlig's boys the night before. The King won't be denied. If the bargain falls, your strangers will return to an empty village." The Elder stepped away from him. "Now go to Ceana. Prepare her. I'll ready the draught."

Marchal gazed at him for several seconds, then nodded jerkily and stumbled off. Dughan stood where he was, as if watching him go. Then, without warning, he glanced back over his shoulder.

Sheppard resisted the urge to move. He knew exactly how well he was hidden. He stood, his borrowed coat making him one with the shadows, until the Elder had turned back towards the lodge and hurried away.

He stayed there for quite some time afterwards, too.

Night fell swiftly on M3T-211. The particle layer robbed the sky of reflected light, rendering the sunset an ugly, pallid thing that lasted minutes at best. By the time Sheppard and Keller made their way to the village gates it was almost entirely dark.

A small crowd had gathered to see them off. Keller said her goodbyes to the village healers: she had left them medical supplies, along with instructions for follow-up care. While she spoke, Sheppard stood quietly and searched the crowd for Ceana and Marchal.

He didn't see them.

Finally Sul Dughan stepped forwards and took their hands in his. He thanked them for their efforts, expressed a hope that they would return soon, and bade them farewell.

After that, with no further ceremony, the gates were closed and barred against them.

They walked away in silence, Sheppard picking their way with a tactical flashlight. Only when he was certain that they could neither be seen nor heard from the village did he find a place to stop.

"You buying any of this, doc?"

"Not a damn word. I don't know about you, but I am getting a serious *Wicker Man* vibe from that place." Keller folded her arms, bouncing a little on her toes. They had been allowed to keep the coats, but with the meager sun hidden the wind had turned even more bitterly cold. "Seriously, John, there's something sick happening here, and that little girl's life is in danger."

Sheppard nodded upwards. "You see any moons?"

"Through that crap? Not a chance."

"Yeah, that's what I thought. Lunar alignment my ass." He reached up to his headset. "Wright? How are you doing up there?"

"It's a little fresh, sir. Are you on your way?"

"There's still things to do down here, but we need some wheels. Dial home, brief Colonel Carter, and then gate back here with a jumper ASAP. Fly it through cloaked and home in on our position."

"Affirmative, Colonel. Anything else you need?"

"A couple more marines couldn't hurt. Oh, and night vision goggles. How's McKay holding up?"

There was a slight pause. Then: *"Doctor McKay went back to Atlantis two hours ago, sir."*

"Huh." Sheppard rolled his eyes. "Figures."

"You could at least have invited me."

Sheppard gave his binoculars a tweak. Far below him a shapeless blur sharpened into a staggering bundle of dark clothing, lurching haphazardly from wall to wall. Another drunken villager making his solitary way home. "You wouldn't have enjoyed it."

"That's not the point," McKay snapped. "Anyway, how do you know I wouldn't? I can party hard."

"Seriously?" Sheppard lowered the binoculars to stare at him. "Did you actually just say that?"

"Yes, but if you try to tell anyone I'll deny it forever."

Sheppard returned his attention to the village. He had been watching the streets for an hour, while Keller remained in the jumper with Wright and the two marines she'd brought. "Have a little patience, okay? Trust me, there's something nasty going on down there and I want to know what it is. What's your hurry?"

"My hurry?" McKay stuffed his hands under his armpits, somewhat theatrically. "One, I'm cold. *I* didn't go to a party and get a funky new coat. Two, did you realize that stray particles are constantly filtering down from that mesospheric boundary? All the time we're hanging around here we're breathing about eight parts per million of the stuff."

Sheppard blinked. "Is it dangerous?"

"Probably not. In the short term."

"What about the not so short?"

"Put it this way; I'd be really surprised if anyone down in that village has the right number of toes. Are you seeing anything?"

"No, I think everyone's sleeping it off by now. We should be able to get back down there without being —" He froze. "Damn it. Hold on."

A light had appeared on the beach. It was a small thing, a bobbing, fluttering spark, pale yellow in the darkness. As Sheppard watched, another approached it. Lanterns, carried along the edge of the cove towards the jetty.

One spark lifted high enough to illuminate the face of the man carrying it. "Dughan. What a surprise."

Marchal and Ceana held the other two sparks, of course. Sheppard twitched the binoculars left and right, but saw no-one else. Just the two men, bending to untie the ropes of a small fishing boat, and the child watching them in what must have been stark, mute terror.

Sheppard folded the binoculars. "We're leaving."

The villagers might have lied about many things, but the approaching fog was not one of them. A bank of vapor had been heading towards the cove before the fishing boat had set sail. Now the stuff was so dense that Sheppard was in danger of losing visual contact altogether.

Luckily, he didn't need to see Dughan's boat in order to follow it. McKay was at the sensor board, keeping a careful track of the vessel's position, while Sheppard kept the cloaked jumper in level flight about two hundred feet up. It took all his skill: the particle layer was having a strange effect on the machine. It was jittery and unstable, twitching like an animal in the crosswinds.

Beneath him, the sea leapt and writhed. Sheppard thought about Ceana, already frightened at the prospect of some unknown ordeal, now being flung about in that tiny, fragile vessel. The fact that Dughan set sail on such a night proved that the man was dangerously insane. Still, he and Marchal must have been sailors of considerable skill. The boat had been travelling straight and true across that furious sea for an hour.

"Son of a…" That was McKay, suddenly sitting bolt upright at the sensor board. "Guys? I'm picking up a power signature from that boat."

Keller's face was dead white, and she was holding onto her seat arms very tightly indeed. "That's impossible."

"Well, I'm looking right at it, so clearly not." Sheppard heard blipping sounds as McKay worked the board. "It's small, something hand-held. If it wasn't the only energy source down there I'd never have seen it, but I'd swear it's Wraith tech."

"Worshippers?" asked Wright quietly.

McKay raised a hand. "Ah, on that subject, has it occurred to anyone that we might be following them into something dangerous? Like a really big bunch of Wraith?"

"Sir," Wright was behind Sheppard now, one hand clamped hard onto the back of his control seat. "Doctor McKay's right. There could be anything ahead of us, a whole city of Wraith worshippers. We should get ahead of them, scope the place out."

"Not a good idea." Keller shook her head. "We could lose the boat altogether."

"We can home back in on the energy source."

McKay made a noncommittal sound. "I don't know, it's pretty weak. I might not be able to find it again if we veer off."

"But we've already extrapolated their mooring point. Why

not land there, wait for them and then grab them as soon as they arrive?"

"Because they could change course. Or sink." Despite her obvious discomfort, Keller's face was set hard. "We still need to find out what they're doing. They were talking about the whole village being in danger. If we jump in too early lives could be at risk."

Wright threw her hands up. "Doctor, if there are Wraith down there *our* lives could be at risk!"

Sheppard didn't speak. Keeping the jumper in the air was requiring too much of his attention. Besides, he had nothing to tell them, no answers to their concerns. Just the ugly feeling that, whatever he feared was ahead of them, the truth was going to be far worse.

When the boat's voyage finally ended, it was in a place more bleak and unlovely than anything Sheppard had seen on Ceana's island.

There was no beach below him, no sheltered cove, just a jagged tangle of wave-beaten rock tumbling randomly down into ferocious, foaming waves. The only artificial structure in sight was a tiny, battered stone jetty, barely long enough for Dughan's boat.

Just before the jumper set down, McKay picked up another set of energy readings. Weak and diffuse, riddled with artefacts from the particle layer. All he could tell for certain was they were probably emanating from a hill some distance inland. So when Sheppard spotted the three lanterns held by Ceana and her escort, he was less than surprised to see them heading directly for the same spot.

There was a narrow path leading up from the jetty, but it was steep, its surface treacherous. The three villagers could not have been aware that they were being followed, and with only the pale light of oil flames to guide them, they made their way slowly. Before Ceana had reached the base of the hill Sheppard had the girl clearly in sight.

He put up a hand, fist clenched, dropped to one knee as the rest of the team halted. He heard scuffling as McKay edged closer. "Are you liking the look of that place any more I am?"

"Not really." Through his image intensifiers the hill was a looming silhouette. At its base, heaped rock rose into a low escarpment, but above that the surface became oddly regular. Sheppard turned his head slowly, following the shape it cast against the flat green-black of the sky, and found himself picking out features that had little to do with natural terrain.

What he had taken to be a sloping cliff to the south was starting to look very much like a drive nacelle. Caves dotted along the top ridge could have been intakes, weapons ports. Broken trees, twisted and sagging from the hill's northern point reminded him of sensor spines.

Eventually, he could deny it no longer. There was no hill on this island. "It's a goddamn Wraith ship."

McKay nodded, his goggles bobbing. "Small," he breathed. "Five hundred meters, maybe less. Supply ship?"

"Does it matter?"

"Not any more," whispered Wright. "It's not going anywhere. Look at that thing, it's a wreck."

The marine was right. Not only was the downed starship utterly dark and silent, but Sheppard could see now that its back was broken. The forward hull lay flat against the ground, but the stern was tilted over at almost thirty degrees. The midsection was a tangle of shattered carapace and broken rock, a ghastly, eviscerating wound that laid the vessel's innards bare.

As he watched, the first of the three lanterns vanished into the starship's torn belly. "Damn it."

"Come on!" Keller was already starting forwards. "We can't lose them!"

Sheppard didn't like the idea of barreling straight into a Wraith warship, even one so obviously crippled, but Keller was right. The interior of the ship would be a maze. If he lost sight of Ceana now, he might never find her again.

"Doc, hold up!" He surged forward, began running after Keller. "We need a plan!"

"No we don't!"

He growled in frustration, but the others were already on his heels. "Okay… Wright, shadow Keller. Rodney, stick with me. Lewis, Mexter, you stay at the entrance and make sure nothing follows us. And if things get noisy, come in hot."

By the time he had received acknowledgements from the others he was already at the base of the escarpment. Around him, great shards of stone reared skywards, deep rock torn up by the vessel's catastrophic impact to spear the hull in a thousand locations, but an amplified flicker of lantern light led him between two boulders, under a broken spar of granite bigger than the puddle jumper.

Beyond this, the ship's carapace was rent open, a gaping tear easily big enough to walk through. Sheppard could see, as he clambered through, that it had been crudely widened.

From the outside in, he wondered, or the inside out?

He scampered forwards, into a narrow, vaulted passageway. There was light ahead of him, a sickly yellow glow, and he switched off the goggles, tugged them free to dangle from their strap.

The walls around him were gnarled, ridged and pocked like the inside of a diseased bone. He glanced across the passageway and saw Wright move in front of Keller, her P90 aimed into the gloom ahead.

There was no sound, other than the drip and patter of water from the walls and, behind him and far more distant, the sea's muted roar. Sheppard moved quickly towards the nearest corner, peered around it to see the black hem of a villager's coat vanish around an intersection. "This way."

Ceana was being taken directly towards that queasy glow.

Sheppard followed, silent now, communicating with the others only by hand signal. They moved with him, in teams of two, one pair covering the other in case of ambush, but no threat arose. Had it not been for that increasing light, Sheppard might have believed the ship entirely dead.

As they moved to the next corner, McKay drew his breath in sharply. They were passing a series of deep sockets in the walls; vaguely leaf-shaped, taller than a man, filled with a dry, rotted tangle of tubes. Gaping like gray, bisected wombs.

Wraith hibernation chambers. All empty.

On the far side of the passage, Keller put a finger to her lips, then pointed to the next intersection. *There*, she mouthed.

Sheppard stepped over to her, leaned around the corner.

Past the intersection, the passageway opened out into a high chamber. Half the space had collapsed long ago, walls and ceiling crumpled together, the deck gouged brutally apart. What remained was dotted with dozens of hibernation chambers.

Some were empty and dark, like those in the passage. Ceana, Dughan and Marchal stood before one that was not. A Wraith soldier, masked and armored, stood behind the glassy shell of its womb, wrapped in pulsing umbilicals and bathed in that vile light.

The light shone on Ceana, too. She had already taken off her coat; without it, dressed in a plain wool shirt and britches, she looked heartbreakingly thin and small. But she was standing close to the chamber, unbowed, gazing up on its occupant with undisguised loathing.

"I'm ready," she whispered. "Give me the draught."

"You're sure?" That was Marchal. His voice shook as he spoke. "You know I'll take your place if you —"

"Don't make it harder on her, lad." Dughan stepped past him. The Elder had a bottle in one hand, and was holding it out to Ceana. "It's sour," he told her gently. "But drink every drop."

"I know." She took the bottle from him and put it to her lips.

Sheppard saw her grimace, her white face creasing in disgust as she gulped the stuff down. He almost hurled himself at her to rip the bottle away, but he had hesitated too long. If the draught was poison, Ceana's small body was already rife with it.

He watched her hand the bottle back to Dughan. "Quickly, Elder," she said. "Before I sleep."

Dughan gazed down at her for a moment, his eyes brimming with what looked to Sheppard very much like pride. Then he reached out to a panel on the wall and hit it hard with the side of his fist.

The panel chimed dully, a thick, rasping sound as the transparent shell began to grind painfully upwards. The chamber was in poor repair, Sheppard realized, just like the rest of the ship. Hundreds of Wraith must have already died there, trapped, suffocated or starved as their support systems failed.

This one, though, was very much alive. Sheppard saw it lurch out of the chamber, massive fists bunching. Its masked head dipped towards Ceana.

"Master," Dughan said, bowing and gesturing to the girl. "She is for you. Feed, and be strong."

There was no doubt now. The villagers were engaged in some sickening bargain with the Wraith trapped here, waking them one by one, offering their children as meals with only a soporific draught to dull the pain of their ending. In return, their village was spared.

That bargain ended tonight. Sheppard stepped around the corner, smooth and fast, the P90 centered on the Wraith's center of mass and his teammates spilling out after him. "Back off, pal. Breakfast is cancelled."

The creature snapped around to face him. In front of it, Ceana stood with eyes wide, her mouth open in shock. "John? What are you doing?"

"Trying to save your life." The Wraith was too close to her. If he opened fire the ricochets from its armor would tear her apart. "So meet me halfway and get away from that thing."

"No!" she screamed. "Go away!"

Before he could answer the chamber was full of bodies, all yelling at each other. Keller was reaching out to Ceana, trying to coax the child away from the hulking alien at her back. McKay was moving towards a vantage point closer to the hibernation chamber, while Wright was circling the group, trying to get a clear shot around the shouting, confused villagers.

Only the Wraith was still.

The situation had gone very bad, very quickly. Sheppard cursed himself. He should have listened to Wright, intervened earlier. "Ceana…"

She was shaking her head at him. "You shouldn't be here."

"Just let us help you!"

"You can't," she said dully, and then the strength went out of her. She sank to her knees.

Fleetingly, Sheppard had a clear shot over her head. He squeezed the trigger, sent a clattering burst into the Wraith's shoulder, but then Marchal was in the way, running towards his daughter, howling her name.

The Wraith caught him by the jaw, stilling his cries. Then it span him clear around and smashed the flat of its other hand into his back.

The blow was perfectly aimed, brutally delivered. It took Marchal off his feet, whirled him through the air and straight into Sheppard.

He tumbled in a tangle of limbs and curses, the weight of the villager's body slamming him backwards into the passage, knocking him to the floor. He heard a yammer of gunfire as he fell, Wright's or McKay's, possibly both. Then a solid impact, a cry of fear.

Sheppard rolled out from under Marchal, dived back into the chamber.

Wright was down, sprawled, and the Wraith had Dughan by the throat. Sheppard brought the P90 up again but there wasn't even time to aim before the creature leapt, the old man still in its grip, down into a gaping rent in the deck.

He ran to the edge, saw no movement. "Aw hell."

"Okay," McKay muttered, aiming nervously down alongside him. "That didn't go so well."

Wright was sitting up. "Sorry, sir, it was just too fast."

"Ceana's drugged," Keller called, from the other side of the chamber. "But she's all right. Marchal's in bad shape, though."

"See what you can do for them." He slung the P90, looking for a route down through the tangled wreckage. "Wright, stay with her. Once Marchal's stabilized, get everybody back to the jumper."

McKay stared at him. "Where are you going?"

"After Dughan. Come on."

They found the Elder within a few minutes. He was crumpled against a wall on the next deck down, his coat torn open, his skin desiccated and stretched like dusty paper over his bones. Sheppard gazed at Dughan's eyeless ruin of a face and tried not to feel sorry for the old man, but a meal for Wraith was no way for anyone to end their days.

There was something lying next to the corpse; a hand-sized slab of glossy carapace, its screen glowing faintly. Sheppard picked it up. "Tracker."

"Yeah, must be what I spotted from the jumper." McKay took it from him. "Looks like it's homed in on some kind of beacon — probably how they navigate here through the fog."

"There's a beacon running on this ship?"

McKay shrugged. "Automatic distress call from the crash? Whenever that was. Too weak to pick up unless you know what you're looking for, especially with the particle layer." He tossed the thing aside. "You know what bugs me, though?"

"Being right all the time?"

"No, I'm perfectly fine with that." McKay gestured upwards. "All those hibernation chambers, the empty ones. You think Dughan's people woke them up?"

"Sure looks that way."

"So where are they all?"

Sheppard opened his mouth to answer, realized he didn't have anything to say, and closed it again. The ship, however, chose that moment to speak for him. No sooner had his jaw snapped shut than a high, piercing scream began to echo through the vessel, a liquid shrieking, painfully loud. Sheppard grimaced, resisting the urge to clamp his hands over his ears. "Now what?"

"Alert siren." McKay was looking around wildly. "Our buddy from upstairs is trying to warn the rest of the ship."

The Wraith had only just woken, Sheppard thought. It might not even know that the vessel was on the ground, let alone broken and deserted. "Could he open the other hibernation chambers?"

McKay was striding across the deck. He had spotted a panel set into one wall, a dull lens of glassy, corroded chitin. "I don't know. Maybe."

Sheppard watched him tapping at the lens, saw icons swim and shift under its surface. "I guess stopping him might be a good idea."

"What do think I'm trying to — Oh."

"Oh?"

"As in 'Oh crap.'" McKay was staring at the lens. "You know what I was saying about the beacon being too weak to get through the particle layer? Well, Buddy's just increased the signal strength by a factor of about ten thousand."

Sheppard was almost impressed. "That's smart, for warrior caste."

"Yeah, I've heard people say the same thing about you." McKay began stabbing at the control surface again. "Seriously, it's broadcasting clear out of the atmosphere. If there are any other Wraith nearby…"

"Oh, today just keeps getting better." Sheppard peered into the lens, saw strange shapes moving there, like plankton under a microscope. "You can shut it down, right?"

"Not from here. I can't access emergency systems on this." McKay stepped back. "We need a major control link. Which is probably where Buddy is right now, if he's not already out

waking every other Wraith he can find. In either case we—"
His eyes widened. "No! Wait, I've got it!"

"Never doubted you for a second." Sheppard watched McKay's fingers dancing rapidly over the lens. "While you're at it, can you shut that damn racket off?"

"Nope. Emergency system. But what I can do is access the power plant Buddy's using. Route it away from the beacon." The panel chirruped thickly and changed color. "There."

"What about the signal?"

"Well, a few seconds' worth is still propagating outwards, so there's a chance more Wraith could arrive. Basically, the sooner we get everybody off this planet the better."

The alarm slowed, deepened to a grinding bellow, then went silent.

"Oh no," said McKay quietly.

"What?" Sheppard frowned. "Alarm bad, no alarm good. Isn't that right?"

"Usually, yes." McKay prodded at the panel, this time with no obvious effect. "But not today. Like I said, the emergency systems should still have power. If they haven't, that means…"

Far off, in the distance, thunder rolled.

"Energy feedback. The ship's too damaged to contain the bypass."

"How long?"

"Until it goes reactor-critical?" McKay spread his hands. "I'd guess slightly less time than it'll take us to get out of here."

Sheppard grabbed his shoulder, turned him and began to propel him down the passageway. "Still okay with being right all the time?"

"I'll let you know."

Thankfully, McKay's calculations were off by some degree. Sheppard was able to get McKay all the way back to the entrance wound before the first explosions began to tear their way through the ship, and was clambering in through the puddle jumper's rear hatch when the Wraith vessel finally succumbed to its own internal energies.

He looked back, saw the south edge of the ship vanish in a billowing cloud of fire, a rippling detonation that tore along its length in no more than a second. He felt its heat wash over him, the fizzing hammer of its shockwave, and dived forwards, hitting the door panel as he flung himself, headlong, at the controls.

He had seen stone rising in the explosion; at a distance, no more than fragments of shadow, but Sheppard knew that untold thousands of tons of rock were in the air. He wanted to be away before any of it came back down again.

He dropped into the control seat, swept his hands over the board. "Everybody hang on!"

The jumper surged to life. He took the drives to full power, felt the ship whirl up into the sky, heard the startled cries of the other occupants. This was no time to be gentle, though. Boulders were already slamming into the ocean below.

And then they were out over open sea. He looked back. McKay and Keller were gaping at him, Wright and the other marines clutching at every handhold they could find.

"Now, that wasn't so bad," he grinned. "Was it?"

Light flooded through the forward port. Outside the ship, night had turned into a brief, blinding day.

There was just enough time for every alarm on the jumper to start howling at once before the second, and infinitely more powerful blast wave picked the vessel up, spun it around a few times, and then hurled it mercilessly down at the dark and boiling sea.

Much later, Keller tapped Sheppard on the shoulder. "Marchal's regaining consciousness," she whispered.

"Great." He unfolded himself from under the control board, and stood up. "How is he?"

She shook her head sadly. "Go easy on him. I don't think we've got long."

"Thanks, doc." He glanced down at McKay. "Okay to take a break?"

"Sure." McKay had a selection of the jumper's control crystals spread out on the deck in front of him. "I'm gonna be a while with these anyway."

Sheppard stepped carefully past him, then followed Keller to the aft section, rolling his head around on his shoulders to straighten out the kinks. He had been contorting himself into various access panels almost from the moment the jumper had come to rest, stripping out crystals so that McKay could realign them before carefully slotting them back into place. Together they had managed to restart life support, but the engines and sensors were still offline.

The explosion had lashed the jumper with a huge electromagnetic pulse, knocking out almost every system instantly and dumping the vessel onto the seabed. Sheppard was trying very hard to forget that there were a couple of hundred feet of water above him.

Marchal was on a bench in the jumper's aft section, draped in a silvery thermal blanket. His face was slack, gray-white, but his eyes were open and focused on Sheppard. "Where's Ceana?"

Sheppard crouched next to him. "She's right here."

The villager couldn't turn his head. The Wraith's blow had smashed his spine. "Is she well?"

"Yes," snapped Wright, from the sensor board. "No thanks to you."

Sheppard glared at her, but Marchal just chuckled weakly. "She drank the draught. She was safe. As soon as the monster sipped from her he'd be out like a candle."

"You mean you can drug Wraith during feeding?" Keller glanced back at Ceana, still curled unconscious on the opposite bench. "How long does it last?"

"Long enough for the journey." He coughed. Crimson threaded his chin. "To the cave of bones..."

Sheppard frowned. While a sedative that could knock out

a feeding Wraith might be useful in the future, Keller's medical curiosity was getting in the way of more important issues. "Look, hold up. You were using Ceana as *bait?*"

The man's reply was little more than a whisper. "Can't bring in a catch without bait, two-wrist."

There was a faint whining sound from the front of the cabin, a flutter of light. Sheppard saw McKay and Wright leaning over the sensor board. He touched Marchal's shoulder, a moment of reassurance that the man probably couldn't feel, and leaned around the bulkhead door. "Anything?"

McKay was tapping nervously at the board. "Sensors are online. Um…"

"Problem?"

"I don't think so. Just picking up a lot of movement." His eyebrows went up. "Whoa. Something's going over us."

"A big something?"

"Either one big something or a lot of little somethings."

"The explosion must have stirred up all the sea life for miles," said Wright. "Probably just squid."

As she spoke, something slithered past the forward viewport. Sheppard looked up, and for a horrible instant thought he saw something peering in at him. Then it was gone, a ragged shadow darting away into the gloom.

It could only have been a fish, but the half-glimpse he had of it left him profoundly unnerved. "Nice work, people. But just in case there's anything out there big enough to think we're food…"

Behind him, Keller whispered his name.

He turned back to her. She was dabbing at Marchal's lips with gauze, and it was coming away red. At her touch, the man moaned softly. "The Mainlanders."

"Try not to talk," Sheppard told him.

Marchal's jaw worked. "We warned them, but they sailed out too far, fished too deep. Woke something…"

"The Wraith?"

"No. The Wraith brought us here. Like cattle. My father's father…" He sucked in a breath. "He found the village. Empty. They…"

Keller was readying a syringe. "Marchal, hold on."

"Don't go back," the villager whispered. "They're awake now. Don't go back."

Keller did her best, but there had never been any real hope. She kept working on Marchal even while Sheppard was piloting the jumper up and out of the ocean, only stopping once they were in the air. Maybe, he thought later, she had wanted his final moments to be in daylight.

At cruising speed it took only minutes to get back to Ceana's village. Sheppard had expected the little community to be in chaos, the villagers milling in terror. The explosion must have been clearly visible, even through the fog.

There were no panicked crowds to greet him, though. He set the jumper down on an empty beach.

The fog had thickened overnight. A solid wall of it met him as he stepped out the cargo door, the sudden chill harsh in his throat. It felt like a physical weight, oppressive. It deadened sound, halted the air. There was no wind at all now.

Even the sea was silent.

Keller trotted down the ramp to join him. "Where is everyone?"

"Hiding, probably." He checked the P90, settled his headset more comfortably over his ear. "Look, you'd better stay with Ceana. We'll find the villagers, try to set up an evacuation plan."

"John, I've got a bad feeling about this." She hugged herself. "Something's not right here."

Sheppard couldn't help but agree. There was something ugly about the silence, something sinister. He turned back, as if to reassure himself that the jumper was still real and solid behind him, and as he did something small and slender darted from it and scampered away into the fog.

"Ceana?" He squinted into the grayness, trying to see which way the child had gone, but she was already out of sight. "Ceana!"

Wright was in the hatchway. "She just ran straight past us."

Sheppard sighed. "Okay, everybody spread out, full sweep. As soon as you find someone, call in."

He made his way through empty streets, past dark houses with windows shuttered and doors ajar. After a few minutes he gave up calling Ceana's name, or shouting for anyone to answer him. There were no replies, not even echoes. The village was lifeless.

Finally, as he emerged from checking Sul Dughan's lodge, he heard something that was not his own breath or footfalls. High above him, a quiet sobbing.

It took a few minutes for him to find his way to her, up a narrow, rocky path half hidden in the jagged rocks of the cliff face. By then Ceana's weeping had ceased. She stood quietly now, gazing out to sea, her pale skin and bleached wool shirt making her almost one with the fog.

"You had me worried," Sheppard gasped, as he drew close. The path had been steep, and the fog was raw and choking. There was a fire in his chest.

"Sorry."

"Ceana?" She hadn't moved at all. Sheppard wondered how close the edge of the cliff was, and froze. "Where's everyone hiding?"

"They're not hiding. They're gone."

"I don't understand. Gone where?"

"To the Sea Folk."

He shook his head. "Ceana, you don't have to worry about the Sea Folk any more. We blew their ship up. They're all dead."

"You stupid man!" She whirled. "The Sea Folk aren't Wraith! They were here before the Wraith, before the ruins…"

"Kid, listen, that doesn't make any sense."

She sighed. "My people came here on that ship. The Wraith

brought us, but they crashed. Most of them died. My ancestors killed the rest. When they found the village on this island they thought they finally had a safe place to live…" She turned back to the invisible sea. Sheppard noticed that she had her bone flute clutched in one hand. "I was five when people started vanishing. The Sea King had woken, and he was taking his due."

It was a legend, a fairy tale, but she was telling him as though it was a truth she'd known all her life. "Dughan said we should feed him a Wraith. He knew how to make the draught, how to bait them, catch them. Chain them in the cave of bones." She nodded downwards. "There, so nobody would hear them screaming. They heal, you see. The Sea Folk take us quickly, but Wraith last for ages."

Suddenly, everything made sense to John Sheppard. People going mad under the mutating sky, wandering out into the ocean like Dughan had told him. To explain it, a legend of some carnivorous king beneath the waves. The Elder and his chosen few sailing to the Wraith vessel for their sacrifices, baiting them with children, drugging them with the draught. A cave of bones, carved into flutes for their macabre festival.

The Wraith were not preying on the village. It was the other way around.

He wondered how long a Wraith would survive, chained and roped above the wild waves. Weeks, maybe. Months. The thought sickened him. "Ceana, come with us. We'll find your people. You don't have to do this any more."

She looked back at him, over her shoulder. "I played well, didn't I?"

Sheppard realized what was going to happen then, and lurched towards her. But she had already taken her final step into the mist, and was gone.

He ran, as hard as he had ever run, down the path, past the dark, silent lodge and into the cove. He ran to the water's edge, calling her name. Knowing she could not answer.

A hundred feet down onto jagged rocks, into the cold, silent sea. There was no hope. But he waded out anyway. He could not leave her to the ocean.

When he was in up to his knees, he stopped. There was something blocking his way. A shadow, a tall shape in the fog, tattered and dark and as motionless as stone.

A tiny, thin body, pale and broken, was cradled in its arms.

Sheppard stumbled to a halt, brought the P90 up in shaking hands. He had seen this shape before, in the village streets, but this wasn't a costume. Its limbs were not stilts. The ragged edges of it were not sailcloth. And the blank, terrible mask it wore was not carved and painted wood.

The sight of it stopped the breath in his throat. It took all the strength he had left to speak.

"Give her back."

The shape moved, then, its awful head tipping slightly towards him; just enough for him to see that, contrary to what he'd first thought, the Sea King wore no mask. Then the fog heaved, churned by the black waves beneath, revealing for the briefest of times that the water beyond it was peppered with dark shapes, as hunched and frayed as the faceless thing before him. And among those forms, something else, something that could, if he chose to believe it, be the heads and shoulders of human beings, two hundred or more, shrinking away into the ocean as they walked, step by slow, unhurried step, away from the beach and into the domain of the Sea Folk.

But Sheppard could not bring himself to believe that. The thought of it was too vile. And besides, when the fog moved again there were no shapes in the water, no bent and tattered shadows extracting their terrible tribute.

There was just the grey mist and the black sea. He was alone, beneath the dreadful, changing sky.

STARGATE SG-1
When On Earth

Sabine C. Bauer

THE WORMHOLE had disengaged, and the Chappa'ai stood inert. This and the fallen were the only things silent in the entire room. Hil'tac, the last of Apophis's Jaffa who had pursued them lay dead, struck by multiple projectiles from the Tau'ri's weapons. His comrades who followed had been destroyed by the contraption the Tau'ri referred to as an 'iris.' But means notwithstanding, Teal'c was the one who had killed them, and he would have to make his peace with that. Not now, however. Now adjusting to this new world took precedence.

He was accustomed to people keeping their Chappa'ai in all manner of locations — most frequently out in the open for ease of access — but he could truthfully say that he had never in his travels come across an arrangement as peculiar as this. The Tau'ri Chappa'ai sat on a dais constructed of some kind of metal mesh — surely not designed by the Gate Builders — at one side of a square, unadorned, high-ceilinged chamber that was small for its purpose. In fact, it reminded Teal'c of nothing so much as of the inside of a gray box.

Set high in the opposite wall was a wide window, the only one in the room, and behind it Teal'c could see another, darker chamber and people staring down at the mayhem unfolding around the Chappa'ai. A short while ago someone had shouted for 'medics,' and he assumed that this referred to the men who soon after had rushed through the doors carrying what he took to be medical paraphernalia. Jaffa had no use for those, of course, but he had frequently witnessed their application.

These medics had taken away the one called Casey, who had sustained serious injuries when covering their escape from Chulak, and were guiding out several other wounded. Major Kawalski, who had guarded Casey until the arrival of the medics, had refused to go with them and now stood staring, seemingly as adrift in this sea of bodies as Teal'c felt. The room was still teeming with people. In fact, more seemed to be arriving constantly to fuss over the refugees, soothe nerves, inspect minor injuries, and issue directions.

O'Neill, Daniel Jackson, and Captain Carter slowly descended the metal walkway. Teal'c followed hesitantly, no longer sure of himself. Despite the number of people milling about, a path cleared almost instantly as refugees and Tau'ri alike attempted to put distance between themselves and the Jaffa. He was familiar with loathing and fear — after all, until this very day he had been in the service of Apophis — but he had never been distrusted. He could have laughed at the irony of it. As First Prime he had been the most trusted of Apophis's Jaffa when he least deserved that trust. Now, although he was entirely truthful in his allegiance, trust was withheld.

Rankle as it might, he would not question it, Teal'c promised himself. They had a right to be distrustful, and but for one hot-headed, impulsive act — which Master Bra'tac would likely hold up to students to come as an example of how not to arrive at a decision — he had done nothing to inspire confidence in anyone. Not in the snotty-nosed child who stared at him with terror-glazed eyes, not in the old woman who would mutter a quiet curse as soon as she had ducked from his scrutiny. Certainly not in Daniel Jackson who was battling his hatred and not quite succeeding. Perhaps not even in O'Neill.

Beckoned by the short, stout, bald man who had dismissed the team earlier and who seemed to be the leader of the Tau'ri, O'Neill had left the room and presently appeared behind the window in the chamber above. Evidently the Tau'ri leader had desired a more private conference. Just as evidently that conference became heated within a very short span of time. O'Neill's posture bespoke a man barely controlling his temper.

His leader, as was a leader's prerogative, did not find it necessary to exert such control. Clearly, Tau'ri technology was more advanced than Teal'c had originally surmised; the large transparent pane in the window served to smother the sound of the man's angry voice even to a Jaffa's acute hearing.

Teal'c walked over to Hil'tac's body and picked up the staff weapon. His own weapon he had entrusted to Captain Carter, who had taken it away, but habit forced him to follow tradition, even though he no longer knew why. It was a last gesture of respect to the fallen to secure his weapon and pass it on to his next of kin, but here, among the Tau'ri, there was no one to whom he could possibly pass on this legacy.

As he straightened up, he noticed two black-clad warriors approaching him. For a moment he fooled himself into believing that they might wish to extend their welcome, then he saw the apprehension, as well as the steely will to obey their leaders' commands in spite of it. Not an offer of friendship then. They were, however, courteous.

"Sir?" the elder ventured. "We have orders to take you to the infirmary."

"It's routine," added his comrade, a little too brightly. "Everyone who's been off-world has to get a checkup. Alien bugs, you know?"

Indeed, Teal'c did not. Had the Tau'ri had a problem with insect bites while visiting other worlds? And what was an 'infirmary'? Did he strike these people as so physically feeble that he needed to be brought to a place of that name? He carefully kept his face blank, certain that any admission of ignorance or confusion would produce sneers rather than explanations.

The elder warrior's reaction seemed to confirm the wisdom of that choice. He leveled a cold stare at the younger man and barked, "Cut the crap, Jenkins!" Then he returned his attention to Teal'c. Almost. His gaze lingered on the staff weapon in Teal'c's hand. "That's some kind of gun, isn't it?"

"It is not."

"You cut the crap too!" the man snapped. "I've seen those other guys who were geared up just like you!" His eyes briefly darted to the place where the other Jaffa had fallen, then continued to scrutinize Teal'c's armor. They were hard as flint and filled with misgiving. "They shot balls of fire with those sticks!"

Teal'c arrived at another spontaneous decision, as instinctive and potentially ill-advised as the one he had made in Apophis's dungeon. Tradition would have to change. Or perhaps it merely was time for fresh kinship. He extended his arm, shoving the weapon at the warrior — who took a step back and raised his own gun.

"Do not fear. It is quite safe, unless it is pointed at you," Teal'c endeavored to reassure the man. "Take it."

It was the younger warrior, still prone to the rashness and carelessness of youth, who took heart first. Without a moment's hesitation he lowered his gun and snatched the proffered staff weapon. "Wow," he whispered. "Cool!" Almost reverently his fingers glided along the shaft, then they encompassed the thickened center portion, tracing its intricate carvings.

"I advise caution," Teal'c said. "You might —"

He was too late.

The man had inadvertently depressed the trigger. The top of the staff split open to release a menace of blue light. A heartbeat later the charge launched.

Mercifully, the young fool had been pointing the staff back at the Chappa'ai and the scaffold it stood on. Thus, instead of killing or injuring any of the Tau'ri or the refugees from Chulak, the blast merely scorched the railing and sent a glob of molten metal dripping to the floor beneath the site of the main impact. At the same time warning klaxons erupted, replacing the stunned silence in the room with their own kind of mayhem.

"What in the hell is going on down there?" The bellow of a disembodied voice very nearly drowned out the klaxons. Teal'c could not determine where it came from — did the

Tau'ri possess a *vocume*? — but he recognized it as belonging to the Tau'ri leader.

"Sorry, sir! Jenkins was trying to secure the alien weapon!"

"Could have fooled me, Sergeant! Have you tried to *succeed* in securing the weapon? And somebody shut down that god-damn noise!"

"Yessir!" shouted the man — was 'Sergeant' his name? — at the same time as the klaxons ceased their wailing. His face had reddened alarmingly, and he yanked the staff weapon from Jenkins' grasp. "Idiot," he muttered under his breath, then he glared at Teal'c. "You! Mind telling me the trick?"

"There is no trick," Teal'c informed him. "But for now, I would advise against touching any of the engravings."

"No kidding," muttered Jenkins with a furtive glance in the direction of the window and the squat figure beyond. At last, he frowned at Teal'c. "You got any more of those alien gadgets on you?"

There was the *zat'nik'tel*, of course, but recent events suggested that it might cause more unnecessary upheaval if Teal'c admitted to carrying one. Best perhaps, to keep his own counsel. He very much doubted that the Tau'ri, should they find it on him, would identify the *zat'nik'tel* as anything more consequential than a bauble. And they would likely permit him to keep such a bauble. Who knew when it might be of use?

Schooling his face into a neutral expression, he replied, "I do not."

"Just as well," growled Sergeant, and added, "You've got to come with us."

"If you don't mind," Jenkins supplied, which earned him another foul stare from his mentor.

Teal'c had yet to decide if it was intentional. He could not be entirely sure, but if it was, the Tau'ri were either far more cunning or far more tedious than he had expected. Like any Jaffa he had learned early on in his training to memorize any route he took. He had attempted to do so, from sheer force of habit, if nothing else, and found he could not.

Sergeant and Jenkins led him through a seemingly endless succession of corridors. Each of those corridors looked identical to the last, gray and unremarkable. Each of them was crossed by other gray and unremarkable corridors, their monotony broken only by sturdy metal doors that had numbers stenciled on them. At one juncture they entered a transportation device that took them upwards and to another set of corridors, equally gray and unremarkable. By that stage Teal'c had given up even on committing to memory the exact sequence of left and right turns they had taken. It was futile to do so without a reliable point of reference.

At last they turned into a short cul-de-sac. At its end a door opened into a large, brightly lit room where the gray monotony was broken by an abundance of white fabric and the colorful displays of various devices whose purpose Teal'c could not begin to fathom. It reminded him of nothing so much as a dormitory at the barracks, except the cots were uncomfortably narrow and too high.

This had to be the place where the medics had brought at least some of the injured. He was unable to see Casey, but he recognized several other faces, including that of a little girl who had an ugly gash on her forehead and had seemed petrified with fright as she watched him come through the Chappa'ai. Now she was seated on one of those tall, narrow cots, and a Tau'ri man shone a tiny light into her mouth. What could he possibly hope to discover in there? And how would it aid in healing an injury to her brow?

Before Teal'c was able to so much as guess an answer to either of these questions, another man approached him and his escort. His garb was similar to that of the person who took care of the little girl. Presumably this indicated that the man worked in this... infirmary?

"Evening, fellows," he offered cheerfully and, with a nod at Sergeant and Jenkins, added, "How about you guys just get out of the way? Guard the door or something? I'll take care of him, and get him ready so the doc can have a look at him."

Jenkins shrugged and cast a questioning glance at Sergeant whose frown suggested that he either disliked the proposal or was considering it with more diligence than warranted. Finally he sniffed. "Sure. Why the hell not? We've got his gun, and it's not like he can get out of here."

This last piece of information was cause for alarm. For the first time since his arrival, Teal'c consciously registered the fact that he had yet to see a window or a door that did not lead into more windowless spaces — or any sign that there actually was such a thing as open air, wind, rain, and a sky on this world of the Tau'ri.

Was the planet's surface poisoned? The atmosphere unbreathable?

Teal'c had seen such planets. Some, though inhospitable, had been beautiful — in a lethal fashion. Some even had had inhabitants, burrowing deep underground and huddling in sealed caverns, much as the Tau'ri appeared to do. Unlike the Tau'ri however, those people had borne the telltale signs of poison: skin covered in sores, thin, bleached hair, red-rimmed eyes, any number of indicators betraying that their world would kill them before long. Not so the Tau'ri. They all appeared to be in perfect health — or, as Daniel Jackson's flawed vision proved, as healthy as anyone could be without a symbiote.

"Alright, pal! It's you and me!" exclaimed the infirmary worker. He seemed to be unduly thrilled about this. His left eye closed and opened again, which had to be either a nervous tic brought on by excitement or a Tau'ri gesture intended to signal jocularity.

"Indeed it is not," replied Teal'c, resisting an absurd impulse to mimic the man's eye-blinking. "It would appear that there is a great number of other people in this room."

"Trust me to pull the shy one!" The man jovially slapped Teal'c's shoulder. "Come on, buddy. We've got a private room for you."

"I am not shy. Also, I advise you do not touch me without warning. I am a trained warrior. I may misconstrue your intentions and accidentally harm you."

"I very much doubt that," the man replied on a laugh. He was either a fool or supremely confident. "I'm tougher than I look."

Teal'c very much doubted that. However, he considered it unwise to prove his point; the Tau'ri would almost certainly take exception to it. So he kept silent and waited for what was to come.

What came was something of a surprise.

The man sighed, his shoulders slumped a little, and his demeanor changed markedly. "Okay. I guess the chirpy bedside manner thing doesn't work for you. So how about we try the straightforward approach?"

"That would be appreciated."

"Well, that's something." He reached out, reconsidered, and let his hand drop. "Right… right. Look, we decided it might be better if we took you to a private room. Folks here" — his arm described a sweeping circle that encompassed this peculiar room and everyone in it — "well, they're kinda worried about you."

"I understand." Teal'c had surmised as much. If the furtive glances and ducked heads had not been revealing enough, he had heard all he needed to hear. The curtains that were drawn around many of those strange high cots could not stop anxious whispers and angry snarls from floating around the room.

"Mostly about that… snake-thing?" his talkative companion supplied. "The critter you carry in your… womb?"

"Pouch."

"What?"

"We refer to it as a 'pouch.'"

"Ah… *We*?"

"My people. The Jaffa."

On hearing the name, a woman with the bearing of a clan leader, who stood by a cot across the room, glared at him with eyes full of hate. Then she slowly, deliberately tore her gaze away, spat on the floor, and stared back at him. Teal'c averted his eyes. He remembered her from the dungeon on Chulak. Her son, a bright, plucky child of about ten, had been one of the chosen. Teal'c had taken him.

His escort cringed and began ushering him along. "Sorry 'bout that. Don't know what's gotten into her…"

"I know what has… gotten into her." Using the phrase, whose meaning Teal'c had only deduced from the context, was a gamble, but one he would have to take regularly from now on if he was to adapt to the Tau'ri and their idiom. When no reaction was forthcoming, he presumed that he had used it correctly. "I know," he repeated, "and it is none of your doing. There is no need for you to feel sorry."

The man did not reply. After all, there was nothing that could be said. He led the way in silence, into an adjoining corridor — gray and unremarkable — and after a few steps came to a halt in front of an unmarked door. He opened it and showed Teal'c inside a small room that held another one of those peculiar beds, two chairs, and not much else.

"Make yourself at home," his companion recommended. "It's not much –"

"It is not."

"But it's yours." The man's eye twitched in another one of its nervous blinks. He marched over to a cupboard, the only item of furniture beside the cot and chairs, and withdrew a thin wad of folded fabric. "Now the fun part starts," he promised cheerfully. "I'll have to ask you to take off your… uh…" — he frowned at Teal'c's armor — "suit and put this on. Once you're done I'm gonna have to take your stuff, 'cos they'll want to take a look at it, but you'll get it back."

"Who are 'they'?" Teal'c inquired, accepting the wad of fabric.

"Oh, you know…"

Evidently Teal'c did not, else he would not have asked, but the man seemed oblivious to this simple logic. He waved his hand indecisively, and his eye twitched yet again. "I'm gonna leave you alone now, so you can change. I'll be back in a few. Meantime, holler if you need anything." With that he disappeared and closed the door.

In a few what?

And Teal'c would most definitely not holler. Jaffa did not holler. Jaffa bellowed to incite fear in the enemy.

Bemused and not a little disturbed, Teal'c began to strip out of his armor. It felt as if, with every familiar piece of metal he unfastened, he stripped away a piece of himself to hand over to the Tau'ri. Some faceless, nameless Tau'ri of nebulous rank who were known only as 'they.'

One thing was absolutely certain: this had not been among the consequences Teal'c had considered prior to arriving at his irrevocable decision. Now that he thought of it, he could not recall considering many consequences at all, which spoke volumes as to O'Neill's powers of persuasion.

No. 'Persuasion' was the wrong word entirely. Because, if truth be told, O'Neill had not persuaded. He had simply been... himself, resolved to do what was right if not necessarily wise. That very bloody-mindedness was what had swayed Teal'c. No one and nothing could withstand such a force, and it had swept him along like a maelstrom.

And now?

With a Jaffa's finely honed sense of irony, he permitted himself to snarl at the question. Now Teal'c, son of Ronac, was standing in a cramped chamber, beyond question guarded and naked as his mother had birthed him, attempting to discover an effective way of wearing a garment — some kind of shirt? — that would barely have clothed a child, let alone a full-grown Jaffa. On a small fabric tab inside the collar a group of letters spelled out "XXL." Teal'c doubted that this was of any instructive value. He tentatively slipped one arm into a too-short sleeve, then the other. The shirt was too tight across the shoulders and would not meet up in front, even when he fastened the three sets of ties. This would not do at all.

He unfastened the ties and stripped again.

Was this shirt supposed to be worn back to front, exposing his *mik'ta* to anyone who cared to look? Surely not. Even the Tau'ri had to be more dignified than that.

Finally he decided that, irrespective of the Tau'ri custom in regard to garments such as this, he was going to fashion it into a loincloth. It struck him as the only way of preserving at least a modicum of decency.

He had barely managed to secure the sleeves around his hips when, upon a brief knock, the door flew open and his guide reappeared.

The man came to an abrupt halt in the doorway and stared, eyes wide. He opened his mouth, as if about to say something. His gaze drifted to Teal'c's face, upon which his mouth closed and his rather protuberant Adam's apple moved rapidly as though he was swallowing something.

At last his capacity to speak returned. "Neat idea," he declared, sounding disingenuous. "Real neat… uh… The doc'll be here any minute now, okay?"

It was not. Or perhaps it was. Who could tell? Since Teal'c could not begin to fathom what the arrival of a 'doc' might herald or how to plan for an event that was supposed to occur at any minute — what a singularly useless measure of time! — he could not possibly determine whether or not anything was okay.

At least his new friend did not insist on an answer. He had turned away and busied himself by gathering Teal'c's armor to take it only the Tau'ri knew where. It appeared that the task was more onerous than he had anticipated. His face had reddened, and he was staggering under the weight of the chain mail and protective plates.

"Do you require assistance?" Teal'c asked, since courtesy seemed to demand such an offer.

"No," panted the man. "Thanks. I'll handle it." Knees buckling he disappeared into the corridor.

Moments later Teal'c heard a loud crash and some surprisingly imaginative swearing. Several of the suggestions were anatomically quite unfeasible, even for the Tau'ri. Although he had a fair idea of what had occurred and hardly required confirmation, he struggled against the temptation to leave the room and see for himself.

His inner debate was interrupted by a new arrival. A female this time. Teal'c was pleased about this. Other than with Captain Carter, he had not had any close contact with Tau'ri females. Experience showed that, if you wished to find out facts about a race rather than warlike boasts, you were well advised to talk to their women.

The first thing that struck him about this one was her size, or rather the lack thereof. She was diminutive, and her reaction on seeing Teal'c was markedly different from that of his guide. She remained unimpressed.

A glint of amusement — amusement? — in her eyes, she observed, "Interesting look. It definitely rates extra points for imagination." Then she sobered. "My apologies. We really have to do something about those gowns."

This was a *gown*?

"It appears I have a great deal to learn about Tau'ri fashion," Teal'c observed carefully.

Her reply was a chuckle. "Trust me, these things have nothing, *nothing*, to do with fashion, and thank God for that! We'll see about getting you some clothes that actually fit you just as soon as we're done here." Her gaze dropped to his bare feet. "Boots, too, though that might be a challenge... For now, would you mind just sitting down on the gurney to let me have a look at you? By the way, I'm Dr. Frasier."

While Teal'c complied with her request, she kept on chatting. "It shouldn't take too long," she promised. "And then we'll assign you quarters and you can get some rest. I realize you must be tired and that having to go through this first is an imposition. But we need to protect both you and ourselves."

The thought of a creature as delicate as this woman protecting anyone, let alone a Jaffa, would have been laughable had she not sounded so serious.

"I do not require protection." The moment he said it — as gently as he could manage — he realized that his might be untrue after all. The *zat'nik'tel* he had meant to retain for defense in a potential crisis was still attached to his armor's belt. A beginner's mistake that should not have been committed by someone as seasoned as Teal'c.

Dr. Frasier mistook his frown. "I don't mean physically. I doubt you need any protection on that score. It's a question of health. You may carry alien organisms that are harmful to us — apart from the obvious, I mean," she interjected with a slight wince. Evidently someone had informed her about the larval Goa'uld he carried. News traveled as fast among the Tau'ri as they did among any other people. "Or you could have picked up some Earth bug that might be harmful to you."

Were all Tau'ri afflicted by an obsession with pests?

"None of your insects could possibly harm me."

"Oh!" That light, brief laugh rang out again. "Not that kind of bug. Microscopic organisms — bacteria or viruses — that cause disease. We call them bugs." She had plugged an odd metal hoop into her ears. From it dangled a second piece of metal that was joined to the hoop with a thin plastic hose.

Since she pressed the piece of metal to his chest, Teal'c deduced that she probably had not plugged her ears in order to avoid having to listen to him. "Those… bugs cannot harm me either. I do not succumb to disease. Nor do I require rest."

"Sure you don't," she murmured, giving the impression that she concentrated on sounds that were transmitted by the piece of metal through the hose and to her ears. "Heard it all before. None of you guys ever gets sick or needs rest."

"That is correct. An opportunity to *kelno'reem* would be welcome however."

Her head snapped up, and she stared at him. "An opportunity to *what*?"

"*Kelno'reem.*" The woman's expression indicated that she was unfamiliar with either the word, or the concept, or both. Teal'c searched for the simplest way of explaining an act that came as natural as breathing. "It is a state of intense concentration but, at the same time, an absence of conscious thought."

"You mean meditation?"

"No." When he left it at that, she looked at him expectantly, her gaze forcing him to continue. This silent form of compulsion struck him as a powerful, vastly effective method of interrogation. "Meditation may aid in achieving a state of *kelno'reem*, but it is a mere shadow thereof. In *kelno'reem* my subconscious is in control, allowing me to commune with my symbiote."

"Ah, yes… your symbiote." It appeared to fascinate her. Frowning with concentration, she studied his pouch flaps. "So, this is where you keep the… Goa'uld implant? The symbiote?"

"Indeed."

She hesitated briefly, as if again expecting him to add something. When nothing was forthcoming, she asked, "Is it safe?"

"Exceedingly so. My life depends on the symbiote's well-being."

"That's… not quite what I meant. Would it be okay if I… uhm… examined the inside?"

"You may." Teal'c lay back on the odd bed he had been requested to sit on. He nodded at the healer. "Do not concern yourself. The symbiote is too immature to desire a host."

"That's good to know." She was unlikely to be wholly reassured, but she fought valiantly not to show it. He was beginning to develop a grudging respect for her.

She lightly pushed against one of his pouch flaps, then the contact firmed. Her frown deepened. Whatever she might have discovered, she had not foreseen it.

Deciding to ignore the examination as best he could, Teal'c let his thoughts drift back to the dawn of this singular day and the way the passage of time, swift and relentless, had been dragged before his very eyes, showing him dread — as deep-seated as it was overwhelming — where it had never before occurred to him to dread.

His son was growing up and nearing his *prim'ta*.

"Happy news, my husband!"

Drey'auc's face had shone with joy. A joy Teal'c did not feel. Instead he had experienced a sense of dismay so deep that he had trouble concealing it from his wife.

To his disgrace, he winced.

"I'm sorry! I didn't mean to…" Dr. Frasier froze momentarily, and her voice trailed off before she could explain what it was that she had not meant. Then she composed herself and resumed the briskness that appeared customary for her. "I don't want to hurt you," she said. "So you'll have to let me know if I'm causing you pain or discomfort. I'll be as careful as I can."

Unlike everyone else he had encountered in this place so far, Dr. Frasier seemed unafraid, which was remarkable in one unarmed and physically unimposing. Teal'c could snap this small, delicate woman in half without breaking a sweat. In the past he had had no compunction about doing so to people who caused him pain or discomfort. After all, he was Jaffa.

She seemed utterly oblivious to what that meant.

"Interesting," she murmured, more to herself than him, then she straightened up. "Look, Mr. T…" Suddenly she blinked, shook her head, and gave a soft chuckle.

Teal'c failed to see any cause for levity, and he decided that the Tau'ri sense of humor had to be a far cry from that of the Jaffa.

The woman's face sobered. "I'm sorry, Mr. …" She gave up with a sigh. "How do you pronounce your name again?"

"There will be no 'Mister' necessary."

At that moment the door swung open, and through it Teal'c

could see the guards he had known to be there, as well as a rather more welcome figure.

"Just 'T', huh?" O'Neill entered the room without being bidden and approached Teal'c's cot, nodding in approval. "That actually could work, you —"

"Not for me, Colonel!" Dr. Frasier stood barely tall enough to reach O'Neill's shoulder, and this only because she wore the most outlandish footwear Teal'c had ever seen — absurdly raised at the heel and pointed at the toes. At any rate, what she lacked in height, she made up for in audacity.

As far as Teal'c had been able to determine, O'Neill was the First Prime of the Tau'ri leader he served. And yet, this woman did not seem to be cowed by his position. A reproving look on her face, she declared, "I like to do my patients the courtesy of addressing them by their proper name."

"I am not a patient!" Teal'c interjected at the same time as O'Neill blurted, "*Patient*? Is there anything wrong with him?"

"No!" replied Teal'c and Dr. Frasier in unison, although the woman sounded as if she were almost annoyed about it.

"In that case, Doctor, you might wanna curb that understandable curiosity and check on some of your more dented clientele." O'Neill cocked a thumb over his shoulder, presumably indicating the occupants of the larger, less private room, most of them refugees from Chulak. "Mr. T here is done. Come on, Teal'c, I need to introduce you to an Earth ritual. It's called Happy Hour."

Happy Hour?

If it was in any way related to the rituals designed to engender felicity among the Jaffa, it would involve a measuring of strength and skill, one man against another, with the winner deriving happiness from victory, and the loser dying happily and well and surrounded by praise for his bravery.

His interest sparked, Teal'c pushed himself up to sit and swung his legs off the bed. "I shall be honored to accompany you, O'Neill. Will there be a contest?"

O'Neill's eyebrows shot up as he took in Teal'c's costume, but he refrained from commenting — a feat that, by Teal'c's estimate, took him an inordinate amount of willpower. Then a keen, calculating look stole across his face. "A contest?" he said at last. "Depends. We could hit O'Malley's. If Big Molly's there, she's always game for shots. But I'm warning you. Last time she knocked *me* on my butt. I couldn't see straight for three days after."

Dr. Frasier gave him an exasperated look. "If either one of you is in here with a stinking hangover tomorrow morning, don't expect any tea and sympathy from me!"

"My faith forbids me to drink tea, Doc" — O'Neill's solemn tone struck Teal'c as slightly suspect — "and I wouldn't dream of expecting sympathy."

Teal'c was intrigued. Obviously, the Tau'ri denied combatants medical care for injuries sustained during the ritual duels. Indeed a harsh method of teaching caution in a race that could not avail itself of the healing properties of a symbiote. Of course, the efficacy could not be disputed. Even Master Bra'tac would be impressed.

The thought of his old friend and mentor triggered another sudden pang of wistfulness, but Teal'c resolutely shoved it aside. Regret would not magically bring his family or Bra'tac any closer, therefore it was futile. He had made his choice, and he would have to live with it.

"I am ready, O'Neill," he said firmly. "Lead the way."

"*Ready*?" O'Neill's gaze scanned Teal'c from head to toe. "Aren't you forgetting something? Like… pants, maybe?"

Teal'c cast a brief glance at the guards by the door. "Your men took my outer garments and footwear. Apparently they are deemed dangerous and require examination," he added with a twist of irony.

Whatever it was O'Neill muttered under his breath, it did not sound flattering to the soldiers' intelligence. His gaze snapped back to Teal'c. "As well as your weapons?"

"I considered it wise to surrender my possessions voluntarily." Noting O'Neill's scowl, Teal'c felt obliged on the one hand to prevent an incident and, on the other, to continue neglecting any specific mention of the *zat'nik'tel*. "You would have been expected to hand over your weapons, had you wished to enter my encampment, O'Neill. It precludes complications."

"That's what you think," O'Neill growled. Then he relaxed and caught the eye of the woman. "You think you could rustle up some scrubs for him, Doc? Else he'll only feed into all those *National Enquirer* reports of half-naked aliens boogieing around top secret US Air Force facilities."

Dr. Frasier's lips twitched. "We may have a set of xxx-larges back in the storeroom, but they'll still be snug I guess. And we don't have any shoes. Just booties."

"Never mind. I just want to get him decent enough to head up to supplies where we can grab some BDUs and a pair of boots."

"BDUs?" She cocked an eyebrow. Apparently there was some special significance attached to beedeeyous.

"As far as I'm concerned, he's part of my team," O'Neill declared, looking mulish.

It coaxed another smile from Dr. Frasier. "You know what, sir? I think I like you."

"Don't jump to conclusions." O'Neill grinned. "You haven't treated me yet."

"That's true. Then again, you haven't been my patient yet. I'm sure you'll be a pussycat, Colonel. Follow me!"

While Teal'c was grateful for the more adequate clothing Dr. Frasier had procured, these 'scrubs' were worse than merely snug. They were as tight as a second skin and too short in the arm and leg, forcing him to walk with an old man's stiff-legged gait. The ridiculous flare of fabric around his bare feet — the items the Tau'ri called 'booties' — only compounded the indignity.

The guards were still padding along like a pair of well-trained hounds, and O'Neill had not spoken since they had left the area of the infirmary. Teal'c sensed the anger boiling in him. The signs were minute, but they were there for everyone who cared to see — tense shoulders, stiff back, a small muscle ticking in his jaw now and again. As a purely ethnological observation it was fascinating: Tau'ri and Jaffa did not differ at all in this respect.

Teal'c wondered if it might improve Daniel Jackson's opinion of him if he shared this observation, and almost laughed at his own folly. He had taken the young man's wife. Should anyone dare to take Drey'auc from him, he would tear the offender limb from limb, and there was no observation in the universe that would have the power to mitigate his rage.

Of course, there was the question of what Drey'auc would think of her husband now. And what she would do. Teal'c attempted to deny his fear for her — after all, there was nothing to connect Drey'auc, or Rya'c for that matter, to his act of treason. Drey'auc of the Morning Glades had influential friends. He had to believe that she and her son would be safe.

But would she maintain her allegiance to a husband who was *shol'va*?

Teal'c attempted to push the thought away, but it refused to melt into oblivion. Instead it brought him back to his own rashness and the knowledge that he should have considered the consequences of his actions more carefully. Then again, he had hardly had leisure to do so. Hesitation on his part would have meant the death of O'Neill and the other Tau'ri.

Why had the life or death of these prisoners mattered when the lives or deaths of hundreds before them had not?

Had it been O'Neill's insane refusal to give up hope in a situation where one was best advised to suspend hope and prepare to die well?

Teal'c realized that he might never find an answer, that it had merely felt right and compelling at that moment in time. Whether it remained to be right and compelling would have to –

O'Neill had stopped so abruptly that Teal'c, lost in ruminations, almost collided with him. He gathered himself and managed to take a step back, just in time for O'Neill to whip around and glare at the guards. The men came to a halt, a little shuffling and insecure.

They were of the black-clad variety of warriors, like Sergeant and Jenkins. Teal'c had noticed that the colors of the Tau'ri warriors' garments varied, but he had yet to discover the relevant rules. The most reasonable assumption was that the colors denoted clan affiliation.

Undoubtedly, at this precise juncture in time, these men devoutly wished to be safe at the hearths of their clan. Teal'c could all but see them wilt under O'Neill's stare. If truth be told, he himself would not wish to be at the receiving end of it.

Leaden silence rolled through the corridor, and under the low ceiling the tension between O'Neill and the guards turned the air into a compressed and stifling mass.

But the men did not budge, and at last one of them spoke. "Uh… sir?"

He received no answer. Instead O'Neill continued to stare. Teal'c himself had never stood on this kind of ceremony, but he had known and served under First Primes who would not abide lower ranks addressing them unless they had been spoken to first. Could O'Neill be one of those? And how would the man fare, now that he had stepped out of line?

O'Neill's eyes narrowed, and his stare grew even more intense. "Do I know you, Airman?" he growled.

Concerned for the well-being of the forward warrior, Teal'c wished he were familiar enough with Tau'ri customs to know whether it was appropriate for him to intercede. Familiar or not, action had to be taken. He could not let –

"I dunno, sir. But I sure as hell know you." The man grinned.

What was the fool doing? Did he not realize that he was dicing with his life? No inferior rank had ever addressed a First Prime in this way — none who had lived, at any rate. Teal'c's own father had been killed for far less than that.

"Oh, for cryin' out loud!"

What was that supposed to indicate? A ritual invocation of impending grief? Teal'c could make as little sense of it as he could of the odd look on O'Neill's face.

"Lowenstein?" The enigmatic look dissolved into a grin that was at least as wide as that of the offending warrior. "Who the hell decided you were suitable for a posting here?"

"Apparently you did, Colonel. Something about a list you had to draw up?"

"Crap. Didn't think anybody would actually read it… You're only on it because I was running out of names, by the way."

"Naturally, sir." Impossibly, the man's grin grew even wider. "You don't wanna underestimate General Hammond, sir. The guy reads stuff…" The grin dimmed at last and, with a tilt of the head in Teal'c's direction, he added, "Including his own orders, if you know what I mean, Colonel."

"Starting to," O'Neill acknowledged soberly. After a moment's pause for thought, he spread his arms in an apparent attempt to look harmless. Unsuccessfully so, as far as Teal'c was concerned. "So, now that we got reacquainted, obviously you know that you can trust me."

"Oh yes, sir!" Lowenstein snorted loudly enough to make his comrade wince. "As far as I could throw you, sir. I was there when you ran rings around those Ba'ath boys in Iraq, Colonel, remember? And I was with the team that dragged you home when we finally managed to find where they kept you… more dead than alive, I might add. Don't try to kid a kidder. What do you need me to do, sir?"

"I need you to decide that my vast expertise and exceptional common sense are sufficient to guarantee the… safety… of our *peaceful* and valued guest here, and that he won't require an escort to the storeroom that merely diverts valuable resources from where they're needed. Which means that, when I tell you to leave us the hell alone in… oh" — O'Neill threw a perfunctory glance at his wristwatch — "about thirty seconds or so, you'll follow my orders."

Lowenstein pinched the bridge of his nose, scrunched his mouth into a moue, and wrinkled his forehead — all in a show of strenuous deliberation, Teal'c presumed. Finally he said, "I guess I could do that, sir… provided we make it 'pigheadedness' and 'a pinch of crazy' instead of the expertise and common sense stuff." The man's grin flashed briefly, then he turned serious, slanted another look at Teal'c and asked, "You're absolutely sure, Colonel?"

"Positive, Sergeant."

"Yessir!" Then, to his comrade, "Let's go, Sanchez!"

The man he'd called Sanchez opened his mouth as if to argue, but thought better of it. He shrugged, in a long-suffering way that suggested that he was used to his comrade's caprice. Then he fell in behind Lowenstein, who after a moment's pause turned back to face O'Neill once more.

"Permission to speak freely, sir."

O'Neill's eyebrows shot up. "You require permission now, Sergeant? Since when?"

Lips twitching in an effort to suppress another grin, Lowenstein replied, "I dunno. Just thought it was the polite thing to say… Sir, you may wanna consider trusting General Hammond. He's one of the good guys. Our kind of people."

"So noted, Sergeant. And thanks. I'll take it under advisement."

Lowenstein nodded and he and his comrade turned to leave. O'Neill watched the two men walk away until they had reached the end of the corridor and disappeared.

Finally in a position where he might ask for information without being taken for a dolt, Teal'c tried to prioritize his questions according to the potential importance of their answers.

"How do the Tau'ri know where they are going on their world?"

O'Neill blinked slowly and shook his head, as though attempting to dislodge some kind of blockage. "Come again?"

"Whereto, O'Neill?"

This time the reply was a sigh. Perhaps Teal'c had been wrong to assume that questions could or should be asked. But then O'Neill shook his head a second time and said, "Okay... sorry, Teal'c. How do we know where we're going?"

"Indeed. I have previously met troglodyte races but your burrows seem to be exceptionally..." He struggled to find a descriptor that would not sound insulting and at last settled on "uniform."

"You mean 'boring'?"

Teal'c felt a flush creep up from his toes. Some people claimed that Jaffa were incapable of blushing. He wished they were here to witness it. Or perhaps not. At any rate, he opted for honesty, especially since O'Neill seemed to be quite aware of the monotony of his abode. "The thought had crossed my mind."

"I bet. But I still don't–" A sudden flash of inspiration lit O'Neill's eyes. "Wait a minute! You think this is it? Seriously?"

"I would not presume to jest about someone's home."

"Yeah. A person's home is their mothership or something, right?"

"For some persons, yes."

The look on O'Neill's face indicated that he did not wish to further discuss such persons. Or perhaps it was a Tau'ri's understandable envy of the Goa'uld's superior design. "Well, this" — a sweep of O'Neill's arm encompassed the corridor and, by extension, dozens of its ilk — "isn't the mothership. But for now you'll have to take my word for it. We need to get you some clothes."

More corridors. However, there were fewer people. While Teal'c was reluctant to admit it, the absence of an escort had put him at ease. O'Neill, at least, seemed willing to trust him, and there was a surprising amount of solace to be found in this particular Tau'ri's trust. The warriors they encountered along the way — several more of the black-clad clan, some in the dingy kind of green O'Neill himself wore, and yet others in a sandy color that was marbled with whites and grays—showed O'Neill the respect accorded to a First Prime and otherwise went about their business without displaying any undue curiosity or attempts at interference.

At last O'Neill stopped outside another unmarked metal door, took the thin rectangle of plastic he wore on a piece of cord around his neck, and inserted it into a slit in the chunky piece of metal that was fastened to the wall beside the doorjamb. It struck Teal'c as an oddly simplistic and antiquated way of securing access, but it worked smoothly enough. The door slid open, and they entered a room that was filled with tall metal shelving units. The shelves in turn held stacks of clothing of various descriptions and orderly rows of foot- and headwear.

"It's not exactly Paris," remarked O'Neill, sounding vaguely apologetic, "but we should be able to find something that fits."

Paris was a minor—a very minor—Goa'uld who had possessed the bad sense to abduct a rival's consort, thus causing entirely unnecessary and absurdly drawn-out complications in that particular sector of the galaxy. The fool was known for his taste in fine clothing, but how O'Neill—or any of the Tau'ri for that matter—could possibly have known about it was a mystery to Teal'c.

They made their way to the back of the room, to a set of shelves that held fewer items than the others.

"X-Large section," O'Neill observed as though this explained everything. Then he chose several folded items of clothing as well as some footwear that looked supremely uncomfortable. "These should fit. If they don't we're gonna have a problem…"

"I shall endeavor not to cause any problems, O'Neill. Thank you." Teal'c took possession of the items handed to him and studied the color. The dingy green. "Will your clan be agreeable to my wearing their color?"

"What?" O'Neill had been busy trying on various types of head coverings and spun around abruptly, wearing an oddly shaped helmet. "Will my clan *what*? What clan?"

"Does not the color of the garments indicate one's affiliation?"

"Uh… yeah. Yeah. Kind of." He took off the helmet, tossed it back on the shelf, and nodded at the clothes in Teal'c's hands. "These are BDUs — a battle dress uniform. They belong to the Air Force. That's my… uh, clan. Yours, too, if you like. Up to you. I mean, if you wanna join the Marines, I –"

"What are Marines?"

O'Neill frowned. "How about you go and get changed? I'll explain later."

Teal'c retreated behind a shelf unit and tried on the new clothing. Beedeeyous. At least O'Neill had solved that particular mystery. Battle dress uniform. Recalling the offer of Happy Hour, Teal'c presumed that, although these garments obviously derived their name from being worn in battle, they also were the preferred vesture for the ritual fights. He attempted a brief sequence of *lok'nel* moves and found the garments' fit adequate and nonrestrictive, albeit somewhat short in the arms and legs. Despite their awkward looks, even the boots were comfortable, and when he went to find O'Neill again, Teal'c felt ready to participate in Happy Hour.

O'Neill had picked out more items, including a backpack into which he shoved several metal cylinders he retrieved from various pockets of his pants, as well as a cap of soft, warm yarn that he held out to Teal'c. "You'd better put his on," he said, tapping a finger to his forehead.

Indeed.

None of the Tau'ri, not even the warriors, were wearing tattoos, and it clearly was a wise idea to blend in more seamlessly by concealing his own. Teal'c put on the cap, pulling the rim down to his eyebrows.

"Sweet." O'Neill nodded approvingly. "It's you, T."

Unsure of who else he might conceivably be, Teal'c opted for a noncommittal reply. "It is indeed."

"Uh… great. Let's go." The backpack slung across his shoulder, O'Neill headed for the door. After he had shooed Teal'c through like a mother *triq'joc* would shoo her chicks, he fell in beside him. "Listen, Teal'c. From now on out until I tell you otherwise, don't talk if there's other people around. Anyone we meet, you just nod at them and otherwise follow my lead. It's important."

A rite of spiritual preparation for the Happy Hour, no doubt.

"As you wish, O'Neill." Since there was indeed no one else around and since he had ascertained that O'Neill had not entered a preparatory state of meditation, Teal'c felt it was appropriate to ask another one of those burning questions that had arisen in the short while that he had spent among the Tau'ri. "Am I correct in assuming that 'Sergeant' is not a name?"

"Ah, no… I mean, yes, you are correct. 'Sergeant' is a rank."

"What is a rank?"

"You guys have ranks, right? I mean, you're what? What is your position among the Jaffa?"

"I am… I *was* First Prime of Apophis."

"Meaning what?"

"I fulfilled the same function and enjoyed the same privileges as you do. You are First Prime of the stout, loud system lord, are you not?"

O'Neill missed a step and stumbled. When he caught himself and spoke, his shoulders shook and his voice sounded oddly constrained. "Yeah… except, we don't call ours system lords. We call them generals. Probably because their eyes don't do that weird flashy thing. The… uh… stout, loud one is called General Hammond. Hammond's his name."

"I see."

"So, you were First Prime. What about the guys under you? The men you commanded?"

"They are warriors."

"Yeah, I got that, but what about the hierarchy? Who was in charge when you were off sick?"

"I do not get sick."

"Come on, Teal'c! Just work with me here. Who's next in command after you?"

"The oldest of the warriors. He is the one with the most experience."

"So you've got no command structure, instead seniority goes by age?"

"As the word implies, yes. Although the most senior among us no longer commands. He teaches."

"Ah. See, we handle it a little differently. Age doesn't determine seniority. Merit does. Mostly. Of course, you always get the guys who know how to pull strings."

Teal'c could not begin to fathom how the pulling of a piece of thread might in any way contribute to a man's standing as a warrior, but he decided against closer inquiry. Things were sufficiently confusing already.

As no answer or comment was forthcoming, O'Neill continued. "Basically, a sergeant is in command of a group of about ten guys. In terms of admin it's a little more complicated than that, but you –

"Sorry, T, we'll finish this later. Remember what I told you. Keep it zipped, don't make eye contact, and try to be invisible."

O'Neill was staring ahead, to the point where the corridor terminated in a small lobby. This place Teal'c could identify. The transportation device could be accessed from here. And there were people waiting for the cabin to arrive.

After O'Neill's caution, Teal'c had expected some form of difficulty to arise. In actual fact, nothing happened. Following O'Neill's instructions to the letter, he avoided eye contact and pretended to be elsewhere. Specifically, he chose the Morning Glades on Chulak, and his first meeting with Drey'auc. She had made him laugh that day, at a time when he thought he had lost that particular facility completely.

Their journey in the cabin took longer than anticipated, interrupted by frequent halts to allow others to enter or leave the device. When it finally came to a stop at station "11"—this according to the figures that lit up on a small panel set into the wall—there was only one person left besides O'Neill and himself.

The woman exited ahead of them and approached a desk where two guards were stationed to show them the plastic rectangle—apparently identical to O'Neill's—she wore around her neck. The guards examined it carefully.

O'Neill tugged at Teal'c's sleeve and steered him into a corridor that led away from the transportation device, the desk, and the people. As soon as they were out of sight, he increased his pace, almost to a run. Whether it was directed at himself, whether it was directed at somebody else, Teal'c had a strong suspicion that O'Neill was engaging in some kind of subterfuge. But, absence of people notwithstanding, this likely as not still fell under the same directive: he was to follow O'Neill's lead. Therefore he ran.

At last O'Neill came to an abrupt stop in front of an unmarked metal hatch—as gray and unremarkable as everything here, except O'Neill himself—that was inset into a wall. The hatch had to have been well maintained, for it swung open absolutely silently, revealing a dimly lit shaft and countless metal rungs leading down. And as many again, leading up.

To the planet's surface? Was it habitable after all? Or had O'Neill received orders to get rid of the Jaffa by stranding him in what might well be an unbreathable atmosphere or a vast number of other deadly conditions?

"Let's go!" hissed O'Neill. "I know it looks funny, but now is not the time to explain!"

"Which way, O'Neill? Up or down?"

"Up. Sorry about the climb. I got us as close as I could, but this is the only way if we want to get back in."

Whether or not he wished to 'get back in' was yet to be decided, Teal'c thought as he slipped into the hatch and started climbing. However, he was sure that he would find a means of remaining wherever they were going if he felt it suited his purposes better. Then again, this shaft might merely lead to yet another maze of gray, unremarkable corridors.

Behind him he heard O'Neill close the hatch and follow up the rungs.

Before long Teal'c managed to find a rhythm of movement that allowed him to slip into a light meditative state. While it made the climb less taxing, it had the disadvantage of slightly dulling his senses. It explained why he very nearly struck his head on an obstruction that closed off the shaft.

"Look for the handle!" O'Neill suggested from below. "It's right in the middle. Turn left to unlock it. But wait for me to help you open the hatch — it's heavy as sin!"

Teal'c decided that he did not wish to wait with a solid metal blockage over his head. He turned the handle as O'Neill had indicated and pushed. The hatch opened smoothly and without much effort.

"Holy crap! What did you eat for breakfast?"

O'Neill's question briefly took Teal'c aback, because he couldn't remember. This day seemed to have gone on forever, and breakfast appeared to be utterly inconsequential. "Steamed *plak'norel*," he answered at last once it came to him.

"Ah, yes. That explains it…" O'Neill muttered behind him. "Sounds hearty. Now move!"

Teal'c moved.

Not least because, on opening the heavy lid that closed off the shaft, he had been enveloped by a blast of fresh, cool air that smelled pleasantly of rain and a dozen other, less familiar things.

Fresh, cool, breathable air.

So the Tau'ri did, after all, have a world worth living in.

Above rose the indigo vault of the night sky and to the west a last, faint echo of the day outlined the jagged knife edge of a mountain ridge. They had emerged near one of the peaks, and below them tall trees descended into blackness. The sky was dotted with countless stars, clustered in a broad, bright ribbon that spanned from horizon to horizon.

O'Neill came to his side and gazed up as well. "We call it the Milky Way. It's an arm of our galaxy." After a moment, he asked, "Can you find Chulak?"

"I cannot." Much like the gray corridors beneath the mountain, this Milky Way afforded him no point of reference he could recognize. He was lost, perhaps irrevocably.

Beside him, O'Neill stirred and dug something from his backpack. In the faint starlight, Teal'c could make out a shiny metal cylinder, moist with condensation. O'Neill pulled at a small latch on the cylinder's top. It opened with a hiss, and he handed the cylinder to Teal'c to repeat the entire process with a second one.

"This is called 'beer'," he explained, clinking his cylinder against Teal'c's. "Cheers and welcome to Earth! You're supposed to drink it." He proceeded to demonstrate.

Teal'c followed suit. The beer's flavor was tart and a little sweet, and the liquid had a fizzy quality that bit his tongue. All in all it was unexpected but not entirely unpleasant. Oddly like the Tau'ri.

As though he had read Teal'c's thoughts, O'Neill said, "This isn't what you expected, is it? I guess by now you realized that I can't make good on my promise. They won't let you stay at my place." He wandered to a nearby rock and sat. "One day I'll show you this world, I swear, but for the time being we'll have to make do with this. But we've got beer, so let's call it Happy Hour."

This was Happy Hour then?

Again, Teal'c found himself surprised, and he understood that there would be considerably more surprises in his immediate future. He walked over to O'Neill and took a seat next to him.

"It is different from what I imagined. But different is not necessarily bad. It is merely unexpected. Cheers!"

It also was beautiful.

And it might, in time, justify the decision Teal'c had made so rashly, just as this strange, unpredictable warrior next to him might, in time, become a friend.

STARGATE ATLANTIS
Close Quarters

Melissa Scott

RONON Dex leaned forward in his seat in the puddle jumper, watching the Ancient warship grow as they approached. It looked a lot like the Lanteans' own ships, which made sense since they'd borrowed both the basic design and a lot of the technology, the boxy hull pale against the stars. Of course, it was pretty much derelict, or the Travelers who had found it wouldn't have traded its location to Atlantis. But the scientists seemed to think there was a chance that it could be repaired at least well enough to bring it back to Atlantis, and no one was going to turn down the chance of getting another warship. Even if it did mean dealing with the Travelers.

Teyla looked back at him from her seat beside Lorne, and Ronon gave her a polite smile. She had been very determined that he should accompany them, even though this wasn't his usual sort of mission. Ronon suspected it was because she was worried that he had been hurt by Jennifer's rejection and wanted to keep him distracted. He found that he appreciated the thought: it had been more than a decade since anyone had felt the need to watch over his feelings — Milena had considered him man enough to handle that on his own, and surely he was by now — but it was good to know that someone cared. Not that his heart was broken, either. Bruised, certainly, and he didn't think it was just his ego; he was genuinely fond of Dr. Keller. Nor did he blame McKay, he just wished she had chosen him instead.

Teyla gave him a very marked smile, and Ronon realized Lorne had been speaking for some time. He smiled back, nodding — they'd been talking about the work on the ship, hadn't they, and how far it had come? — and Teyla turned back to Lorne.

"You see? I told you Ronon would be happy to help."

Ronon kept his smile steady with an effort. All right, he'd deserved that. He just hoped he hadn't agreed to anything too unpleasant.

"Dr. Zelenka could probably use him," Lorne agreed, and Ronon relaxed. He liked Zelenka, and spending time with the little scientist usually meant that McKay wasn't present.

The jumper slid into the docking bay, the doors closing smoothly behind it. Both the gravity and the atmosphere seemed ordinary enough, and Ronon allowed himself to relax. All in all, he preferred gate travel to the incalculable uncertainties of spaceships. Besides, ships were a little too… Wraith-like, when you came right down to it. Only the Travelers and the Wraith lived in space.

Lorne lowered the back ramp, though he stayed at the controls to talk to someone on the radio. Ronon threaded his way between the crates that filled the back of the jumper to where Teyla was waiting. She started off without comment, leading him between two more jumpers and then across the bay and into what looked like a main corridor. As that door slid closed behind them, she cleared her throat meaningfully, and he glanced down at her.

"All right. What did you sign me up for?"

"You were very kind to volunteer to assist Dr. Zelenka in examining the hull structure," she said austerely, but there was laughter in her eyes.

Ronon suppressed a groan. "Really?"

"Oh, very definitely." Teyla paused at a cross corridor, then turned to her left. "I will take you to the control room, I expect he will still be there."

"Thanks."

Ronon trailed along in her wake, wondering exactly what he'd gotten himself into. It looked as though they'd brought a pretty good-sized science team on board, there had been four jumpers in the bay, counting their own, and even if at least one more of them was carrying supplies, that added up pretty quickly. This wasn't exactly something he was trained for, but it made Teyla happy and it was at least different from doing nothing on Atlantis, where he was a little too likely to run into Jennifer. Which, he supposed, proved Teyla's point, though he wasn't sure he was ready to admit it just yet.

The control room door opened before Teyla could pass her hand over the sensor, and McKay burst out, looking over his shoulder so that both Ronon and Teyla had to step sideways to avoid a collision.

"No, no, no, that's a complete waste of time, and I'm not sparing anyone to do it."

"Good afternoon, Rodney," Teyla said and McKay blinked.

"What? Oh. Hello. I have work to do —"

And he was gone again. Ronon suppressed a snicker, and followed Teyla into the control room.

"And good afternoon, Dr. Zelenka," Teyla said, with her usual bland smile.

Zelenka pushed his glasses up on his nose. His hair was disordered, as though he'd been tugging at it, but he managed to answer calmly enough. "Good afternoon, Teyla. Ronon."

Ronon kept his face sober with an effort. "Doc."

"Did you bring the bridging kit?" Zelenka asked. "And Dr. Sommer?"

"We came with Major Lorne," Teyla said. "Dr. Sommer was not with us. But I believe there was — bridging equipment? — in one of the other jumpers."

Zelenka said something sharp in his own language. Czech was, Ronon thought, an effective language for cursing. "If Rodney has gotten him first —" He stopped, shaking his head. "It's all very well to re-invent the Ancient's hyperdrive, but if the hull isn't sound, we still won't be going anywhere."

"Ronon has said he would help with the frame survey," Teyla said, and Zelenka gave Ronon a sympathetic glance.

Before he could say anything, however, the control room door slid open and Sheppard appeared. Teyla's smile widened as she murmured a greeting, and Sheppard visibly swallowed whatever he had been going to say.

"We came out with Major Lorne," Teyla said, and Ronon grunted agreement. "Mr. Woolsey thought I might be of help if there were any discussions to be had with the Travelers."

Sheppard gave a rueful smile, rubbing his chin. "You might, at that. I'm never quite sure where we are when we're dealing with Larrin."

We know. Ronon swallowed the words as unkind and not entirely true.

"And Ronon volunteered to help Dr. Zelenka," Teyla said.

Sheppard lifted an eyebrow at that, and Ronon felt his face heat. But the most Sheppard would think was that he'd been bored; Ronon could deal with that.

"I could certainly use him," Zelenka said. "Since Rodney has stolen all my other assistants already."

"That's fine by me," Sheppard said. He looked at Teyla. "Did Radek tell you about the drones?"

She shook her head.

Sheppard grinned. "This ship is full of them, hundreds it looks like."

"If they will fit in Atlantis's systems," Zelenka interjected. "This is a much older ship, and many of her systems are unfamiliar. The drones do have some differences."

"But it's definitely worth a try," Sheppard said. "Right now, my biggest concern is to get them back to Atlantis, and that means taking them by jumper. If you'll stay here to deal with the Travelers, I can take three jumpers on each run."

"Surely that is excellent news," Teyla said

"Yeah." Sheppard looked genuinely happy. "We should be able to replace a lot of the drones we've expended."

"If they will fit," Zelenka said again. "Dr. McKay has not yet looked closely at them."

"And he can't be bothered to do it while he's doing whatever it is that he's doing right now," Ronon said. The others looked at him, and he spread his hands. "What?"

"True enough," Sheppard said. "My plan is, we try the drones on Atlantis. If they don't work, and we get this ship working, we fly it back to Atlantis and reload the drones there. If we can't fix it, we see if we can adapt the drones to work on Atlantis."

"And if that does not work," Teyla said thoughtfully, "and we brought some of them back here, we might be able to set up a very effective sort of trap should we need to deal with the Wraith in that way."

Zelenka nodded slowly. "We would not need the frame to be completely intact to fire a drone salvo. But we would not get more than one shot without making repairs."

It was a good idea, Ronon thought. Lure the Wraith, then fire all the drones at once. The Wraith cruisers certainly couldn't stand up to that kind of attack and even the strongest hiveship would suffer serious damage.

"Let's not get ahead of ourselves," Sheppard said. "Let's see if we can use them on Atlantis first."

"Yes," Zelenka said.

"If I take three of the four jumpers — How many people have you got working here, doc, a dozen?"

"Not so many." Zelenka reached for his laptop. "We need equipment more than people at the moment. Five, counting myself and Rodney. And if you leave us Teyla and Ronon that will make seven. We could certainly fit into a single jumper in case of an emergency, and with Rodney and Dr. Tanaka we will have two people on board with the ATA gene."

"That was the thought," Sheppard said. "Teyla, I'll leave you in charge. I don't expect there to be any trouble, but if there is something, like if the Wraith show up —"

"I will put everyone onto a jumper and we will either cloak

and hide or we will return through the Stargate," Teyla answered. "Do not worry, John, I do not expect trouble, either."

"Where the Travelers are concerned, that's usually when we get it," Sheppard answered, but he was smiling. He reached for his radio. "Lorne. How's it coming with loading those drones?"

"Piece of cake," Lorne responded, his voice only a little distorted by the radio. "We've got the first jumper loaded already, and it shouldn't take long to do the second."

"Load the third as well," Sheppard ordered.

"Sir, there's just me and Porter to fly them. Well, except Dr. McKay, but —"

"I'll take the third," Sheppard said. "If there's a problem here, Rodney will have to take over."

"Yes, sir," Lorne answered.

"You can be the one to tell him that, Colonel," Zelenka said.

Sheppard grinned. "Oh, Rodney will be fine. I'll just go talk to him myself."

"I will go with you," Teyla said, and the control room door closed behind them.

Ronon looked at Zelenka, who dropped into the nearest chair, shaking his head. "Look, doc —" he began, and Zelenka lifted a hand.

"No, no, it's a good plan, as plans go. It's just not the one I thought we were following."

"I'd like to help," Ronon said. "But I don't want to be in the way."

"And you can be a help, I think," Zelenka answered, with a quick smile. "You understand the problem, yes? We have to find all the places that the ship's skeleton is stressed or broken outright, only I do not have enough people to do it manually. So if you would start with these files —"

Ronon suppressed a groan, and seated himself at the indicated console. A screen lit, showing a model of the ship rotating in space, and Zelenka pushed his glasses more securely onto his nose.

"This is a — Well, essentially it's a stress scan of the ship. We placed a tone generator as close to the nose as we could get it, and then recorded the vibration throughout the ship's frame."

"That was smart."

"Thank you." Zelenka touched more keys, and the image on the screen stopped spinning, colors appearing along its length. "What I need you to do is flag every point where the metal shows red — this bright red, here."

Ronon squinted at the screen. There was quite a bit of red on the model, mostly at points where one or more lines crossed, and he gave Zelenka an uneasy look. "Is this thing safe?"

"Mostly? We are leaking some atmosphere, but not much. Not enough to change our orbit, at least not in any reasonable time frame. As long as we don't try to fly it, we should be fine."

"All right." Ronon reached for the mouse, began moving it around the screen, clicking on the red patches to expand them, and drawing circles around the points where the color flared brightest. "Hey, doc? Wouldn't it be more efficient to have the computer do this?"

"Probably." Zelenka didn't look up from his own screen. "But I don't have time to write that program just at the moment, and you are a perfectly reliable substitute."

"Thanks," Ronon said, doubtfully, and went back to work.

He worked his way down from the nose to a point a little before the control room, the number of weak points that he had marked making him feel as though he ought somehow to move more carefully, or at least sit more lightly in his chair. He felt as though he were inside a cracked eggshell, the spring eggs that they had bought filled with confetti for Founders' Day. He jumped as the control room door slid open, but it was only Teyla, coming back from the docking bay.

"Colonel Sheppard is ready to return to Atlantis," she said.

Zelenka nodded, adjusting his headset, and moved to a different section of the controls, activating the main viewscreen so that it showed the Stargate hanging above the curve of the planet. "Rodney. Colonel Sheppard is about to leave. Are all your people clear of the area?"

"Yes, we're fine," McKay answered.

Ronon tuned out the rest of the familiar conversation, looking up only when the Stargate whooshed open. One after the other, the three puddle jumpers disappeared into the roiling blue light, and then the gate winked closed.

"Well," Zelenka said, and Teyla nodded.

"It is good to restock the city's weapons."

"Yes —" Zelenka broke off as half a dozen lights flashed to life on his console. His hands moved busily over the keys, and he swore under his breath. "Someone is dialing the gate."

A moment later, the Stargate whooshed open, and a battered ship tumbled through. It hung for an instant against the stars as the gate blinked out behind it, and then thrusters fired in ragged sequence, irregular flashes of light across the scarred hull. They winked out, leaving the ship nearly motionless against the stars.

"Wraith?" Ronon asked, and managed not to reach for his weapon. Something was very wrong.

"I don't feel any," Teyla said, and she was cut off by a screech of static from the communications system.

Zelenka swore again, adjusting the frequencies, and abruptly words came clear.

"— Lanteans still on the Ancient ship, please answer! If anyone's on board, come in, please!"

Zelenka touched a key. "This is Zelenka. Identify yourselves, please." He muted the system, and looked at Teyla. "Do you recognize the ship?"

She shook her head. "It looks like a Traveler ship, but I don't recognize it. It's not one of the ones we have dealt with before.

"Thank the Ancestors, the Lanteans are still there!"

Ronon could almost hear the speaker shake himself, controlling fear and excitement.

"Atlantis personnel, this is Tarris, Housing Officer of the

Traveler ship *Great Astala*. We collided with the *Sunstar*, she's holed, and we suffered catastrophic drive failure and are venting atmosphere. I've brought off the children and some of the women, but we're out of power and we're losing the ship — "

"Rodney, you are needed on the bridge," Zelenka said, into his mic, and touched the keys again. "I understand you, Tarris. You say you have survivors on board?"

"We're the lifeboat," Tarris answered. "But there are another two hundred people back on *Astala*, and we can't get them off — "

"We don't have enough ships to rescue all your people at once," Zelenka said. "We can take off some, but it will take several trips. How badly is your main ship damaged?"

"*Astala* lost the main drive," Tarris said again. "She's in an unstable orbit. If we don't get power back, we're going to enter the atmosphere and burn."

Ronon looked over his shoulder as the control room door slid open, admitting McKay. The scientist slid into a seat next to Zelenka, for once not interrupting, and Zelenka frowned at the screen.

"How long do you have?"

"I don't know. The engineers were trying to get the maneuver drive back but they weren't having any luck — " Tarris stopped, and Ronon could almost hear him hauling himself back from the brink of panic. "Ok. They're telling me maybe four hours? Five? Not much more than that."

"All right," Zelenka said. "That gives us a little time to plan." He hit the switch that closed the channel and looked at McKay. "You heard?"

"Every word." McKay was already typing figures into a laptop. "Do we know anything at all about this ship of theirs? Besides that it's a Traveler ship, which means it's a jury-rigged collection of improbably wired and extremely dangerous components that have finally given out on them?"

"That seems to describe it, yes," Zelenka answered.

"The first thing must be to get the people off," Teyla said.

"We can't," McKay answered. "We've only got the one puddle jumper, it'd take ten trips at least. And where would we take them?"

Zelenka opened communications again. "Tarris. Are you sure there's no room on your other ship?"

"We're sure. *Sunstar's* environmental systems were damaged, she's barely able to take care of what she has."

"What exactly is wrong with your power plant?" McKay demanded. "What did you do to it?"

"We didn't —"

"Do you have any schematics?" McKay reached for his laptop. "Any record of what happened?"

"I can send you what we have." That was a new voice, a light contralto that could have been a very young man or a slightly older woman. With the Travelers, Ronon thought, it could be either. Any Traveler who showed a talent for ship maintenance was promptly pressed into service.

"Got it," McKay said, watching the data spooling onto his screen. He spun the laptop so that Zelenka could see the screen. "If this is really what's wrong — and I grant you, it's a big if, this data is pretty ratty — we can fix it."

Zelenka studied the screen for a moment, then nodded. "Yes. Yes, we have everything you would need."

"Once we get the engine back on line, we can stabilize the orbit, and everything will be fine." McKay scowled at his screen. "And if we need to — We have lifeboats here, right?"

"Yes," Zelenka said, "but they're not — their engines won't take them further than the planet."

"I know that," McKay said. "But if we have to, we can ferry the rest of the Travelers back here. I don't want to try to put them on this ship —"

"Not given the state of the hull, no," Zelenka said.

"But there are, what, five lifeboats? We can transfer them to the lifeboats temporarily while we get this ship out of trouble."

Zelenka nodded. "Yes, ok, that will work. I will start loading the jumper —"

McKay shook his head. "You're not coming."

"Oh?" Zelenka looked up sharply, ready to protest, and McKay went on as though he hadn't spoken.

"I need you to stay here and launch the lifeboats. I'll take the rest of our team — and Teyla, she can organize the rescue — and we'll handle the repairs."

"Who will fly the puddle jumper?" Teyla asked. "Rodney, you cannot do that and fix their engines —"

"Of course not. Dr. Tanaka has the ATA gene, she can fly the jumper."

Ronan looked at Teyla. "Do you want me to come with you? I can help corral the Travelers."

Teyla tipped her head to one side, visibly considering. "No. The Travelers must be used to emergencies in space, they will not panic. And we need all the room there is."

Ronon nodded, and swallowed his automatic protest. She was right, of course. They could fit two Travelers into the space he'd occupy in the jumper, and he wasn't going to be any help with the repairs.

"Did you hear that?" McKay demanded. "We're coming to you."

"We heard," Tarris answered. "And thank you."

Zelenka watched the puddle jumper leave the docking bay and accelerate toward the Stargate. It had taken less than an hour to assemble the supplies and load everything onto the remaining jumper, but that was time that was running out on the *Astala*. And on the ship that was *Astala's* 'lifeboat', hanging in space between the Ancient ship and the Stargate. Tarris had not complained, but the scanner confirmed that they were pushing the limits of their life support systems.

And that, he told himself sternly, was their problem to deal with. His job was to launch the Ancient lifeboats in preparation for the jumper's return. He scrolled through Ancient menus, muttering to himself. Yes, there it was, the section of the manifest that dealt with emergencies, and there was the section on the lifeboats. All five of them were present, though the hull around both three and five had suffered damage. He checked the scan, frowning, but none of the stress lines showed completely red. According to the system, the lifeboats should be fully stocked, but they'd already discovered that the computer was not entirely accurate. Prone to wishful thinking, Rodney had said, glaring at the empty tool sockets as though it were a personal insult. But Radek was inclined to think that the Ancients were just as bad about falsifying checklists as most people. It wasn't until your life had depended on the most obscure tool in the kit that you really understood how important they could be. And, besides, there were a few things the lifeboats would need that the Ancients didn't supply.

"Ronon. I need you to make sure that the lifeboats are in fact in place and fully supplied."

The big man rose, nodding.

"Also there are oxygen candles in the locker beside the door. Take — let's see, two for each lifeboat — take ten of them and share them out."

"Ok." Ronon turned toward the door. It was nice, Radek thought, to deal with someone who didn't need to argue about absolutely everything —

The lights flickered. Radek looked up sharply, then reached for his laptop, switching to internal scans, but there were no alarms. The naqqadah generator was in place, powering the ship's systems; the gravity field indicators glowed green, and they weren't losing any more atmosphere than they had been.

The lights flickered again, and then blinked out. The emergency lights came on at once, but half the consoles were dead.

"Doc?" Ronon said.

"I don't know." Radek glared at the displays as though he

could make them work by mental force. "We've lost everything but emergency power."

"Damn."

Radek took a deep breath, considering the displays. Everything was down except the emergency systems, and they, too, were showing warning signs. But the naqqadah generator was fine, and the connections said they were still good. If they weren't, he and Ronon would have to get down to the engine room and replace them by hand. But, for now, try rebooting, he thought, and typed in the sequence of commands that would bring the naqqadah generator back into the system. The response flashed across his screen: the generator was receiving his input, but the power wasn't crossing into the ship's systems. Probably that was a physical problem with that particular bridge. But, no, when he pinged it individually, it showed intact. The frequency? Ancient equipment could be finicky about the frequencies it received. The emergency lights wavered, shadows moving across the consoles, but he ignored them. He touched keys again, adjusting the generator's output. Bring it down to the minimum, he thought, tune it to be sure it matches exactly, and then try to reboot…

He entered the last command, holding his breath. The power surged, and the main lights flashed. For just a moment, he thought he'd succeeded, and then everything cut out. In the dark, the chair fell away beneath him as the gravity cut out, and he heard Ronon yell.

He grabbed for the edge of his chair, dragged himself down against it and wrapped his feet around the pillar that connected it to the deck. "Ronon! Grab something and hold on!"

"Trying, doc." The answer came from somewhere near the door, but Radek couldn't waste the time to look even if he had been able to see anything. His laptop, he needed his laptop — needed any laptop, it would be battery powered. It had been on the console beside where he'd been working, and he reached carefully in that direction, trying not to stir up air currents that would drive it away from him. Assuming that all the air was not rushing out — but, no, there was no breeze on his skin. They were not decompressing.

The laptop. He had to find the laptop. He leaned forward, not losing his grip on the seat, and stretched in the direction where he'd last seen it. His questing fingers touched metal, batting it away, and he swore.

"Are you all right?" Ronon's voice sounded closer.

"I'm fine. Hold on to something, you don't want to be drifting if the power comes back." Radek unwound his feet from the chair, grabbed its arm with one hand and stretched again. This time his fingers closed on the laptop's edge, but he flailed for a moment before he could drag himself back against the console. He opened the laptop, and couldn't help a sigh of relief as the screen sprang to life.

In its dim light, he could see Ronon spinning slowly in the center of the room. He wasn't flailing, but working his arms and legs slowly, as though he was swimming in jelly, and Radek hooked his foot around the chair again to anchor himself. Ronon wasn't in immediate danger; his first care had to be for the ship.

The system management program opened, alert windows popping open everywhere. Radek dismissed the least important, leaving the last four open so that he could switch quickly from system to system. Power was definitely out; the naqqadah generator's fail-safe had cut in, and he'd need to restart it. Their own Wi-Fi was running, but that was it for communications; he could talk to the generator, and to the other laptops, and anyone who happened to be on the ship. Except, of course, that it was just him and Ronon. The environmental systems were completely shut down, and there were new stress points showing throughout the hull.

None of that was good, he thought, but the power came first. Without power, he couldn't do anything else. "Ronon! I am going to try to get power back. Try to secure yourself."

"Yeah, I'm working on that."

Ronon sounded faintly breathless, but Radek couldn't spare him a look. He switched to the main power window, studying the readouts from the generator. The power surge had tripped the failsafes, just as it was supposed to; when he pinged the system, there was no sign of damage. He typed in the commands to bring the generator back online, and held his breath as the line that showed power flow began to build.

"Hold on! I think we're restarting —"

The lights flashed on and off, then on again, and the gravity field surged, his body suddenly twice as heavy as it should be. He heard Ronon yell, and swore himself as he fell painfully against the edge of the chair. He clutched the laptop against his chest, trying to switch windows, the deck heaving under him, his weight fading and then returning to pin him against the chair and console. The program refused to connect to the Ancient systems, and he dragged himself to the next control station, trying to read the flickering screens. There, he thought, there was the problem. He touched keys, closing one damaged circuit, and, before he could compensate, the ship seemed to whirl sideways into a spin, flinging him out of the chair and toward the ceiling.

He landed hard, lay for a moment crowing for breath: the corner of the laptop had caught him in the diaphragm, knocking the wind out of him. The lights were coming back on, slowly but surely, and he managed to sit up, wincing. It wasn't the ship that had flipped, he thought. Instead, the gravity field had reversed itself so that he was sitting on what had been the ceiling, the laptop still clutched to his chest.

"Ronon?"

There was no answer, but in the growing light Radek could see him sprawled against the bulkhead beside the hatch.

"Ronon! Are you all right?"

This time, Ronon moved, cautiously stretching arms and legs. "Yeah — ow. I've hurt my leg. Not broken, I don't think."

"Good." Radek reopened the laptop, sighing with relief at the unbroken screen. The news, though, was less than good. Power was flowing steadily again, but that was about the only thing that was working correctly. Air was moving, but the environmental readouts showed that the ventilators were off line. "Ok, this is not good."

"What?" Ronon was sitting up against the far wall, wincing as he felt his way down his left leg.

"The surge in the gravity field has opened more breaks in the hull." Radek switched windows again, calling up the hull scan, and swore at the results. "Damn it, it's all in pieces. I don't know how long it will hold."

"Can we get to the Traveler ship?" Ronon asked.

"Communications are out," Radek answered. "And they didn't have much in the way of maneuvering power. We could get to the lifeboats, maybe."

"You're going to have to help me," Ronon said, after a moment. "My knee's not going to take my weight."

And I can hardly carry you. Radek swallowed the words, looked around the control room. Surely someone had brought a first aid kit? Yes, there it was, the bright plastic impossible to miss, stuck to the bulkhead beside what had been the lower curve of the hatch, completely out of reach. Ronon followed his look, and for just an instant his expression was bleak.

"At least we have one," Radek said, and pushed himself to his feet. The gravity field felt fairly stable, the new 'deck' solid beneath him, but he grabbed a carryall that someone had left behind and stuffed the laptop in it, then slung the bag over his shoulder. They could not afford to lose the laptop. With it secured, he made his way to the bulkhead, and stretched as far as he could. The first aid kit remained tantalizingly out of reach. He turned, scanning the control room. "Something to stand on…"

"Me," Ronon said.

Radek looked at him sharply, then realized the other man

was right. None of the other furniture could be reached; it was all bolted to the deck, or what had been the deck, and hung overhead useless and unhelpful. "Are you sure?"

Ronon held out a hand and Radek took it, wincing in sympathy as Ronon tried to pull himself to his feet.

"Maybe not —" Radek began

Ronon gave a wincing grin and began scooting himself along the deck until he was positioned beneath the first aid kit. "Ok. On my shoulders."

"I'm not so sure this is a good idea," Radek said.

"You got a better one?"

"I do not."

"Just don't step on my leg," Ronon said, and held out his hands.

Radek took them, then put his right foot on Ronon's shoulder.

"Go on. You can do it."

"This is not precisely what I studied for," Radek said, and pushed himself up. He got his left foot in place, and stood for a moment, wobbling, nerving himself to release Ronon's hands.

"Doc…"

"Yes," Radek said, and made himself let go. He wavered alarmingly, then found his balance by resting one hand flat against the bulkhead. Ok, he told himself, reach up. It wasn't that far, but it took an effort to stretch for it, knowing that his boots were digging into Ronon's shoulders, pressing him hard into the deck. He took a deep breath and got his hands on the corners of the first aid kit. It was an awkward grip, and not much leverage; his first tug nearly knocked him off Ronon's shoulders. Ronon reached up, steadying him with a hand just above Radek's knee, and Radek tried again. This time it came away easily. Ronon released him as he started to sway, and Radek jumped clear, landing awkwardly on the decking.

"Nice," Ronon said, and held out his hand for the first aid kid.

Radek passed it over. "There should be splints, I think? And also anti-inflammatories for the pain."

"Yeah."

Ronon was sweating lightly, and Radek gave him a worried look. "Are you all right?"

"I'll be better when this is stabilized," Ronon answered. He pulled out an object that looked like a much folded ladder and shook his head. "You're going to have to help."

"Yes." Radek wished his first aid training had been more recent but together they got the splint unfolded and locked into the correct configuration. Ronon continued to claim that nothing was broken, and there was certainly no obvious break nor any sign of blood. By the time the straps were fastened, Ronon was leaning back against the bulkhead, his eyes flickering closed, and Radek rummaged in the kit for an injector. "Anti-shock," he said. "You need it."

For a second, he thought Ronon would protest, but then he nodded. "Go ahead."

Radek jabbed the injector's pointed end into Ronon's bared forearm, wincing at Ronon's grimace of pain. "Sorry—"

"I'm fine."

He didn't sound it, but Radek wasn't going to contradict him. Instead, he busied himself fitting everything back into the first aid kit, giving Ronon time to recover and the drugs time to work. After a moment, he heard Ronon take a deep breath.

"Ok. You said, the lifeboats?"

"They are still here and still intact," Radek answered. "And I don't trust the gravity field or the integrity of this hull. If we can get to one, and launch it, we can stand off and wait there for Teyla's return. We might even be able to free the other lifeboats in case they are bringing the Traveler refugees—"

The sound of an alarm cut off his next word, and he snatched his laptop from its bag.

"What is it?"

"Hull breach," Radek said, typing frantically. "One of our patches gave way; the gravity shift was too much for it. I'm trying—oh, no."

Red lights flashed on the screen as a series of airtight bulkheads sealed, though the control room door mercifully remained open.

"What?"

"The emergency systems have sealed the ship's core," Radek said. "They operate automatically to close off any breached section. Unfortunately —" He poked the keys again as though he could force a better answer, but the image remained stubbornly the same. "We are cut off from the lifeboats."

"There has to be a lifeboat for the control room crew," Ronon said. He was feeling steadier now, and shifted his weight experimentally. Yes, he could stand, if Zelenka steadied him, and that meant they could move.

"Yes, and that station isn't far," Zelenka answered. "But that's the one the Ancients used when they abandoned this ship."

Of course it was. Ronon sighed. "Ok. You're sure we can't get to any of the others?"

"Every way I would try, there are at least two sealed doors between a lifeboat and us. Or a compartment open to space, plus a sealed door."

"Can we just stay here?"

Zelenka shrugged. "We might be all right. But if the gravity field acts up again? The hull here is not very secure. And we are venting atmosphere."

"How long do we have?" The ship breaking apart, spilling them out into cold space… The image lifted the hairs at the back of Ronon's neck.

"I don't know. There's no way to tell." Zelenka tapped his knuckles thoughtfully against his mouth. "There is — The forward drone compartment is empty now, but it was meant to be airtight and to stand up to the strain of launching the drones. And it is on our side of the sealed doors. That would be the safest place."

"Can we get there?" Ronon felt his spirits lift. If they could just do something — anything — it would feel less as though they were just waiting for the ship to collapse around them.

"If you can walk," Zelenka said. He tucked the laptop back into its carrier and held out his hands. "I will help as much as I can."

"I can walk," Ronon said. To prove it, he started to haul himself upright, but fell back as pain lanced through his knee. He breathed through it, assessing it the way he'd learned when he was a Runner: sharp and hot, but not the agony of an actual broken bone. He shouldn't try to bend the joint, but there was a good chance that, with the splint in place, the leg would hold his weight.

"I'm not convinced," Zelenka said, looking at him over the top of his glasses. "We would be safe to stay here as long as the gravity stays constant."

"What are the odds of that?"

Zelenka shrugged. "Even?"

"Not good enough."

"There is also no guarantee that the drone compartment will be safe."

"But it's more likely to hold together."

"Yes," Zelenka said. "But I can't promise that, any more than I can promise that the power won't fail again or that the gravity won't go haywire. Or for that matter that it will. Also, I must point out, I can't carry you."

Ronon grinned in spite of himself at the image that conjured for him. "You don't have to. Just help me up."

Zelenka looked distinctly dubious, but held out both hands. Ronon took them, drawing his good leg under him, and heaved himself to his feet. Zelenka staggered, but held firm. Ronon caught his balance, resting one hand on the bulkhead, and Zelenka stooped to collect the first aid kit, adding it to the bag with his laptop.

"Well, this is progress," he said. "Can you walk?"

Ronon took a careful step. It hurt — damn, it hurt — but

the splint kept his knee from collapsing under him. "Yeah."

"That's good," Zelenka said. "Because, while I hate to mention it, the power levels are starting to drop."

"How long?" Ronon took another step, wincing, and braced himself against the edge of the hatch.

"We are running under the emergency protocol," Zelenka answered. "That means that power goes first to sustain life, for example, environmentals, and then gravity and then lights and communications. The program is supposed to sense when one of those components is off-line — like the ventilation system, in our case — and shunt power to the next priority instead. According to this computer, that's what's happening, but –" He shrugged. "That assumes the power is reaching the ship's systems correctly, and that has been our problem all along."

Ronon eyed the hatch. With the gravity reversed, he was going to have to lift his injured leg over the coaming, and that — was not going to be pleasant. He took a deep breath, bracing himself. "Can we fix the generator?"

He lifted his injured leg, managed to get it up and over, and stuck there, unable to shift enough weight to that leg to bring his good leg through.

"Allow me," Zelenka said, and flattened himself against the opposite side of the hatch so that he could slither through. "Ok, put your weight on my shoulder –"

Ronon did as he was told. Zelenka staggered but recovered, and Ronon managed to drag his good leg through the hatch. Pain jolted through him like a bolt of electricity, and he fell back against the bulkhead, breathing heavily.

"You asked about the generator," Zelenka said.

Ronon managed a nod. Any distraction would be welcome.

"Maybe we could fix it. My guess is that the connections have been compromised in some way — not disconnected, everything indicates that they're physically intact, but they're not putting through enough power to sustain the ship's systems." Zelenka stepped back through the hatch, still talking.

"Unfortunately, however, the generator and the controls for the power supply are all on what is now our ceiling, and I do not think I can reverse the gravity again without doing even more damage to the hull."

"So we wait for either Sheppard or Teyla to get back," Ronon said. The pain was fading again, back to a manageable level, and he took an experimental step. It hurt, but not so badly.

"That's right," Zelenka answered, popping through the hatch again, a second carryall slung across his body.

Ronon blinked, recognizing it as the thing he had been going to get — was it really less than an hour ago? "The oxygen candles?"

Zelenka nodded. "Let us hope we won't need them."

"Yeah." Ronon straightened. Was the faint whisper of air against his skin getting stronger? He put that thought aside and looked down at the little scientist. "Which way?"

Zelenka consulted his laptop. "Left."

Ronon braced himself against the wall and took a halting step. His leg throbbed, but the splint held his weight. He took another, and another, trying not to think about how much it hurt, and how far he had to go. He'd been through worse, he told himself. He'd been hurt more badly, and he'd been in more danger. At the moment, no one was trying to feed on him, and that was an enormous improvement.

He ran out of wall then and ground to a halt, breathing as hard as if he'd been running. He could feel air moving against his skin, definitely stronger than before, almost a breeze, and for a second the breath caught in his throat.

"Left again," Zelenka said.

Ronon straightened, flinching as the movement jarred his leg, but managed to make the turn into the next corridor. What had been a touch of air was now a solid breeze, and he lifted his head. "Doc?"

"Yes, I feel it. We must hurry if you can."

"I can." Ronon made himself move faster, lurching forward

heedless of his leg. They crossed another corridor, and then a third, and finally turned left again, into a narrower corridor that ended abruptly in a sealed door. Zelenka said something under his breath and waved his hand at the sensor. The door didn't move.

"Doc?" For a moment, Ronon wished this were the sort of problem he could solve with his gun. He understood about shooting Wraith, understood the subtle leverage of strength and firepower and intimidation that usually kept him from having to shoot humans, and none of that was the slightest bit of use to him now.

"This door sealed when the emergency bulkheads closed," Zelenka said, hauling out his laptop. "If Rodney was here, or Colonel Sheppard, they could just tell it to open again, but we don't have that option."

"Uh-huh." Ronon blinked hard. His leg hurt worse than ever, spasms running along the muscles, and he was grateful for Zelenka's voice distracting him.

"I should be able to enter the system here and override it," Zelenka went on, fumbling one-handed with a length of fine cable. "Yes, good, there's a port — Damn."

"Trouble?" Ronon said, and closed his eyes. Just once, couldn't things go right?

"The system isn't acknowledging my codes — no, not my codes, it's not acknowledging the port. And that, in fact, is very bad."

"Yeah." You didn't have to be a scientist to understand a problem this simple: if the port wasn't working, there wasn't any way to open the door. Moving air tickled his skin, more than there should be and in the wrong direction to be the ventilators starting up again. He stared at the control panel, bigger than usual, with an extra set of colored buttons above the sort of displays he was used to seeing on Atlantis.

"If I can just — Damn." Zelenka shook a pinched finger. "Ok, that cable isn't compatible."

Ronon waved his hand at the sensor in turn, in the faint hope that somehow Zelenka hadn't managed to set it off. The door stayed stubbornly shut. Zelenka ignored him, rummaging in the bag that held the computer, and finally came up with another cable that ended in a flat disk.

"What's that?"

"An experiment." Zelenka laid the disk flat against the control mechanism. "We were trying other ways to connect to Ancient devices besides having to tie ourselves to them with cables."

"Does it work?"

Zelenka shrugged. "We'll— Ah."

"Progress?" Ronon looked hopefully at the door, but it didn't budge.

"Of a sort. The door mechanism is functional. I just can't get it to accept my input."

"Oh."

Under their feet, the deck shivered, the barest hint of a vibration. Ronon shifted uneasily, trying to take more weight off his injured leg, and a low groan, metal on metal, came from the ship's stern. Zelenka whispered a curse, checking his laptop, and shook his head.

"The change in internal pressure is putting more stress on the frame. I don't know how much longer the hull is going to hold together. If I cannot make the lock recognize me — Maybe I can cut in and activate it manually?"

"No cutter," Ronon said.

"No. That would be the problem." Zelenka set down his laptop and reached for the bag that held the oxygen candles. "These burn hot, but if it's hot enough? I don't know."

It made sense, Ronon thought. They'd had cutting torches on Sateda that burned bottled gases, and the Lanteans had smaller, stronger versions; if anyone could figure out how to do it, Zelenka would be the man. He stared at the lock, wishing he had the ATA gene. Without it, none of the Ancestors' technology would respond to him, and he was absolutely useless.

And that was so frustratingly typical of the Ancients, cutting themselves off from lesser beings —

He stopped abruptly, his eyes focusing on the colored buttons above the main lock. "Doc, wait. What do those do?"

"What?" Zelenka froze, the candle opened but not yet ignited.

"Those buttons, above the lock." Ronon pointed, supporting himself with his other hand. "Are they part of the lock? There's nothing like them in Atlantis."

"No," Zelenka agreed. "They seem to be part of the lock, but I can't make any of it work."

Ronon tipped his head to one side. They were tantalizingly familiar, a memory momentarily out of reach — The game, he thought, the game that had been all the rage his last year in grammar school. You had to figure out the next color in the sequence from the colors that had come before. "I think I know how that part works," he said. "You pick the next color."

Zelenka set the candle back in the bag with the others. "If that's right, it would certainly be better." He ran his hand gently over the row of buttons, and shrugged. "I think they'll move. Do we have to get it right the first try, or do we get more than one attempt?"

Damned if I know. Ronon swallowed the words. "In the games you do. But one mistake resets everything." He stopped, feeling the color rising in his face. "There was a game like this, when I was a kid."

Zelenka nodded as though that made perfect sense. "The anthropologists back at the SGC talked about Ancient knowledge surviving in nursery rhymes and children's games. Why shouldn't it be true here? Don't try to move, just tell me what color to select."

That was the trick, wasn't it? Ronon squinted at the band of color printed above the first button. Red, yellow, red, blue, red, orange, red… "Purple."

Zelenka pressed the button, pressed it again to cycle through the series of colors, stopping on purple. The band lit up, and he made a pleased sound. "Oh, very good."

The ship groaned again, a dull, grinding noise that set Ronon's teeth on edge. He ignored it, concentrating on the next pattern. Blue, yellow, red, yellow, red, blue, yellow, blue… "Yellow."

Zelenka pressed the button, and the strip lit again. "Yes."

Was the air moving faster now, rustling across his skin? Was there a different smell? Ronon shoved those thoughts aside. "Blue."

The next strip lit under Zelenka's touch. The next sequence had gaps in it, as though the paint had been scratched away. He frowned at it, trying to work out what was missing, deduce the sequence from the gaps. "Red?" he began, and shook his head. "No, wait!"

Zelenka froze.

"Nothing. Skip that one and go on." Ronon considered the next line of colors. "Definitely red."

Zelenka cycled through to red, and both strips lit. They were all on now, and Ronon held his breath. There was a grinding of metal from inside the bulkhead. Slowly, shuddering, the door began to move — and stopped, leaving an opening not much more than a hand span wide.

Zelenka said something pithy in his own language, and put his shoulder to the door. It gave another inch or two, and stuck again.

"Let me try," Ronon said, before he could think better of it, and leaned hard on the door. It didn't move, and his knee gave way under him. Zelenka steadied him.

"I do not think that is going to work." He reached for his laptop, unfolded it, and began typing. "It says there's nothing wrong with the mechanism. Something's jammed it from the other side, perhaps?"

The deck shivered under them, a vibration that seemed to travel from one end of the corridor to the next. The hull groaned again, and there was a distinct popping sound. Zelenka swore again, working his keyboard one-handed, and abruptly a breeze swept across Ronon's skin, strengthening perceptibly.

"We're in trouble," he said, and Zelenka nodded.

"The breaches in the hull have gotten worse. We have maybe fifteen, maybe twenty minutes of good air left."

Radek took a final look at the uncompromising numbers on his screen, then closed the laptop. They were in the core of the ship, in a section that remained more intact that others, but that wouldn't save them unless they could get into an airtight compartment. There were no airtight bulkheads between them and the nearest breaches, and the most recent scan showed dozens of tiny fractures all around them. And if any one of them became large enough, the pressure differential would shatter the hull entirely. "The drone compartment is designed to be airtight," he said. "If we can just get in —"

Ronon nodded, and heaved at the door again, but fell back, wincing. "It's jammed pretty good."

"Yes." Radek tried to see into the compartment, but the emergency lighting didn't seem to be working. He worked his shoulder into the opening, feeling cautiously along the inside of the door to see if he could feel the blockage. There was nothing, and he stepped back, reaching for the laptop. "I'm going to try closing and opening it again, see if I can work whatever is blocking it loose."

He touched keys, and the door slid shut, the grinding noise much less evident. That was a hopeful sign, Radek thought. It should mean that the mechanism itself was intact, and the problem was something external. He entered the command to open the door again, and it slid back, only to jam in the same place. Or maybe not, he thought, and in the same moment, Ronon said, "It moved."

"Good." Radek cycled through the sequence again and yet again. The grinding noise was worse than ever, but Ronon was right, the door was opening just a little further. He ran the sequence a fourth time, and the door stopped with a screech of metal. "Ok, not so good."

"You could get through that," Ronon said.

"Maybe." Radek shrugged off his shoulder bag, and then stripped off his jacket. If he could get through, and could clear the jam enough to let Ronon pass…? It was worth a shot. He turned sideways, put one leg through the gap, and then his shoulder, turning his head as he tried to slide through. He stuck for a moment, something sharp digging into his chest, and then he forced himself through, tearing his shirt and drawing a long scratch across his ribcage. He dabbed at it, swearing under his breath — a little blood, not much; good thing he'd had all his shots — and tried to get his bearings in the unlit compartment. As his eyes adjusted, he could see a faint flash of light from the center of the floor: the original ceiling fixture, he guessed, broken by falling debris when the gravity field failed and then reversed.

The flicker of light was just enough to reveal a hulking shadow resting against the door. The next time he had a mission off Atlantis, he would be sure to bring a flashlight, he told himself, and looked back out into the corridor. "Ronon! Hand me that candle."

The Satedan passed it through without a word. Radek planted the magnetic base against the bulkhead where it would be out of the way and still, he hoped, cast enough light to be useful, and pulled the ignition tab. The candle hissed and sputtered and burst abruptly into blinding white light. He blinked, and as his vision cleared, the shadow resolved itself to a tangle of lifting gear, cables and pulleys and the twisted frame of a hoist that had fallen against the door mechanism. It didn't need to be moved very far, that was the good news, but… He studied the pile of wreckage for a long moment, looking for a weak point. Yes, there, that beam: if it shifted a few centimeters toward the center of the compartment, the door should surely open. The trick would be to move it.

He leaned his weight against it, but it was dishearteningly solid. If only Ronan could make it through the gap, but if he could, they could simply seal the door again behind them. He tried again, exerting his full strength, but nothing moved. The hull moaned again, a dull noise that was as much vibration as sound, and the light of the candle wavered slightly.

"Doc?"

Radek hurried back to the gap in the door. "Are you all right?"

"Yeah." Ronon's tone wasn't as confident as his words. "But I think we're losing more air."

Radek cursed again. "Yes, I believe it. Just hang on, I can move this in just a moment."

"Maybe I can get through," Ronon said, and wedged his shoulder into the gap, only to fall back, wincing.

"Give me my laptop," Radek said. He would find a way, there had to be a way, but while he was figuring it out, he needed to set up the laptop to work the door controls from the inside. His hands moved without conscious volition, attaching the new cable, typing in the commands and adjusting the tolerances. The window opened, and he allowed himself a sigh of relief.

"Better take these, too," Ronon said, and shoved the bag that held the oxygen candles through the gap.

Radek accepted it automatically, dragging it to one side so that it would be out of the way. There were still pulleys on the floor and on what was now the ceiling, an elaborate block and tackle system intended to ease moving something larger than the drones. Or, perhaps, to move the things the drones were loaded into? It was hard to tell. Most of the hoist had broken free of its moorings, but at least the main block and tackle was intact. If he could just free one end of the cable —

He hauled on it, and staggered back as it came free, the pulley wheels running freely. That was good, and he traced the other end into the tangle, hauling on it until it stuck fast. If he had a cutting torch — and that was something else he was going to carry the next time he went off Atlantis, assuming there was a next time. He killed that thought. He didn't have a torch, and he was running out of time.

He wrapped the free end of the cable around his waist, to be sure his efforts didn't drag it out of the sheaves, then tugged at the other end to gain some slack. He looped that around the biggest beam, angling it to get the best leverage, then walked back toward the opening, pulling in the cable to bring it taut. It came fast at first, the wheels clattering, and stopped abruptly, the cable singing as it snapped tight. He put his full weight on it, felt the metal give, and then stick fast again.

"Doc," Ronon said again. "The air, it's going. Seal the door."

"We do not do things that way," Radek said, breathlessly, and hauled with all his strength. The metal moved, and he pulled again, hanging from the cable to get every last gram of force. It moved, it definitely moved, but was it enough? It would have to be, he thought, and reached for his laptop. "I think we have it."

"It's too late," Ronon said. "Seal the damn door."

"Don't pass out, I can't carry you." Radek typed the command into the computer, and the door began to move, sliding back on its track. Ten centimeters, twenty-five… it jammed again, but surely the opening was large enough. "Come on!"

He could feel the air flowing past him, the candle sputtering. Ronon lurched forward, and Radek caught his arm, steering him through the gap and into the shelter of the storage compartment. Ronon shook himself, leaning hard against the wall, and Radek reversed the door. It slid closed with a solid thunk. Above them, the oxygen candle guttered, and Ronon slid down the wall, grimacing as he settled himself on the floor.

"Are you all right?" Radek checked the bag with the oxygen candles. They had a dozen left; he could spare another to replenish the atmosphere they'd lost. He dragged one out, stuck it to the wall, and pulled the tab. It flared to life, casting a second set of wavering shadows, and Radek turned his attention to the other man. "Let me see."

"I'm ok," Ronon said. "Just my leg."

"Yes —" The hull groaned again, and Radek reached for his laptop. "I think — Yes, we're still holding together, though we're losing atmosphere everywhere." He allowed himself a deep sigh, and slumped to the floor beside Ronon. "But this compartment is intact, and we still have emergency power. That means we should keep gravity, at least for a while."

"That's good, right?" Ronon sounded exhausted, and Radek made himself reach for the first aid kit.

"Yes. We should be fine until either Teyla or Colonel Sheppard returns. Now, let me take a look at your leg."

"There's nothing more you can do," Ronon said. He rested his head against the wall. "Unless you've got any of those pain pills?"

"Yes." Radek found them, measured out the tablets.

Ronon palmed them, swallowing them dry. "Thanks."

"We should be all right —" Radek began, and Ronon shook his head.

"Don't say it."

Radek laughed under his breath. "Perhaps not."

"When do you think they'll get here?"

Radek shrugged, reaching for his laptop. "Who knows? But hours, not days."

"That's something."

The dry humor in Ronon's voice was oddly encouraging. "Yes, well," Radek said. "I did not bring anything with me to amuse myself with."

Ronon shifted, reaching into his pockets. "Cards."

"You brought playing cards?" Radek looked doubtfully over the top of his glasses.

"I was planning teach Martinez and Sloan how to play catch-as-catch-can," Ronon said. "But Teyla decided I needed to come on this mission. They were in my pocket."

"I'm not exactly sorry," Radek said. "If you hadn't been here, I don't know if I could have gotten that door open. I wouldn't have known that was part of the lock, much less figured it out."

"It wouldn't have done me any good if you hadn't gotten the

door unjammed," Ronon answered.

That was not something Radek really wanted to think too much about. "Can two people play this game, catch-as-catch-can?"

"Not so much." Ronon sounded faintly relieved at the change of subject. "But there are other games."

"Good," Radek said briskly. "You can teach them to me."

Sheppard peered at his laptop's glowing screen, night rising outside Atlantis's windows. It had been a long day, but a much better one than it might have been, considering everything that had gone wrong. Nobody had been killed, and Carson promised Ronon's wrenched knee would be fine in a week or so. Ok, they hadn't been able to save the Ancient warship, but Rodney had managed to repair the Traveler ship in the nick of time. His fingers moved, typing quickly. *Dr. McKay's assistance ensures that the Travelers will continue to cooperate with Atlantis mission objectives*: he thought that was pretty good report-speak for 'and now Larrin *really* owes us one.'

Unfortunately, the Ancient warship's hull proved to be unstable and the ship unsalvageable. However, we were able to remove all useable parts and return them to Atlantis. (See attached inventory.) And that pretty much covered it, because there wasn't any room in the official report for the moment of pure adrenaline when he came back through the wormhole to find a Traveler ship in orbit and the Ancient ship dark and silent, or for the sheer relief of finding Zelenka and Ronon alive and not seriously hurt. He couldn't suppress a crooked smile, remembering how his team had found the two of them, sitting quietly in the drone compartment, cards in hand and a pile of improvised counters in front of Zelenka. That was something else that wasn't going in the official report: don't play cards with Zelenka. He'd let them figure that out the hard way.

STARGATE SG-1
Time Keeps on Slippin'

Keith R.A. DeCandido

This story takes place between "Nemesis," the third-season finale of Stargate SG-1, *and "Small Victories," the fourth-season premiere.*

FOR MAJOR Samantha Carter, it was always a question of multitasking.

Under normal circumstances, it would be the easiest thing in the world to keep track of three things at once, even if those three things were remembering how much time had elapsed, keeping herself alive while under heavy fire, and paying attention to the vibration of the ship around her. The latter was particularly important, as those vibrations would increase when the ship in question, the Asgard vessel *Beliskner,* was touching the stratosphere.

Complicating matters, though, was the second part. Even at the height of the Gulf War, she'd never been under fire quite like this. Hundreds and hundreds of mechanical spider-like creatures that Thor of the Asgard referred to as "Replicators" were skittering toward her. By her side were Colonel Jack O'Neill and Teal'c. The sound of metal on metal from the Replicators' movements, the mechanical humming of the creatures, both sounding a hundred times over, combined with the hum of the active Stargate behind her and the reports of two SPAS-12s and her own GAU 5/A all firing over and over on semi-automatic to keep the Replicators at bay.

The close quarters of the chamber on the *Beliskner* made it as loud as anything Carter had ever experienced, the cacophony making it nigh-impossible to concentrate enough to focus on one thing, much less all three.

Somehow O'Neill managed to shout over all that. "Carter!"

"Not yet, sir!"

They had transported the Stargate from Cheyenne Mountain to the *Beliskner*, and Teal'c had manually dialed it to another world. She had already sent the stasis pod with the very ill Thor through the Stargate. Now she was waiting for the right moment for them to join him: soon enough for the friction of atmospheric entry to aid the explosives Teal'c had planted on the hull in destroying the ship, but not so long that the selfsame friction would burn off the explosives. Then O'Neill would set off the detonator and they'd step through the Stargate to safety while the *Beliskner* was destroyed along with all the Replicators.

She hoped.

The vibration in the deckplates increased, and the right amount of time had elapsed, and Carter really hoped that the former wasn't because of the thousands and thousands of replicators moving across the deck.

"Now!"

O'Neill stopped firing and pulled the detonator out of a pouch, Teal'c shifting his field of weapons fire to cover the colonel.

He pushed the button and cried, "Let's go!"

All three of them dove through the Stargate. Carter did a right shoulder roll that would have made Sergeant Nadaner back at the Academy proud, but she still wrenched her shoulder, as the ground was far lower than expected. Most Stargates had a ramp or stairs or were buried partway into the ground, but this one was apparently off the ground but without easy access. When they went home, they were going to need to take a big step up to go through.

The wormhole closed with a swish, and Carter looked around as she scrambled to her feet, favoring her right shoulder as she did so. She saw a large plateau with several trees and bushes, and a small lake. Thor's pod floated in the air near the DHD. In the distance, she could only see mountain tops covered in snow. The sky overhead was full of clouds, but the sky over the horizon was oddly — well, blurry.

"Everyone okay?" O'Neill asked, yanking his safety goggles off his face. With bullets and blown Replicator bits flying all over the place, the eye protection had been necessary on the *Beliskner.*

"I am fine, O'Neill," Teal'c said. After taking his own goggles off, he removed the magazine from his SPAS-12 and replaced it with a fresh one.

"Me, too, sir." Carter looked over at the Jaffa. "Teal'c, where are we?"

"P4X-234. I chose an address that could be manually dialed with the greatest speed and efficiency."

"Good thinkin'." O'Neill headed to the DHD.

"Sir, I wouldn't bother dialing home." Carter took off her own goggles before gingerly shouldering her rifle. "Remember, *we* just used the main Earth gate. It'll take at least a day or two for them to get the beta gate out of storage and install it."

O'Neill blew out a breath. "Right." The second gate that Carter and O'Neill had found in Antarctica had been in storage ever since those rogue N.I.D. agents were caught using it. "Maybe the Asgard will come and fetch Thor and give us a lift. Meantime, I *really* hope that P4X-234 is a friendly planet."

"It should be." Carter, though, was dubious even as she said it. "Teal'c, are you sure that's where you dialed?"

Teal'c sounded more than a little nonplussed. "Indeed."

"I'm sorry, I don't mean to doubt you, but — well, the reports SG-4 made last year were that the gate was on an island. This is on a mountain." Carter looked around. "But this area matches the description perfectly otherwise. The lake, the trees, the bushes. Captain Zerelli even reported that the water in the lake was drinkable and the fruits on those bushes were edible."

"Good," O'Neill said, heading for the lake, "'cause I'm starving and thirsty. Carter, did SG-4 find any people?"

Carter shook her head. "No, sir, but it was just a big ocean all around. For land like this to just show up around it would take millennia of continental drift."

O'Neill was cupping water from the lake into his hands. "Ahhh. I needed that. All right, let's take a few minutes to relax. I, for one, could use a break."

Carter smiled. "Well, sir, you did want to go fishing."

With a snort, O'Neill fell more than sat on the ground next to one of the bushes. He was still in the civilian clothes he'd been wearing when Thor beamed him to the *Beliskner*. They had all been on vacation while Dr. Daniel Jackson recovered from an appendectomy, but then the crisis with Thor and the Replicators happened.

Her smile falling, Carter added, "I just hope the Asgard ship was completely destroyed."

"Not a helluva lot we can do about it now." He picked a few berries off the bush and popped them in his mouth. "Mmm, tastes like boysenberry."

"Well, that's good," Carter said.

O'Neill shook his head. "Actually, I hate boysenberry. So please, have as much as you want." He pointed at the bush. "Let's all catch our breath, eat, drink, and be merry, and then we'll do some recon."

Carter and Teal'c both sat alongside O'Neill. The berries didn't taste anything like boysenberry to Carter, but she didn't contradict the colonel. As for Teal'c, he bit one, swallowed it very gingerly, and then intoned, "My symbiote allows me to go many days without food."

"You don't like boysenberry either, huh?" O'Neill sighed. "All right, since you're not eating, Teal'c, you start the recon."

Clambering to her feet, Carter said, "I'll go too, sir. I want to examine the area around here, see why it's so different from what SG-4 reported."

O'Neill threw up his hands. "Yah sure youbetcha," he

said in the same bad Minnesota accent he'd used to try to convince her to come fishing with him.

With a chuckle, Carter followed Teal'c as they headed toward the edge of the clearing.

But when Teal'c got to the edge of the grass line, he suddenly disappeared.

"Teal'c!" Carter was only two steps behind him.

When she passed the edge of the grass, however, Teal'c was nowhere to be found, but the sky was no longer blurry. Instead, there was a certain amount of cloud cover.

On the ground next to her were Teal'c's rifle and zat'ni'katel.

"Sir," she started as she turned around, but when she looked back at the plateau, O'Neill wasn't moving. The colonel was in the midst of getting up from the ground, but he looked frozen in place.

"Colonel!"

O'Neill didn't respond, didn't move, didn't budge. Carter started to move back toward him —

— and couldn't. It was like there was an invisible wall — or, more likely, a force shield — keeping her out of the plateau.

Cadet Samantha Carter who graduated the Academy at the top of her class would have been utterly baffled by the current situation, convinced that someone was playing a trick or that perhaps she was going mad.

Major Samantha Carter, though, had spent the past three years as part of SG-1 and not only wasn't baffled, but was pretty sure she had figured it all out already. To prove it, she bent down and picked up Teal'c's rifle. The SPAS-12's magazine was completely empty. He had just reloaded it when they came through the gate — there was no way he could have shot all those rounds, even on semi-automatic, in the two seconds between his "disappearance" and Carter going through that apparent force shield.

For whatever reason, time was moving at a far greater rate away from the Stargate than it was on the plateau. The colonel *was* moving, but relative to the speed at which Carter was now moving, it was like he was standing still.

Teal'c could have been there for hours before moving away, and it would have appeared to Carter as if he'd just disappeared.

She noticed something else on Teal'c's rifle: blood.

Looking down on the ground, she saw more blood. The trail continued down the mountain. Carter didn't have Teal'c's tracking ability, but even she could follow that...

She turned to make one more attempt to get through the force shield, even shooting her GAU 5/A at it, but the rounds just ricocheted off, and she stopped for fear of being hit with one.

If Teal'c was hurt, her first priority was to find him and try to rescue him. If she was lucky, O'Neill wouldn't have finished getting up by the time she got back. She hoisted both Teal'c's rifle and her own, wincing at the pain in her right shoulder, and kept the zat'ni'katel in her right hand. The zat had been of no use against the Replicators, but she figured it was best for her primary weapon to be a non-lethal one, at least to start.

Eventually, the blood trail thinned to the point of uselessness, but by then she was in sight of a large city in the valley between this mountain and the next one over. There were no other signs of civilization, though she did see disturbingly large animal tracks here and there on the ground.

Even as she worked her way down, so many thoughts vied for attention in her head, and, just as she had on Thor's ship, she kept them all going in her mind at once.

The astrophysicist in her wondered how this planet could possibly function, with one section of it moving at a different rate of time. She was no geologist, but she imagined the stresses alone would tear the mantle apart.

The soldier in her thought back over the battle on Thor's ship, hoping that the explosives Teal'c placed on the *Beliskner* were enough to destroy the ship and the Replicators, thus saving Earth. She had a very real concern that the plan hadn't worked and by the time Stargate Command got the beta gate up and running, they'd be going back to an Earth that was overrun by Replicators.

The space nerd in her, the one who asked her parents for a telescope for her fifth birthday, was once again grooving on the notion of walking on alien soil. It had been three years since she set foot on Abydos after going through the gate for the first time, and the thrill of placing her boots on a planet that wasn't Earth had yet to diminish. She truly hoped it never would.

As she got closer, she noticed that the far end of the city had a huge industrial complex that was powered by four massive engines, all of which had what appeared to be geothermal taps. Also, the entire city, except for that complex, was surrounded by a stone wall. The buildings inside seemed to be made of refined metal, for the most part, and Carter found it an interesting juxtaposition of styles between the architecture of the wall versus that of the city.

She spied a metal portcullis embedded in the stone wall, guarded by two men, both of whom were as bald as Teal'c, and also had little tufts of blond hair on their chins. Carter was amused by the fact that these people, on a planet billions of miles from Earth, had also developed the soul patch as a fashion statement. They were armed, so Carter figured it was best to not escalate matters by showing off her own weaponry. She holstered the zat.

The men held up their weapons, which looked like Civil War-era pistols. "Halt!" one cried.

Carter held up both hands. "My name is Major Samantha Carter. I come from a place called Earth. I came through the Stargate, and I'm looking for a friend of mine who I believe was brought here hurt."

Looking at each other briefly, one of the guards said, "Describe your friend."

"Taller than me, bald, with a golden symbol of a serpent on his forehead."

Now the guards nodded at each other. "The *feraq* victim," one said.

The other removed a small device from his pocket and put it

to his throat. "Hem ten, this is hem fifteen. We need an escort to the hospital."

A tinny voice sounded over the small speakers of the device. "Acknowledged, hem ten. Escort will arrive shortly."

"Wait here, please," the guard said as he pocketed the device. "Someone will take you to your friend in the hospital."

Carter nodded.

The other one asked, "You said 'Stargate'? Is that what you call the ring in the oasis on the mountain?"

Allowing herself a small smile, Carter replied, "Yes. We use it to travel to other worlds. There's an entire network of them." She decided to venture a question of her own. "What's a *feraq*?"

"Vicious beast that roams the countryside. They're why our ancestors built this wall, in fact. Your friend saved the lives of two idiots who were out trying to capture one of the beasts without a hunting license."

"Yeah, Macri took those two in *right* off," the other guard said with a chuckle. "They thought your friend was one of us, on account of his lack of hair."

"Speaking of which, with hair like that, what do you *do*, exactly?"

Carter blinked. "I'm sorry?"

"Well, your hair's way too long for you to be a menial, and too long for a tradesperson. And it would need to be longer for you to be a scientist."

Suddenly, Carter wished Daniel was here. He would be fascinated by the contradictory architecture, and would probably have a theory about why they had sophisticated communications technology but ancient firearms. Plus this whole adjust-your-hair-length-to-fit-your-job thing was bizarre to say the least.

Another man with a shaved head and a blond soul patch stood on the other side of the portcullis.

One of Carter's guards said, "This woman is to be taken to the *feraq* victim at the hospital. She's one of the ones he said would come for him."

Carter smiled. Teal'c must have told them about her and O'Neill both.

A guard pulled another device out of his pocket and pressed a button, causing the portcullis to rise.

"Come with me, please."

The streets of the city were made of cobblestone, and most people walked, though she saw a few wagon-wheeled carriages that were powered by tiny batteries. Apparently, they never developed the combustion engine, but went straight to electronics — and skipped over the notion of radial tires or asphalt.

The hospital was a surprisingly small building. There were no subdivided rooms, but simply one huge hall filled with beds. It took no time at all to pick out Teal'c, as he was larger than anyone else present and the only one with the gold symbol of Apophis on his forehead.

While the patients had a variety of hair types, Carter noticed that the people walking around the hospital all seemed to have either crew cuts — these appeared to be maintenance personnel — or kind of shaggy hair that hung near their necks. Based on what the guard said, these were the doctors and nurses.

One such, with shaggy black hair, was standing by Teal'c. "I really wish," she was saying, "that we could study you in more depth, but that would require dissection, and I don't think even you could recover from that."

"Indeed." He looked up at her approach. "Major Carter."

"Teal'c. Are you okay?"

"I am fine."

The doctor smiled. "He's more than fine. I'm Tan Xirale. Anyone else who was as badly wounded by the *feraq* as Teal'c here was would be dead by now. The blood loss alone would have done it, given how long it took them to carry him down the mountain."

"I'm glad you're okay, Teal'c. But we need to get back up the mountain and figure out a way to get through that force shield."

"Actually," the doctor said, "you should talk to my sister.

She's the Chief Scientist of the city, and she can probably help you — and you can probably help her."

Teal'c was free to go, and Xirale's workday was done, so she led them to her sister's office, which was only a few streets away.

This was another building with very few divisions in the room, but many desks. Apparently they weren't big on private office spaces around here. Xirale brought them over to a woman with similar features, as well as the same color hair, also down to her shoulders, but much curlier. The woman in question was holding what looked like a laptop monitor without a keyboard, operating it by touching the screen.

"Sam Carter, Teal'c, this is Tan Nardah. Nardah, Teal'c is the patient I was telling you about."

Nardah frowned at her sister. "I thought you said he was attacked by a *feraq*. He's looking mighty healthy."

"I am a Jaffa," Teal'c said.

"Which means he heals fast," Carter added with a smile. "Unfortunately, it's just him. If it had been me who was attacked by the *feraq*, I'd probably need a lot more of your sister's help."

"Carter here," Xirale said, "is a scientist."

"Astrophysicist, actually." Carter pointed at the screen of her device. "That looks like a schematic of the machine on the outskirts of the city."

Nardah nodded. "It is."

"What's wrong with it?"

"The short version? It's broken."

Carter peered more closely at it. "Looks like the geothermal taps are working beyond their capacity."

Now Nardah turned and regarded Carter with appreciation. "Okay, when I saw your hair, I just assumed Xirale was joking about you being a scientist."

Chuckling, Carter said, "Sorry, where I come from, hair doesn't indicate job."

Teal'c did his trademark head-tilt. "That is not entirely correct, Major Carter. The Air Force to which you belong requires hair be a certain length, and Jaffa tradition holds that First Primes must remain hairless."

Nodding to concede the point, Carter said, "Still, I can be a scientist with hair like this. What does the engine do? Provide power?"

"I wish. No, this thing sucks up all our power — but without it, the entire planet would blow up."

Carter blinked. "The tectonic stress from operating in two different timestreams?"

Now Nardah frowned. "Excuse me? I mean, yes, tectonic stress, but we haven't been able to determine why it's happening."

"Is it localized under the mountain where the Stargate — the ring is?"

Nardah set the device down on her desk. "You can't possibly have known that from looking at this schematic."

"No, but I know where the temporal displacement is. Something is causing time to slow down on this planet — except for the area around the Stargate. We had a team come to this world a year ago, but then the Stargate was on an island."

Shaking her head, Nardah said, "The best geological evidence we have is that this mountain has been here for two thousand years. But there've been a lot of tectonic shifts in those two thousand years, and the ocean has receded considerably, but —" She shook her head. "How can time move at a different rate in one section of the planet?"

"Naturally? It can't. But there are lots of technologies that we barely understand that have done stranger things. We've seen devices that can move to alternate dimensions, that —"

Xirale held up a hand. "I hate to interrupt, but I need to get home. I assume I can leave these two in your care, Nardah?"

"Try to take them away from me," Nardah said with a grin. "Carter, you may be the answer to our prayers. The machine has been able to stave off the tectonic stresses — without it, the entire continent would collapse, and possibly the entire planet would be destroyed — but we haven't been able to figure out the cause."

Carter nodded and glanced at Teal'c. "I might be able to help you with that — if you can help us with our problem. We need to get through to the Stargate."

"We gave up hope of getting through to the oasis decades ago, but it's been long enough that some fresh eyes might actually help." Nardah put her left hand over her heart. "I promise that I will aid you in your quest, if you will help us in ours."

Matching the gesture, assuming it to be the equivalent of shaking hands on a deal, Carter said, "I promise to do likewise."

"As do I," Teal'c said, without the gesture.

For the next several hours, Nardah showed Carter the workings of the machine, as well as the geological scans of the mountain and its environs.

Eventually, a man who resembled Nardah and Xirale both, but had a shaved head and a blond soul patch, entered the office. "Sister, it's time to go home."

Nardah closed her eyes and sighed. "Macri, you *really* don't have to escort me home every night."

"As long as you're receiving death threats, I tend to disagree."

Teal'c, who had been eating a meal Nardah had had delivered to the office, rose to his feet. "You are one of the officers who arrested the men I rescued."

Macri nodded. "I'm Tan Macri. My other sister tells me that you two came through the ring?"

"Indeed. Please explain your reference to death threats."

"It's nothing," Nardah said before Macri could answer.

"It's *not* nothing," Macri said in a long-suffering tone that reminded Carter a great deal of some of her arguments with her brother Mark. "There's a faction of people who believe that the machine should be dismantled, that it's consuming too much power for not enough gain."

"They're idiots. The earthquakes that will result from turning the machine off will destroy half the city." Nardah shook her head. "I'm tempted to turn it off just so they can see how catastrophic it would be."

Macri frowned. "Please tell me you're not serious."

Nardah regarded her brother with amusement. "I'm not serious. Entirely." She then looked at Carter. "There's an inn nearby, but I suspect that you don't have any currency that we take, given that you're from another world and all. However, I have an extra room in my dwelling, so the pair of you can stay with me in my guest room."

"Actually," Macri said, "why doesn't Teal'c stay with me? I assume you two will be geebling about the machine at all hours, and based on the glazed look that Teal'c had when I came in here, he might enjoy staying with a peace officer more than he would a pair of scientists."

Teal'c bowed his head. "Your offer is greatly appreciated, Tan Macri. I accept."

"And I accept your offer," Carter said with a grateful smile.

The next several weeks were at once fantastic and frustrating for Carter.

The machine was a device of exquisite design. Nardah was not the designer — that was her mentor, a now-deceased scientist named Yor Bestra — but she was the one who maintained it and who had made many improvements to it over the years. It was only staving off the inevitable. With each passing year it required more power to keep the tectonic stress and volcanic activity in check. Still, it did its job superlatively.

What frustrated her was an inability to figure out a way to stop the tectonic stress permanently, or a way to get through the force shield. The more time passed, the more the mountain's ever-changing geological structure due to its moving at a different rate of time than the rest of the world, the more unstable it all became.

Equally frustrating were the constant barrage of protests against the use of the machine. Carter was mostly exposed to it in the form of e-mails that were sent to Nardah, as well as flyers and graffiti she saw on the walls of the city. (She couldn't actually read them, but Nardah translated, albeit bitterly.)

Teal'c had been serving as an unofficial advisor to the peace officers, showing them some Jaffa techniques in hand-to-hand combat that they had never developed here. Meanwhile, Carter had been letting her hair grow out so she'd fit in more with Nardah and her co-workers at the science institute.

One day, Mardah, Macri, and Xirale all had dinner together, leaving Carter and Teal'c to share a meal alone for the first time in weeks.

"Have you made any progress in penetrating the force shield, Major Carter?"

Carter shook her head as she popped a bit of *feraq* chop into her mouth. "None. Most of the technology on this world is geared toward information storage and communications. Some of that has bled over into other technology, like powering their version of cars, but they've developed very little tech that directly affects the environment. Most of their tools are mechanical, they've never invented air conditioning or heaters — but those touchscreen devices can store five times as much information as the mainframe in Cheyenne Mountain." Realizing she was burying the lede, she chuckled. "You know, by now, Colonel O'Neill would have interrupted me, made some kind of strangling noise, and told me to get to the point already."

"It has been my observation that you do reach the crux of the matter eventually."

She held up the mug of fruit juice in mock toast. "Well, thanks for that. Anyhow, the crux of the matter is that I need some kind of wave modulator and a frequency jammer that I can fine-tune to try and disrupt the force shield. I've actually been working on the design for that, but they don't have the manufacturing capability here to do it." Carter shook her head. "The hilarious part is, I can only design it because the computers here are so good. The modifications are based on how the wormhole interacted with the solar flare when we got sent back to 1969, and the studies they made at Area 51 of the quantum mirror before General Hammond destroyed it."

Teal'c nodded. "Impressive."

"Not really." Carter blew out a breath. "Right now, it's all theoretical. I don't have the means to build what I need. We're just barely earning our keep here helping the Tans. That's one good thing; I've been able to help increase the efficiency of the machine, though I wish we had a real engineer here to give it a once-over. This is way out of my league."

"I have found, Major Carter, that your league encompasses more than you give yourself credit for."

"Maybe." She shook her head and finished off her meal. "The good news is that we have plenty of time. I went up the mountain yesterday, and the colonel hasn't even finished getting up off the ground yet."

Carter was sitting at the desk that Nardah had issued her — right next to Nardah's own — in the science institute, when the large monitor attached to the ceiling came to life.

Glancing over at one of the other scientists, Carter asked, "What's that?"

"Level-one council session," the scientist said, sounding bored. "The articles of law say that all such sessions have to be broadcast so the people can be aware of how the council functions. Mostly it just shows us how incredibly boring council sessions are."

It didn't take long for Carter to come to a similar conclusion to that of her colleague. But then, governmental procedure had never held any interest for her. She came from a military family where you followed orders handed down through the chain of command. Carter generally preferred the simplicity of a briefing to the tedium of a meeting. For one thing, she had yet to encounter a military operation that was ever in any way improved by a politician's getting involved, from that congressman during the Gulf War who decided to go on a fact-finding tour that included Carter's unit and nearly got himself killed in the process, to Senator Robert Kinsey's attempt to shut the SGC down two years ago.

The only part of the broadcast that was in any way interesting was the fact that politicians here wore their hair in topknots, making them all look vaguely like samurai from feudal Japan.

However, one item on the agenda did grab her attention. A councilor named Kif Mirak asked to speak before the council on the subject of shutting down the machine. A majority of the remaining council agreed to let him speak, and then he stood.

"I would like to urge the council to once again take a vote regarding the shutting down of the machine. I am aware that the last ten votes have resulted in the resolution failing, however the latest power consumption reports have been issued, which prove beyond a shadow of a doubt that the machine itself is simply consuming more power, with less impressive results.

"The fact of the matter is that the machine is a failure. It doesn't do what it's supposed to do, and it's been doing it less and less well at greater and greater cost for years now. We need to shut it down and find a new way to stave off the geologic stresses that the science institute claims the machine is stopping.

"While we're at it, we should also pass a resolution to have an independent study commissioned to see if the machine is even necessary. The problem may well have been resolved by the machine, and the continued running of it simply a boondoggle from the science institute to pour currency into their coffers to fix a problem that is already solved.

"Now, I don't wish to impugn the good names of the people in the science institute — I'm sure they're all fine, ethical people. But the fact of the matter is that we only have their word for the fact that the machine works. I think an independent study is necessary, which means shutting the machine down.

"I also believe that the two aliens should be detained until we can determine for certain where they came from and what their agenda is. I'm aware that the male alien saved the lives of two of our citizens, at grave risk to himself, but I'm also aware of the fact that the power consumption of the machine has increased tenfold since the female alien's arrival and since she started 'consulting' with the science institute."

Carter just stared at the screen in confusion. The rate of increase of the machine's power consumption was consistent over the past several years. Yes, it had increased since Carter's arrival, but on the same track it had been on before she started working with Nardah.

There was a vote on all three of Kif's resolutions. To Carter's relief, the only one that passed was the independent audit of the machine — which was also the only one of the three that was reasonable. However, she was disheartened to see that the resolutions to detain her and Teal'c and to shut down the machine only lost by one vote each.

That night, both Teal'c and Macri, as well as two other peace officers, showed up to escort them home. At Carter's questioning look, Teal'c said, "There are crowds gathered in the plaza that sits between this location and Tan Nardah's dwelling."

"And the death threats went through the roof after Kif's idiot speech this morning," Macri added. "As it is, we're taking the long way home."

"What difference does it make?" Nardah asked. "The resolution didn't pass."

Carter shook her head. Just because she didn't like politicians didn't mean she didn't recognize their tactics. "It doesn't matter. The vote was very close, and Kif wouldn't have made that speech if he didn't know he would strike a nerve with it. We need to be careful."

Nardah sighed. "It's ridiculous, it —"

Macri threw up his hands. "Nardah, someone tried to kill you today!"

Carter's eyes went wide. "What?"

"Someone sent a bomb here to the science institute. We intercepted it in time, and with Teal'c's help, we were able to track who delivered it. They've been arrested, but the point is, *someone sent a bomb here*. This isn't just random people being cranky and sending you threatening mail. This is *real*."

Teal'c said, "The explosive device was also accompanied by a note which specifically said that Major Carter and myself should be put to death for crimes against the city."

Closing her eyes, Nardah let out a slow, steady breath. "Dammit. All right, Macri, you win. I know you've wanted to put a permanent guard on Carter and me, and I've resisted, but I'm done with that."

"With your permission," Teal'c said, "I would like to volunteer for that duty."

Macri smiled. "I was already going to ask you to do it."

Turning to Carter, Nardah said, "I'm afraid I owe you an apology, Carter, and I also need to inform you of something I should have told you about."

Frowning, Carter asked, "What's that, Nardah?"

She sighed. "In the sub-basement of the institute, we have a repository of various devices, experiments, and the like. You might be able to modify one or more of them to make that wave modulator you've been tinkering with."

Carter opened her mouth, but Nardah put up both hands and cut her off.

"I know, I know, I should've told you sooner, but — well, I thought it was a fool's errand, and besides, I was being selfish. I didn't want you to go back to the ring and leave us forever. You've been a blessing, Carter, and so've you, Teal'c. My brother has never gushed about anyone the way he gushes about you."

Macri winced. "Nardah…"

"Oh, stop it, Macri, you *have* been gushing. But it's not fair to either of you." Nardah went to her desk and took out a keysquare. "This will access the sub-basement. Now I can't guarantee that you'll find what you need, but —"

"But I might." Carter accepted the keysquare. "Thank you, Nardah. And thanks for your honesty."

"I'm just sorry it didn't come sooner."

"Fine," Macri said impatiently. "Now if we're done being all emotional, let's get you two home."

They did indeed take a more roundabout route home, but when they turned a corner of a side street, there was a huge crowd of about two dozen people armed with various knives, plus one woman with a pistol.

Standing at the center of the crowd was Kif. He appeared unarmed, which Carter unkindly figured was to cover his own ass in case things went badly.

"Please, Officer," Kif said, "do not stand in the way of justice."

Macri actually sneered at Kif, a facial expression Carter applauded. "How exactly is mob rule 'justice,' Councillor?"

"Your choice is simple, Officer," Kif said as if Macri hadn't spoken. "Hand the aliens over to us or accept the consequences of refusing."

"Well done, Councillor, you just officially threatened a peace officer. You are hereby bound by law."

It was Kif's turn to sneer. "Don't toy with me, Officer. I'm a member of the council, you can't arrest me."

"Actually, I can." Macri unholstered his own weapon and pointed it at Kif. "The articles of law specify no exemptions."

"How naïve. Put the pistol down, Officer."

The other two officers also raised their pistols, and Teal'c held up his zat, activating it to the ready position with an electronic click. Carter wished she had her weapon, but consultants to the science institute didn't generally walk around armed. Her rifle was back at Nardah's dwelling.

The woman with the pistol also raised hers and aimed it at Teal'c. "Put it down, alien."

"Congratulations, citizen," Macri said to the woman, "you too are bound by law along with the councillor. Anyone else want to join them?"

"I haven't done anything wrong." The woman snarled. "The articles of law don't say anything about threatening aliens. Or, for that matter, shooting them."

She cocked the weapon. Carter immediately dove for cover, grabbing Nardah and pulling her to the ground as well.

Teal'c, though, stood his ground.

Macri cried, "No!" and leapt in front of Teal'c, just as the woman pulled the trigger.

The other two officers also fired, with Teal'c firing the zat.

But Macri blocked Teal'c's shot, so he went rigid from the zat's electric shock just as the bullet from the woman's pistol slammed into his chest.

The woman also fell to the ground, bullet wounds in her chest and head from the other two officers.

Kif immediately turned and ran, and the rest of his mob panicked as well. The street was clear in moments, except for the bodies of Macri and the woman, as well as Nardah, Carter, Teal'c, and the other two officers. One of the latter had a communication device at his throat calling for medical aid.

Teal'c was kneeling with Macri's body cradled in his arms. "He has no pulse."

Nardah just stared at Teal'c, seemingly unable to comprehend what Teal'c had just said. "You mean, he's — he's dead?"

"Indeed. I am sorry, Tan Nardah. I did not wish for this to happen."

"It's — it's not your fault, Teal'c." She turned toward the now-empty street where Kif had stood. "I know exactly who to blame, believe me."

For Carter, it was always a question of multitasking.

This time, though, it was to keep from falling asleep. She had spent days being questioned about the incident on the street, and attending hearings, and testifying in what was referred to as an inquest. However, when she wasn't actually testifying or answering questions, she was sitting in the gallery. All work save for the barest maintenance had ceased on the machine pending the inquest results.

Carter had been able to go to the sub-basement during one

of the recesses and make a quick inventory. Now she was juggling in her head how to kitbash some of the prototypes she found down there to do what her temporal waveform modulator was supposed to do; how they could reconfigure the geothermal taps; what to get Cassandra for her birthday; wondering whether or not O'Neill had gotten to his feet yet; hoping they consulted her notes at the SGC when they installed the beta gate; wondering who created the Replicators in the first place; and wishing that Councillor Ren Ympiz didn't talk in quite so dull a monotone.

However, Carter did put all the various thoughts aside when Ren announced that the inquest was at an end and a decision had been reached.

"While Councillor Kif's methods were deplorable, we do not wish to condemn his beliefs solely because he expressed them poorly."

Carter winced and gave a sad look to Nardah and Xirale. Their brother was dead. That was a lot more than a poor expression of beliefs.

"It is the ruling of this inquest that Kif Mirak be stripped of his councillorship and imprisoned for a period of twelve years. It is the further ruling of this inquest that the audit of the machine will continue and that an observer appointed by the council will look over all work that occurs involving the machine for the next three months and make regular reports to the council. And it is the final ruling of this inquest that Tan Macri died a hero, and will be honored in the plaza, and this day of every year shall be deemed Tan Macri Day in his memory."

On the one hand, Carter was glad it was over, and glad that Macri was being honored for his sacrifice. On the other, she wasn't thrilled about the observer.

She was even less thrilled the following morning when the observer arrived. He was one of the council, a man named Ain Anred. He approached Carter and Mardah, and said without preamble, "I just want you to know that I find this entire project a waste of time, and that I voted to have it shut down and to have you and that other awful alien put in chains. Your job is to convince me that I was wrong."

Carter raised both eyebrows and sighed. "Great."

The first day was primarily spent explaining what they were doing. Three years of dumbing things down for the other members of SG-1 served Carter in good stead, as Ain had a sub-O'Neill-level of understanding of anything scientific.

And then at the end of it all, he asked, "Why can't we just shut the blessed thing off?"

"Because," Nardah said impatiently, "the only reason we're all still alive right now is because of this machine. If we turn it off, nothing will stop the collision of the tectonic plates and the earthquakes will destroy the city."

"And you have proof of this?"

"We have mathematical models that conclusively—"

Ain shook his head. "You misunderstand me, Tan Nardah. I'm not speaking of models you made up on your computers. I'm talking about physical proof. Actual real-world proof."

"Councillor," Carter said, "if I understand you correctly, the only way you'll believe that it'll cause earthquakes if we turn the machine off is if we actually turn it off and we get earthquakes?"

"I believe, alien, that you have summed it up nicely, yes. I would like to propose that you shut the machine off for a day so we can see what it is actually doing."

Nardah stared at him. "That's insane."

"Nonetheless, I think it would go a long way toward proving the machine's usefulness."

"So not satisfied with getting my brother killed, you and your fellow imbeciles want *more* dead bodies on your hands?"

Ain put his hands on his hips. "I will not be spoken to this way!"

Carter stepped between the two of them. "It doesn't matter. With respect, Councillor Ain, you don't have any authority to give us orders. Your sole purpose is to observe and report your findings to the rest of the council, correct?"

Reluctantly, Ain said, "That is so, yes. But I still think—"

"I don't care *what* you think," Nardah said. "Now I've answered all your stupid questions. From this point forth, you can just observe. If you have any questions, ask Carter. I'm done talking to you."

With that, Nardah left the room in a huff.

"Her behavior will go in my report," Ain muttered to himself.

Carter stared angrily at the councillor. "Her behavior is because she just lost her brother—to a person who used a lot of the same rhetoric you're using right now."

"Have a care, alien. Your presence will not be tolerated forever."

And then Ain followed Nardah out of the office area.

Shaking her head, Carter muttered, "Better not be forever."

That night, she went back to Macri's former dwelling, which Xirale and Nardah insisted that Teal'c and Carter use. As a peace officer's dwelling, it was more secure than most. Even with Kif disgraced, a lot of his attitudes still prevailed, as Carter's conversation with Ain had proven. Better to be safe.

"Teal'c, I think I may have—what is that on your chin?"

The Jaffa raised an eyebrow.

Then Carter grinned as she realized that over the past few days, he had grown a soul-patch and dyed it blond, just like the peace officers. "You're growing one of those beard things?"

Nodding, Teal'c said, "Tan Macri died saving my life. I am growing this patch on my soul in order to honor his memory."

Carter nodded. Then she pulled out her minicomputer. "I think I may have found a way to build my waveform modulator. Apparently, years ago, someone experimented with making a sonic weapon that he wanted to sell to the peace officers. But he never was able to properly weaponize it; he just made a gun that makes a subsonic noise that might give a few people a headache."

"How does that assist in your endeavor, Major Carter?"

"It's the delivery system I need. I've already got a power source and something I *think* I can convert into a dimensional shifter like the one in the quantum mirror. I should be able to get this together in the next week or so."

"I am grateful to hear that, Major Carter."

"Yeah." She sat down on the couch. "I just hope I still have access to the institute for that long." Then she told Teal'c about Councillor Ain.

"It would seem that Councillor Kif was not the only opponent to the machine."

"No. And it's ridiculous. It's like those people back on Earth who dismiss evolution saying 'it's just a theory.' A theory isn't 'just' anything, it's a conclusion based on detailed, hard data that has been gone over with a fine-tooth comb. But the only evidence Ain will accept is an actual disaster!" She shook her head. "I'm sorry, I didn't mean to rant."

"You may rant all you wish, Major Carter."

She smiled. "Thanks, Teal'c. Truly, I don't think I'd have gotten through this without you."

"You would not have been in this situation were it not for me, as it was I who chose to dial this world."

"True." She got up from the couch. "I'm going to take a bath." Another technological invention that had passed by this world was the shower, but they valued baths quite a bit, and tonight, Carter definitely needed one.

Ain observed Nardah and Carter for two months. During those eight weeks, Carter and Nardah managed to find a way to streamline the geothermal taps' work, and for the first time in years *decrease* the power used by the machine. That, if nothing else, did a great deal to shut Ain up, which made everyone happy. (Except Ain, but few in the science institute were all that concerned with the councillor's happiness.)

In her spare time, Carter also finished constructing the

prototype for a temporal waveform modulator. Her military training forced her to give it a designation, and she went with TWM-1.

When she got to the top of the mountain, she saw that O'Neill was not only upright, but also staring angrily at a spot where there wasn't anything she could see.

"Why is O'Neill staring at the air?" Teal'c asked her.

And then Carter saw it. Or, rather, didn't see it. "Where's Thor's pod?"

"Perhaps it moved through the field into the same time stream that we occupy."

Carter shook her head. "It hasn't been long enough. The anti-grav units on that pod kept it slow-moving for Thor's health. It can't have moved to the force shield in the time since we've gone through. Besides, if it had gone through, the colonel would've chased it."

"Indeed." Teal'c raised his eyebrow. "Perhaps the Asgard were able to locate Thor and transport him to their ship."

"And not take the colonel?" Carter sighed. "Well, let's test the TWM-1, and then maybe we can ask him."

She fired the converted sonic pistol at the force shield, and then picked up the test object: her safety goggles.

The goggles bounced off the force shield just as the bullets had that first time. "Dammit."

She tried the three other settings on the TWM-1, but none of them worked. The sonic pistol's design was only for four settings, and changing that wasn't really practical.

Carter frowned. "I thought I found the right range of wave modulations to make this work." She stared at O'Neill, still standing with his mouth open in a look of grumpiness. "Maybe I have the time ratios wrong. I need to get back and try another—"

Her musing was interrupted by the ground shaking beneath her feet.

"What the hell—?"

She lost her footing, but Teal'c reached out to grab her arm and steady her, but then another quake hit, twice as rough as the first.

Pulling out her binoculars, Carter glanced down at the city to find that the machine's lights had gone dark.

"I don't believe it! Some idiot turned the machine off!" And she had a pretty good idea who the idiot in question was.

Another quake, and this time Carter and Teal'c both fell to the ground. Luckily, they were high enough up on the mountain that there was very little danger of anything falling on their heads.

That was the final quake, and Carter again peered through her binoculars. The machine's lights were coming back on.

"C'mon, Teal'c, we have to get down there."

"Indeed."

By the time they finished the long trek down the mountain, the peace officers and medical personnel had things mostly under control. They still provided assistance, Teal'c's strength and observational ability and Carter's field medical training proving beneficial.

Carter finally made it to the science institute after nightfall. Nardah was there drinking something alcoholic. "Carter, where the hell've you been?"

"I told you I was—"

Nardah waved her off, her brief moment of anger burned to ashes. "Right, right, up the mountain, testing your new toy. Sorry, it's been a bad day. We had a power outage. Apparently, Ain saw that we had reduced the power needs for the machine, so he had the council authorize less power for the machine overall. But he got the figures wrong—of course—and it took too much away. So the machine shut down." After gulping down some of her drink, Nardah added, "The good news is, Ain has his proof now that the machine is vital. With any luck, he'll recommend that we keep the machine going."

"With any luck. Have any more of that?"

Smiling, Nardah poured another glass of the drink, which Carter recalled was named *yeriz*.

Then a buzzing noise interrupted them. Nardah put a communications device to her throat. "Yes?"

"Tan Nardah, this is Officer Ham Solvig. I'm afraid that we have some bad news. I believe you were searching for Councillor Ain Anred?"

"Yes, I was concerned about his wellbeing."

That surprised Carter — but then, something bad happening to the councillor would probably translate to something bad happening to the science institute.

"His wellbeing is quite poor, I'm afraid," Ham said. "He's dead."

Carter's second time experiencing an inquest was more exciting than the last, but it also made her realize how much better boring was in the grand scheme of things.

One councillor testified: "According to Councillor Ain's reports, the staff at the science institute was abusive toward him. More than once, he felt that his life was in danger."

An aid to the council, who wore a topknot, but one that was much shorter than those of the councillors: "I reviewed Councillor Ain's figures, and they were enough to cause the machine to shut down from lack of power. The councillor told me that they were the figures provided by Tan Nardah and the alien woman. I believe that Tan Nardah and her colleagues deliberately had Ain be responsible for the temporary deactivation of the machine so they could make him look foolish."

Nardah muttered to Carter in the gallery, "No, the universe made him look foolish."

Carter snorted in agreement.

The testimony continued in that vein, with only Nardah herself providing the truth. "The figures we supplied to the councillor were correct and would not have shut down the machine. But while I'm sure that Ain Anred had many virtues, a head for mathematics was not one of them. He barely understood the principles that Sam Carter and I laid out for him. It's not a surprise that he got the numbers wrong. Councillors, I am sorry for what has happened, but it was an accident. And this accident has also proven just how necessary the machine is."

After all the testimony was taken, Councillor Ren said, "The council will deliberate, and take into full consideration the testimony given today, as well as the allegations of manipulation of data. We will render the rulings of this inquest tomorrow."

The crowd filed out of the government building, and as soon as they got outside, Nardah turned to Carter and Teal'c. "How close are you to getting through to the ring?"

After glancing at Teal'c, Carter said, "I've readjusted the TWM-1 to four new possible waveforms. I think it stands a good chance of working this time."

"Then go — get up to the mountain at first light and go through. Because I can guarantee that, based on Ren's tone, the council is *not* going to be favorable toward us."

Carter hesitated. "Nardah, we can't just —"

"Yes, you *can* go. You *need* to go. This isn't your world, and this isn't your fight, it's mine. I appreciate the help you've given me, but I think this last incident will bring a lot of our good work to an end."

"Nardah, I —"

"No, Carter. No goodbyes. I've already said goodbye to my brother unwillingly, I won't do it for the pair of you. Just *go*."

The next morning, Carter and Teal'c put on the fatigues that they'd been wearing when they'd boarded the *Beliskner*. Neither of them had said they were going to do it, and Carter wasn't surprised that Teal'c was thinking the same thing as her. They also made sure to grab plenty of food and drink, in case they did make it through. "O'Neill will, I suspect prefer these to boysenberries," Teal'c said.

"Indeed," Carter said with a smile.

As they reached the plateau on the mountain, Carter saw that O'Neill hadn't changed position, but he had closed his mouth.

She tried the first setting, tossed the goggles. Nothing.

Then the second setting.

On the third setting, the goggles flew through, but hovered in midair as soon as they crossed the event horizon.

And then the ground started to shake, far more violently. The very rock of the mountain started to split apart, and Carter and Teal'c both fell to the ground.

Teal'c shouted over the din of the quaking earth. "We must go through, Major Carter!"

Her first thought was of Nardah and Xirale, but her next was that she didn't want to die on this time-displaced mountain, and the quakes were getting more intense, no doubt in response to the lessened influence of the machine.

So she dove toward the plateau at the same time that Teal'c did.

This time, her shoulder roll was perfect.

"*There* you are!" O'Neill cried. "First Teal'c disappears, then you disappear, Carter, then the Asgard come and take Thor away, then you come back." He frowned. "What happened to your hair?"

Carter blew out a breath. "It's a long story, sir." She glanced over at Teal'c.

However, the Jaffa was staring at Carter's hands. "Where is the TWM-1?"

"The what?" O'Neill asked, legitimately confused.

Glancing around the clearing, Carter saw no sign of it. "Dammit, I must've dropped it on the other side! I was hoping to go back, but without the TWM-1…"

"Might it still be on the other side?"

"With those quakes? There's no guarantee it'll still be there, and besides, it's been *years* now."

His hands at his temples as if to stave off a headache, O'Neill asked, "Will someone *please* tell me what the hell's going on? Teal'c, why do you have a soul-patch?"

"As Major Carter said, O'Neill, it is a long story."

"Well, we've got plenty of time," O'Neill snapped. "I'd kinda like to hear it."

"Yeah, *we* have plenty of time." Carter glanced back at the mountain with a heavy heart.

For each of the next six days, SG-1 continued to dial Earth, only to have the wormhole fail to engage. In the interim they also used some rocks on the plateau to create a makeshift staircase so they could approach the Stargate without clambering up the bottom of the circle.

By the fifth day, Carter was fully convinced that the SGC *hadn't* read her instructions on the computer, or didn't look for them until it was too late.

Over that time, Carter noted that the topography of the ground around them changed subtly.

And then, six days after Carter and Teal'c returned, there was a glow around the perimeter of the plateau. Suddenly, two women were standing on the other side of the force shield.

"We did it!" one woman cried.

"They're still here," the other said.

"You've been here for a week?" the first woman said. "We thought the ring was a portal to another world. Shouldn't you have left by now?"

"Uhm," O'Neill said.

"I don't know, sir," Carter said, genuinely confused. It should have been the better part of a century since they were in the city.

"You two must be Samcarter and Talc?" the second woman said. "Wow, I really thought you'd be taller."

Carter frowned. "Who are you?"

"I'm Ellasan, and this is Freygar. We're scientists, and I have to say it's a great honor to meet you, Samcarter. When we found the records of your work in the ruins of the old city, specifically of the TWM-1, it was the breakthrough we were looking for. We finally were able to work out a way to stabilize the planet."

"Stabilize — You mean the whole planet is on the same time stream now?"

Ellasan nodded. "Yes! Oh, I'm so glad you're still here. We have to go back and report our findings, but we'd love to stay in touch with you now that we can reach the ring."

Freygar started moving back to the mountain. "We will be back soon. Please don't go anywhere."

O'Neill stared down at Carter. "You look sad, Carter. You do realize that those two women just saved their planet from likely destruction thanks in part from your notes, right?"

"I guess, it's just…" She trailed off.

Teal'c came to her rescue. "Ellasan mentioned the ruins of the old city. That can only mean that the city in which we resided has been destroyed."

Carter added, "Which means that Nardah and Xirale are dead. And the city was probably destroyed right after we came back through here because the council turned the machine off." She shook her head. "Such a waste."

O'Neill put a hand on her shoulder. "It's been, what, a hundred years or so since you left? Good chance those two would've been dead by now no matter what."

"I suppose, sir."

"Look at it this way, thanks to you two, SG-1 has saved two planets in one week."

"Assuming," Teal'c said, "that we did succeed in our mission. It is possible that we have been unable to dial Earth because your homeworld has been destroyed."

"Thanks, Teal'c," O'Neill said with a sigh. "Nice job helping me with the cheering up."

Ellasan and Freyga did return, and Carter's hypothesis was confirmed: the council had shut off the machine, and the resultant earthquakes destroyed the city. The geologic disasters spread to other parts of the world, and they traced it to this mountain. Finding Carter's research in the ruins led to them understanding the temporal disturbance. They used Carter's notes on time dilation, on the Stargate's solar-flare-related time travel capability, and on the quantum mirror that all accompanied the TWM-1 specs to help guide them in the right direction toward bringing the planet back into temporal alignment. It helped that they'd been doing their own experiments with temporal physics, as well.

All this meant that P4X-234 now moved at the same speed through time as the rest of the galaxy.

"We'll have to send a team back at some point," Carter said, "and try to find out what it was that slowed time down on the planet in the first place. It's got to be technological, but we were never able to find the source."

"Some other time, Carter," O'Neill said. "Right now, it's time to futilely dial the gate again."

Just as he had four times a day every day since arriving at P4X-234, O'Neill dialed the six chevrons that corresponded to Earth and the seventh chevron that was the symbol for P4X-234, the point of origin.

But this time, the wormhole engaged. Carter almost didn't believe it when she saw it. She fumbled for her GDO to transmit SG-1's identification code so they would open the iris.

"About time," O'Neill said. "I could use a shower."

With feeling, Teal'c said, "Indeed."

Carter smiled, and the three of them walked up the makeshift rock staircase and through the gate.

As soon as they materialized on the ramp, greeted by General Hammond, Daniel Jackson, and a bunch of airmen, O'Neill said without preamble, "Well, it's about time!"

STARGATE ATLANTIS
Consort

Amy Griswold

Thousands of years before the Atlantis expedition, the Wraith rule victorious over a galaxy abandoned by the few surviving Ancients, but they face a new and deadly threat: attack by the Asuran Replicators. Fighting to save his queen's hive from destruction, Guide, the Wraith later known to the Atlantis expedition as 'Todd', searches for a way to turn the tide of war...

GUIDE wrestled his dart into a steep turn, arrowing between the hive and the Asuran cruiser through a hailstorm of glowing Asuran drones. As he had hoped, a cluster of the tiny hunting weapons fixed on his dart, streaming after him in his wake and away from the Wraith hive's fragile hull. The hive had taken heavy damage in the Asuran attack and was dangerously weakened on its starboard side.

Three other darts were following his lead, moving to draw off more of the drones as he rolled his own ship to keep the pursuing weapons a few heartbeats from his dart's tail. He could feel the other pilots' satisfaction as the drone weapons veered away from the hive, and feel them begin their own evasive maneuvers. Swift's dart was hindmost, and he hesitated a moment too long before beginning his turn; in an instant his dart was swarmed by the Asuran weapons, shattering as they burst against its fragile hull.

Guide wrenched his mind away from Swift's as his agony flared and then moments later ended. Poorly named, he thought, and perhaps also poorly led. They had come out of hyperspace nearly on top of an Asuran battleship, and fled in the direction Guide had advised as best, directly into the waiting ambush of three smaller cruisers. Pinned between them, they had been a sitting target, and all their maneuvering had only opened up one narrow chance to break for open space.

It meant bringing the hive all too close to one of the cruisers, with only the darts to keep the Asuran weapons from battering the hive's hull apart. The queen was at the controls of the hive herself, bringing it about on the precise course that might let them escape. The readouts streaming across the inner surface of the dart told him that course was true, but he hardly needed them. He could feel Snow's mind brushing his, and trusted her cool confidence in the course she had plotted.

And yet it still seemed too easy. Another dart was shattering under drone weapon attack, a ripple of fear spreading through the thinning dart wings. He shut his mind to all of it, watching only the readouts, trying to think.

The drone weapons were familiar horrors, but they weren't the worst ones the Asurans possessed. The nanites that made up their own bodies had that distinction, able to swarm like tiny parasites through the flesh of men or hive ships, consuming it like so much meat to build more abominations like themselves. They were harrying the hive, trying to cripple it, but they might not need to if they could offer an attractive enough distraction. Like the possibility of escape.

Guide flipped his dart on its axis, diving back toward the hive. He reached out with his mind to collect the nearby pilots at the same time as he spoke the orders that would stream across their own screens and whisper in their ears. He rolled, bringing them over the top of the hive to its damaged starboard side, which Snow was skillfully keeping angled away from the nearest cruiser.

He saw it then, a tiny ripple in his sensor readings, a tiny insect of a shuttle drawing next to the hull. A parasite infested with a deadly disease. If even one Asuran made it aboard, if one nanite penetrated the flesh of the hive and began replicating itself there, they were all corpses walking.

My queen, he said, and reached for Snow's mind, forcing himself to the center of her attention. He could feel her anger, and some part of him flinched from it, but he forced his mind open to hers, showing her what he saw, what the hive's damaged sensors had not. The Asuran shuttle was drawing closer, its landing gear reaching out like claws for the hull. Far too close.

He felt her understanding, immediate and horrified. *Our hull damage hasn't begun to regenerate. If you open fire on the shuttle, you'll breach our own hull.*

Yes, he said, and brought the dart around into the only possible line of attack.

For a moment she hesitated, and then he could feel the cold calm of decision, numbing ice for his own raw nerves. *Open fire on the Asuran shuttle.*

He dove on the shuttle, adjusting his angle until the last second, trying to find some line that would make it safe to fire. There was none, and he fired regardless, one burst rather than a spitting rain of energy. The first shot went home, straight into the shuttle's main propulsion, and his heart leapt as he saw it begin tumbling as he had hoped, away from the hive.

He pursued it, putting his dart between it and the hive's flesh. The hull was still holding, and every heartbeat brought them further away from its wounded flank. Two more darts were falling in behind him, one properly, one a fraction off its line, its inexperienced pilot wobbling on his course in his terror.

Correct course, he snarled at Bloodred, putting all the force he could behind it, but the boy was deaf with his own fear. He should never have put him in a dart, Guide thought, not an untried young blade barely out of the crèche, but they had so few pilots left —

The Asuran shuttle rolled, one thruster coming back online, and even as he fired, shattering its bridge compartment, it fired its own energy weapons in one last dying burst, tearing into Bloodred's dart. The dart rolled wildly, tumbling end over end, and then drove at speed into the hive ship's weakened hull.

Vapor streamed from the vented compartments as the hull tore, a long rip widening as the hive strained into its next turn. Within, clevermen and drones would be desperately seeking a way farther into the hive, those who hadn't died at once of explosive decompression. The hive would stop them, sealing off the damaged compartments. He had seen it before, the marks of men's claws in the flesh of sealed hatchways, dead men who had fought and failed to save themselves from the hive's relentless instinct to keep those in undamaged sections alive.

There was no time to think of that now; the Asuran shuttle was tumbling harmlessly at last, its passengers no threat as long as they were frozen by the chill of space, but the drone weapons were still harrying the hive. Snow was bringing them back on course to slip through the gap between the Asuran fields of fire, the hive handling badly now but holding together. Guide signaled the remaining darts to shield the hive.

Return, Snow signaled. He protested wordlessly, and felt the force of her mind bending him to her will, not angry, but grimly determined. *We must jump to hyperspace as soon as we are clear. We cannot afford to lose all the darts. Retrieve your men.*

He collected as many as he could, arrowing for the dart bay. Several of the darts bruised the deck in their landing, damaged or piloted by men trembling with fatigue and the consciousness of their losses. He cracked open the canopy and climbed out, steadying himself carefully as he did so; he was trembling too, and couldn't afford to be seen to stagger.

He felt the jump to hyperspace, a sickening wrench, and counted the darts. Twelve were missing, destroyed or left behind. He counted again, hoping for a better answer, and then snarled as someone pushed past him without apology.

It was Seeker, and Guide bit back his reprimand; for all that the man was a cleverman and not a warrior blade, they were friends of long standing, and did not stand on ceremony. Seeker reached to help two drones extract a wounded pilot from the canopy of his dart. The man's face was badly burned, his breath irregular.

Will he live?

Probably, Seeker said, long fingers at the man's throat to take his pulse. His mouth tightened, and he turned and drove his claws without warning into the chest of one of the drones. It growled a protest, but didn't fight Seeker as he drained its strength. Seeker turned and tore through the wounded pilot's shirt with his claws, pressing his feeding hand against his chest. The man gasped, and then began to breathe more steadily, though only the very edges of his burn showed signs of healing.

Take him to the feeding cells first, Seeker told the other drone. *Then to the infirmary. I'll follow.* The drone obeyed, its fellow staggering in its wake.

With the hull breached, we're lucky we made the jump to hyperspace, Guide said.

Seeker shook his head. *We nearly didn't. Spark says he can't keep us in hyperspace more than a few minutes.*

So Spark says.

And so I say, Seeker said, with a flare of temper. *The internal tissues of the hive can't heal while they're exposed to vacuum. Hyperspace is even more damaging to them. We must set down at the first opportunity, unless you'd like the hive to die.*

There was another wrenching lurch as they came out of hyperspace. Guide pushed men aside to reach the nearest console, and relaxed a fraction as he saw their location: a system with no inhabitable worlds, but with one rocky satellite that held enough of an atmosphere to make their repairs possible. It was a clever choice on Snow's part, a place where the Asurans had no reason ever to go.

The repairs were the first priority, he told himself, and didn't let himself think yet about where the hive would be left after that.

The lights were still dim hours later, and acrid smoke hung in the chill air. Guide found Seeker working to repair a ragged tear in a supporting bulkhead, where the walls strained painfully away from each other, dripping ichor, and gaped too wide to heal without tending. He was up to his elbows in the wound, wrestling its edges together with Bramble's help.

Two blades were hunched against the corridor wall outside the door of the empty game room, its interior too dark for games, if anyone had the heart for them. They stood with shoulders together, watching in sullen exhaustion as the clevermen worked.

Help them, Guide said.

Thunder raised his head, stubborn challenge in his eyes. *It's no part of our work.* Bonesnap kept his own eyes closed, his head back against the wall.

Guide snarled at them, too tired himself to leash his temper. *What work do you see that you'd be more fit for?*

We've done our part.

You're done when I say you're done.

Thunder bared his teeth. *Do you say so?*

Would you care to argue that?

Thunder put his hand on his knife, considering it. Seeker raised his head, his hand stilling, although he didn't turn. Thunder saw that as well as Guide did, and turned his head with a snarl. *We're done when you say we are,* he said. *But we're tired. Let us be.*

You can rest when the hive is mended. Help Seeker.

Little you care, Bonesnap said hoarsely, opening his eyes at last. They burned hot when he turned on Guide. *My brother is dead, but your pet cleverman stayed huddled safe in the depths of the hive like the coward he is.*

Seeker rose, at that, and turned with his hand on his own knife, leaving Bramble wrestling abruptly with walls that threatened to close in on him. *I can hear you, you know,* he said, deceptively mildly. Thunder looked appalled, reaching out to hold Bonesnap back, but Bonesnap shook his hand away. Bramble shrank back against the hive wall as if trying to master Seldom-Seen's gift of passing unnoticed in a crowd.

They were heartbeats from a fight that would at best draw Snow storming from the zenana to forbid it, and at worst end with more men dead senselessly on the deck.

Enough, Guide said, and stepped between them, drawing his own blade in the same motion and pressing it to Bonesnap's chin. The man froze, his throat working under the point of the knife. *Must we do our enemies' work for them? Are you that eager to die? I am sure you could have spent your life in battle if you tried. Now your death will buy us nothing.*

We fought for the hive, Thunder said.

As did we all. He lowered the knife, putting it deliberately away without taking his gaze from Bonesnap's face. *Beg Seeker's pardon.*

I won't require it, Seeker said. His face was smeared with ichor and ash, and he looked desperately tired.

Guide ignored that. *He is the Queen's pallax,* he said. *You will treat him with due respect.*

Bonesnap looked for one moment as if he were about to question the judgment of a queen who chose clevermen as favorites among her zenana, and then as if he thought better of it. *I beg your pardon,* he said, bending his head without grace.

Granted, Seeker said, with a smile that bared teeth.

He's grieving, Thunder said in more appeasing tones.

Grieve when the work is done, Guide said, and herded them over to help mend the hive wall.

When the tear was spliced well enough that Seeker judged it would hold, and the blades and Bramble had departed for other duties, or at least to shirk somewhere not under Guide's eye, he retreated for a moment into the darkness of the gaming room. Seeker was there already, turning one of the scattered game pieces around in his fingers.

I see why neither of those two will be Consort, Seeker said.

The hive had no permanent officers, a source of tension at the best of times. Young queens like Snow attracted young and disaffected men from dozens of other hives, all competing for her favor. In the years since he and Seeker came to the hive as young men themselves, with nothing but ferocity and their wits to recommend them, Guide had maneuvered his way to something like leadership of the hive's blades. It was no easy task to lead men born to different lineages with old rivalries between them, but he succeeded better than any other could. He was the queen's acknowledged pallax, one of her especial favorites among her zenana.

And still not Consort. Nor, at this rate, was he ever likely to be.

I don't worry about that, no, he said. *Although Bonesnap's not usually so erratic.*

All the same, it was stupid.

Yes.

You didn't have to interfere, Seeker said.

Would you have preferred me to let you stab each other?

Maybe, Seeker said. He tightened his fist around the gaming piece, claws digging into his hand. *I might like to stab something, at this point.*

Do you expect me to beg your pardon?

Would you? Seeker said.

No, Guide said. He leaned back against the wall in the darkness and let himself sag under the weight of his own exhaustion. *How many dead?*

Twenty-one men. Twelve were pilots lost with their darts. We lost seven in the section that decompressed. Of the other wounded, I think all have died who are going to die. Wreath will be a long time healing. I've put him into hibernation. Flicker may not recover vision in his left eye. I had to excise too much of the nerve for it to fully regrow.

Then I can't put him back in a dart.

I expect not, Seeker said. His voice was flat. *I don't have a good count of the drones. We may have lost as many as half when that section decompressed. Seldom-Seen will be able to give you a precise count. He's... not happy.*

Furious was likely to be closer to the truth. The Hivemaster Seldom-Seen took a special interest in the drones; Guide had to admit he could rarely tell one from another, but to the Hivemaster they were somewhere between pets and brothers. They were his blood kin, after all, born of his mother's flesh and the hive's, however unintelligent they might be.

Let the Hivemaster mourn them; Guide was busy calculating the extent of this disaster. They were left with enough men and drones to man the hive, once it was repaired enough that they could risk venturing back into territory crawling with Asurans. One more such battle, and he doubted that would be the case. And the dart wings were at half strength, a third of their strength in better times; there was a limit to how much he could rely on them to shield the hive, however willingly he spent the lives of his men.

One more such battle, one encounter with a stronger hive whose queen saw them as weak for the taking, one mistake, one piece of pure bad luck, and it would all be over. He would die defending Snow, of course, as he had in his first romantic dreams about her when they met; he found now that the reality paled severely beside the idea of serving her while still alive.

So what do we do now? he asked, a question he would not have dared ask in anyone else's company. But the room was deserted and cold, and the hum of minds aboard the ship too clamorous for anyone outside this room to sense his indecision and call it weakness.

We have to have a better defense against the Asurans.

Ask Spark why he hasn't come up with one yet, Guide snapped.

I have, Seeker said, in a tone that suggested he was choosing to ignore the crackling resentment under Guide's words. Spark was Snow's other especial favorite among her zenana, and at first Guide had dismissed him as a serious rival because he was a cleverman and not a blade. A miscalculation, like so many others of late. *He says these… things… are as much alive as machines. They function like living organisms — they take in nourishment and reproduce.*

Then why haven't you come up with a solution yet? Guide asked, but without heat.

Because they're not alive the way a man or a hive ship is alive. I can't engineer a weapon or a virus to affect their tissues. They don't have tissues; they're mechanical. Nor can I cloud their minds. It would be like trying to communicate with a human cargo ship, made out of dead metal. They think because they're programmed to think, not because they have living brains.

Programmed, Guide said. He picked up another of the scattered game pieces and set it back on the board with a click. *Can they be reprogrammed?*

I don't think so. At least, I don't think we can do it. Their programming is regularly updated — we've learned that much — and the new code spreads out virally to all other nanites within range. In theory, such a virus could spread to all the Asurans.

In theory?

We have news from a hive that brought an Asuran prisoner aboard to try. Their results were… not promising.

Did they find out anything of use?

Not many survived. The data we obtained from the survivors suggests that the virus would have to be introduced into a central data core in order to have permanent effects. Otherwise, it would simply be overwritten when the next periodic update from the core occurred. The core itself cannot be programmed remotely. It serves as a repository of untouched base code, in case someone tries to do just what we have been trying to do.

And where would we find the data core?

On the Asuran homeworld, Seeker said. His expression showed that he followed Guide's thoughts already, and didn't like them one bit. *Surrounded by thousands of Asurans who would kill us if we came anywhere near their system, which, I may point out, is guarded by more ships than we could muster if we had a dozen hives at full strength.*

And did the report specify the location of the data core?

I don't know, Seeker said, which Guide assumed to be a spectacular untruth; he would certainly have insisted on reading the report for himself, even though the physical sciences weren't his specialty. *Spark would know better than I.*

Then I will ask him, Guide said. He caught Seeker's arm as Seeker turned away from him. *Can I count on your help?*

Don't you always? Seeker didn't look up at him.

That's not an answer.

Seeker finally raised his eyes to Guide's. *Yes. If Spark thinks he can do it — and if he'll agree to anything that's suggested by you — then, yes. It's the best chance we have.* He let out a breath. *Do try not to get us killed.*

Getting killed is not part of the plan.

You have a plan?

I'm constructing one.

Ah. There was a flicker of humor under the words. *You realize you still have to talk the Queen into this?*

I was relying on you to do that, Guide said.

Perhaps I ought to stab you, Seeker said, but Guide was already on his way out the door.

Seeker found Snow in the empty zenana; no one was lounging there now, playing at games or telling stories or hoping to attract Snow's eye. Those who weren't working were sleeping like the dead. Snow paced alone between the couches, her long hair clean now and falling loose down her back in a spill of flame.

She raised her head as if startled to see him. *Seeker. Are all the wounded resting? If so, you should be resting too.*

You should be resting yourself, he said.

She shook her head. *I can't sleep now.* She looked for a moment even younger than her years, less like a young queen in the first flush of her power than an uncertain girl too tired to bend anyone's mind beneath her own.

He crossed to stand behind her and rested his hands on her shoulders, expecting a rebuke that didn't come. *It will be all right,* he said.

She didn't laugh, but he could feel a flicker of bitter amusement in her thoughts. *And what in the world makes you think that?* She drew herself up under his hands, straight and stiff as a blade. *I have led us to nothing but death.*

Guide has a plan, he said.

She turned at that, looking up at him, curiosity starting to bring some life back into her face. It was the virtue or vice they both shared, the insatiable curiosity that had led her to choose clevermen as her pallaxes, men who sought answers and new ways of doing things rather than leading men into battle. Except for Guide, and for a blade, Guide had always had an incisive and restless mind.

And what plan might that be?

A way to reprogram the Asurans so that they will stop their war against us, Seeker said, hoping as he spoke that he wasn't promising more than Spark could deliver. *I believe Spark and I can do what he suggests.*

She stepped back to consider him. *And what aren't you telling me?*

My queen?

Presume I'm in no mood for games.

It can only be done at the Asuran central computer core, Seeker said.

On the Asuran homeworld.

Yes, my queen.

She took a breath, and then let it out. *And how does he plan to accomplish this?*

The details are still being worked out.

You mean he doesn't know yet.

I'm sure he will have an excellent plan, Seeker said.

He had better, Snow said. *I will not allow him to throw away all your lives in an attempt to impress me.*

That's not why he's doing it, Seeker said.

He wants me to name him Consort. Which I have told him I can't do until he proves himself worthy of it. I can't entrust the hive to a man simply because he pleases me as pallax. No matter what my feelings may be.

He understands that.

Does he?

Most of the time, Seeker said. *I understand, anyway.*

And you support his cause.

As he supports me in my ambitions.

That's not why you support his cause.

And his desire to be Consort is not why he is prepared to risk his life to save us all.

I know, Snow said after a moment. *There isn't much choice, is there?* She spoke with frank honesty, as if they were two clevermen speaking together. If they had been, he thought, they would have been friends.

No, there isn't, he said.

Then tell him to bring me a plan, Snow said. She turned away again, leaning back deliberately into his hands, and he rubbed her shoulders, digging in his claws. *My Seeker,* she said. *You know I couldn't ever name you Consort. We're too much alike.*

Make me your Master of Sciences Biological, then, he said. *If we return.* It was entirely the wrong way to ask, too blunt and very nearly a command. No one with any sense of self-preservation commanded queens. But then Snow had always admired audacity.

If you succeed, she said, *I believe that I will.*

Spark was crouched in front of one of the main power nodes, testing a mended conduit. He was even dirtier than Seeker, which Guide hadn't thought possible, and his hands were patchy with the marks of healing burns.

You should rest, Guide said abruptly.

Thank you for your concern.

It won't help us if you make mistakes.

I won't make mistakes. Spark rose from his crouch to consider Guide. *What do you want? I can't fix the ship any faster.*

We're spaceworthy again, Guide said. *As soon as the bridge crew have had a few hours' rest, we'll be leaving.*

But it's such a scenic rock.

Guide snarled at him. *This is not the time for your humor.*

Should I save it for another time? Because I may not be a strategic genius, but at this rate I can't see that we have much more time left.

We did our best.

I know that, Spark said, no mockery in his voice now. *The dart pilots did their best, I did my best, the queen did her best. And it wasn't good enough.*

I know you're good at what you do.

Compliments, now. We must be dying.

Will you listen for once in your misbegotten life? He bared his teeth, and Spark adopted a posture of respectful attention that might conceivably have been taken as sincere. *Seeker tells me the Asurans can be reprogrammed,* he said. *Hypothetically. Can you do it?*

No, Spark said. *Reprogramming an individual unit won't work, because when the base code updates — *

Suppose you had access to the Asuran data core.

Hypothetically? He thought for a moment. *Yes, I could do it.*

You mean you think you could do it.

I mean I know I could do it. I've gone over the report we got from the clevermen who tried it before. They were close to a solution, except for not having access to the data core, and where they did go wrong, I can see how to fix the problems. I have no doubt that I can create a computer virus that will rewrite the Asurans base code to make them leave us alone. But we don't have access to the Asuran data core.

Leave that to me.

You're crazy, Spark said at once. *If we so much as enter the same system as the Asuran homeworld, they'll detect us. A hive ship isn't exactly easy to hide.*

We aren't going in a hive ship, Guide said. The plan was coming together as he spoke, and he hoped it proved to contain no gaping holes. *We're going to steal a Lantean ship.*

How will that help? We won't even be able to fly it.

They had some ships that didn't require Lantean pilots, didn't they?

Well, yes, some little freighters designed for human pilots without the Lantean genetic markers, but those ships are pieces of junk. I could probably get one working, but it won't have any weapons.

Good, Guide said. *We don't want it to appear to be a threat. We want it to appear to be a derelict.*

They'll still come investigate. Even scrap metal is food for them.

How fast?

Maybe not instantly.

All we need is to get far enough in-system to be able to launch darts.

You can't go by yourself in a dart, Spark said. *As attractive as that idea sounds to me. You're going to need me to go with you. I can't talk you through this. And we'll need at least one other cleverman who knows something about computer systems. We'll have to work very fast.*

The darts are for you and your men as well.

I repair ships, I don't fly them, Spark said.

You won't need to.

Spark paled abruptly as he followed Guide's thought. *You're crazy. You really expect me to trust one of your pilots to drop me off with a culling beam, and then trust them to pick me up again? Even if they survive that long.*

They'll be picking me up as well.

Do you trust them not to leave you down there?

I do, he said. If he hadn't given his own men reason to want him safely back aboard the ship, he didn't deserve to lead them.

The problem is, I don't trust you, Spark said. *Suppose this works. And I wouldn't place any bets on that, because it's going to take some time for the code push to propagate even locally, and while we're waiting around, anyone who's noticed what we're doing is going to be trying to kill us. But even supposing this does work, what possible incentive do you have not to just leave me conveniently behind?*

The good of the hive, Guide said.

It was a long moment before Spark replied. *Find me a ship we can fly.*

Write your code. And make it good.

It'll be good. Dark amusement flickered under the words. *The queen won't like it if you get me killed.*

Guide bared his teeth at him. *I know.*

The auxiliary control room was little bigger than a sleeping room, wound through with tangled conduits and cradled in the flesh of the hive. Its control console was wreathed in cables and partially disassembled, but it had never been used in Guide's memory; the chair nestled in one corner of the room doubled as both sleeping couch and control chair, with all the contacts needed to communicate with the hive.

The room appeared to be unoccupied, the chair in shadow.

Seldom-Seen, Guide said. *I need to talk to you.*

Illusion dissolved like fog, revealing Seldom-Seen sprawled in the chair, head back and eyes closed, his hands on the neural contacts. Deception was his gift, the gift of Osprey's line perfected to a height few men could master. It was a gift that would have been of great use to a blade. Guide was never certain whether a blade was what his mother had in fact intended to breed when she had taken a pallax with Osprey genes; what she had gotten was a son with the illusion gift in its fullest expression, and not the slightest talent or inclination for battle.

Seldom-Seen opened his eyes. He looked haggard, as if in pain. Probably he was; the hive was still protesting its injuries strongly enough that even Guide felt it like a faint discordant whine in the back of his mind, and he was far less attuned to its moods. For Seldom-Seen, the damage to the hive probably felt like an open wound. *What do you want, Guide?*

What do you know about the Asuran sensor capabilities?

A reasonable amount, Seldom-Seen said. He shook his head as if trying to clear it and raised one hand from the neural contacts, although he left the other one in place. *What do you want to know?*

Suppose I wanted to conceal several darts and men aboard a Lantean freighter and make it appear to be abandoned, Guide said. *At what range would the Asurans be able to tell we weren't what we appeared to be?*

Seldom-Seen put his head to one side, considering. There was little resemblance between Seldom-Seen and his sister in the cast of their features, but despite that, for a moment he looked very much like Snow. *They'd have to be fairly close to detect the men,* he said. *Close enough to pick up thermal variations within the ship, or to pick up audio that made it clear there were people aboard. But the darts are made of different materials than a freighter. Reasonable enough for cargo, but their shapes will be distinctive on any kind of scan.*

What can we do about it?

The light of interest kindled in Seldom-Seen's eyes despite his discomfort. He had made a particular study of all forms of concealment, not only those that used his own individual gift. *A number of things,* he said. *For concealing the men, you'll either need to lower their apparent body temperatures — a protective suit with cooling features would do it — or surround them with warmer objects to confuse the thermal imagery.

Audio is even easier to mask with a white noise generator. I can build you what you need.*

And the darts?

You're going to need to break up their silhouettes. Cover them in similar materials to create different shapes, and surround them with a variety of cargo if you can. The more confusing the sensor readouts are, the more time you can buy. He chewed on one claw thoughtfully. *Let me talk to Spark,* he said. *If we know what particular features of darts the Asuran sensors are designed to look for, we may be able to actually make some structural alterations that will slow them down in identifying what they're seeing as darts. The Asurans may be complicated machines, but they're still machines. They're slower than we are at pattern recognition.*

Guide sensed hesitation behind his words. *But?*

But I can only buy you time. No matter what you do, they'll see through the deception eventually. And you'll never be able to use the same trick again.

Time is what I need, Guide said. *If Spark isn't exaggerating what he can do.*

Spark doesn't usually exaggerate. Seldom-Seen shook his head at Guide's expression. *He tells the truth about what he can do. He's just not modest. Or tactful. But he's very, very good.*

You actually like him.

Yes, I do. I think he's good for the hive. And good for the other clevermen, even when he sets them on their ears. It means they stretch themselves trying to keep up with him.

You support him as Consort, then?

Seldom-Seen looked as if he were choosing his words with great care. *I would like to see this matter settled,* he said finally. *Without anyone leaving the hive. You won't find another specialist in the physical sciences as good as Spark. But there's not another blade aboard who men will follow the way they'll follow you.* He shrugged. *And if you go, your cousin Seeker will go, and we haven't got another specialist in the biological sciences who can match him.*

I don't want anyone to leave the hive.

Don't you?

Guide dug his claws into his palms, but the answer was the same as before. The good of the hive came first. *No.*

Then maybe it won't come to that. Seldom-Seen put his head to one side again in that expression so much like Snow's. *He'd make a useful ally, if the two of you ever stopped wanting to kill each other.*

As Master of Sciences Physical?

Seldom-Seen shrugged. *He'd be good at the job. And that would leave Seeker for Master of Sciences Biological — *

And you as Hivemaster.

Which would leave you Consort.

With your support?

I would support an alliance of the three of you, Seldom-Seen said very carefully.

An alliance of the four of us would be unbreakable. Who would dare challenge us?

No one. But allying myself with rivals who are at each other's throats is less attractive. Work out who's going to be Consort, don't get Spark and Seeker killed on this lunatic mission, and you have my support, for what it's worth.

The support of the Hivemaster is worth a great deal.

Seldom-Seen nodded, acknowledging that. *Then bring them back alive.*

The cargo ship looked persuasively like a heap of junk. Spark prowled around the echoing cargo bay, hoping that its pitted doors would remain intact until they reached their destination and then open when they needed them. The queen would be unamused if they failed at their mission because they had to blast their way out of their own ship.

I trust that won't be necessary, Snow said, stepping through the cargo bay doors. Spark swept a bow, inwardly kicking himself for having been so absorbed in his preparations that he hadn't noticed the queen's approach.

I'm sure it won't, he said.

How sure?

You can rely on me, he said. He looked around, shaking his head at the ship. He found Lantean technology interesting — it had taken skill for them to build spaceworthy ships out of dead metal alone, without any of the biotechnology that made a hive ship live and grow. And their power systems were still worlds beyond anything the Wraith could possibly match.

But this was not a battleship, fueled by a ZPM and fitted out with the flower of Lantean technology. Even in the days when the Lanteans had dominated the galaxy, this had never been more than a workhorse freighter, entrusted to some human pilot to ferry grain or ore between worlds more easily than it could be moved through a Stargate. It had been abandoned on a world that had been heavily culled; the few humans who lived there now made their living scavenging in the wreckage, and had no interest in spaceships.

But you can make it fly? Snow asked, following his thoughts.

I can make it fly.

Spark turned his attention to the dart, considering it critically. They'd modified the nose and the wings considerably, making its general shape blunter but adding jagged spikes that broke up its clean lines. The result was an aesthetic nightmare, and wouldn't handle as well as an unmodified dart, but it should take the Asurans a few precious minutes to recognize it with certainty as Wraith.

The other two darts were already in their storage containers, boxy and hard-lined as the Lanteans and most humans preferred, and filled with the same materials that made up the darts themselves. It should buy them time. He wished he knew how much.

And conceal our presence?

I've modified the hull and the interior bulkheads to mask our thermal signatures. It will be uncomfortably hot, but not harmful. Seldom-Seen's devices will mask our sound, although we should try not to make noise. It should work.

Snow ran her hand over the new angles of the dart's wing. *You're not just saying this to impress me.*

I'm saying it because it's true.

And are you doing all this to impress me?

Which answer would you prefer? he replied. He refrained from saying that it was unlikely to matter, as odds were none of them were coming back.

The truth, she said.

I'm doing it because it's our best chance, he said. *And to impress you.*

Snow smiled a little. It softened the sharp lines of her face, and he dared to catch at her sleeve, offering her his mental picture of the two of them together, lightning flashing in the distance through silently drifting snow.

Spark, she said, freeing her sleeve running her claws across the back of his hand. *You don't really want to be Consort.*

Yes, I do.

To spend all your time overseeing the dart wings and mediating quarrels between bickering blades? That would be a waste of your talents.

There are hives with clevermen as Consorts. It's been done.

I'm not afraid of doing things that haven't been done before, Snow said. *But think it through. How much time would you have for your laboratory, your work? What chance would you have to experiment? Other people's quarrels tire you.*

My own quarrels tire me, Spark admitted. It was entertaining to bait Guide, and sometimes irresistible, but they were locked now in a rivalry as wearying as a stalemated game of Towers; he could hold his own, but saw no way to secure the victory.

You don't want to be Consort.

No, he said slowly. *But I want you.*

And if I chose to make my most troublesome pallax Master of Sciences Physical?

I would accept, of course.

It would displease me were you to leave the hive. Were he to leave her, he thought she meant. Or at least hoped.

Then wish us luck, he said.

Guide slid into the control chair of the human ship with distaste; it was no pleasure to fly such a vessel, but its operation was clear enough. The controls were simple enough for even the human pets of the Lanteans to master.

Spark and Seeker were quarreling without heat, and had been doing so since they came aboard, in what he supposed was their way of working out their nerves. It did nothing for his own, and he tried his best to ignore them.

And where is the other man you promised to bring? Seeker said. *If you believe me to be an expert at computer programming, you are mistaken.*

I thought you considered yourself an expert on everything, Spark said. *But all you have to do is input the code when I tell you to. The hard part will be dealing with whatever security they have protecting the main core, and Glisten is coming to help me with that. He's on his way.*

He is not, Snow said, stepping through the hatchway from the cargo compartment. She was dressed for battle, in a long leather coat that came only to her ankles instead of sweeping the floor, a stunner belted at her side. *I am here instead.*

Seeker spoke as Guide was still rising from his seat in shock. *Surely you don't mean to come with us.*

Her eyes were on Spark. *Will I not serve as well as your man?*

You are as good a programmer, he said, and then seemed entirely at a loss for how to continue. His own eyes sought Guide's, as if even the most unlikely of allies might help him at that moment.

You can't, Guide said.

Snow turned on him at once, and he felt the force of her mind bearing him down like crushing ice. He staggered, struggling to resist sinking to his knees. *Will you now instruct your queen?*

No, he said hoarsely. The pressure eased a fraction, and he went down to his knees voluntarily at her feet, turning his face up to her. *I am yours to command. Always, until death. But our queen is the life of the hive.* He shook his head, his eyes on her face. *What will this victory profit us if you die achieving it? It will be the end of the hive as surely as if we failed.*

But not the end of the Wraith, Snow said. *If the Asurans are not stopped, they will consume us to the last man, and feast on our bones. They will achieve what the Lanteans could not — to wipe the Wraith from the face of the galaxy as if we had never been.* She raised her chin and walked fearlessly to the command chair, not a desperate girl now, but a great queen, at peace with the road that lay before her. *If that is our fate, we will buy the lives of our brothers and sisters, and they will remember our names.*

He turned his face away, unable to speak, and she reached to touch his cheek. *My Guide,* she said, in a tone that she had not before used when anyone else could hear. *And my clever lords of the zenana. If I lost you all, what hope would there be for the hive even if I lived?* She let her hand fall, and the touch of her mind was a steadying wind, now, bearing him up on its cold wings as he stood. *But I do not mean for us to die.*

He stepped back and bowed low, motioning her to take the command chair. *My queen.*

Snow settled into the chair, arranging the skirts of her coat around her. *Let us go,* she said, and touched the controls that would set their course for Asuras.

There was little to do on the journey, and Seeker found that it was indeed uncomfortably hot. Once they reached the outer edges of the Asurans home system, Spark forbade all unnecessary movement, even shifting away from overheated bulk-heads and interior furnishings. *Seldom-Seen's devices are good, but let's not push them.*

Snow cut their thrust at what Spark judged to be the outer limits of the Asurans' sensor range, and left them drifting on a course that would bring them within dart range of Asuras. Guide stood, ignoring Spark's glare, and went back to the cargo hold to ensure that the pilots were ready. Seeker followed, glad of any excuse to move about, and Spark narrowed his eyes.

The pilots were stationed by their darts, ready for the sig-nal to pull away the crating that surrounded them and pre-pare them for flight. Seeker exchanged a measuring glance with Thunder, and a more neutral one with Obsidian, who he barely knew. The third was Flicker, and Seeker winced to see that his left eye was still clouded and misshapen.

I doubt he has full vision, he said to Guide, keeping the thought firmly between the two of them.

The dart can compensate, Guide said just as privately. *And who else would you have me choose?*

Seeker gestured acknowledgment of the point; they had few enough choices left, and Guide was the best judge of his remaining men. Still, he hoped for another pilot himself.

We're coming into sensor range, Snow said, and they all froze; despite trusting Seldom-Seen's devices, Seeker found himself reluctant to breathe.

Guide's expression was watchful, as if counting off the sec-onds until they came into dart range. Seeker could only wait, trying to resist the temptation to chew his claws.

Still no sign of Asuran activity, Spark said. *Maybe — no, here they come.*

I see it, Snow said. *A small ship moving toward us at no great speed.*

They haven't recognized us as Wraith, Spark said in sat-isfaction.

Yet, Guide said. *Ready the darts.*

Once you do, we've lost the element of surprise.

Guide is right, Snow said. *There is no more time. We cannot risk being discovered before we launch the darts.*

The blades were already moving, stripping the casing away from the darts. Snow came through the hatchway from the bridge, followed by Spark, as the pilots climbed into their darts and closed the canopies.

I've modified each of our stunners to use a different energy signature, Spark said. *You'll get two or three good shots apiece, no more. After that, the Asurans will adapt.*

We know, Guide said. He nodded to his pilots. *You know what to do.*

Seeker stiffened against his will. He had seen the culling beams used many times, but never experienced them himself, and he flinched at the prospect despite knowing he would feel nothing while in the pattern buffer until he reached the surface. If he ever reached the surface. To die without ever being aware of it, to be energy and then to be nothing —

The culling beam touched him, and then he was in an unfamiliar corridor, with high bright walls of blue glass that looked out over a vast city. Far above, a dart was pulling out of a dive, its wings flashing against blue sky. He let out the breath he hadn't been aware he was holding and turned to look for their target.

The Asuran city was cold and painfully bright. Guide shivered in the sudden chill as he looked around. The others were all there, although Seeker looked unsteady and Snow bemused. He doubted anyone had ever risked using the culling beams on the queen before.

Spark bounced on his heels with what might have been either eagerness or nerves, his thoughts crackling like his namesake. *This way,* he said, and set off up the nearest stairs.

Snow flanked him with Seeker a step behind, and Guide followed to cover their rear. Once they halted on a landing, frozen by the sound of footsteps in the corridor beyond, but no one came to investigate.

We don't have much time, Spark said. *They're going to run an internal scan eventually and notice that we're here.*

Guide could feel Snow's frown. *How much farther?*

The next landing, Spark said, and they hurried their pace.

At the next landing, Snow looked out and pronounced the corridor clear. *Which way?*

Straight across, Spark said.

They crossed into a room flooded with colored light. High windows bathed the room in blue, and the Asuran computer core glowed like a fire, plated in many-colored glass. Whether that served some function or was their idea of ornament, he didn't know, and now wasn't the time for curiosity. *Get to work.*

The walls were lined with computer consoles, and Spark approached one at once, with Snow following at a second station. Seeker took up a third, running his fingers dubiously over the input device. *What do you want me to do?*

Nothing, until we get into the system, Spark said. *Then input the code. You're not going to be able to interface your scanner with the Asuran system, so you're going to have to retype it from the scanner's readout.*

I know the code, Seeker said.

Guide could feel Spark's skepticism. *If he says he does, he does,* Guide said. Seeker's memory was near perfect, whether or not he understood the commands written into the code.

All the same, copy it from the scanner, Spark said.

When?

Soon.

Guide held his stunner at the ready. *Hurry.*

Spark's fingers flew across the input device. Snow was working steadily as well, but more slowly, hesitating occasionally over the Lantean symbols on the keys. They were close to their own lettering, but not identical, and arranged in a different pattern. She and Spark had their minds open to each other, and Guide could catch only flickering hints of symbols he couldn't understand.

Now, Spark said abruptly. *We're in, do it now.*

Seeker drew out his scanner and propped it on the console, typing rapidly.

They know we're in, Spark said, and Snow added almost in unison, *They see us.*

The door, Guide said, and fired quickly at the control panel by the door. It spat sparks, and the whole room shuddered, the lights above flickering. Seeker's scanner toppled to the floor, and he ignored it, typing in the code from memory.

You had better know what you're typing, Spark said.

I know everything, remember? Seeker said without slowing.

Snow tossed her head, torn between amusement and frustration. *If we survive, I'm going to kill you both.*

Hurry, Guide snarled. There was the whine of an energy beam in the hall outside, and the crack in the sealed door lit; someone was cutting through it with a weapon. He went to one knee behind the central core, the only possible cover in the room, bracing his stunner for the best aim.

The whine rose to a shriek, and a section of the door fell inward. An Asuran stepped in after it, in form very much like a Lantean or a human, but too perfect, every hair in place and every fold of his clothing falling without disarray, no sign of emotion on his unmarred face. He lifted his hand, and as Guide watched, it sharpened until his arm ended in a blade.

Guide raised his weapon and fired. The Asuran didn't stagger or crumple; he froze, and then fell like a toppling pillar, hitting the floor as stiffly as a statue. The next two were already through, walking toward him unhurriedly and without hesitation. He fired again, and again; the first shot told, another Asuran dropping, but the third only rippled against the Asuran's chest as if her flesh were made of water.

You said three shots, he growled.

I said two or three, Spark said. He threw Guide his weapon, a poorly aimed throw, but Guide managed to snatch it out of the air even so, throwing down his own useless stunner. He raised it and fired.

More Asurans were stepping through the door, or flowing through it, the rearmost pouring like water through the bottleneck formed by their fellows and then reforming inside the door. Guide fired, and fired again. This time it was the fourth shot that rippled harmlessly against the chest of an Asuran woman, who looked down as if in mild curiosity and then sharpened both arms to dagger points, lunging toward him.

He dropped and rolled, throwing himself to the other side of the computer core. *Seeker!*

Seeker threw him his own weapon without turning to look, better aimed even so; he was reminded for a moment of their childhood games, clambering through the corridors of the hive where they were born. He caught the stunner and fired, once, twice, a third time.

It's done, Seeker said.

Spark was backing away from the Asurans, his scanner raised as if it could defend him. *It'll take seven minutes for the code to propagate.*

We don't have seven minutes, Snow said.

We might, Guide said. He scooped up one of the useless stunners and threw it at the window. The glass shattered, and he could see sunlight outside. Not another interior room, then, which was all he needed to know.

Seeker followed his thoughts all too quickly. *There might be a thousand-foot drop out that window.*

Would you rather let them consume you?

We would not, Snow said, and made for the window. One of the Asurans was in her way, and she fired her own stunner, their only remaining weapon. He dropped, and Guide moved quickly to follow her, with Seeker at his shoulder.

Snow pushed Seeker past her. *Jump,* she said. He did,

without looking back, to the sound of splintering glass. Guide could feel the sting of his cuts and a heartbeat's terror at falling, and then his scrambling landing on some ledge or outcropping below. It was good enough for him, and he took the stunner from Snow's hand. *Go,* he said, and she made as if to argue, and then nodded and dived through the window herself.

He turned to motion Spark through, and saw him throw himself back against the wall as one of the Asurans lunged at him with a sharpened hand. He skewered Spark's coat rather than his flesh, and Spark tugged away, his mind flaring panic.

Guide fired, and Spark ripped free of the Asuran as the creature froze in place. He threw himself out the window, and Guide followed, letting the useless scanner fall as he flung himself into open air.

There was a moment's disorientation as he fell, and then a ledge was coming up faster than he expected. He struck it hard, and nearly rolled off and kept on falling. Then hands were catching at him, Snow pulling him back from the ledge and urging him up the stairs to a high causeway open to the sky. He let himself lean on her by necessity, feeling bones broken, and then feeling them knit, equally painful.

One dart was diving toward them, only one, but there was no time to mourn the loss of the other two. He stood, bracing himself for the chill of the culling beam, and then snarled in bafflement as the dart swept past them and down to a skidding landing on the causeway.

He ran toward the dart, not sure whether he wanted an explanation or the pilot's blood. The canopy opened, and Flicker leapt out, his bad eye bloodshot and his face pale. *They've raised the shield. We can't get out.*

He looked up and saw that the sky, which had been blue, was now a patchy bronze, not the brilliant gold of the Lantean shields, but certainly still enough to stop something as fragile as a dart.

Three minutes, Spark said.

Too long, Guide said. Doors were opening, now, more of the Asurans moving toward them from a distance, and some of them had energy weapons. *We'll never last so long.*

At least we can distract them, Snow said. *Make them spend their three minutes.*

Maybe we can do better, Spark said. *If this city is patterned after Lantea, it'll be ringed by shield emitters. But their shield is nowhere near the strength of the Lantean one. All we need is to take out one shield emitter, and I think we can punch through.*

I'll try, Flicker said.

No, Guide said, pushing past him to climb into the dart. *I will.*

He launched the dart and pulled it into a long banking turn, sweeping back over the others. He could see them through Snow's eyes, standing shoulder to shoulder, Spark and Seeker guarding Snow's back with Flicker out protectively in front of her, hissing his defiance at the oncoming Asurans. He thumbed the culling beam on, and they dissolved into its beams. He had been aware of them all, a whisper in the back of his mind, and now all was cold and silent.

He turned the dart toward the city rim, pushing it for speed. It shuddered under his hands, its modifications making it far less maneuverable in a tight turn. The canopy crawled with warnings; the Asurans were launching drone weapons, their sleek deadly forms pouring out from the city center. If they had any doubt whether this was a Wraith craft, they knew it now.

The dart's display was signaling a shield emitter at the shield's edge, although, unlike Lantea, the city continued beyond the shield, a sprawl of cold jagged buildings as far as his instruments read. It was surely designed to protect against an attack from outside the shield, not from within; that was his advantage. But the drones were already homing in on him, and he dared not slow the dart as he approached the wall of energy that would smash him if he was a moment too slow in his turn.

He fired as he dived on the shield emitter, the dart spitting energy beams that struck home without weakening the shield. Closer, he had to get closer, although every instinct was warning him to pull out of the dive. He kept firing as the dart's warning systems began to scream, the shield looming like a wall.

At the last second, he pulled out of the dive, skimming the surface of the shield as he fought to keep the dart steady in the turn. He brought the dart around, but the drone weapons were close behind him, making their turns more sharply than he could in this misshapen craft. There would be no hope of a third pass.

He dove on the shield emitter again, firing as he neared it, letting the dart's systems scream their warning. One more second and there would be no chance of pulling out of the dive. He drove onward, firing again.

New readouts crawled across the dart's displays, a marginal weakening of the shield. It had to be enough. He resisted the instinct to wrestle the dart into a too-sharp turn that would only set them spinning, and held it on its course directly into the shield.

It was like hitting water at high speed, an impact like a full-body blow and then a moment when the controls responded as sluggishly as if he were struggling through thick liquid. Then they were through and rising like an arrow toward the sky.

The dart shuddered as they broke the planet's atmosphere, damage warnings streaming across the canopy; this might well be its last flight. But it was handling better as he cleared the atmosphere. He set a course in the opposite direction from the remains of the freighter, preparing to signal the hive to retrieve them.

He aborted the motion even as he began it. Multiple Asuran cruisers were moving toward him, closing in on the dart from all sides. He might evade them for a while, if the damaged craft would hold together, but he could never hope to outrun them. And the hive was no match for even a single cruiser in its weakened state. He would not summon it to its death.

He queried the dart urgently for time elapsed since takeout. Three minutes twenty seconds. He hissed as the cruisers closed in. He had been a fool to trust his life to Spark's experiments, and now he was going to pay with his life and the queen's. And all for nothing. He gritted his teeth and set a ramming course for the bridge of the nearest cruiser. He would make the Asurans pay at least some small price for all their lives.

Two other cruisers adjusted course, expecting this tactic, and the dart shrieked warnings as he came into their field of fire. He braced himself for impact, keeping the dart on its deadly course. At least the wreckage of the dart might reach its target.

No impact came. No shots were being fired, he registered even as the dart's proximity alert warned of imminent impact.

He wrenched the dart out of its dive, clearing the cruiser's hull by a hair's-breadth. He arrowed between the cruisers, and they ignored him as if he were only a piece of floating debris, breaking out of their attack formation to resume parking orbits around Asuras. He skimmed between them unheeded, and then past them, out toward empty space, and the hive, and home.

The queen stood before her throne, her blades and clevermen assembled before her. Their ranks were thin, but they need not be so for long, not in the hive that had freed their people from the pestilence of the Asurans. Guide intended to choose carefully from among the young blades who would swarm to join them. He could afford now to take only the best of pilots, and only those he could envision ever trusting at his back.

We have won a great victory today, Snow said, and clamoring pride rose all around her like thunder. *May there be many more such, by the efforts of our hive, and of my lords of the zenana.* She reached out her hand to Guide, and he came to kneel at her side, pride and longing burning as if it could consume him from within. She took his hand and raised him to his feet, and he could feel her own joy, like snow leaping silver on a wild wind. *My Consort.*

Approval rose again, thunderously. If there had been any who doubted her choice, they did not doubt it today. He looked sidelong at Spark, who smiled sideways for a moment, and then bowed to him without mockery.

And my masters of the sciences, she said, motioning to Spark and Seeker, who both bowed considerably more theatrically before going down on one knee to her. Seeker had warned that the hive itself was still dangerously weakened; they would have to go carefully for a while. But there would be time now for the hive to heal, and Seeker and Spark were already plotting the improvements they wished to make to its structure once it had grown strong again. Some of their plans sounded entirely unwise, but Guide trusted that Snow would restrain them both from excesses of experimental zeal.

Seldom-Seen stood off to the side near her throne, for once visible but still not making any effort to attract attention; Guide caught his eye, and he nodded. He had his allies, then, and such allies as few could boast. Only a fool would challenge all the ship's senior officers so long as they stood united.

She means to keep him as her pallax, you know, Seeker said privately to him as Snow raised Spark to his feet, letting her fingers linger in Spark's for a long moment for everyone to see.

I know. It made the moment less than perfect, a twist of jealousy underneath his satisfaction, and yet — if Snow had bent to Guide's will in this regard, she would have been less than herself, less than a great queen. *But we need him.*

Do try and remember that.

"My lords of the zenana," Snow said aloud, amusement in her tone; if she had overheard, she gave no other sign. "Attend me."

She ascended to her throne, and he came to stand at her shoulder, Spark and Seeker and Seldom-Seen standing beside her as befitted the ship's officers.

"Set our course, my Consort," she said.

"As my Queen commands," he said, and strode down the steps of her throne toward the bridge, his heart lifting with every step as if on the wings of a winter wind.

STARGATE SG-1
Perceptions

Diana Dru Botsford

COLD METAL pierced his skin, bringing wave after wave of pain. Liquid sloshed, movement becoming possible in ways that it should not. He bent, arced, thrashed against a host no longer made of bone and cartilage.

Realization dawned when he bumped into the walls of a symbiote tank. Still… He could not see. He could not hear.

If only he could not feel.

He refused the relentless pressure, fought to deny the sounds and images filling his senses.

Until he could fight no more.

"Do not resist," *boomed a voice in the dark.*

A black-hooded figure filled his view, its face obscured in a swirling miasma of energy.

"I am your lord, Anubis."

1. Denial (n): {*psychology*} — *a condition in which someone will not admit that something sad, painful, etc., is true or real. The first reaction following loss.*

"Closer. Closer." Colonel Jack O'Neill braced his disrupter against the empty Goa'uld queen tank, taking aim at the oncoming super soldier. After a wicked fire-fight, SG-1 had retreated inside Anubis's latest drone factory — a chamber of horrors with slick marble floors, granite walls and a sky-high ceiling. The disrupter had enough juice for one more shot. That was all he'd need. That and a hundred yard dash through the tunnel ahead of them to the Stargate and his team would get home in one piece.

SG-1 would make it to the gate. Their first mission since Janet Fraiser's funeral wasn't going to fail.

The doc's death had hit them hard, but they'd been hit before. Loss always sucked, he knew that. He had the T-shirt, a whole closet of them, to prove it. What he'd had enough of was missions gone bad. It was time for a win.

While a mission in the win column wouldn't bring Janet back, it would move SG-1 forward. The team wasn't gelling anymore. This first mission back was supposed to give them the chance to do just that.

But first, they needed to get to the gate.

The air reeked of burnt ozone. Smoke filled the tunnel leading to the gate ahead of them as well as the one to their rear. The solitary drone advanced, red plasma bursts erupting from its wrist weapon. The thing was a killing machine, both literally and figuratively.

The super soldier stomped across the central chamber, its black metal boots clanging against the marble floor. Obviously, the silent element of surprise wasn't a factor. Anubis trained these living machines to tromp all over the galaxy, hence SG-1's visit to do a little damage to the System Lord's new factory. Anubis may have skipped town, but apparently he'd left some house-sitters. If it wasn't for the disrupter Carter and her dad cobbled together, SG-1's collective asses would be toast.

Two drones down, one to go.

"Close... Closer," Jack promised his team.

Teal'c flipped on his staff weapon from his position behind a neighboring column. Crouched beneath the tank, Carter and Daniel hugged their P90s. All of them as ready for the fight as Jack.

Screw MacKenzie and his two-bit shrink shop. 'You need time to process. Time to accept,' the SGC's resident psychiatrist had blathered on before the team headed out. As if SG-1 hadn't dealt with death before. No, what SG-1 needed was a win.

Hell, if anything, Fraiser's death was fuelling this mission.

Anubis was the latest in a line of sanctimonious megalomaniacs that needed to end. What better motive was there than wanting to hit that slimeball where it counted?

The super soldier stomped across the marble floor, searching left and right. Jack sucked in a breath, leveled the disrupter, and waited for it to get a wee bit closer. He'd shoot the thing dead and get his team home.

According to Jacob Carter, Anubis called them 'Kull Warriors.'

Well, kull this —

Jack squeezed the trigger. The disrupter's cobalt blue energy arc smashed into the drone straight on. The thing collapsed. A mechanical doll with its battery yanked out.

"Plant the C4, Carter, and let's get out of here." He holstered the spent disrupter and stood up. He winced as a spasm twisted his guts, a reminder that, even with a few weeks off, his wound from the P3X-666 fiasco still wasn't healed.

"Daniel, Teal'c, grab whatever you can carry that's useful —"

"Useful how, Jack?" Daniel crawled out from under the tank. "There's nothing here."

"There's gotta be something."

Teal'c strode to a box beside the tank and slid the lid back. He pulled out a shiny red crystal as big as a baseball. "This central control crystal might aid Major Carter's research."

"Now you're thinking." Jack turned toward Carter.

She hadn't budged from beneath the tank. If anything, she hugged her rifle tighter.

"Carter. The C4?"

"Sorry, sir." Out came the C4, the receiver, and the remote transmitter.

"You all right?"

"Yes, sir." A barely perceptible swallow.

Jack took the C4 gear, knowing a lie when he heard one. They'd barely spoken since the funeral, and when they did, Carter would only talk about Cassie, not Fraiser. It was the proverbial elephant in the room; big enough that they couldn't ignore it, too impossible to accept.

He offered his free hand to Carter. "A hundred yard dash down the tunnel, Major. Last one through the gate buys dinner."

With a faint smile, she scrambled out from under the tank. "Dinner sounds good, sir."

While Carter packed up the crystal, Jack took care of unfinished business. He pressed the C4 against the tank, plugged in the receiver and pocketed the remote. "I'm thinking tacos—"

A bolt of red plasma shattered the tank.

Jack slammed his eyes shut, feeling more than seeing the tank explode across his face and hands. A shard nicked his left eyebrow, others sliced across his palms as he covered his face. Heart hammering, he dived under the tank stand, warm, wet liquid running down his face. He dashed the blood from his eyes, lacerated hands stinging as he grabbed for his P90 hanging from its harness. But the rifle slipped from his fingers, his hands slick with blood.

Wiping them on his BDUs, Jack ignored the pain and raised his rifle. Repeated blasts erupted from the tunnel leading to the gate. Inside it, he could make out the silhouettes of at least five more super soldiers firing on the team.

A bolt shot toward Daniel, but Teal'c pushed him out of the way just in time. He returned fire, but his staff weapon was barely keeping the enemy from closing in. Then another super soldier slipped in to their left, aiming his wrist-weapon at Teal'c's back.

"Watch out!" Daniel swung his P90 toward the drone, spending the better part of a magazine keeping the thing at bay.

Jack's neck felt wet. He should probably worry about that, but at the moment he was more concerned with how his two guys were covering each other's backs but leaving themselves wide open to—

Where the hell was Carter?

"Colonel!" She dived under the tank, but not before letting

loose a stream of bullets that could take down a stampeding…

Elephant.

But they weren't fighting elephants.

Or were they?

Spots clouded Jack's eyes. Even through all the plasma fire and bullet reports, he felt woozy. He needed a nap. "We need to get to the gate, Major."

"Not possible, sir." Carter grabbed his left hand and pressed it against his neck. He could feel wet, sticky stuff seep through his fingers.

Daniel and Teal'c joined them below the tank stand, both out of breath. The drones kept up their barrage.

"The Stargate is unattainable, O'Neill."

"Yeah, I get that, Teal'c."

"And yet we continue to pursue that objective."

Fair point.

Daniel ripped open a field dressing from his tac vest. "How you doing, Jack?"

"Peachy." Jack wrapped it around his neck. "Any of you know another way out?"

The drones kept on shooting. Their shots hit the granite walls, sending rocks and dust down into the inner chamber. Unlike their recently deceased buddy, these drones just held their positions blocking SG-1's retreat.

"We'll never make it to the gate!" Daniel shouted over the enemy fire. "There's too many."

"Find a way," Jack mumbled. God, he wanted to sleep. He wanted to get through that gate, eat a juicy steak, and take a long nap. "Can we backtrack around; dial home before they figure it out?" When no one said a word, he spoke louder. "Carter?"

The major pulled out her scanner and turned a knob. Her eyes widened. "I can't get us to the gate, but…"

"For crying out loud, what then?"

Another plasma bolt smashed into the neighboring wall panel creating a man-sized hole. Wires and tubes sizzled and sputtered inside. It was all too noisy. He just wanted to forget how the day had gone to hell in a handbasket and —

"Sir, there's an empty Tel'tak cargo ship down the tunnel behind us."

Jack didn't want to ride in a stinking Goa'uld ship. He wanted to gate home.

The view from under the tank slid sideways. Or rather, Jack did.

Daniel pulled him back up. "Okay, well… The other tunnel seems clear, but Sam, you're sure there's no one on board?"

Carter stuffed the scanner into her vest. "The power's on, and there's no discernible life-forms on board."

"And you don't find that the least bit convenient?"

Jack groaned. Since when had Daniel become so negative? "So… No elephants, I take it?"

"Sir?"

More plasma fire. He rubbed his eyes, but the fireworks kept on coming. "So… No Stargate."

"No, sir. No Stargate."

2. Anger (n): {*psychology*} — *a strong feeling of being upset or annoyed at oneself or others because of something wrong or bad. Once in this stage of loss, the individual recognizes that denial cannot continue.*

Sam led the way onto the cargo ship, one eye on her scanner. Anubis's super soldiers hadn't followed their escape, but Daniel was right: the ship was too convenient. The drones had blocked the tunnel to the gate, firing into the chamber, but their shots barely ever came close. It really was too easy an escape. She knew better, but still… What choice did they have?

And what had she been thinking, cowering under that empty Goa'uld queen's tank like a cadet? She hadn't even thought about her scanner until almost too late.

That wasn't like her.

Teal'c laid Colonel O'Neill down beside an aft bulkhead. Sam hated seeing the colonel that way. Hated seeing him sprawled on the ground. That was how she'd found Janet during the battle on P3X-666. Stretched out. Dead. Gone.

A glass shard had nicked an artery below the colonel's jaw, but Daniel was already on it, using his trauma kit to clamp the small gash. He ripped open a clot pack and applied it to the wound, then a pressure bandage. Swift, measured. Of all of them, he seemed to be handling their situation the best. He displayed no emotion. No anxiousness.

No sign of the Daniel who once wore his heart on his sleeve.

He administered a mild stimulant to keep the colonel alert. Sam silently approved. That shot would buy them enough time to travel to the Alpha Site and then gate back to the SGC where Janet could…

"Damn it." What was wrong with her? She knew Janet was gone. And she knew better than to have been knee-deep in that drone factory without monitoring their situation.

Get a grip, Sam.

Teal'c took the pilot's seat and began the engine's warm-up cycle. The ship responded with a steady hum. "Should we not insure the Tel'tak does not contain a recall device before — ?"

"Just get us out of here." Sam laid down her pack carrying the salvaged crystal and stormed to the central console behind the cockpit. Teal'c raised an eyebrow at her hasty response, but he was a big guy. He'd do what needed to be done.

The thrusters rumbled to life. She grabbed a guardrail and held on as the ship lifted off.

So far, so good. Unclipping her P90, she secured it beside the console and popped the side panel open. A dozen crystals pulsated inside, blue, yellow, and green ones as long as her forearm. Shorter white crystals, connected to spools of black wires, surrounded the larger brackets. Everything checked out.

If she could avoid any more mistakes, they'd get the colonel home.

She pulled out her scanner again and double-checked the internal wirings. No recall device, but also no cloaking mechanism. She glanced over at Daniel and his patient. The blood had been sopped up from Colonel O'Neill's neck and, though his face had drained of color, his eyes were open. His chest rose and fell more steadily, too.

The colonel would make it. That's all that mattered.

At Daniel's urging, the colonel drank from his canteen. Daniel turned toward Sam. "At least he isn't mumbling about elephants anymore."

"Good." She snapped the panel back into place. "Keep him that way."

"Sam—"

"Keep an eye on that wound, Daniel." She knew he wanted to help, but unless he had a Stargate in his back pocket, he needed to focus. They all needed to.

A glance out the forward canopy revealed they'd left orbit. The ship swept past two lifeless moons locked in a push-pull orbit around a cyan gas giant. The view was almost hypnotic, until the steady thrum of thrusters yanked her back to reality. "Teal'c, why haven't you engaged the hyper-drive?"

"I am attempting to do so, Major Carter." Teal'c swiped down on the control interface. Nothing happened.

"Come on!" Sam strode to the navigator's chair and studied the HUD display. All systems appeared normal. "It should work."

Teal'c tilted his head. "And yet, it does not."

Sam slammed her fist down on the controls. "That's not possible. You're doing it wrong!"

"Carter!"

She spun around. Colonel O'Neill had managed to push himself up to a sitting position. His glassy-eyed gaze knocked her breath away.

Through the silence that followed, the sound of the thrusters and her pounding pulse kept their grip on her, pushed her forward because SG-1 had to survive. They'd gotten into trouble; it was up to her to get them out.

"Consider what you've been through. Eventually it has to take its toll."

She shoved away Janet's voice. Now wasn't the time to think about what she couldn't change, only what she could. "Sir, what if—"

"Take it easy, Major. We've gotten out of worse."

"I'll take a turn piloting." Daniel stood up and smiled. Almost. Thinly guarded, the corners of his mouth never really turned up. "Teal'c, why don't you help Sam in the engine room?"

Teal'c grabbed his staff weapon and was at her side in less time than Sam had to protest. She could do this alone. She didn't need help.

She hesitated. "What about the colonel?"

"I'll come with." Colonel O'Neill pushed himself up.

A moment's wobble, a hand on the bulkhead. His face gray as stone. As happy as Sam was to see him upright, he'd lost too much blood.

"No, you don't." Daniel nudged him back down.

Sam looked away, unsure of what to do, what to think. How to feel. She wanted it to stop. All of it. No more deaths. No more loss.

"Major Carter?" Teal'c presented her with her P90, and then strode toward the engine room.

Sam clipped her P90 to her harness, torn between helping the colonel and fixing whatever kept them from jumping into hyperspace. She knew going to the engine room was the responsible thing to do, the rational thing to do.

Daniel gave her an encouraging nod and turned his attention back to the colonel. "Come on, Jack. You can keep me company."

"And miss out on all the fun? Hey, Carter…"

Sam's stomach clenched, but she forced herself to look him in the eye. "I know, sir. Get a grip."

"Or not. Just… Stop looking down that rabbit hole so much."

She heard his unspoken words: stop thinking about Janet's death. Move forward. Live here. Live now.

If only it was that easy.

"Sir…"

"Go on, Carter. Play with the engines. You like that sorta thing, remember?" The colonel gave her a smile.

The tightness in her chest loosened. Colonel O'Neill was right. With a nod to Daniel, she headed off for the engine room. She'd fix the hyper-drive and they'd get out of this mess. Like the colonel said, they'd gotten out of worse.

She paused at the archway, glancing back as Daniel unzipped his pack and pulled out a paperback book and pencil. He handed them to the colonel. "That'll keep you out of trouble."

From the archway, Sam couldn't see the book, but, for the colonel's sake, she hoped it had something to do with *The Simpsons*. Maybe Siler packed it as a gag gift.

Colonel O'Neill stared at the cover, his smile dropping into a tight scowl as he tossed the book across the deck. "Don't push it, Daniel."

It was a crossword puzzle book.

"Major Carter!" Teal'c's shout came from the engine room. It sounded like trouble.

Releasing the safety on her P90, Sam dashed down the connecting corridor. She should have scanned the entire ship. Was there an intruder on board? What had she missed this time?

She turned the corner into the engine room, weapon raised. Teal'c stood inside, his staff weapon aimed. Both the primary and secondary hyper-drive compartments were slid open. Black cables dangled from each drawer, leading to what had to be at least a hundred-gallon tank.

Inside that tank swam another, more pressing puzzle.

A fully matured Goa'uld symbiote.

3. Bargaining (v): {*psychology*} — *to negotiate or come to terms. A reaction to feelings of helplessness and vulnerability. This*

stage of loss involves the hope that the individual can some-how regain control in order to undo or avoid a cause of grief.

Teal'c activated his staff weapon, its electrical charge a promise that the abomination inside the symbiote tank would soon be put to an end. He had gone to the engine room, hoping to allow his bone-weary soul a moment's pause, and in doing so perhaps provide Major Carter with an opportunity to do the same. He knew she had felt Janet Fraiser's death keenly, all of SG-1 had. The doctor's funeral and subsequent memorial had been only a first step toward the healing they required.

Eliminating the immediate threat so that they may return to the SGC was now a necessary second.

"Don't shoot it!" Major Carter stepped closer to the tank.

Teal'c did not. Nor did he deactivate his weapon. He under-stood her need to grasp the situation, but as O'Neill would say, one could never trust a Goa'uld.

Even one thrashing as wildly as this. Metal spikes pierced its pale skin, two above the serpent's head and more along its body. Wires from those spikes led to a knee-high metallic black box on the floor beside the hyper-drive compartments. Thick cables led from the box up into each drawer, where they were fused into the very brackets that controlled the crystals. In the wall above, a circular lens glowed blue.

Clearly, there was danger here. He swung the staff weapon toward the black box. "At least allow me to disable its connec-tion to the hyper-drive."

"I don't think that's a good idea." Major Carter approached the box and knelt. She pulled out her ever-present scanner. "Not until we know what we're dealing with."

He knew precisely what they were dealing with: a false god without a host. Without a face by which to lure innocents to quench its all-consuming thirst for bloodshed.

His thumb hovered over the staff weapon's trigger. "Can

you not determine its purpose once it is disabled and we have safely entered hyperspace?"

"I wish it was that simple."

It was that simple. Why could Major Carter not see that? There were times Teal'c wished the Tau'ri would recognize their fragility. Dr. Fraiser's recent loss should have served as a reminder. An indelible lesson that, yes, risks were worthy of the taking, but they should be calculated. Considered. Planned properly.

Teal'c raised an eyebrow, taken aback by his musings. If he'd said the same aloud to Master Bra'tac, or even to O'Neill, they would have accused him of behaving like an old woman.

"*Ah… Sam? Teal'c?*" Daniel Jackson called over the radio. "*Everything all right?*"

"We are endeavoring to determine the situation," Teal'c replied. He briefed their teammate on their condition. "Are there any enemies in pursuit?"

"*Nothing yet.*"

"Do you wish me to take over piloting?"

"*No. I'm fine.*" A moment's pause. "*Keep us posted.*"

Even Teal'c could not ignore the brevity of Daniel Jackson's response. He exchanged glances with Major Carter.

She shrugged. "Daniel's been pretty quiet since… Since Janet's death."

"They were close," Teal'c offered. Indeed, it had been his observation in the weeks before Janet Fraiser's demise that Daniel Jackson spent much of his free time with her and her daughter, Cassandra.

In the weeks since, he had turned inward. Not withdrawn, but not as quick to engage in non–mission-related concerns.

Healing would take time. For all of them.

"Teal'c, I'm sorry about biting your head off earlier."

"My head is intact, Major Carter." He met her sorrowful gaze and added, "Your apology is appreciated."

She examined a cable emanating from the tank, then

looked up from her scanner. "Do you know anything about why Daniel's so eager for the colonel to do crossword puzzles?"

"I do not." Teal'c shifted his staff weapon to his other hand. "Janet Fraiser had several such books in her office."

"Yeah," she whispered.

"Major Carter, the symbiote?"

"Right." Biting her lip, she returned to studying the scanner. "I'm willing to bet this uses the same technology as Anubis' super soldiers. The nutrient tank houses the Goa'uld, which in turn controls key systems. Somehow, the symbiote's cybernetically tied into ship's functions."

She touched the cable. A blue wave of energy shot outward, throwing her back against the far wall.

Teal'c ran to her side. "Are you all right?"

She gave a swift nod. "The tank's got the same shielding mechanisms as the super soldiers. Either that, or there's a feedback loop somewhere in the system." She stood and rubbed her hand. "I don't think your staff weapon's going to do much good."

Glancing back at the symbiote, he discovered that its thrashing had subsided.

He shared his observation.

"The shock must have spooked it. I have a hard time believing a blank slate symbiote, like the ones used in the super soldiers, could manage something as complex as a hyper-drive."

She strode over to the hyper-drive compartment, as if the attack on her person had never happened. Raising her scanner over the black box, she then followed the cables extending from its base up into the drive's compartments.

Teal'c once again aimed his staff weapon toward the tank. "You yourself made it clear that O'Neill requires immediate medical assistance."

"He does…" She peered into the open primary hyper-drive drawer. One cable from the box was threaded up into the drawer and wrapped around the primary control crystal. Kneeling by the box once more, Major Carter aimed her scanner at its base as surely as his staff weapon was aimed at the tank. Her brow furrowed. She turned a scanner dial and repeated her task.

"Major Carter?"

"Hmm?"

"If O'Neill was here, he would express impatience."

"I know, Teal'c." She rocked back on her heels and frowned. "I just... I just don't know how to fix this. Not yet."

There had to be a way. Of this Teal'c was certain. SG-1 had not come this far or risked so much to be left stranded. He eyed the now-still symbiote. "Perhaps the electrical surge that harmed you can be used to permanently disarm the Goa'uld's stranglehold. Perhaps there is some unguarded cable. An unshielded crystal to — ?"

"Not that I can find. The shield extends from the nutrient tank to the hyper-drive's control crystal." Major Carter stood up, her attention returned to the black box. "I'm pretty sure that if we kill the symbiote, the ship wouldn't work at all, and it's not only the hyper-drive I'm worried about. Look up there." She pointed to the computer core and then to the life support systems against the rear bulkhead. Black cables led from each down into the nutrient tank. "As much as I hate to admit it, the design's without flaw."

"Oh, I can think of one flaw."

O'Neill had arrived. He leaned against the doorway, his eyes never leaving the tank. "If that slimy snake in the tank controls the ship, why did it let us lift off?"

4. Depression (n): {psychology} — a state of feeling sad marked by inactivity, difficulty in thinking and concentration, and feelings of dejection and hopelessness. During the fourth stage, the grieving person quietly separates to bid their loved one farewell.

Daniel slumped in the pilot's seat, hands on the control globe, and waited. The ship wouldn't go into hyperspace, he still had thrusters, but so what? It wasn't like there were any neighboring planets or moons with a gate. SG-1 was stuck, as usual. Sam would figure out how to fix it. As usual.

An asteroid loomed off the port bow. With a bit of gallows humor, he considered changing course to bring the ship closer. The last time he'd seen an asteroid up close, it had nearly been his final resting spot.

A morbid thought. He knew better. He should be used to the pain, he should be used to saying goodbye.

He swallowed hard at that realization. "I never got to say goodbye."

"*Nor I.*"

Daniel glanced over his shoulder. "Did you say something?"

Jack wasn't there. The crossword puzzle book lay on the floor, the pencil beside it. Broken. As if someone had stepped on it.

Fine. Jack could ignore the puzzle book. He was a grown man. While he was at it, he might as well ignore Daniel's efforts to keep him alive.

God, he was tired. Soul tired. He recognized the symptoms and he knew the only cure was time. Eventually, he'd get used to the loss, but it would still leave a hole.

It always did.

He pulled out his radio. "Teal'c, is Jack with you?"

"*Hold on, Daniel,*" came Sam's voice from the radio. "*The colonel might be on to something.*"

Daniel stuffed the radio back in his pocket. Leave it to Jack. He'd lost a great deal of blood and still refused to give up. Daniel appreciated his "never say die" attitude, tried to live it. Especially since his own return to life.

"But sometimes it isn't enough," he said aloud.

A rattling sound came from the intercom grid next to the HUD controls. "*They attempt to disengage my connection to the ship.*"

Daniel sat upright in his seat. "My connection?"

"*They will not succeed. Anubis is too clever.*"

Daniel yanked his radio back out. "Um, guys… You better get in here."

"*I had heard Samantha Carter was quite brilliant, but even she cannot —*"

Daniel stared at the intercom. "Who are you?"

"*I am Penthos of the Tok'ra.*"

"Penthos… The Greco-Roman spirit of —"

"*Grief.*"

Under different circumstances, he'd have smiled at the irony.

"And I'm Santa Claus." Jack stumbled into the cockpit with Teal'c's aid. "Daniel, who ya talking to?"

"*I know of all of you, Colonel O'Neill. Daniel Jackson. Jacob Carter's daughter, Samantha, and the Jaffa, Teal'c.*" Another sigh. Deeper this time. "*SG-1's exploits are known throughout the Tok'ra's spy network.*"

"Yeah, so?" Jack shrugged, nonchalant as ever. "Last I checked, we'd made the galaxy-wide Goa'uld news, too. That doesn't prove anything."

"You know my father?" Sam asked.

"*We met shortly before my final assignment. Selmak and I were born of the same queen-mother.*"

"Egeria," Teal'c said. "That is also not unknown to the Goa'uld."

Penthos groaned again.

"Are you in pain?"

"Goa'uld or Tok'ra, Daniel, he'd have to be," Sam whispered. "Anubis punctured the symbiote's hide with at least a half-dozen conductors."

"*Eight, to be precise, Jacob's daughter.*"

"I'm sorry, I —"

"Don't go feeling sorry for it, Carter." Jack sank down into the navigator's chair. "It's still a Goa'uld."

"And we're still stuck on a ship incapable of hyper-drive," Daniel reminded him. "Goa'uld or Tok'ra, shouldn't we —"

"What? Do you want to negotiate with the thing?"

"O'Neill, would it not be prudent to see if this Penthos could be of assistance?"

Daniel nodded in agreement with Teal'c.

"Fine." Jack leaned back in the chair and closed his eyes. "Have at it."

"Wait a minute, Daniel." Sam slid into the pilot's chair and enabled the HUD. "Penthos, if you're really a Tok'ra, can you tell us the coordinates for the base you were stationed at before... Before losing your —"

"Before losing my host?" Another groan. This time thinner, more ragged. *"For the sake of my fellow Tok'ra, I cannot. While the Tau'ri were willing to share coordinates for their Alpha Site, you are many and my people few."*

Jack's eyes snapped open. "What's an Alpha Site?"

"Please, Colonel O'Neill. The Tok'ra knew of its location. Your General Hammond had offered sanctuary if ever the need arose."

Daniel was satisfied. "Sounds like a Tok'ra to me."

"Indeed," Teal'c said. "A Goa'uld would have lied, providing us with false coordinates."

"I am not Goa'uld!"

Daniel raised his hands, unsure if Penthos could see the peaceful gesture for what it was. He turned around, searching for a lens that might indicate if the symbiote could see as well as hear.

There. Over by the HUD. A blue-tinged round camera lens, about two inches in diameter. Penthos had been watching them since they'd come on board. Why hadn't he said anything until now?

"Uh, hello." Daniel waved at the lens. "We'd like to believe you, but..."

"You require a demonstration of my good faith. I understand."

The ship lurched forward. Daniel glanced out the window, and there it was, the prism-like streaks of hyperspace.

"Nice job." Jack peered up at Sam. "Any way to tell whether that thing's taking us farther into Goa'uld territory?"

Sam keyed the HUD. The translucent grid displayed a star map with a series of dashes leading from the center toward a cluster by the top-left corner. "That's Cassiopeia. From there it's only 11,000 light-years to home."

"*Its nearest solar system contains a Stargate on the fifth planet that will take you home.*"

"Penthos… If that's really your name…" Daniel sat down on the steps behind the pilot chair. "If you're Tok'ra, what happened to your host?"

"*Haider sacrificed his life so that I could complete our mission,*" Penthos whispered. Then, stronger, flatter, he continued. "*Several months ago, we infiltrated Anubis' base on Tartarus—*"

Sam gasped. "My god… You're the spy who gave away the Alpha Site's coordinates."

"*Never. I would rather die.*"

"But you didn't." Jack stabbed a finger at the intercom. "You're still alive. Carter here almost lost her life to one of Anubis's goons thanks to you. Over a hundred of my men did die, along with a few dozen of your Tok'ra buddies and a slew of Jaffa rebels."

"O'Neill, it is possible that Anubis probed Penthos' mind as he did Thor and Jonas Quinn."

"*If what the Jaffa says is true, I am deeply sorry, Colonel. I have no memory of the time between my capture and being placed in the tank controlling this vessel.*"

"Which happened how, exactly?" Daniel asked.

Penthos sighed and the ship shuddered in response. "*Upon reaching Tartarus, my host and I posed as a minor Goa'uld in the hopes of obtaining intelligence on how the System Lord manufactured his warriors. One of Anubis's Jaffa discovered our presence as we retrieved vital information from the data banks.*"

"And yet you live to tell the tale," Teal'c said.

"*Half of who I was is no more. The other half ensnared in a device of infinite pain. Would you call that living?*"

Teal'c bowed his head. "I would not."

"*We used the Jaffa's zat'ni'katel to render him unconscious, but within moments the room filled with super soldiers. It was Haider who urged me to leave him, to hide within the Jaffa's pouch until there was a way to escape into another host. He removed the Jaffa's prim'tah. I protested, but Haider insisted. He knew word of how Anubis engineered the Kull warriors must be sent to our people.*

"When Anubis wrenched me from the Jaffa… *He could not have known that I was Tok'ra. To him, I was merely a symbiote to do his bidding. To Haider, I was — His final selfless act before dying was to save me, but now… Now I am alone. I am — Ahhhh!*"

The deck keeled sideways. Daniel grabbed hold of the central console. Teal'c did the same while Sam gripped her chair. Jack began to tumble out of his, but managed to hold on. Outside, the stars streaked by, but at a more stuttered rate.

"Sam?"

"Something's wrong with the hyper-drive." Sam half-walked, half-crawled toward the console as the ship righted itself.

"Penthos?"

"*I will not permit Anubis to use me so! Please, you must disconnect me. I cannot separate from the pain.*"

Was it physical or had the loss of Penthos' host become too much? Daniel knew how loss could swallow a person whole, but his experiences had to pale in comparison to losing half of what made a Tok'ra complete.

He turned to Sam. "There's got to be something you can do."

"The tank's tied directly into the main crystal. If I…" She glanced at her backpack and her eyes lit up. "Penthos, do you have any control over the shields blocking access to the drives?"

Penthos didn't answer.

The ship shuddered a third time and then settled down, its, jagged streaks replaced by smoother, more normal luminescent lines. The hyperspace window had been restored.

"*I cannot lower the shields around my tank, but I believe the main compartment can be accessed. Is it possible? Can you end my existence?*"

The pleading in his voice tore at Daniel, at a wound barely begun to heal. There were times he wondered whether the Stargate program was really worth all the loss.

Sam snatched up her pack and pulled out the red crystal from Anubis's clone factory. "If we drop out of hyperspace, I can bypass the tank's control by replacing the drive's main crystal. That would at least take some of the stress off Penthos until we can get him to the Tok'ra."

"Now wait a minute!" Jack pushed himself out of his chair. "Won't we be sitting ducks?"

"I don't think so, sir. The minutes we've spent in hyperspace should have taken us several light-years away from any threat from Anubis."

"As far as we know."

"O'Neill, would not Penthos' rescue aid our current situation with the Tok'ra?"

"Teal'c's right, Jack, and whether you like it or not, we need to get you to a doctor."

Jack collapsed back in the chair. "I suppose."

Daniel turned back toward the intercom. "Penthos, you haven't said anything for a while."

"My life will not end."

"No." Daniel recognized it was more a statement than a question, but he answered with as much optimism as he could muster. "If Sam succeeds, we can take you back to the Tok'ra."

He left out that they'd need to find the Tok'ra first. There'd been no word from any of them since the alliance fell apart. Not even Jacob.

"I ask a favor in return. That someone remain in contact with me while Jacob Carter's daughter endeavors to bypass the hyper-drive."

"We'll take turns," Daniel promised.

"Then we are in agreement." A sudden jolt and the ship dropped out of hyperspace.

Jack grinned, barely. Daniel recognized the attempt for what it was: bravado. "Carter, does the intercom work in the cargo hold?"

"It should, sir, but —"

"I'll go first then." Jack struggled to his feet again.

Daniel felt his eyebrows shoot up. "You?"

"Sure. Why not? Teal'c, fly this bucket while Daniel helps out Carter. Penthos can keep me company in the cargo hold so we stay out of everybody's hair."

With a silent nod, Teal'c sat down at the helm.

Daniel took Jack's elbow, guiding him up and out of the cockpit. The fact that Jack didn't resist spoke volumes.

"You're not exactly at your best, Jack."

"That's never stopped me before."

Daniel pointed at the lens and whispered, "And you hate the Tok'ra."

"Hate's a pretty strong word." Jack didn't even bother to glance at the lens.

"Well, as far as words go, it fits the —"

"Come on, Penthos." Jack shrugged off Daniel's hand and headed for the cargo-hold. "Let's go chew the fat."

Daniel watched him leave, hoping Jack would hold back his typical anti-Tok'ra sentiments.

Teal'c turned the ship to face a swollen red giant. The old star hung in space, a bloody ink stain against the black of space. "There are currently no enemy ships in our area."

"Hopefully, it'll stay that way." Sam left for the engine room, her pack slung over her shoulder.

Daniel followed until he heard a crunch beneath his feet. He lifted his boot. Underneath was the broken pencil he'd given Jack. The crossword puzzle book lay beside it.

He picked them up, wondering exactly what 'words' Jack would have for Penthos.

5. Acceptance (n): *{psychology} — Coming to terms with the inevitable. Embracing the opportunity to make peace. A highly individualized stage not necessarily achieved by everyone.*

The blink of an eye. A shift in one's thoughts.

The change of one perspective for another.

A jagged current rippled across Penthos' skin. He pushed the pain aside, enabling the cargo hold's sensor lens so he might see Colonel O'Neill. He wished to understand why this man was both admired and disdained for his methods.

Penthos zoomed in on the man's features. Tiny cuts covered much of O'Neill's gaunt face. While a first impression would show an injured human sprawled out in repose to recover, Penthos noticed the agitation that lay within. Long fingers toyed with a bloodied bandage on his neck. Legs crossed and uncrossed.

"Well?" *O'Neill glared into the camera.*

"You are older than expected." *And yet, so young. So impossibly young.*

Haider had been like that.

The cargo hold doors slid open. Daniel Jackson strode in, holding a black and white book and two pieces of yellow-painted wood.

"Everything all right in here?" *The doors slid closed behind him.*

O'Neill turned his gaze toward his subordinate. "Give it a rest, Daniel."

"Says the pot to the kettle." *He offered the book and wood pieces to O'Neill.* "If you and Penthos run out of things to talk about… Well, maybe you could try filling in a few of these."

O'Neill did not move.

Daniel Jackson lowered his voice, but Penthos could still hear. "You know she would've wanted you to keep doing them."

"In a manner of speaking, she outranked me." *O'Neill's eyes narrowed.* "You don't."

"No… I don't."

A silence fell between the two men. Penthos could not tell if it was one born of companionship or woe. Daniel Jackson broke the peace, dropping the proffered objects into O'Neill's lap.

"Think of it as a way to honor her memory."

Daniel Jackson departed, his final words affirming Penthos' decision.

Jack stared at the crossword book, hating everything it represented.

"Does Daniel Jackson's insubordination trouble you, Colonel O'Neill?"

Jack snorted. "If you only knew."

"And yet I detect humor in your voice. I am not familiar with Tau'ri mannerisms, but you appeared to smile in response to my question."

"What's your point?" Jack tossed the book aside. He'd volunteered for babysitting duty to keep the Goa'uld out of everyone else's hair, not to be psycho-analyzed by a snake.

"I suppose I have no point other than that I, too, have struggled with subordinates not understanding the need for a clean chain of command. Subordinates who meant well, but—"

"Look, the last thing I need is command advice from a..." He stopped himself from saying the G word, but it wasn't easy.

"Does the book carry great meaning amongst the Tau'ri?"

"This thing?" He scowled at the book. "More like it carries a proverbial pain in my butt."

"How can a book be so problematic for the great Colonel O'Neill?"

"The 'great Colonel O'Neill,' huh?" Jack recognized a failed suck-up when he heard one. He thumbed the radio in his tac vest. "Carter? How's it going in there?"

"Penthos is as good as his word, sir. We've managed to isolate the line feeding into the control crystal without getting shocked. I just need to—"

"Yeah, I don't need the details." He glanced up at the blue fish-eye lens on the wall. If keeping it distracted would get them home, so be it. "Let me know if the situation changes. The faster we're outta here, the better."

Dropping his hand from the radio, he felt his fingers brush against the crossword puzzle book. The Goa'uld wanted company? All right. He could do that.

Opening the book to a random page, he picked up the leaded pencil half. "Right then, let's start easy. One across: three letter word for 'feline.' Well, that's simple. 'Cat.'"

"Please explain. Is your book some sort of dictionary?"

"Nope. It's a game." He explained the basics, but then it occurred to him… "Goa'uld language and English aren't the same, are they?"

"I am not Goa'uld, Colonel." The wall speaker rattled; Jack tried to ignore how much it sounded like a sigh.

He scribbled in the word 'cat.' "Next up: a nine-letter word for 'puzzle.' First letter would need to be a 'C.' If it's too hard for ya—"

"As a spy within the Tok'ra network, I have learned many languages."

"Including ours?"

"Enough to know that the word you seek is 'conundrum.'"

"That works." Jack tucked away the fact that a Tok'ra spy knew how to spell Earth-English and penciled in the word.

"Is this a common custom amongst the Tau'ri?"

"Custom?" The next word wasn't too hard. "Seven across, five letters for—"

"Daniel Jackson said performing this puzzle would 'honor her memory.' I wish to learn more about honoring memories of the fallen. Whose memory did he mean, Colonel?"

"No one you know."

"You have lost someone. I have lost someone."

"Yeah, well. Who hasn't?" Jack slapped the book shut. "This is ridiculous. I'm not playing crossword puzzles. Not with a snake. Not with anybody."

The speaker rattled again. *"Was my capture by Anubis the cause of her demise? She must have been a fine warrior. A soldier worthy of—"*

"Janet wasn't a soldier," he muttered, wishing Penthos would just go away. "She was a doctor. She patched us up. Kept our guts from spilling out all over—"

"So her battles were not on the field."

"No, they weren't."

"Was she brave?"

He stared at Penthos' lens. The lens stared back.

"They didn't get any braver." Jack re-opened the book.

Sam stepped around the black box, giving it a wide berth. The cables coming from the nutrient tank to the box were still hot, but the cables feeding out to both hyper-drive drawers were offline. Thanks to Penthos, she and Daniel had managed to isolate the cables leading to the original control crystal. Now it was simply a case of replacing the crystal with the one they'd retrieved from Anubis's factory. The trick was using a small enough tool to bend back the brackets without damaging them.

"Be careful, Jacob's daughter," Penthos warned. *"Any static fed back into the isolated cables could electrocute me."*

"Got it. Keep the nutrient tank clear of any discharge." She reviewed her kit, confirming her worst fear. She didn't have the right tool. "Daniel, did you bring your archaeology kit?"

"On a mission to blow up a drone factory?"

"If I had a small enough tool…" She wiped her forearm across her brow. The tank's high humidity made the engine room feel like a sauna. She examined the brackets surrounding the cable-wrapped crystal. "Something like a miniaturized pick or —"

"Promise you won't tell Jack?"

Sam looked up. "So you do have your kit."

"Never leave home without it."

"Even when our mission had everything to do with stopping Anubis and nothing to do with ancient ruins?"

Daniel wiggled his eyebrows. "Busted."

With a laugh, she waved him off to retrieve his kit from the cockpit.

"I have not heard that sound in a very long time."

Sam peered at the lens over the hyper-drive drawers. "It's been awhile for me, too."

"Because you lost Janet?"

Sam stiffened. Of course… The symbiote must have heard everything since they'd first come on board.

"Jacob's daughter —"

"It's Major Carter, actually, but if you're related to Selmak, I guess that makes us almost family so… Call me Samantha or Sam." She forced a grin she didn't quite feel.

"Family. Are all of SG-1 a family?"

"In a manner of speaking." The grin came more easily. "Pretty much all of Stargate Command's like that. Aren't the Tok'ra?"

"I would die for the Tok'ra."

Sam squeezed her eyes shut against the remorse in Penthos' voice. "I think, if anything, Janet's death has brought home that maybe it's more important to live. Getting angry won't fix things," she realized aloud.

She opened her eyes and gazed at the symbiote in its tank. Penthos' red and yellow serpentine eyes stared back at her. "Let's get this crystal swapped out so we can take you home, okay?"

The eyes blinked in what she could only assume was agreement. *"Samantha, is there a Tau'ri significance involving death and crossword puzzles?"*

"God, no." She picked up the primary cable leading into the box. "Daniel must have his reasons —"

"To honor her memory?"

Sam cocked her head. "Different people find different ways to ways to remember those they lost."

"I suppose I must find my way."

Just as she needed to find hers. "So do I," she whispered.

With a flick of his tail, Penthos turned his back to her. Sam was just about ask him if everything was all right when Daniel strode in.

"Will this work?" He held up a miniature trowel, no longer than five centimeters. The end had a gold-plated spade.

"Daniel, why the crossword puzzles?"

"Oh, that…" He went over to the hyper-drive drawer. "Janet made Jack do them every once in a while. Ever since he stuck his head in that Ancient Repository."

She joined him by the drive. "What on Earth for?"

"To make sure Jack's mind was intact. The Asgard might have removed the Ancients' knowledge, but—"

"Janet wanted to make sure that was all they took."

"Yeah. She was clever that way." Frowning, he pointed the miniature trowel toward the jerry-rigged crystal.

"Careful!" She plucked the trowel from his hand. "We need to avoid sending any charge through the cable. Here, help me swap these out." She handed him the new crystal.

Sliding the trowel between the two closest cables, she reached for the nearest bracket, and—

"Whoah!" Daniel pointed at the nutrient tank, where Penthos was listing to one side.

"But there wasn't any spark!" Sam pulled the trowel back out. "Penthos, are you all right?"

The deck surged upward, throwing her to the floor—a hand's breadth away from the charged black box. Daniel managed to keep his footing and helped haul her back up.

"*Major Carter,*" Teal'c called over the radio. "*Has the hyperdrive been repaired?*"

Sam thumbed her radio. "Not yet. What's going on?"

"*We're under attack!*" Colonel O'Neill barked. "*One of Anubis's motherships, and it's coming in fast.*"

Teal'c knew the only way for SG-1 to survive would be if he took the Tel'tak underneath the mothership to avoid its most forward guns.

"How the hell did they find us!" O'Neill emerged from the cargo-hold and slid into the navigator's seat.

"Is it not obvious?" Twin balls of plasma shot toward them, confirming Teal'c's decision to dive. He pushed the cargo ship down below the massive disc forming the center of the mothership. Although gun banks covered the many spikes protruding from the mothership's belly, the cargo ship had the advantage of maneuverability.

"Damn it," O'Neill growled. "They tracked the ship."

"Indeed."

Once beneath the dome, a gun bank pivoted in their direction. Teal'c rolled the ship onto its side so the shields would spread the blast, minimizing impact.

"You're sure we don't have any weapons?" O'Neill asked.

"None."

Teal'c spun the ship around, heading back the way they had come. He gripped the control globe as plasma rounds from the mothership's port side grazed the bow. The cargo ship shuddered, tossing O'Neill from his chair.

"Hold on!" Teal'c yanked back on the control globe, well aware that the artificial gravity might falter. More weapons fire erupted from the mothership, but went wide. Teal'c glanced quickly at O'Neill. He'd pulled himself back into his chair, blood trickling down his collar from beneath his bandage.

"Keep 'em guessing, T." O'Neill thumbed his radio. "How much longer, kids?"

"*Working as fast as I can, sir!*"

"*Holding the ship steady would help,*" added Daniel Jackson.

"Funny man. Carter, what's left to do?"

"*I've replaced the crystal, but the hyper-drive won't work until I reconnect the cables.*"

"Then what's the problem? Connect them. Teal'c — watch out!"

Rapid-fire bursts riddled the space ahead. Teal'c banked right.

The HUD flickered, but held. Teal'c headed toward the mothership's aft region where he'd spotted a lack of gunnery.

"*Sir,*" Major Carter shouted on the radio, "*with the artificial gravity acting up, Teal'c has to keep the ship steady or any attempt to reconnect the cabling could kill Penthos.*"

"He's trying, Carter." O'Neill wiped away the blood pooling at his collarbone. "How the hell did that oily-skinned snake manage to find us way out in the galactic suburbs?"

Teal'c decelerated as they neared the mothership's rear thrusters, six plasma guns swiveling around to meet them.

Pushing the control globe downward, he pitched the ship head over tail. The ship responded, heading back toward the center of Anubis's ship.

"How you holding up, Teal'c?"

"I am uncertain how long we can sustain this pace."

"*You must connect the hyper-drive. Even if it ends my life.*"

A shower of sparks all but drowned out Penthos' proposal, but Teal'c heard him.

As did O'Neill. "It's not happening, so drop the noble Tok'ra suicide talk."

The central gun loomed ahead. It dropped farther from the dome and spun toward them. Teal'c banked left and went back toward the aft thrusters.

Jumping up from his seat, O'Neill came to stand beside him. "I've flown a few kamikaze missions in my day. Get up."

Teal'c gratefully obliged. O'Neill climbed into the pilot's seat and gripped the control globe with fervor.

"*I am prepared to die, Colonel O'Neill. Are you prepared to live?*"

A flinch from O'Neill was the only response as he began a pattern of alternating forward pitches and sideways rolls. The mothership's artillery continued to shoot, but O'Neill's tactics aided them in escaping any direct hits.

"*I have lived my life. I would honor —*"

"*Jack, don't listen to Penthos!*" cried Daniel Jackson. "*Just hold the ship steady. We're almost —*"

The ship jolted sideways, a support beam plummeting to the deck behind them.

"The ship can sustain little more damage." Teal'c glanced at the blue lens he had come to identify with Penthos. The situation was dire. With regret, he knew it fell upon him to provide the unconsidered option. "I understand the bond that has formed with the Tok'ra Penthos, but —"

"I wouldn't call it a bond, T, but come on! It — He's a Tok'ra, not a Goa'uld. I doubt he even knew the ship was being tracked."

Another hit. More sparks rained down across the cockpit.

"*You are all fools,*" Penthos boomed, his voice deeper. Cruel. "*Lord Anubis wastes his time with you.*"

"Excuse me?" O'Neill asked. "We're trying to save your Tok'ra ass!"

"*I am not Tok'ra,*" Penthos hissed through the intercom. "*I am Goa'uld, servant to Anubis, greatest of the system lords!*"

Teal'c's hand shot to the zat'ni'katel in his leg holster.

"*A tracking device on board this Tel'tak has informed Lord Anubis of your every move toward the Tau'ri's new Alpha Site.*"

"Sonofabitch," O'Neill growled. "I knew it. Never trust a snake."

"*But you did. You trusted me. The great Colonel O'Neill — a bloodied fool who plays at games. Teal'c the Shol'vah, so mindless in his following of your every move. And worse! You set a female to counter technologies far beyond your understanding.*"

The ship pitched forward, and with it, O'Neill. Teal'c grabbed his arm to pull him back, but O'Neill shook his head and gestured at his hand. He'd covered Penthos' lens beside the HUD.

"Go!" he mouthed, gesturing toward the engine room.

"*Even half alive, I bested you.*"

Teal'c raced for the engine room, dodging support beams and wires hanging from the ceiling as he ran. Penthos' words from when first they met echoed in his memory.

"*Half of who I was is no more.*"

Friend or foe, Teal'c saw no other choice.

The whole ship felt like it was falling apart. Daniel crouched with Sam beside the hyper-drive in disbelief. Dangling cables sparked, liquid sloshed over the nutrient tank's sides as noxious vapors hissed from exposed vents in the collapsing ceiling. The engine room was a nightmare, made all the worse when Teal'c showed up, a charged zat behind his back. His intention was clear.

"*You are fools to believe Lord Anubis would permit such an* easy escape," Penthos' droned on. *"He preyed upon your naiveté. Your weakness. Your inability to see the truth."*

But Daniel refused to believe his words. Eight years of dealing with the Goa'uld had taught him their penchant for obfuscation, for deception, and Penthos' loss hadn't been a lie. Grief didn't work that way. If anything, it forced truth into the open.

"Penthos!" Daniel stood up, aware of Teal'c's wary eyes on him. "It doesn't have to be this way! We can help—"

"Daniel," Sam warned. "There's no time."

"I serve—"

Teal'c whirled toward the lens and shot it twice. The glass shattered and, with it, Penthos' vision.

"Do it now, Major Carter."

Sam threw a pained look at Daniel, then plugged the cable into the drive. She jumped back, grabbed her radio, and gave the symbiote its death sentence. "Hyper-drive is online, sir!"

An electric arc sizzled along the cable, enveloped the black box, and then rushed toward the nutrient tank. The symbiote thrashed, banging its body against the tank's sides.

The ship lurched forward. A moment's disorientation hit Daniel, followed by a microsecond of nausea.

Jack had kicked in the hyper-drive.

Daniel peered at the nutrient tank, its shape half lost in the hissing vapors that still leaked from the damaged ship. Penthos, the symbiote, had sunk to the bottom, his eyes still open.

Teal'c holstered his zat. "There has been enough loss."

Daniel couldn't disagree. He stepped closer to the tank, struck by how Penthos' yellow eyes seemed to focus on him. "Sam, is he...?"

"He's dead, Daniel." She slid the hyper-drive drawer shut.

"I'm not sure if that's what I was asking."

She handed him his tool pouch with a sigh. "One thing's for sure."

"What's that?"

"In the end, I'm grateful."

Daniel turned toward her, surprised. "For what?"

"For being alive."

He heard nothing. Saw nothing. Felt nothing.

A bottomless ache filled his senses. An ache for the life once joined with his.

A life no longer lived. A life duty-bound.

A life now honored.

Two days after returning to Earth, Jack managed to spring himself from the infirmary and go home. Carter and Teal'c set the table inside, while on the back deck Jack lectured Daniel on the finer points of grilling the perfect burger. Below freezing temperatures and heavy clouds threatened a last round of snow before winter gave up, but after spending three days stuck inside that sauna of a cargo ship and another two in the SGC, Jack opted to forgo a jacket. Daniel bundled up in enough layers to thaw a snowman.

If push came to shove, Jack would never be sure whether Penthos had been a Tok'ra or a Goa'uld. In the end, he'd been a snakehead and just as bombastic as the rest of them.

Or had he?

He dropped another burger on the grill, knowing full well that if Carter hadn't connected the hyper-drive, they'd be as good as Daniel's efforts at dinner: burned, toasted, dead.

It'd been a lousy mission with a lousy ending.

SG-1 still needed a win, a check in the victory column. Tonight, playing games and munching on food would have to do the job. Having the team's honorary member join in was just the ticket to make sure that happened.

"Hey, Jack?" Cassie called out from the living room. "Since when is 'bore' a four letter word for a precalculus class?"

Why were teenagers always so nosey? He could have sworn he'd stuffed that crossword book where the sun don't shine.

Spatula in hand, Daniel raised a Teal'c-like eyebrow. "Four-letter word?"

"Flip the burger before it burns, Daniel."

"You do it." Daniel shoved the spatula into Jack's hands and ran inside.

Jack turned the burgers over and followed, prepared for inevitable jibes from the team. Cassie sat over by the fireplace, next to the stack of newspapers he used for kindling. She had the crossword book open in her lap. Carter sat beside her, and while her hundred-watt beam of a smile usually outshined any other, the shades of a grin on Cassie's face for the first time in too long put the Major to shame.

"The answer is 'trig,' doofus." Cassie grabbed a pencil from the coffee table and scribbled in the right word.

"Right, what was I thinking?" Jack waved a finger in the air. "How about some *Trivial Pursuit*? Cassie, pick the category. Sports, science, history—"

"One word to go, sir." Carter peered over Cassie's shoulder. "Thanks to a little help."

"If I may?" Teal'c took the book and joined Daniel on the couch.

"Now hold on a second!"

Teal'c leafed through to the dog-eared pages at the end.

Well, crap.

"O'Neill, did you refer to the answer key in the back?"

Daniel started to laugh, but Jack shut him down with a proper O'Neill glower.

"Let's make this interesting, sir." Carter exchanged glances with Cassie. "I'll bet you can't finish the puzzle without referring to the answer key."

"Hmmm, a bet, you say? What're the stakes?

Cassie shot her arm in the air. "How about pie?"

"Apple or lemon meringue?"

"Winner's choice?" Cassie's grin widened just the smallest fraction.

"Deal."

Cassie grabbed the book before Teal'c could fork it over.

She opened it back up. "Okay… Five letters. An ancient unit of capacity equal to a hundred gallons."

Jack knew the answer, but what the hell? He'd milk it. "Five letters, hmmm."

"Here's a different clue," Cassie offered. "Bald. Wears a short-sleeved shirt."

Teal'c raised an eyebrow. "Is General Hammond in your crossword, O'Neill?"

"Funny. Let's see. Ancient units. Short-sleeved shirts. Bald —"

"Come on, Jack!" Cassie's grin dropped away. "You know the answer."

"Hmmm, that's a toughie." He grabbed a Guinness from the coffee table. Four faces stared at him as he screwed off its cap. Four faces that warmed up his home and made every trip through the gate easier.

And harder.

"Is it 'homer?'"

"Bingo!"

"And here I thought we were playing a crossword puzzle. So, lemon merengue it is."

"Not so fast, sir." Carter grabbed a newspaper from the kindling stack.

He frowned. "Apple, then?"

"How about double or nothing?" She opened the newspaper, ripped out a page, and held it up.

It was another damn crossword puzzle.

"You're on, Carter." Jack flipped the bottle cap into the fireplace. "Two pies are always better than one."

"But no help this time." Carter eyed her teammates. "From anyone."

"Even me?" Cassie asked.

Carter shook her head. "Especially you."

The two exchanged million-watt grins.

In Jack's mind, there wasn't much more of a win than that.

STARGATE ATLANTIS
Pleasure Cruise

Geonn Cannon

THE SHIP moved slowly across the pale blue sky, skimming across clouds until it blocked out the sun. She ignored the grubby fingers pinching the tailfins, the skinny, sun-kissed arm that stretched down from the rocket to her own body lying in the grass. Samantha Carter lay on her back just beyond the willow tree's shadow, head tilted back and one eye squeezed tightly shut as she plotted the vessel's trip across the heavens. She didn't like the toy very much, since it wasn't an accurate representation of Apollo 11, but it was close enough that she could imagine. She had a very good imagination.

She could hear her parents talking with their friend, George, on the porch. They were having a barbecue, but it wasn't the Fourth of July. Sam dropped the rocket and sat up, grass trimmings falling from her hair and clothes as she looked toward the house. She could see her mother and father, their features obscured by smoke rising from the grill. Something was off but she couldn't figure out what. She stared at her mother and wondered why her presence seemed so miraculous and wonderful. She could smell the smoke very strongly, and her head hurt from being in the sun too long.

"Hello, Sam."

She looked up at the lean and lanky figure of George Hammond. He'd served with her father in Vietnam and, according to her mother, had saved his life. He was dressed casually for the barbecue in a bright yellow shirt and shorts, but somehow she knew he would look more familiar in a uniform. She cupped her hand over her eyes as she looked up at him. She didn't remember him being so broad-shouldered or so capable of blotting out the sun. He was like a monolith. And he sounded strange. Older than he should.

She smiled and waved. "Hi."

He crouched and she saw he was still young, his red hair trimmed close to his head in the military style her daddy had. He gestured at the rocket with his chin. "Apollo 11?"

"Sort of. They got a lot of things wrong."

George chuckled. "Well, I'm sure they did the best they could. Maybe one day you'll get to fly the real thing."

Sam smiled. "I hope so! Daddy said they went to the moon right after I was born so the road would be ready."

"You'll get there, Sam. I know you will." He looked up into the sky. "It might take you a long time to get to the moon, but you're going to go so much farther... and do so much more."

His voice had changed again, and when she looked at him it was hard to see his face. She squinted, feeling oddly lightheaded. Something had gone very wrong, but she couldn't remember what it was. There had been alarms, and people counting on her to make the right decision. Engines were... She looked back at the toy rocket and knew she needed to move it. They were in great danger.

"What are you going to do, Sam?" Hammond asked softly.

"Sir?" she said. Her voice sounded different, too. She cleared her throat and leaned back, hoping that stretching out on the grass again would help settle her head.

She started to slip out of her seat, and tightened her grip on the armrests before she could tumble to the floor. Her eyes widened as consciousness flooded back to her. The memory of the strange barbecue and the stranger conversation with General Hammond...

That didn't really happen, did it?

She couldn't remember ever having that conversation with him, but it didn't matter; the autumn backyard was fading fast and she focused on the situation at hand.

She was... what? Where? She was aboard the *George Hammond*, her ship. But where was her crew? The bridge was vacant and smelled of smoke. A quick visual scan didn't show any critical damage, but she remembered their systems had overloaded. Thin tendrils of smoke wafted up from a few stations but she saw no evidence of a spreading fire. The ship was too silent, too completely still in the wake of whatever catastrophe must have happened, so her first thought was that she'd ordered an evacuation. It took her a moment to remember the layout of her seat's controls, pushing back the fog of her bizarre dream. She activated the ship-wide intercom, clearing her throat before she spoke.

"This is Colonel Carter. Anyone who is still aboard, contact the bridge immediately with your situation. I repeat, this is Colonel Carter. All hands, contact the bridge immediately."

She didn't truly expect a response, and she couldn't sit and wait for one. After making sure she wasn't physically injured she stood up and moved to Major Marks' station, stumbling and catching herself on the edge of his monitor as she maneuvered down into the seat.

Power levels were dangerously low, weapons were depleted, and the shields had been completely knocked out. Asgard weapons were... That's right, they were on the way back to Earth to have the Asgard weapons repaired. They were still in the Pegasus galaxy but there was little Atlantis could do even if Sam got a message out. She rested her hands on the controls and closed her eyes.

"Okay. Try to remember," she muttered. "We were on our way back from Atlantis. Marks was talking about…something."

She furrowed her brow and closed her eyes as she tried to remember.

"I'm not saying I expect anything as fancy as what they have on the show," Marks said, "but it would be nice to have the distraction."

Sam fought the urge to smile. "We went to a lot of trouble to stock a library of books and movies to fill these long slogs between galaxies. We don't need a holodeck, Major." They had been through hell the past few months, and it was nice to have a simple, uneventful cruise to wind down. Moments of pure relaxation were rare and to be treasured when they happened to pop up, because for every Goa'uld defeat there was an Ori threat looming in the shadows. But relaxation was one thing, frivolous luxury was another.

"Maybe not *need*," he conceded, "but it would be nice. And the Asgard database probably has the technology to make it happen."

"Even if it does, good luck getting the budget to have it installed."

"Wouldn't that go through General O'Neill?"

Sam raised an eyebrow. "Actually, now that you mention it…"

Captain Kleinman interrupted her thought. "Colonel, we have an unidentified bogie coming up fast on our position."

She turned to face him, any trace of humor fading from her voice. "It's tracking us through hyperspace?" Since defeating the Ori they had yet to encounter another race in either galaxy with the capability to track the Asgard core when the hyperdrive was engaged, but anything was possible.

"Yes, ma'am," Kleinman reported. "At the rate it's coming it will overtake us in approximately three minutes."

If it was gaining on them in hyperspace then outrunning it obviously wasn't an option. The only chance they had was to stand their ground and fight. Sometimes the bully just needed to see his prey stop running to show his true cowardice.

"Take us out of hyperspace. Shields and weapons at the ready." The lights dimmed as they returned to subspace, red emergency lights flashing as Marks checked his instruments. "Major?"

"No matches on the database. Doesn't look like anyone we know, Colonel."

"Sound general quarters. Open a wide frequency." She stood and stepped forward. "This is Colonel Samantha Carter of the United States vessel *George Hammond*. We extend—"

Her spiel was interrupted by a blast from the other ship's

weapons. The lights flickered as Marks reported. "Shields down to…" The awe in his voice was hard to miss. "Down to seventy-three percent, ma'am."

"From one blast?"

"Apparently so."

"Our new friends pack a wallop," Sam muttered. She almost said they'd never encountered anyone with that kind of firepower, but something gnawed at the back of her mind. "Major Marks, evasive maneuver beta. If we can't outrun them, maybe we can make sure we're more trouble than we're worth."

"Aye, ma'am. Executing beta."

Sam had just returned to her seat when the ship was rocked again by two consecutive blasts. The force of it nearly knocked her feet from under her, and she held tight to the chair to keep upright. A station to her left overloaded in a shower of sparks. She took a moment to ensure that no one had been injured before speaking again. "Shields?"

"Forty-one percent, ma'am."

Kleinman said, "The ship's changing position, Colonel. It's targeting our engines."

"Return fire," Sam said. If their opponent was powerful enough to knock their shields out so fast, they wouldn't get anywhere with half-measures. "Give them everything we've got."

"Aye, ma'am." A moment later Kleinman reported. "Ma'am, they're destroying the missiles before any of them could make contact. The alien ship is undamaged. Should we cease fire?"

"Yes," Sam said. The back burner of her brain, the part General O'Neill claimed was always working on three different problems at once, was busy searching for that nagging memory of a past mission where something similar had happened. The *Odyssey*? No, it had been before that. The *Prometheus.* "Captain, do we have a visual of the ship?"

If Kleinman had ever answered, the memory remained lost for the time being. Sam's strange sense of déjà vu lingered as she stared through the viewscreen at the empty space stretching out in front of them. But space wasn't a horizontal plane and whatever had attacked them could still be around. She accessed the sensors and discovered something very large hanging immobile just beyond their visual range, objectively above their position. She recognized the shape of it without having access to her report from the SGC.

Five years earlier she had been part of the mission to retrieve the *Prometheus* from a planet where it had been forced to make an emergency landing. The return journey was slow going, due to mandatory cool-down periods between hyperspace jumps. During one of their stops they were overtaken by a vessel extremely similar to the one currently looming over her. The entire crew had jettisoned in escape pods only to be snatched up and taken prisoner by the unknown aliens. She was overlooked and left behind, unconscious with a head injury, because she was in a shielded portion of the ship. This time her exclusion had to be more deliberate. But why?

"Hello again," she muttered. She opened a channel and spoke at full voice. "This is Colonel Samantha Carter of the Earth vessel *Hammond* requesting a response from the unidentified vessel." She paused, sucking her bottom lip as she scanned the empty air in front of her. "I don't know if you can hear me, or if you understand me, or if this is even getting through. But you obviously stopped just short of destroying us so… Thank you for that. I assume my crew has been transported to your vessel. I'd like to begin negotiations to get them back."

Silence.

"They're not going to answer."

Sam closed her eyes. "Oh, great…"

She turned slowly to see Rodney McKay looking at the front viewscreen as if he could see the alien vessel outside. His face was twisted in an expression of dismay that almost bordered on pain. Last time she'd encountered these beings, her head injury had caused her to hallucinate team members who weren't actually present. This time, though she didn't know what had rendered her unconscious, it seemed the modus operandi was the same.

"Hello, McKay. You're probably right. So I'm going to head down to the 302 bay and see if any of the fighters are operational. They can't get me back to Atlantis, but they'll be better than just sitting here waiting for rescue. At the very least I might get out far enough that someone will find a distress signal. Maybe one of the Traveler's ships will hear it, or—"

"The *Mary Celeste*," McKay said as he trailed along behind her. "The USS *Proteus* in 1941... Uh, the *Nereus* a month later. All ghost ships. Airplanes, sailing ships, all going missing so often we have the Bermuda triangle myth. All this running around in space, all the ships we've thrown out into the cosmos, it was bound to happen. We were bound to have a ghost spaceship eventually. I always figured I would be on board when it happened. And oh, look. Here I am."

"The *Mary Celeste* was found, but her crew was missing." Sam didn't focus on the fact that she was currently the only crewmember whose whereabouts were known. "And the other ships were victims of extenuating circumstances. You said it yourself, the Bermuda triangle is a myth."

McKay said, "Yes, extenuating circumstances. Like a giant ship that just knocked out the most advanced ship in our fleet like it was a Big Wheel? We are completely hooped!"

She grimaced. "Why do you always have to be such a doomsayer?"

"I point out the worst-case scenario. That has value. Especially when everyone is looking to me for some kind of miracle. You don't know the kind of pressure that comes with that expectation."

Sam snorted and rolled her eyes. "You do realize who you're talking to, right? 'Sam will figure it out. Sam blew up a sun. Sam can learn an alien culture's complete language and technology in five minutes and fix things.'"

"Do you realize who *you're* talking to?" McKay said. "I'm not even here right now. This is just… I don't know what this is."

Sam had to admit she was a little confused by that as well. "Last time I thought I was suffering a head injury. I assumed I was just talking to myself, hallucinating the people closest to me so I could work through the situation."

McKay straightened his shoulders and preened a bit. "The people closest to you, eh?"

She glared at him as she accessed the lift to descend to the 302 bay. "But that's obviously not the case this time. The aliens have copied their previous behavior down to the last detail—disabling the ship, taking the crew, leaving me behind. The only question is why."

"Interrogation."

Ronon spoke from her left side. He was staring straight ahead, arms crossed, expression frozen as it tended to be when he was trying to work something through in his head. A quick scan of the lift revealed McKay had vanished. She had a feeling that Ronon had never really warmed to her, but she was still glad to see he was part of whatever was going on in her head. McKay did have his value, but Ronon was a warrior. Sometimes a situation needed a strong arm more than a quick mind.

"You think they took the crew to interrogate them?"

"No. Well… maybe. I think they're interrogating *you*. Maybe everyone else is still on the ship and you were the only one taken. Or you were all taken, and right now you're all seeing the same thing: yourselves, alone on the vessel, trying to figure out how to get home. And whoever took you is watching to see what you do."

Sam smiled. "Teal'c said the same thing last time."

"Did he?" It didn't really sound like a question, just a mere acknowledgment of what she'd said.

Sam thought for a moment about the possibility that he was right, but it didn't strike her as plausible. "No. I don't think that's the case. Last time I came up with the solution to free us from a gas cloud, and they needed me to implement it to free them."

"Gas cloud?"

"Yes. I suggested we take cover inside the cloud hoping the alien ship wouldn't follow us inside. I was wrong. Fortunately, we both ended up trapped inside of it."

Ronon said, "So the cloud is why the aliens didn't destroy your ship last time. You got them out and they felt obligated to you."

"Maybe."

"Makes you wonder what stopped them from taking you all the way out this time."

The elevator arrived at its destination and Sam stepped out of the lift. Directly ahead of her she saw a blonde woman, about her height, wearing the flight suit of a crew member. Even from a distance Sam could see the patch wasn't the *Hammond*'s. She stepped closer and the woman's features came into focus as she began to speak.

"Major Erin Gant, United States Air Force. Currently assigned to the *Prometheus*. This is my record of the events that occurred on January 16, 2004. To the best of my knowledge, sir."

"I'm sure it will be fine, Major," General Hammond said.

Sam remembered Gant's fidgeting as she tried to remember anything from the alien ship that might be helpful. "Colonel Ronson sounded the evacuation, so we got to the escape pods and jettisoned out. Unfortunately the cloud we'd taken refuge in affected them the same way it had *Prometheus*. Our engines died and the alien vessel scanned us. After that… we were back on the bridge. I could tell time had passed but I didn't remember anything that happened in between the two events."

"That's what you said in your initial report. In the time since, have you remembered anything else?"

Gant brought her hand up to her mouth and chewed on her thumbnail. She and the rest of the crew had been the prisoners of an unknown race that had managed to disable the ship with no effort whatsoever. All of them claimed to have no memory of their captivity. Even though they had been returned unharmed, it wasn't difficult to imagine the possibilities. Sam had spent a good portion of the return trip questioning her own sanity, lying in the infirmary and trying to determine if the visitations had been simple figments of her imagination, interference from the aliens, or something else altogether.

She hadn't come up with an answer then but it seemed like she might get a second chance at finding out the truth. She let the memory of Gant's interrogation fade but she held on to the memory of General Hammond a moment longer than everything else. The news of his death had come as a shock to everyone. She hadn't had the opportunity to process the loss before the Wraith showed up and threatened the planet, but these long slogs between Earth and Atlantis gave her plenty of time to think about life without General Hammond.

As if he was cued by her thoughts of him, the image or ghost or whatever it was turned to look at her. "Hello, Sam. You've come a long way from Jacob's backyard, haven't you? Did they get this ship right?"

"Yes, sir," Sam said. "I made sure of it."

Hammond chuckled.

"I wish you could have been here to see it, sir. I made sure it was given an appropriate name: the *George Hammond*."

"I'm honored. Although I'm surprised that you didn't name it after your father."

Sam smiled. "Commanding a ship named after my father? Even with hazard pay I couldn't afford all the therapy that would require. Besides, dad was a soldier in the war against the Goa'uld, just like I was, and he served under your command. We all did." She realized she still didn't understand what was happening, or what these visions really meant, but she'd spent the months since Hammond's death thinking about all the things she hadn't had a chance to say. Now she it felt like she had the opportunity to make up for that error.

"Sir, I didn't request the name because I'd known you for so long, or because of what you meant to me. I requested it because, without you, there would be no *Daedalus*-class warships. There would be no Atlantis, no Stargate program to speak of. You kept it afloat, you kept us safe, and you let us do what needed to be done. When you died, I thought… No, I knew. I knew that you had to remain part of the program going forward, even if it was just in spirit."

"I only gave you room to do what you did best."

"You gave me the confidence to do my best, sir. Now…" She looked around. "I don't know if I'm up to this challenge."

Hammond dropped his head and his shoulders shook with a quick chuckle. When he looked at her again he wore that reassuring smile that had gotten her through so many trials. "Sam, I don't think you've ever seen a challenge you didn't overcome. And if Plan A doesn't work, then you'll have a Plan B waiting." He put a hand on her shoulder. "You'll do fine, Sam. You never do anything else."

"Thank you, sir."

She reluctantly left him and continued on her journey. She couldn't spend any more time trying to remember bits and pieces of the past incident. Even if there was something useful in Major Gant's testimony that she couldn't remember, her current situation took precedence. If there was something to be found in the memory, her subconscious would keep chipping away at it while her body did more practical things. She continued on past the hallucination of Hammond and entered the hangar.

The 302s seemed intact, and she approached the nearest one as McKay entered the hangar behind her. "Why are you wasting your time up here? If the aliens are capable of disabling your entire ship and grabbing the crew, why would they leave you with ships capable of escaping? And, even if they were operational, it's not going to do you any good. The range on these things? They'll never get you all the way back to Atlantis."

"I can't just ignore the possibility of a working ship, Rodney. If they'll fly, I could use one to confront the alien vessel. I could force them to respond to my attempts at communication."

"Oh, brilliant plan, Colonel Kamikaze. Just fly up and slam yourself into the side of a ship the size of Australia. I'm sure that'll teach them a lesson."

"Yes, compared to them I'd be an ant. But a strategically placed ant can ruin a picnic."

McKay crossed his arms over his chest, huffy. "Okay, well, what if you poke them and they just ignore you?"

"Then I find the nearest planet with a Stargate. Or I intercept the Intergalactic Gate Bridge. The station is gone, but I can use the dialer in one of the ships to head home and deliver a report."

"You'd leave your team behind?"

"If it was necessary to gather a big enough force to get them back, absolutely." She climbed onto the side of the ship, opened the cockpit, and settled into the seat to check the instrument panels. Rodney might be a manifestation of her pessimism, but she refused to let herself be discouraged when the engines proved unresponsive. "And if the engines are down, I can try sending a distress signal…"

"But communications are down too, right?" McKay said.

She shook her head and hauled herself out of the cockpit. "Failure is just the elimination of one possibility. And whether this is me sorting through my own mental processes, or an alien attempt to probe my reactions, I'll still get useful answers to whatever questions I ask. I just have to decide if getting the knowledge is worthwhile if I'm potentially sharing it with the interrogator. Checking every option also provides me with information about the enemy."

"Like what?"

"Like now I know they managed to disable the 302s. That's an impressive feat. I'd like to know how it was done."

McKay's expression changed as she climbed down, his features twisting into a mixture of revelation and dread. "Oh.

Oh, no. Maybe they didn't have to do anything to the ship at all. Maybe the 302s are perfectly fine. Maybe the *Hammond* is perfectly fine. If they're making you see me, then who knows what else they can make you see?"

"You're not helping. Follow me if you're coming."

He turned on the ball of his foot to follow as she walked past him.

"If you have to be here, you could be a little more help. You're just going around and around in circles. Last time this happened, SG-1 helped me figure out a solution."

"Actually, they presented conflicting theories that you eventually had to tune out in order to solve the problem."

Sam sighed. "Right. I had to learn to listen to myself. The aliens are putting together a morality play just for me." She turned a corner and stopped in her tracks.

Standing between her and the lift was Lieutenant Samantha Carter. Green, naïve, and so eager to please that she snapped off a salute before she realized the commanding officer in front of her shared her face. Sam blinked at Lieutenant Carter, who slowly dropped her hand.

"Wow."

"This isn't real," Sam said. "So it doesn't mean anything."

"Doesn't it?" McKay said. "This is the little girl who dreamt of visiting the moon, whose only ambition was to fly on a rocket ship to outer space. It was what she worked her entire childhood for, and then… boom. *Challenger*. The carpet was ripped out from underneath her feet. She took a job that would get her as close as she could get to her dream, but it wasn't the same. She worked in an office at the Pentagon. Hardly the life she'd imagined. Look at her! The word Stargate doesn't mean anything to her. Bright-eyed and bushy-tailed, this young Carter. So fresh and full of life. Vital. Supple…"

Sam glared at him. "Getting creepy, McKay."

He cleared his throat. "Right. Sorry. The point is, you never gave up. Even when the fleet was grounded you swore you would get up there someday. And now look at you."

"The Amelia Earhart of the SGC?" She stepped around her past self and continued on.

The corridors of the ship were ominous when empty, dimly-lit, and running on the bare minimum of emergency power. She returned to the bridge and checked to see if the alien ship had done anything. While her attention was on the screen, someone stepped around in front of the station to look out the viewscreen. She didn't have to look up to know who it was; she knew him by his gait and the way he folded his arms as he craned his neck in an attempt to lean out far enough to see the enemy ship.

"Any ideas, Colonel Sheppard?"

"A few. They're acting strangely, don't you think?"

Sam considered the question. "How so?"

"Well, look at your last encounter with them. The *Prometheus* was just sitting there, no engines to speak of, a fraction of their size, and they ran up and started pounding on you with everything they had. They knocked out your shields, they blew up your missiles before they could explode harmlessly against their shield. You didn't stand a chance against them. Then you ran away, and they chased you."

Sam nodded. "Right."

"But they didn't have to chase you this time. There's no cloud that you're both stuck in. So why did they stop? Why are they just sitting here now?"

"You have a point."

"Maybe they want you to surrender."

"They obviously don't," Sam said. "They refused to respond when I opened a channel."

Sheppard shrugged. "Maybe they don't communicate in a way we recognize. Maybe they think you're the one refusing to respond to their messages."

Sam closed her eyes and pressed her thumb against the bridge of her nose. "It doesn't make sense. They're a civilized race."

"What makes you say that?"

"The ship!" Sam said. "Any race that reaches these technological heights has to be doing something right."

Sheppard said, "What about the Wraith? What about the Ori? Just being advanced doesn't mean you're immune from being a jerk."

"But they proved their true nature last time. We made a deal and they followed through on it. They gave back the crew and left without attacking us any further because I helped them out of the cloud. And that proves they're capable of understanding me because they were able to make the deal in the first place."

Sheppard nodded. "Okay. So they're capable of listening to reason."

"But their behavior doesn't fit. They walked up, punched us in the face, and then listened to reason? They chased us into a cloud they must have at least suspected would affect their ship. Why would they be so aggressive and then simply back off?"

"Maybe the aggression had a different purpose. They stopped short of destroying you when they could have done it easily."

None of it added up. She laced her fingers on the back of her neck and stretched.

"I don't know why you're trying to figure this all out by yourself," McKay said.

She stifled a groan of frustration.

"It's a pointless exercise when you have access to my vastly superior brain. Of course, if this is just a projection of your own thought process, then it will be a poor substitute for the real thing…"

Sam sat up and turned to face him. "Can it, McKay!"

He blinked and took a step back. "Wow. That was really angry."

She stood up and faced him. "Yes, it was. I've been nice; I've tried to be a reasonable person when it comes to you —"

"You once told me to go suck a lemon."

"But this time, this one time, I don't have to worry about

hurting your feelings. You. Are not. Smarter than me. And I'm not smarter than you. It's ridiculous to turn intellect into a competition. I'm wiser because I've spent more time at the SGC, because I've failed more and learned from those failures. You're better at calculating the potential fallout and finding a way around it, but I'm more creative when it comes to solving problems. We're not at odds, Rodney, we complement each other. When you say you're smarter than me, what you're really saying is that you're better than me. And when gender is the only real difference —"

"Just because my reproductive organs are on the inside..."

Sam recoiled from the echo of her own words, glancing to the left in time to see a ghostly image of Captain Samantha Carter fading from view. She looked at McKay, who appeared to be bracing for further attack. She squared her shoulders and shook her head.

"No. I don't have that chip on my shoulder anymore. I don't have to prove my place here to anyone, least of all you." She met McKay's eye. "You're threatened by me, so you posture and preen. We're better than that. You've earned your place and I've earned mine. I'm not going to let you distract me from the task at hand."

She turned back to the monitor and saw Sheppard watching her.

"You and I don't have any issues," she said, "so I don't know what you want from me."

"Who said you were supposed to work out your issues?"

She stepped down off the platform and faced Sheppard. "Something is going on here, and it's not internal. It's not a problem with me physically because I feel fine."

"So why is this exactly like it was last time?"

Realization dawned. "It's not. It's not like last time, because last time... there was a little girl. She helped me." Sam had a vague recollection of the girl's name, but it slipped away from her when she tried to grasp it. "She's the one who gave me the idea for the bubble that got us out of the cloud."

Sheppard looked around the bridge as if he expected a child to appear. "Doesn't look like she's going to be offering you help this time around."

"No," Sam said. "I'm in a different place now. They wouldn't send a child."

"And you know this because…?"

She thought for a moment. "The alien ship never intended to destroy us. If they had, they would have just blown the *Hammond* out of the sky once our shields were down."

"Maybe they wanted the crew," Sheppard suggested.

"They have the crew. They don't need to keep the ship intact for parts. What possible reason could they have for sitting there staring at us?"

McKay spoke up again. "Testing us. Seeing how you react, what you try to use to escape. Figuring out our technology."

"Oh, please. They knocked us down without breaking a sweat. We don't have anything they could want. So it's not about technology." She realized what he had just said. "You're right. They're seeing how I react."

"You just said—"

She shushed him and he fell silent, proving to her that he was indeed a hallucination. She felt like she was onto something but she needed a few seconds to think it through. Normally she did it silently but talking out loud had helped last time. She looked at McKay and used him as a proxy for the aliens.

"You don't care about our technology. You care about *us*. You took away our ability to run, to defend ourselves, and to fight back. You stripped us of everything that got us here, and then you stepped back to see what we would do. This is a test, isn't it?"

"You would be surprised how many people just sit down and give up."

Sam turned to see Colonel Sheppard standing in front of the viewscreen. His posture was more solid this time, his cadence business-like and soothing. Though he still looked like the man she knew, he was just a mask somebody else was wearing. McKay had disappeared and she had a feeling the ruse had run its course.

"So you are the same race from the encounter five years ago."

"We are. It's peculiar for us to encounter the same person twice in rapid succession like this, particularly at such an extreme range. You're very far from home, Samantha Carter."

Sam nodded. "So are you really here? What is this? A hallucination? A projection?"

"It really doesn't matter one way or another, does it?"

"I suppose not. It would put my mind at ease, though."

He smiled. "I'm not really here. We're communicating through your mind. My behaviors, my conversational tics, are based on your perceptions and memories of people. Your mental construction of John Sheppard is very clear. He seems to be the closest you know to an equal."

Sam chuckled. "Oh, if only Rodney could have heard you say that."

"He is your intellectual equal, but John Sheppard has intelligence and a military background."

"I suppose you're right." She'd never thought about it that way because he didn't flaunt his intelligence like McKay did, but maybe that was why she liked him so much. She'd had other soldiers under her command but she'd never worked with anyone as long or as closely as she had with Sheppard. Maybe their relationship had been so easy because they were kindred spirits. She wished she'd spent more time with him when she was assigned to Atlantis. "Okay. At least that answers one of my questions. Who are you?"

"That's definitely not important."

"You're not even going to tell me your name?" He only smiled. Sam considered having a silent standoff with him to see which of them broke first, but she had a feeling he had infinite patience. "Okay, then. Can you at least tell me why? You must have recognized the technology when you scanned us. Whatever test you're running, you must have known we already passed it."

The thing that wasn't Sheppard nodded. "You did pass. But this ship is far more advanced than the one we found you aboard last time. You've been outfitted with technology acquired from the Asgard, a once-great race now extinct. Many of us were curious about beings who had come so far, so fast."

"And leaving me behind again was just luck of the draw?"

"Yes and no. We did not single you out because of who you are. But you were left behind because in both instances you were the most experienced and most intelligent member of the crew. You were the most likely candidate to pass our test."

Sam tried not to scoff. "I'm flattered. I guess."

"The Tau'ri have been attracting our interest a great deal over the past few years. After centuries of quiet, suddenly everything is thrown into turmoil. The Goa'uld are remnants of the past, the Ori have come and gone, and even the Wraith are in upheaval. When you first appeared in our awareness we believed you were children playing with forces far beyond your ken. We anticipated horrific ramifications spreading out like ripples on a pond. But you surprised us. That is what prompted our first interaction. We wanted a closer look at you."

"I'm glad we passed muster."

He inclined his head slightly. "Some of us were still skeptical, so we decided we would check up on you again. The pessimistic among us were worried when we saw how reliant you were upon Alteran and Asgard technology. In the past, we would have labeled the Tau'ri scavengers, like the Goa'uld, and restricted your access to such wonders."

Sam raised an eyebrow. "Restricted us? What, you're the parents of the galaxy?"

"We ensure those who steal power can't use it against those who are less advanced."

"Excellent job stopping the Goa'uld; almost everything they used was taken from the Ancients. Where were you guys then?"

A shadow passed over Sheppard's face. "We were unable to

stop the Goa'uld's initial rise to power; problems in our own galaxy preoccupied us. But we saw what devastation they caused and vowed to do everything we could to ensure that it never happened again. Now we pay close attention when small civilizations begin reaching out into the galaxy."

"Races like humans."

He nodded. "You were, and are, a very young race. You tear your planet apart with wars and send your soldiers out into the galaxy with guns and explosives and weapons of mass destruction."

Sam said, "We don't go looking for fights, but we want to be prepared for the ones we find. You didn't put those weapons on your ship for the aesthetics."

"True. Possession of weapons doesn't inherently make one evil. That's why we strip them away, disable your ships, and watch to see how you react."

"Last time you got yourselves stuck in a cloud. Was that part of the test?"

Not-Sheppard laughed. "Actually not. Your ship fled and we were simply trying to close the distance so we could beam away your people. We weren't expecting them to launch escape pods, and we very nearly didn't take the risk to enter the cloud after you. For all the time we've been doing this, your race was the first to even come close to escaping."

"I suppose that's a point of pride."

"It was definitely meant as a compliment. We liked you on our first encounter, Samantha. You were interesting to us. Soldiers blending with scientists, brains and brawn protecting one another — there was a balance to the extremes that we found fascinating. And you in particular, being a scholar and a soldier at the same time, were an unusual combination. Many of us were interested to see which would take precedence, your scientific mind or your urge to fight. You chose brains over brawn."

Sam shrugged. "I try to make that my default. It's not always possible."

"Unfortunate, but you are correct. The true measure of a species is how they use the weapons they do possess. The Tau'ri have had a peculiar history with their large-scale weapons."

"Even on our own planet," Sam said. "What would have happened if we failed?"

"You saw what our ships are capable of."

"And you're the one calling other races brutal."

Not-Sheppard gave a non-committal shrug. "We consider ourselves the protectors of those who can't stand up for themselves. There are powerful races in the galaxy who could abuse that power to obliterate smaller worlds and take them over, just like the Goa'uld did."

"And who makes sure you're not abusing the power?"

He acknowledged her point with a nod. "We have authorities we answer to, just like everyone else. If we overstep our bounds I'm sure we'd hear about it from our allies among the great races."

"From the Nox?"

He smiled. "There have always been powerful, advanced races in the galaxy. Some of them are very old, like the Alterans, the Nox, the Asgard, or the Furlings. When they formed their alliance, they had just scratched the surface of what's out here. After everything you've encountered, both here and in Pegasus, do you really believe there have only been four great races?"

"I suppose you have a point."

"We keep our own counsel, but the races I mentioned are aware of us. They'd let us know if we overstepped."

Sam looked out at the stars. "So what happens to those you deem unworthy?"

"We make sure they're not in a position to hurt anybody else. Usually that requires restricting them to their own planets or their own systems. We cripple their interstellar capabilities to ensure they don't bother the other kids in the neighborhood."

Sam smiled at the comparison. "You really are channeling Sheppard, aren't you?"

He smiled enigmatically, and Sam thought back over everything he'd said.

"It's more than testing our worthiness, isn't it? You're looking for something else."

He nodded. "We look at the people with their fingers on the trigger. Hope, compassion, trust, love: it's critical that all of these things exist in someone who is entrusted with enough power to act like a god."

Sam looked toward the back of the Hammond's bridge and saw it suddenly crowded with people: her father, General O'Neill, Daniel, Teal'c, Janet, Cassandra, McKay, Teyla, Ronon, Keller. They were all people to whom she had entrusted her life and whose lives had been saved by her in return. She loved them all in varying degrees and seeing them all together, even as a hallucination, was almost overwhelming.

"You've lived quite a life, Samantha Carter."

His voice had changed and, when she looked, she saw that he had become George Hammond again. The change surprised her. "You should warn someone before you do that."

He chuckled and looked down. It would be so easy to forget everything that had just happened and pretend he was really there. She again remembered hearing the news from Jack, the punch-in-the-gut feeling that everything had suddenly changed. Losing Hammond had been like losing a parent; he'd guided them through the rough waters of the first years at the SGC, and she had no doubt history would have been much different without his steady hand at the tiller.

He stepped closer to the command chair. "Do you doubt you belong here, Sam? That you've earned the right to sit in this chair and make the hard decisions?"

"No, sir. I'm just not sure I always know the right thing to do. Or say."

"I'll tell you a secret, Sam. Me, General O'Neill, even your father — on a good day, we gave our orders with both fingers crossed and saying a prayer under our breath. I seem to remember you saving the world a few times in the same position. Wild-eyed, crazy ideas with only a small chance of working."

Sam nodded. "I know, sir. But you have no idea how comforting it was to know that you were there as a safety net if things went wrong. And now you're gone, I'm not sure I can do this without you. Who am I supposed to turn to when I need help? When I'm feeling unsure of myself? We have the Icarus Base now, and I got to deliver some of the personnel once it was operational. But they're babies. Children."

Hammond smiled. "How do you think I felt the first time I sent you through the Stargate? You were still the little girl playing with plastic rockets as far as I was concerned. If you think I had it all together back then, when we first started, you're sorely mistaken. It was meant to be a cushy assignment to ride to my retirement and it turned into one of the most important posts in the galaxy. There were days I didn't want to get out of bed."

"Right," Sam said. "But that's not true. You're just saying what I hope is true."

"You knew George Hammond. I'm drawing from your memories of the man. Do you doubt he was conflicted?"

"No. He was. Any good man in his position would be."

"And any good person in your position would be wondering the same thing you are."

"Is that the point of this whole exercise? Looking for hubris and knocking people down a few pegs if they aren't humble enough?"

Hammond shrugged and held his hands out. "The Goa'uld acquired power wherever they found it. They used that power to position themselves as gods. We couldn't stop them from doing that, and billions of people paid the price. The universe was forever changed in the wake of their rise to power. So, when we find races like yours, who are on the threshold of becoming great, we step in and test them."

"What is the test? Shut everything down and watch me run

around like a chicken with my head cut off for a few hours?"

"You sought answers. You looked for ways to not only save yourself, but to save those who had been taken. And, through it all, you sought a peaceful resolution. You've passed the test."

"And if I hadn't? You would be judge, jury, and —"

He stopped her. "We don't execute anyone. If you hadn't discovered a way out of the cloud we would have beamed you from the ship and taken you to a safe planet nearby."

"And then quarantined us on Earth. For our own good."

"For your own good, and for the good of the universe at large. We took away your technology to see if you had earned the right to use it. Strip the Goa'uld of their technology and they become harmless worms with teeth. They're nothing more than bullies who happened to find a bigger stick than the rest of the galaxy. We wanted to make sure the Tau'ri weren't setting themselves up to be equally harmful to their neighbors."

"We're using what we find to help people."

"But in time, even the best of intentions can lead to unforeseen consequences. The most stalwart hero is at risk of corruption."

"Right." Sam sighed. "I think Daniel got this lesson once from a little boy."

"Our methods might not make us popular, but we seek peace for everyone."

"Best intentions?"

He chuckled and nodded. "Point taken. But there are others who would step in if we abused our power. Trust me; there is more to this universe than you've ever dreamed, Samantha Carter. Your race has only just begun to scratch the surface."

Sam nodded slowly. "I think I understand. I'm not sure I like it, but I understand."

"The Tau'ri are doing the best they can to do good things. You might occasionally misstep, you may cause some damage in the process, but no river runs without ripples. Your race is one of the most promising we've ever encountered."

"An Asgard once told Jack O'Neill the same thing. Turns out he was right." She stood up. "The Alliance of the Four Great Races has been pretty much wiped out, but the Nox are still around. And if you really aren't the Furlings…" She gave him an opening to confirm or deny, but he only returned her stare blankly. "Anyway, it might be presumptuous of me, but if you ever get tired of flying under the radar, you'd obviously fit in pretty well with the rest of us. We'd love to have you on our side."

"If only to keep an eye on us, and our technology?"

Sam smiled and shrugged. "Checks and balances, right?"

He chuckled and held out his hand to her. "Indeed, Colonel Carter."

She took his hand, squeezed, and felt a surge of emotion. Her brain knew that it wasn't George Hammond, but her heart was a different story. "I never got to say goodbye to him. Would you mind…?"

"Of course not."

Sam nodded and stepped forward to hug him. "Goodbye, sir. Thank you."

"You're more than welcome, Sam. You made me proud."

Sam closed her eyes against the influx of tears, squeezing him once more before she let him go. She wiped at her cheeks before she looked at him again. He had become Sheppard once more.

"I thought this might be easier."

"Thank you. So do you think our races will encounter each other again one day?"

"Hard to say. In a few short years, the Tau'ri have gone from an isolated geocentric race to intergalactic travelers. You first walked on your own moon less than a century ago. Now you have ships that span unimaginable distances in the blink of an eye, you have stewardship of one of the most advanced outposts in the galaxy… Who knows what distances you'll reach in the future?"

Sam nodded. "Okay. Well, just in case, the next time you

find a ship that looks like ours, scan it first to make sure I'm not aboard before you do your whole song and dance."

Sheppard laughed. "That is far from unreasonable, Colonel Carter. We will do you that kindness."

"Thank you." She cocked her head. "I don't suppose you could also fix the damage you caused so we can get home...?"

He smiled and disappeared in a blinding flash. Sam lifted a hand to block her eyes and, when she dropped it, she saw the bridge was once again populated by her crew. Major Marks was standing in the spot the alien had just occupied, and he frowned as he looked around in confusion. Finally his gaze settled on her.

"Ma'am? What... exactly... just happened?"

"It's a long story, Major. One I look forward to briefing you on once we're underway again. What's our status?"

He returned to his station and sat down, gazing at the screen as he entered commands. After a moment he leaned back in confusion. "Engines are within the acceptable range. We can get underway immediately."

"Captain Kleinman, is the other ship still hanging around?"

"It's leaving just as quickly as it arrived, ma'am. It'll be out of sensor range in seconds."

"Good. Wait until they're completely gone and then resume course back to Earth. We'll discuss our little pit stop on the way. No holodeck required."

Despite his confusion, Marks gave a quick smile at the reference. Sam looked toward him, then past him. Over his shoulder, she saw General Hammond standing in the corridor watching her. She smiled at him and dipped her chin, and he lifted his hand to salute her.

"Let me know when you make it to the moon, Colonel," her father's friend said before he left. "I'll be sure to look up and give you a wave."

"Yes, sir," Sam said, holding her imperfect rocket to her chest with one hand, her mother's skirt with the other.

Kleinman broke her reverie. "They're gone, ma'am."

"Excellent. Take us home, Major."

When she looked again, Hammond was no longer visible in the corridor. She wasn't flustered by his absence; she knew he was still there somewhere. She settled back against the seat of command that had once so intimidated her and waited for the push of acceleration that would return them to their long journey home.

STARGATE SG-1
Off Balance

Sally Malcolm

COMING out of the bend, he opened the throttle and smiled as the bike leapt forward, eating up the empty road. Adrenaline kicked, the needle nosed over ninety, and the thrill of all that raw power brought him alive for a precious few seconds.

Cliffs soared high on his right, sunset casting the rock in shades of burnt orange, turning the landscape alien, other-worldly. And he should know.

He felt a spike of loss — still keen after nine years — and accelerated harder, just to blast the feeling away. He liked speed, he'd always liked speed. His wife had once told him, with a note of fond exasperation, that he was born to be a fly-boy. The memory still made him smile, though it was long ago now, part of his lost life.

Up ahead, he could see a line of mountains — the Collegiate Peaks — and the glitter of Buena Vista's lights scattered through the evening shadows. He'd almost topped ninety-five, and was just throttling back, when he heard the siren wail behind him.

Crap.

He slowed, glanced in the mirror and saw the flashing lights of the patrol car pulling him over. Obeying orders was in his blood and, besides, he knew the drill; this wasn't the first time he'd encountered Colorado's finest. Pulling onto the shoulder, he killed the engine and tugged off his helmet. He'd never been good at feigning contrition, but he did his best as the officer climbed out of his car. Recent experience had taught him that cops didn't like kids with smart mouths.

Tall, lanky, maybe early thirties, the police officer walked with a youthful swagger—the kind of bravado born of a uniform, a rank, and a gun at your side. "You know why I stopped you, son?" the cop said.

"Yes sir." He hated being called 'son' by kids almost half his age.

"I'm gonna need to see your driver's license."

He handed it over and the officer studied it for a moment, then peered at him over the tops of his sunglasses. "Jonathan O'Neill."

"Yes sir."

"You go by Jack?"

"Used to," he said. "Not anymore."

The officer didn't comment, eyes hidden again behind his dark glasses. "Is this your bike, son?"

"Yes sir."

"BMW R1200GS? That's a lotta machine for a kid your age."

He gave a little shrug. "I'm older than I look."

"Says here you're twenty-four. And that's an expensive bike."

"It was a gift," he said, "from my uncle. Uncle Samuel."

And, all things considered, that wasn't exactly a lie. He had to do something with the guilt money that dutifully rolled in each month from the Air Force.

As usually happened, the police officer walked away a few steps and spoke into his radio, probably calling through a check to make sure the bike wasn't stolen and that 'Jonathan O'Neill' wasn't wanted for grand theft auto across all fifty states. Everything came back clean, of course, and in the end he only had to endure a lecture on responsibility from a guy who had no idea what responsibility meant.

It was dusk by the time he was allowed to go, so he turned around and headed back toward Salida. He was a little surprised that the police car followed him all the way into town, only moving on after he'd pulled into the parking lot outside Bosco's Tavern. He guessed the cop didn't have much else to do, and resisted the urge to wave him goodbye. Low-profile was the watchword of his so-called life these days, and sassing the police wouldn't help keep him out of trouble.

Bosco's was dimly lit with plenty of corners to hide in. Jack knew it well; he often came here when he was out riding and he liked its shadows. They made it easy to hide. The food was good too, and he ordered a steak and a beer and ate slowly, trying not to think about much of anything. It was an art he'd perfected during his years in exile. Don't think about what's happening out there in the big wide galaxy, because there's nothing you can do about it anymore. Don't think about whether the people you care about are alive or dead, because you'll probably never know. Don't think about your family, your ex-wife, your lost son — all of them belong to someone else. Don't think about any of it, just live in the moment.

Behind him, he heard a swell of voices — an argument brewing, then fading away. He glanced over his shoulder and saw a woman and a man at the pool table, her with hands on hips and him drunk and unpleasant. Ignoring them, Jack turned back to his meal and took a long swallow of cold beer. It helped that he could buy himself a drink now, even if he was still carded a lot of the time. He'd always looked young for his age, ironically.

But at least the face he saw in the mirror these days was starting to look familiar again. He remembered this face, remembered being this guy. There were fewer scars this time around, but his life since leaving the SGC had been a lot less interesting. The last time he'd been twenty-four, he'd already been a serving officer, a pilot. He'd seen combat. This time? Well, it turned out that after you'd spent seven years on the galactic frontline it was difficult to feel like much else in the world really mattered.

The argument behind him grew louder, but he didn't turn back around despite his instinct to step in. He'd learned to control that impulse too, over the last few years. Yet the rise and fall of arguing voices threaded their way through the music, a baseline of unease that made him edgy. Perhaps that's why he was on alert when the bar door opened and two men in dark suits entered. He clocked them immediately, watching as they took seats at the bar, ordered drinks, and glanced around the room with feigned indifference. He didn't recognize their faces, but they had military intelligence stamped all over them. A prickle of tension ran along the back of his neck, half disquiet and half excitement. Were they here for him, after all this time? Was he in danger? Was he needed?

"Son of a bitch!" The shout came from behind him, rolled up in a huge crash and a woman's scream.

Jack was on his feet in an instant — just in time to see a man go flying across the pool table, and another leap over it after him, a pool cue clutched like a club. A bottle broke and there was blood. Jack couldn't stop himself.

"Hey!" he yelled, running over. No one paid any attention, the woman was still screaming and the man with the cue in his hand was hammering at the other guy who lay curled in a ball on the floor.

"That's my goddamn wife, you sonofa—"

"Hey!" Jack grabbed the attacker's arm, twisted it behind him until he dropped the cue with a yell, and then turned him fast and shoved him face down onto the pool table. He held him there. "Cool it," he ordered.

The attacker was drunk and obstreperous. "What the—?"

Jack jerked his arm higher, making him grunt in pain. "I said cool it, buddy."

The other man staggered to his feet. There was a gash on his head, blood dripping down his face and into his eyes. He looked dizzy, like he was about to faint or throw up.

"Sit down," Jack barked at him. "You," he said to the woman, "help him."

She stared at him through clumpy black lashes and a fall of hair too blonde for her middle-aged skin. "Look, kid—"

"Do it," he demanded, like she was a new recruit. "Now."

She blinked, but few people could ignore orders given in that tone of voice. He'd spent years perfecting the ideal balance of threat, demand, and expectation. It worked every time, and this was no exception. She helped the guy sit down, watching Jack as if she weren't sure what to make of him.

Then there were staff everywhere and the manager was threatening to call the cops. Jack realized he still had the guy pinned to the pool table and let go, aware of too many curious eyes on him. Heading back to his table, he grabbed his jacket and left before the manager could rope him into talking to the police.

He was halfway across the parking lot when he noticed the car. A black sedan lurked at the far side of the lot, as out of place as the two suits had been in the bar. His blood was still up from the fight, senses heightened, and he knew there was something wrong here. Instinct urged him to run, to grab a weapon and prepare for an ambush. But he had no weapon, so he just kept walking toward his bike, hairs rising on the back of his neck. He'd barely taken half a dozen steps when someone behind him spoke.

"Colonel O'Neill."

He stopped dead. Keeping it nonchalant, Jack turned around. "You got the wrong guy," he said to the suit standing behind him.

"I don't think so, sir." The man took a step forward. Jack recognized him from earlier, in the bar. "Apologies for approaching you like this, Colonel, but we need your help."

Jack glanced around, but the parking lot was empty. "And who's 'we', exactly?"

"The Pentagon, sir. Homeworld Security."

He raised an eyebrow. "Home*world* Security? Never heard of them."

"A lot's changed since you left the program, sir." The suit gestured toward the car. "Please, we don't have long to fill you in."

He glanced over at the sedan, all dark windows and bullet-proof glass. His bike was about twenty yards behind him. He could make it in a couple of seconds, could probably outrun the car. "You know," he said, "my mom always told me not to get into cars with strangers."

The suit nodded and reached into his breast pocket. Jack swallowed and managed not to reach for a weapon that wasn't there. "Major Kevin Hartkans, sir." The man pulled out his military ID and held it up. "Pentagon."

It looked real, but you could forge anything these days. Jack licked his lips, thinking it through. This moment — the recall to active duty — was something he'd longed for ever since he'd left the SGC. And yet… "Where's General Hammond?"

Hartkans's face tightened. "Sir, I regret to inform you that General Hammond passed away two years ago."

It knocked the air right out of him. All he could manage to say was, "How?"

"A heart attack, sir."

He felt a swift, hot flare of anger. George Hammond was gone — had been gone for two years — and Jack hadn't even *known*? They hadn't even let him pay his last respects.

Hartkans glanced again at the car. "Colonel, I'm sorry, but we don't have much time. If you could come with me, I can brief you fully on the situation on our way."

But he wasn't going anywhere, not yet. Not until he knew. "My team," he said in a voice steadier than he felt. "SG-1?"

With a shake of his head, Hartkans lowered his voice and took a step closer. "That's why I'm here, sir."

His stomach plummeted into his boots. "Tell me."

In the dark of the parking lot, Hartkans's face was all shadows. "They're in trouble, Colonel. And they need your help."

"Yup," Daniel said, peering through his binoculars, "we're in trouble."

Teal'c shifted where he crouched next to Daniel. "There appear to be many Oranians converging on this site."

"Yeah, like I said: we're in trouble."

"Well, perhaps they're not here looking for the same thing we are?" Vala suggested. "I mean look at this place — sunshine, ocean. Wonderful views."

Daniel cast a look over his shoulder. "You think they're tourists?"

"I'm saying they might be."

"With guns?"

She shrugged. "It's a dangerous galaxy, Daniel."

Trying not to roll his eyes, he turned back to the road below. There were twenty Oranians, maybe more, in a tight-packed group, heavily armed, with a few outriders serving as scouts. And they were heading directly for the Ancient outpost.

"Looks to me," Mitchell said, "like they know exactly what they're after."

"We cannot permit them to retrieve the device," Teal'c said. "If it were to fall into the hands of the Lucian Alliance…"

No one needed to hear the end of that sentence. The Alliance might have been weakened after their failed attack on Earth, but no one doubted their commitment to removing the Tau'ri threat from the galaxy. And this device might be able to do exactly that.

"So," Mitchell said, "I guess we find the thing before they do."

"Oh good," said Vala, smiling up at the Ancient outpost towering above them. "I do love a treasure hunt."

The empty warehouse, on the outskirts of Colorado Springs, looked nothing like the Pentagon. Jack eyed it suspiciously through the tinted glass of the sedan as it rolled to a stop in the deserted parking lot of the industrial park.

"Don't worry, Colonel," Hartkans said. "This isn't our base of operations."

"Okay," he said, reserving judgment. The driver got out, came around, and opened the door for him with a crisp salute. Jack couldn't deny that it felt good to be accorded the respect of rank again; he hadn't realized how much he'd missed it.

He nodded to the airman as he climbed out, tugged down at the hem of his shirt and wished he had a uniform. "So," he said to Hartkans, "now what?"

The major indicated a small door, light seeping out from around its edges. "This way, sir."

Inside, there were a few boxes, and some communications equipment, and a couple of airmen studying computer screens. They jumped to their feet when Jack approached, coming to attention. "Sir," one of them said to Hartkans. "*Avenger* reports ready."

"Thank you, Phillips." Hartkans turned to Jack. "Stand by for transport, sir."

"Transport? Where are we — ?"

The fall of Goa'uld transport rings cut off the question and in a flare of white light he was somewhere else. Dropping into a defensive crouch, he had to blink several times to make sense of what he saw. He was on a Goa'uld ship, but the people standing looking at him were no Jaffa. They were human, most dressed in the mishmash of leather and sackcloth he associated with off-world populations. Some, though, were in uniform — USAF uniform — and one of them stepped forward.

"Colonel O'Neill," he said. "Relax, you're among friends."

Straightening, but not lowering his guard, Jack took in the stars on the man's shoulder. "General… ?"

"Turner. We haven't met." He gave a thin smile. "That is, I've only met *General* O'Neill."

"You're kidding," Jack said, surprised. "He took a desk job?"

Turner spread his hands, declining to comment. "Let's find you a uniform," he said. "We have a lot to do."

"Yeah, about that," Jack said, glancing around and trying to get a feel for what the hell was going on. "I can't help noticing we're on a Goa'uld mothership."

The general smiled again. "*Former* Goa'uld mothership," he said, gesturing for Jack to walk with him as Hartkans led the way through the corridors of the ha'tak. "We got hold of a number of them after the fall of the System Lords."

"Excuse me?" Jack almost missed a step. "It sounded like you said 'the fall of the System Lords'."

"Yes, Colonel, that's exactly what I said."

"As in… all of them?"

Turner smiled again. "Every last one — even Ba'al, in the end."

"Okay," he said, blindsided. They'd won the war and no one had told him. No one had told him Ba'al was dead. "I guess I didn't get the memo."

"In here, Colonel." Hartkans stopped in front of an open door, through which Jack could see a neatly folded uniform sitting on top of a narrow cot. "These are your quarters, sir."

Jack didn't enter. "Nine years," he said to Turner. "I've been out in the cold for nine years. No one told me George Hammond died. No one told me we won the war against the Goa'uld. No one told me that Ba'al —" He bit that off, uncomfortable with the way it made his voice tighten. There was an awkward silence. Turner clearly didn't know what to say, and Jack guessed this wasn't really his fault. He threw him a bone. "All these years, and nothing — why should I help you now?"

It was Hartkans who answered. "Because you're Colonel Jack O'Neill, sir, and your team needs you."

He turned back to the doorway, to the uniform that lay beyond. He could see the patch on the jacket sleeve: SG-1. "What about the other guy?" he said. "It's his team, not mine."

"General O'Neill left the SGC a number of years ago," Hartkans said. "He's now head of Homeworld Security."

Jack almost laughed. "Well that's ridiculous. I'd never —"

"Colonel," Turner snapped, "put the uniform on and consider yourself recalled to active duty." He looked at Hartkans. "Bring him to the briefing as soon as he's ready."

With that, he stalked away leaving Jack hovering on the threshold. This was what he'd longed for: a recall to active duty, to the life that had been taken from him. And yet. And yet…

"Sir?" Hartkans said. "We don't have much time."

And I don't have much choice. There was no way he would pass up this chance.

At first glance the Ancient outpost looked like a ruin, weathered and crumbling where it perched like a gothic dream on the cliff edge. Its melancholy air appealed to the romantic in Daniel, but, as usual, he didn't have time to relish it or to absorb the architectural wonders on display. The way Ancient structures seemed to defy physics was something he'd often considered, in passing, but had never had time to really pursue. Perhaps one day, when they were all too old to do this anymore, he'd sit down with Sam and figure out exactly how they whisked up the confections of spires and turrets that marked so much of their architecture.

The thought made him smile — a smile that was nudged off his face by Vala elbowing him in the ribs. "Wake up," she said. "We're here."

'Here' was the entrance they'd discovered on their first recon of the planet: a doorway that led down into the preserved lower half of the structure. Carved — again, he'd have to ask Sam how they'd done it — into the solid stone of the cliff, the rooms below were shielded from the elements and remained intact. And it was somewhere in this labyrinth of tunnels and stairways that the device they were searching for lay hidden. At least, that's what Vala's map, and the scan run by the *Daedalus*, told them.

Cam pulled off his sunglasses and peered into the darkness. "We'll need a flashlight," he said.

Daniel smiled at the understatement. "You know," he said, as he reached into his vest for his headlamp, "even if the Oranians do find the device, they won't be able to use it. And, most likely, neither will the Lucian Alliance."

"All they need is someone with the ATA gene," Cam said. "And they're not so hard to find these days."

"Maybe." Daniel switched on his lamp, turning his head so

as not to blind the others. "But for a device capable of exterminating an entire species? The Ancients were careful. I'd be surprised if a weakly or artificially expressed ATA gene would be enough to activate it. And there aren't so many Ancients in the Milky Way these days."

"Either way," Cam said, "I'd rather blow the thing up. Just in case."

Daniel didn't argue with that. Ancient or not, some things didn't deserve preservation.

"I'll take point." Cam switched on his weapon's tactical flashlight, sweeping it across the staircase leading down into the dark. "Vala, show me the map."

"Right here," she said, with the childlike enthusiasm Daniel somehow found both captivating and infuriating. He wanted to tell her that this wasn't a game, it wasn't a treasure hunt... but of course she knew that as well as any of them. This was just her way of dealing. He'd found Jack's irreverence in the face of certain doom equally exasperating.

"Okay," Cam said, looking up from the map. "Vala, stick with me. Teal'c—watch our six. I don't want those Oranians creeping up on us." He glanced at Daniel. "Let's go."

Like everything on the ship, the briefing room was a kaleidoscopic mix of different people, technologies and cultures. A table that might have been lifted from a Pentagon meeting room dominated the space, at odds with the gaudy Goa'uld décor, and around it sat a group of hard-faced people much like those he'd passed in the corridors on the way from his quarters.

When Jack arrived, Turner was in close conversation with another man, tall and lanky. He wasn't in uniform, but his clothes looked like they came from Earth and not the Leather Emporium that seemed to outfit the rest of the galaxy. They turned when Jack and Hartkans entered, and Jack recognized the stranger immediately as the cop who'd pulled him over that night.

"Small world," Jack said.

He got an apologetic smile in response. "Sorry, Colonel, but we needed visual confirmation that you were who we thought you were."

"Take a seat, Jack," Turner said, cutting through the small talk.

He did, keeping a wary eye on the disreputable-looking people opposite. None of them appeared friendly.

"You're the Asgard clone?" a woman said abruptly. She was strongly built, with hard eyes and hair pulled back from an angular face.

"Among other things," Jack said. "And you are…?"

"Balen Tark. This is my ship." She gave him a brazen, appreciative look. "What do you call yourself?"

He hesitated over his first name, like he often did, and settled on, "O'Neill. You can call me O'Neill."

She tossed him a smile, full of teeth. "And what do you want to call me?"

It felt like a loaded question and he had no idea how to respond. Luckily, Turner interrupted.

"Let's get this started," he said, and gestured toward Jack. "As you can see, we've located the —" He cut himself off. "That is, Colonel O'Neill has agreed to help us." He turned to the fake cop. "Devon, give us the rundown, please."

Devon, it turned out, was the Daniel Jackson of the outfit — complete with PowerPoint presentation. "Colonel," he said, addressing Jack directly, "what you probably don't know about yourself is that you possess what we call the Ancient Technology Activation gene, or the ATA gene."

"Catchy name."

Devon smiled, but didn't miss a beat. "The gene — which is very strongly expressed in you — allows you to activate a number of technologies left behind by the Ancients. Now, we've developed a retrovirus that can activate —"

"Devon?" Turner interrupted. "Cut to the chase, will you?"

Devon cleared his throat, frowned, and said, "Yes sir. We've recently discovered an Ancient device that's capable of exterminating an entire species. However, it's clear that the Ancients didn't want this to fall into general use. We think, perhaps, that it was an attempt to find a weapon to combat the Wraith."

"The what?" Jack said.

Turner waved the question away. "Not pertinent to this mission, Colonel."

"The point is," Devon continued, "that we believe only someone with a very strong, naturally expressed ATA gene can make the device work. And we think that's you, Colonel."

"And why would I want to activate a device that can exterminate anything?" he said. "Except maybe mosquitoes. We're not talking about mosquitoes, are we?"

Turner leaned forward, hands braced on the table; he wasn't blessed with a great sense of humor, Jack decided. "You want to activate it, Colonel," he said, "because it's the only way to save your team."

Jack took a moment to absorb that assertion, but kept his face neutral. "By exterminating an entire *species*?"

"Colonel," Turner said, "the creatures holding SG-1 are vicious. They *will* kill them, eventually. But before that…"

He left it hanging and Jack didn't need to imagine the rest. He shifted, feeling uncomfortable — and not just because the seat was hard. "You're gonna need to explain this, General."

Irritation flickered across Turner's face. "SG-1 was sent on a mission to destroy the device, but an Oranian faction got there first and captured them. They're using them as a bargaining chip to leave the planet with the device. Our mission is to stop them."

"With extreme prejudice, I assume?"

"A conventional incursion wouldn't stand a chance, Jack. They'd kill SG-1 as soon as the offensive began. But if a small team could infiltrate the outpost and activate the device…" He gave a quick, nasty smile. "They're all dead and SG-1 walk free."

"How does it work?"

Devon brightened up. "That's a good question, sir. We think that it —"

"It uses DNA," Turner said, talking right over him. "We've calibrated it to Oranian DNA, but the Ancients designed the device so that only one of them — someone with the ATA gene — could initiate the weapon."

Jack scrubbed a hand through his hair, considering the story. "Why me?" he said eventually. "Why not him? The other O'Neill." *The real one.*

Devon and Turner exchanged a furtive look. "Okay," Turner said after a moment, "I'll level with you, Jack."

"Well, that would be nice."

"This isn't exactly official," Turner admitted. "We've been authorized to operate below the radar."

Jack sat back in his chair, tension tight down the length of his spine. It wasn't that he'd completely trusted these people in the first place, but he couldn't deny that he'd really *wanted* to believe that this was the call he'd been hoping for. He swallowed his disappointment and tried not to look like he was on full alert. "So who are you?" he said, looking around the table. "NID? Is Kinsey behind this?"

Turner shook his head. "Kinsey's dead."

"Convenient. Seems like everyone I know is either dead or missing."

"It's been a long nine years," Turner said. "And if we'd had a choice, we wouldn't have recalled you. But we don't. You're no stranger to covert operations, Colonel. Sometimes it's the only way."

He couldn't argue with that, but something still didn't sit right. He caught a tense glance between Turner and the woman, Balen Tark. "And what do you get out of this?" he asked her.

"The Oranians have killed many of our people," she said, leaning back in her chair as if she were about to prop her feet on the table. "My ship isn't called the *Avenger* for nothing, O'Neill."

"You're talking about a weapon of mass destruction."

"By any means necessary, Colonel," Turner said. "You know that."

He did know that, but he also wished he had Daniel here to argue the other corner. Daniel wasn't here, though; he was being held prisoner along with the rest of his team. Apparently.

"Look," Turner said, "how do you think we tracked you down?"

"Facebook?"

Turner's lips pressed into an unamused line. "General O'Neill told us where to find you. He'd be here himself, if he could, but in his position…" He spread his hands. "Jack, look around you. The galaxy's changed. It's not as simple as it was when the Goa'uld had everything locked down. In many ways, it's even more dangerous out here."

In truth, Jack had no way of knowing whether Turner was on the level. He wasn't sure he bought the story that his alter ego was the Big Man in DC. In fact, he wasn't sure he bought a lot of what they were selling him. He was out of his depth and he didn't like it. But he wasn't about to let on, so all he said was, "After we do this, what happens to the device?"

"We destroy it." Perhaps Turner said it a little too fast, or perhaps it was the way his gaze flickered toward Balen Tark, but Jack wasn't sure he believed that either.

He looked at the woman, but her expression was opaque. Jack didn't miss the tense line of her shoulders, however, or the fact that the whole room was holding its breath. He made himself lean back in his chair, look relaxed. "What if I won't do it?"

Turner's expression was flinty. "Then you'd be disobeying a direct order, Colonel."

"I'm not him," he said. "I'm not 'Colonel O'Neill'. You can't give me orders."

"I thought you'd have more loyalty to your team, Jack."

"The SG-1 I knew wouldn't want me to commit mass murder on their behalf. In fact, the Jack O'Neill I knew wouldn't be too happy about it either."

Turner steepled his fingers on the table, letting a moment pass. "You want to go back to drinking alone in seedy bars, Jack? Getting your kicks from riding too fast on the interstate? Because I can send you back there. If you don't have the stomach for this, I can send you back to that life."

Jack held his gaze, trying to get the measure of the man. He wasn't having much luck.

"Or you can stay and help," Turner said. "You can get back into the action, make a difference again. Save your team. Save Earth."

"And then what? Back on the scrap heap?"

Turner shook his head. "We'll find a place for you. The Stargate Program's gotten a whole lot bigger than just the SGC. There are plenty of places where a man of your talents and experience could make himself useful. Hell, there are whole new *galaxies* to explore."

"Is that so?"

"You wouldn't believe what's out here, Jack."

And that was exactly the problem. Hammond and Kinsey were dead? SG-1 was in trouble? The Goa'uld had been destroyed? He — the real Jack O'Neill — was heading up the whole operation from DC? How the hell was he supposed to know what to believe?

He didn't trust Balen Tark, or Devon, or any of them. But Turner was right about one thing: this was a chance to get back into the game, to reclaim something of the life he'd lost. So maybe these guys were NID, or something else shadowy, but maybe that didn't matter. He'd lived as a shadow for a decade anyway, a ghost of himself. Maybe it was time he started salvaging what he could of his life.

He fixed Turner with a hard look, trying not to hear Daniel's warning voice in the back of his head as he said, "So where do we find this doomsday machine?"

"Damn," Cam said, crouching low against the wall and releasing a precise burst of weapons fire up the staircase. "They got here fast."

"You'd be amazed what Oranians can do when they smell profit," Vala said.

"We cannot hold them here." Teal'c was farther down the narrow stairway, wielding his flashlight to try and see into the darkness. "There appears to be a room to the left, less than a hundred meters away."

"We don't want to get trapped," Cam warned.

"Better than dead," Vala said.

Daniel stood up, staying flat against the wall. "Teal'c and I can check it out, see if there's a back door."

Cam nodded, not taking his eyes off the Oranians further up the stairs. "Be quick, or we'll be falling back anyway."

With a nod at Teal'c, Daniel began to run down the steep steps. Teal'c was right; there was a door, and the panel at its side looked like it would open it if there were power. He jabbed at it anyway, to no effect. Behind him, Cam's P90 rattled again, overlaid by the electronic hiss of Vala's zat.

"Any ideas?" Daniel said.

Teal'c just gave him a look. "Stand back, Daniel Jackson." His roundhouse kick looked terrifying, but his foot impacted harmlessly on the door. With a growl, Teal'c threw his shoulder against it. Still nothing.

Daniel's radio crackled. "We're falling back."

Damn it. "Fall back slowly!"

He looked at the panel again. "There must be a manual override," he said. "There must be a way to open a door if the power goes out, right?"

"Perhaps," Teal'c said, rubbing his shoulder.

Daniel got closer to the wall, scanning its surface with his eyes and fingers, looking for irregularities. Ancient design was smooth, sinuous, and it was only as he traced it with his fingertips that he felt the slight ridge in the surface that cut across the whorls. "There's another panel here," he said, and wished Sam was with them. He pressed it and, to his surprise, it moved inward and then opened with a slow slide. Inside there was a simple lever, which he pulled, and the door released and slid open a few inches. "Yes," he breathed.

Jamming his fingers into the gap, Teal'c hauled it open. Daylight flooded out from the small room on the other side, its narrow window looking out over the ocean. Daniel figured that counted as a backdoor. "Cam," he said into his radio, "come on down. There's a way out."

"On our way," Mitchell replied. "So are the Oranians."

Teal'c covered the door, firing back up the stairs as Vala and Cam retreated into the room, then Teal'c pushed at the door, muscles bunching as it slid shut with a click.

"It won't take them long to figure out how to open it," Daniel pointed out.

Two quick shots from Vala's zat left the door mechanism smoking. "Now no one can open it," she said.

Daniel didn't comment on the obvious flaw in her plan.

Cam was peering out the window, still catching his breath from his flight down the stairs. "When you said there was a way out…"

Daniel joined him at the window and gazed down at the glittering ocean. "Hmm," he said. "That's a long drop."

"I sure hope someone brought a rope."

The boom of ocean waves crashing against a cliff face greeted them as they stepped out of the Stargate onto P3X-406, the glare of sunlight on water almost blinding. Jack wished he still had his trusty glacier sunglasses, but that was something else the other O'Neill had kept for himself.

"Spread out," said Balen Tark, and he watched as her people fanned out around the gate, securing the perimeter. They were good, whoever they were. Jack didn't move, though, still savoring the sensation of gate travel — the indefinable frisson of stepping through the event horizon and launching yourself across the galaxy. Damn, but he'd missed it.

Ahead, perching on the cliffs that fell away a hundred meters to the left of the Stargate, stood the Ancient outpost. Gray as the rock it was built on, it nonetheless had something of a fairytale aspect as it teetered over the ocean, its spires glittering in the planet's hot sun. Jack figured there'd be one heck of a view from the guest rooms.

"No welcoming committee?" he said to Hartkans, who stood next to him on the stone steps.

"Oranians are a spacefaring race," Hartkans said. "They rarely use Stargates. They prefer to land a ship instead."

"That's new," said Jack, and tugged the standard issue ball cap lower over his eyes. He missed his own kit. Without it he felt like he was just playing at being Colonel O'Neill. The only things in his pockets that he actually owned were his wallet and the keys to his bike, still parked outside Bosco's Tavern. But the P90 was familiar, at least, and he relished the feel of it in his hands after so long. Until he'd put on the uniform and stepped through the Stargate, he hadn't realized how disconnected he'd become from the man he'd once been.

"You're sure you know what to do, Colonel?" Hartkans said, flinching slightly as the wormhole disengaged behind them.

"It's not difficult," Jack said. "We get into the outpost and find the device. I activate it — killing the Oranians — and then we spring SG-1 from jail." *Assuming they're still alive. Assuming any of this is true.* "What could possibly go wrong?"

Hartkans didn't answer. "Balen," he said instead, "leave some of your people to hold the gate, just in case."

"In case of what?" Jack said.

Hartkans walked down the steps, away from the Stargate, without looking over his shoulder. "In case something unexpected happens."

Jack had a feeling Hartkans was expecting something unexpected.

There'd been a time when rappelling down the outside of an Ancient structure on an alien world would have been a remarkable event, but that time was long past. Now, as Teal'c grabbed hold of his wrist and helped him climb in through the window, what Daniel mostly felt was tired.

"Thanks," he said, shaking loose the cramps in his arms and rolling his shoulders. Vala sat some distance away, back against the wall, chewing on a power bar while Mitchell was studying the door. The room they were in was larger than the one above, with an annex through an archway off to the right.

"Bathroom," Vala said, when she saw Daniel looking. "En suite. No water, though. I checked."

"No power either?" Daniel guessed.

"And no way out," Mitchell confirmed, turning away from the door. "Unless you can open this one too?"

"I can try," Daniel said.

He found the manual override without much trouble, but it was broken. The lever wobbled and was obviously no longer connected to the door mechanism. Daniel sat back on his heels. "So, plan B?"

Teal'c was still at the window, one hand on the rope as if he could will it to detach itself and fall down. "I could attempt to free climb back up and retrieve the rope," he speculated, but Cam shut him down with a wave of his hand.

"We have C4," he said. "We'll just blow the door."

"Well, *that* won't tell the Oranians exactly where to find us," Vala said.

Cam fixed her with a look. "You got a better plan?"

Turned out, for once, she didn't.

The sun was hot — he'd forgotten how alien suns could be hotter or colder than Earth's Goldilocks star — but Jack found he didn't much mind the heat as they took the path from the gate to the outpost. There were definite advantages to this young body he'd inherited: endurance, strength, and undamaged knees were some of the most noticeable. He figured, physically, he was even younger than Daniel and Carter had been when they'd first joined the SGC. Mentally, though, he felt as wise as Methuselah.

An experienced mind in a young body made a potent combination, which was probably why he recognized the approaching sound before the others — the scuffing of boots against rock. "Off the path," he hissed, ducking behind one of the boulders that littered the cliff top.

The creatures who marched past were like nothing he'd seen before. They certainly weren't human. Their faces were reptilian, long and with weird tentacles on either side. There was a group of about five of them, heavily armed, escorting a ragged human prisoner. He glanced at Balen, who was watching them with narrowed eyes and a twitchy trigger finger.

She spared him a look and in a low voice said, "Oranian hunting dogs."

"Dangerous?"

Her grin was savage. "What do you think?"

Jack preferred to keep his thoughts to himself, so he said, "What about the human?"

"Like you," she said. "Perhaps he has the Ancient genetic marker?"

He watched the little party disappear into the distance, swallowed up by the shadows cast by the vast structure ahead. "You guys know a way into this place, right?"

"Of course," Balen said. "There's always a backdoor."

In this case, the backdoor involved a long and perilous climb up a narrow stairway cut into the cliff, with nothing but the ocean waves to break your fall — before they smashed you against the rocks. Nice thought.

By the time he reached the top Jack was sweating, his skin starting to crisp in the intense sunlight. If Carter had been there, she'd have had some kind of scanner to warn them about high UV levels. But, of course, she wasn't there. None of his team was there. They were being held hostage by the creepy reptile guys.

Maybe.

Balen led them through a narrow doorway into a cramped and dark passage. It smelled musty, like damp rock, and abandoned. The rest of the outpost soared above them and Jack figured the basement was as good a place as any to start. "Now what?" he whispered as Hartkans and the rest of Balen's people crowded in behind him.

"The device is several floors up," Hartkans said. "Balen knows the way and we can —"

"Wait. Where's my team?" Not that they were really his team anymore, but still. "Where are they holding SG-1?"

"We'll find them after," Hartkans said, glancing at his watch. It glowed in the dark and Jack could see a timer counting down. "Come on, we don't have long."

"Before what?"

"Before it's too late." Hartkans fixed him with a look. "For your team."

And you know this, how? Jack thought, but kept it to himself. There were far too many unknowns here for his liking.

There were no lights at first, only a faint illumination filtering down the stairs from higher up. But despite the gloom, Jack could see that everything was getting increasingly fancy the further they went: swirly patterns carved into the rock, the steps opening out into a broad staircase, and eventually the lights activating as they passed.

Hartkans stopped, surprised the first time it happened.

"Motion sensor?" Jack suggested.

But Hartkans shook his head. "You did it," he said. "The outpost's responding to your ATA gene."

Jack tried not to be creeped out by the fact that this Ancient pile of stones could somehow detect his genetic code. "I should get some of these installed at home," was all he said out loud. "It would save —"

Something detonated above them. The explosion shivered through the stone stairs, followed by a concussed silence when all Jack could hear was ringing in his ears. "What —?" The clatter of falling masonry cut him off, clouds of dust billowing down the stairs and making them all cough.

"Damn it," Hartkans growled, glancing at his watch.

Balen snarled something in her own language. "You said they wouldn't be here yet."

"There's still time," Hartkans said. "Keep moving."

Jack didn't bother asking who 'they' were. He doubted Hartkans would tell him the truth, and he'd find out for himself soon enough. He unsafetied his weapon and followed as Hartkans started running up the stairs.

The noise of a firefight began to filter through the dust and he could hear energy weapons discharging — a staff blast? "Jaffa?" he called to Hartkans.

"Oranian pistol," Hartkans said, spitting dust from his mouth. He stopped when the stairs reached an intersecting corridor, glancing both ways. "Balen?"

"That way," she said, indicating left. Unsurprisingly, it was the direction from which all the shooting was coming.

"Something unexpected?" he asked Hartkans.

Hartkans' face was tight. "We have to get to that device first," he said. "Everything depends on it."

Jack didn't answer, but did notice the lack of 'sir' in the orders Hartkans was throwing around. He kept his hands on his gun, using it to gesture along the corridor. "After you, *Major*," he said.

Hartkans gave him a cold stare, then looked past him — probably at Balen. "We can't afford to screw this up."

Jack said nothing, but he could sense the weapon aimed at his back and knew he had no choice but to follow as Hartkans crept along the corridor. It was pretty clear what would happen if he didn't cooperate.

Daylight spilled into the corridor up ahead, through the shattered remains of a door that had been blown out from within. He glanced into the room and saw a long slender window and a shard of sunlight falling across the floor, glinting against something silver that lay in the dust: the wrapper from a military issue power bar.

But there was no time to comment because suddenly they were under attack.

"They're behind us!" Balen yelled and Jack spun, dropping to one knee as a streak of gunfire scorched overhead. It was some kind of energy weapon he didn't recognize. Oranian, he guessed from the fact that a group of the bastards was bearing down on them at a run.

"Hold your ground!" Hartkans yelled, and he opened up with his P90 at the same time Jack did. The enemy went down easily, but there were more behind them. Many more.

Jack edged to the side of the corridor, offering a narrower target. "We need cover!" he barked at Hartkans.

But Hartkans wasn't paying attention. "Tark," he yelled. "Get O'Neill to the device. We'll hold them here."

"What—" Jack began, but Balen grabbed his arm and hauled him to his feet. She was strong.

"Come on," she said. "We can end this now."

He hesitated, but Hartkans and the rest of Balen's people were holding the corridor, and going with Balen at least offered him options.

They ran, clambering over the rubble from the doorway, then further on into a clearer section of the corridor.

"This way," Balen said, skidding to a halt. "Shortcut."

He would have missed the narrow opening in the wall, but Balen obviously knew it was there and squeezed through. Jack followed. He doubted it was part of the original Ancient design, but the rough set of handholds cut into the rock was easy enough to climb. Above him, Balen disappeared through a hole, and a moment later his own head was poking into the room above.

Balen was already at the door, pressing her ear against it, as Jack pushed himself up through the hole and stayed crouched for a moment.

On the far side of the room sat a pedestal with something glowing and definitely Ancient on top. Cautiously, he got to his feet. "That it?" he said.

Balen nodded but didn't leave the doorway. "They're out there."

"Who are?"

"Trouble," she said.

Jack moved so that the pedestal was between himself and Balen, but kept his eyes on the device. It was a domed hexagon, with Ancient letters or numbers written on each of its segmented sides. Genes or no genes, he couldn't make any sense of it.

"Activate it," Balen said. "Do it now."

He glanced over at her. "How?"

"Just touch it," she said. "All it needs is your genetic marker."

The device looked innocuous, small — not much larger than a dinner plate. "And this will kill all the Oranians on this base."

"On the planet," Balen said, still nervous next to the door. "Now hurry."

"How many?"

Irritated, she glanced back over her shoulder. "What?"

"How many Oranians on the planet?"

"I don't know. What does it matter? They'll all be dead."

Jack cocked an eyebrow. "That's why it matters."

Balen's eyes narrowed. "They'll kill your friends."

"So you say."

She shifted, turning her back on the door now — perhaps she'd figured out the greater threat was inside the room. Jack's hands dropped to his P90.

"Activate the device," Balen said. "Kill the Oranians, or we'll all die here."

"And what happens when it's done?" He nodded toward the weapon she held loose at her side. He didn't recognize its design, but it looked lethal. "You kill me and make off with the doomsday device?"

Balen bared her teeth in what might have been a smile. "We could be allies, you and I," she said, a lascivious glint in her eye as she strolled closer. "We could do great things, O'Neill. Explore the galaxy, get rich. With this device, we could rule worlds."

"Yeah," Jack said, "I'm more of a hockey fan."

Balen's face hardened. "Activate the device," she said, her weapon coming up in one smooth motion.

"I'm gonna guess," he said, lifting his own gun, "that you need me alive to activate this thing."

"Only barely."

"Thing is," Jack said, "I don't need you alive at all."

"Well that's odd." Daniel stared at the door panel in surprise. "It's working."

"Just means there's power here," said Cam. "The lights are on too."

"Or," Daniel said, "there's someone inside that room with the ATA gene."

"Will you hurry up?" Vala hissed from a dozen yards farther down the corridor. "They're coming this way."

He didn't need her to tell him that, he could hear the gunfire. "Who do you think they're fighting?" he asked Cam.

"It is irrelevant," Teal'c said. "All that matters is destroying the device held within this room."

"Right," he said, smiling at Teal'c's patient reminder to focus. "You guys ready?"

"For what?" said Cam.

Daniel shrugged. "For whatever's in here."

Mitchell raised his weapon, and so did Teal'c. Behind them, Vala backed closer to them, although her eyes were still turned in the direction of the firefight. "Let's just get inside," she said. "Before we have company."

Daniel pulled his Beretta from its holster, holding it low as he pressed his hand on the door activation panel. It shot open and Mitchell was through it immediately, Teal'c at his shoulder. Daniel and Vala followed, fanning out behind them, weapons raised. The door hissed shut.

"Don't move," Mitchell barked, although it didn't look like anyone was moving in the unexpected tableau before them. A woman — Lucian Alliance, by the look of her clothes — stood with her back to them, the Oranian pistol she held aimed at the head of a young, oddly familiar, US airman who had his P90 pointed right back at her.

"Welcome to the party," said the airman, without shifting his focus from the woman. "I hope you brought snacks."

It was the voice that gave him away, knocking the ground out from beneath Daniel's feet. "Jack?"

A flicker of a glance in his direction, then a flash of the same astonishment he felt. "Daniel?"

Jack's weapon wavered for a fraction of a second and the woman pounced, reaching across the pedestal to grab his vest. "Back off!" she yelled, hauling him toward her over the device as she pressed her gun to his head. "Back off, or he dies."

Jack dropped his P90, letting it hang from his tac vest, and flung his arms out wide, as far from the device as possible.

No one else moved.

"I mean it," the woman said, glaring at Daniel. "I'll kill him."

"She won't," Jack said. "She needs me to activate the device. I have some kind of gene…"

"Yeah," Daniel said. "We know."

"You want your friend to live?" the woman said. "Then leave. Now."

Cam threw Daniel a glance, deferring to his decision. Carefully, Daniel lowered his weapon. Mitchell and Teal'c did the same, but Vala was standing directly behind the woman, unobserved. "Careful," Daniel said, his words aimed at Vala although his eyes were fixed on the woman holding the gun to Jack's head. "Easy does it."

"Now back off," she said, shifting a little closer to Jack.

Vala moved with her, silent as a thief.

"Just shoot her," said Jack.

"You're a fool," the woman hissed. "You're turning your back on a fortune."

"Really? I thought we were here to avenge the deaths of your people."

She grinned, showing wide teeth. "What better way to avenge them than by stealing the most valuable weapon in the galaxy from under the noses of the Oranians?"

"Huh," Jack said. "Oranians have noses?"

Daniel almost grinned, touched by bittersweet nostalgia despite the precarious situation — or, perhaps, because of it. He glanced past the woman's shoulder, caught Vala's eye. It was time. The woman must have seen the look because she half turned, but not before Vala's well-placed shot sent her twitching to the floor in a haze of blue energy.

Released, Jack backed away, watching them all with a mixture of doubt and suspicion. Daniel didn't miss the tense hold he had on his weapon.

"Daniel," Vala said, lowering her zat. "What's going on? Who is this guy?"

"I'm Jack O'Neill," Jack said. "Who the hell are you?"

He'd recognized the cold sweep of Asgard transporter technology the moment the beam touched him, dissolving his mind and reforming it someplace else.

Not an Asgard ship, though. Human. *Prometheus*?

He was in what they'd called 'guest quarters' but, despite the soft furnishings and the decent meal they'd provided, the airman stationed outside his door gave the lie to the term 'guest'.

He'd been there several hours. Time enough for the others to mop up the mess on the planet and to put the Ancient weapon permanently beyond use. They were in motion now, travelling faster than light back to Earth, and probably trying to figure out what the hell to do with an extra Jack O'Neill.

Lying on the bed, hands behind his head, he stared out at the blurred star field and wondered whether he should have made a break for it back on the planet. Once he'd reached the Stargate he could have gone anywhere, could have been free. But free to do what? His life had always been about service, and, without that, what meaning would there be in wandering the galaxy? But the thought of returning to his life on Earth, of knowing that incredible things were happening beyond his reach, was profoundly depressing. It was almost enough to make him wish he'd taken Balen Tark up on her offer.

When the door to his quarters eventually opened, he wasn't surprised to see Daniel and Teal'c standing outside. They looked different from how he remembered them — older, changed by experiences he hadn't shared — but they were still the same men. To him, they looked like old friends. Whether they were or not remained to be seen.

He sat up and swung his legs over the side of the bed, but didn't stand as they entered. Teal'c nodded to the airman and the door slid shut, leaving them alone together.

"So," Daniel said after a short silence, "this is a mess."

"I'm guessing," Jack said, "there is no Major Hartkans?"

"Nope." Daniel moved further into the room and took a seat in one of the chairs next to the small desk in the corner. Teal'c remained standing near the door, hands behind his back. He looked odd with hair, the lines on his face more profound, but he still looked like Teal'c.

"Hartkans," Daniel said, "is ex-NID, a former member of a shadow organization called The Trust. Now it looks like he's working with the Lucian Alliance. Balen Tark is one of the new leaders that emerged after their failed attack on Earth."

"And what's the Lucian Alliance?"

"A loose coalition of smugglers, arms dealers and thieves," Teal'c said. "They have grown to prominence in the power vacuum created by the destruction of the Goa'uld."

Jack glanced at Daniel for confirmation. "So that's true,

then?" he said. "Turner fed me a lot of crap. I didn't know how much to believe."

"It's true," Daniel said, "the System Lords are gone." He let a beat fall. "Including Ba'al, by the way. He was executed by the Tok'ra. I saw him die."

"Good," was all he said, because ten years on he still had nightmares and he didn't see them ending just because Ba'al was gone. He pushed a hand through his hair, as if he could scrub away the memories.

"And the Jaffa are free," Teal'c added, with restrained but deep pride.

Jack smiled, though he felt a weight of sadness. "I wish I could have been there to see that."

"You know why you couldn't," Daniel said. "You know why you shouldn't be here now."

"Paperwork?"

"Something like that."

A long beat fell. "So now what?"

"Now you go home." A frown creased Daniel's forehead, the furrows cutting a little deeper than of old. "Colonel Caldwell wanted to beam you to the SGC for a full debrief, but Cam and I convinced him it wasn't necessary."

"I don't know," Jack said. "I wouldn't mind seeing the old place again."

"The brig?"

"Even that."

"Jack…"

"You have no idea!" he snapped. "To know all this is out here and to have no one — *no one* — to talk to about it? No way to help. To be cut off from everything and everyone that matters?" He dropped his head into his hands, trying to keep a lid on it all. "You have no idea, Daniel."

There was a long silence, Daniel for once apparently lost for words.

It was Teal'c who spoke in the end. "There are many things

that matter, O'Neill," he said. "Not all of them are to be found beyond the Stargate."

"There's nothing that matters more than this," Jack said, looking up. "And you know it."

Teal'c lifted an eyebrow. "You were willing to die for the Tau'ri," he said. "Is Earth so perfect that there is no cause there worthy of the same sacrifice?"

"It's different," Jack said. "Out here—"

"There is great evil in your world, O'Neill. I have seen it. There is war, there is suffering, and there are men as cruel and corrupt as any System Lord. Why do you not oppose them?"

"Hey," he objected, "I can't even join the military—I'm barred, remember? And what else can I do? I'm just one man."

"As was I, when first I opposed the Goa'uld." He fixed Jack with a look. "There is always a way to fight for the people of your world, O'Neill."

Daniel gave him a sideways look. "Um, Teal'c? I'm not sure that's such a good idea."

"Why not, Daniel Jackson? O'Neill is a man of great skill and ingenuity. This cloned body he now possesses gives him youthful vitality to complement his experience and wisdom." His attention returned to Jack. "You could make a difference to your planet."

"He could get himself killed."

Jack felt his heartbeat kick up a notch. Maybe Teal'c was right. Maybe he'd been so fixated on what he couldn't do out here that he hadn't considered what he could do closer to home. Iraq, Syria, Somalia, a dozen other hotspots around the world—could he somehow make a difference? Could he help make Earth a planet worth dying to protect? "Well, it's a thought," he said and watched the smile twitch the corner of Teal'c's mouth.

A stomach-lurching shift in the ship's motion made Daniel glance up at the ceiling. "We've dropped out of hyperspace."

"Home already?"

Daniel just nodded to the window behind Jack's head. He turned, standing slowly, breath catching as it always did at the sight of the beautiful blue planet.

"Home," said Daniel.

Jack moved to the window, pressed a hand against the glass. This would probably be the last time he ever saw this sight, ever left the confines of the world below. It was the end. "I miss you all," he said, without looking around. "I miss the SGC. I miss my life." He took a breath, blew it out slowly. "But you don't miss me. Jack O'Neill is still in your lives. And I'm not him."

Neither of them tried to deny it, but he heard Daniel get to his feet and come to stand by his side at the window. "I'm sorry," he said after a while. "It must be very difficult."

Jack just nodded. "Hartkans told me George Hammond died."

"Yeah," Daniel said with a catch in his voice. "A couple of years ago."

"I wish I'd known. I'd have liked to pay my respects." He hesitated before he spoke again, bracing himself for the answer. "What about Carter? She's not with SG-1 anymore?"

"She's okay," Daniel assured him. "She's Colonel Carter now, commanding the *George Hammond*. That's a ship," he added, as if Jack couldn't guess. "Like this one, only better."

Relieved, proud, and a dozen other things he tried not to feel when it came to Carter, he said, "Well, that's pretty cool."

"Yeah." Daniel cleared his throat. "Listen, um, you should probably know that she and Jack are —"

"Don't," he said, cutting him off. "I don't want to know."

Daniel nodded and after a moment said, "And that's why you can't stay. You can't be a ghost in your own life."

"I know that."

"It's tough, but — God, look at you. You're young, you're strong. Don't waste time looking back."

Jack swallowed a retort and turned away from the window. Daniel, older now than Jack was, regarded him with serious eyes. Teal'c, strange with his white-streaked hair, stood watching him from the door. Good men, good friends — but not *his* friends. He had to let them go, for real this time.

He glanced up at the ceiling. They'd beamed him right into these quarters, he figured they could beam him right out again. "So I just click my heels and say 'There's no place like home'?"

Daniel smiled. "When you're ready."

He took a breath. "I'm ready."

"Then take care of yourself, Jack. Stay out of trouble."

"You too."

Daniel tapped something in his ear and said, "Ready to transport in five, four…"

But before the beam activated, Teal'c crossed the room. With a rebellious look at Daniel he said, "Do *not* stay out of trouble, O'Neill. Seek trouble out." He unholstered his zat, handed it to him. "And when you find it, fix it."

Jack turned the gun over in his hands, a slow grin spreading across his face. "You betcha," he said as the Asgard beam swept him away.

Dawn was breaking over the mountains when Jack materialized in the parking lot of Bosco's Tavern, still wearing his BDUs and holding Teal'c's zat in his hands. The air was cool, fresh with promise, and he let it fill his lungs. Eyes closed, he lifted his face to the sun and for a moment he simply existed — young and strong, with life rolling out ahead of him.

A breeze ruffled his hair and he opened his eyes. It was time to begin.

Jogging over to his bike, he dug the keys out of his tac vest before shrugging it off and stuffing it and the zat into the top box. He'd just fired up the engine when an old man with a broom came out from behind the tavern, sweeping early fall leaves.

He nodded when he saw Jack. "We don't open for breakfast 'til six-thirty."

"That's okay," Jack said. "I'm not staying."

Leaning on the broom, the guy looked at him the way old men look at the young — a mixture of envy and indulgence. "And where're you headed so early, son?"

Jack grinned. "Trouble, sir," he said and gunned the engine, turning the bike toward the road and the sunrise. "I'm headed for trouble."

STARGATE ATLANTIS
A Blade of Atlantis

Jo Graham

This story takes place during the last episode of STARGATE ATLANTIS season one, "The Siege" Part 2. While waiting for the Wraith hive ships to arrive, and hoping that Daedalus arrives first, Atlantis' defenders engage in a desperate struggle to prepare the city while dealing with the Wraith commando teams who have beamed into the city bent on sabotage. If they could not have held the city until Daedalus arrived, the history of the Pegasus galaxy would have been very different...

DR. RADEK Zelenka crouched behind a corner, listening. The sweat was running down his forehead into his eyes even though it was decidedly chilly in the depths of the city. There were Wraith in the city. They had known that when he and two of Colonel Everett's Marines had set out from the control room to the chair. The chair room itself was secure — it was the kilometers of corridors between that weren't safe, and Dr. Weir had shut down the city's internal transport system so the Wraith couldn't use it.

And yet it must be done. The chair must be online before the hive ships arrived, and there was no choice but that he go and do it. He had left Rodney to complete modifications to the puddle jumper that was to carry a nuclear warhead, and gone with the Marines.

A nuclear warhead. Radek shook his head. He had been quite determined never to have anything to do with nukes, and see how that had turned out? No, he could not love them for any reason, had always thought he would not use them even to save his own skin, so great a moral evil were they. But, when his skin was indeed on the line, it looked different, as he supposed it always did — another thing he had learned about himself in Atlantis that was not entirely comfortable.

One of the Marines motioned all clear, and Radek got up carefully. "It's good, doc," he said. "Let's go."

They hurried along the corridor until it opened into a wider area, perhaps some kind of former gallery or store, with floor to ceiling columns of twisted opaque and mirrored glass. It was very pretty, but also deceptive as their reflections shifted with each step. One of the Marines saw movement and spun around, the barrel of his weapon rising. As he moved the reflection changed, revealing the movement to be their own.

"Damn," the Marine said.

"Yeah, don't open up in here unless you have to," the other said, gesturing at the columns. "Breaking all that glass will make a hell of a lot of noise."

"It is distracting," Radek said. "For a moment I thought I saw…"

The Wraith stepped out from behind the glass column, a flash of blue light emanating from his stunner. It caught the two Marines in its beam, dropping them bonelessly to the floor.

Radek dodged behind another column. He could no longer see the Wraith or the Marines either, save for one outflung arm where one of the Marines lay unconscious on the floor. There was the sound of the Wraith's footsteps, and Radek risked retreating to another column. The stunner fired again, blue beam illuminating his reflection on another column. The mirrored confusion worked both ways. With a rush, Radek ran for the corridor door, back the way he and the Marines had come. There was nothing else to do. He was unarmed, and he certainly could not drag two unconscious Marines. The best he could do was escape.

The Wraith followed. Radek heard his footsteps behind.

He crouched down, prying the cover off an air vent. He squeezed in, pulling the cover into place behind him. He wiggled backwards on his stomach, trying to get as far in as possible. If he could crawl back far enough that if the Wraith looked in he wouldn't see him…

His questing feet encountered nothing, and he slipped suddenly backward down a vertical shaft, falling perhaps two meters before he landed on his feet. Beneath him a grid gave slightly, and he glanced down, his breath sounding harsh in his own ears. It was a ceiling vent in an unoccupied corridor one level down. Radek went to his knees on the grid. Was this the kind of vent… yes! There was ductwork running in both directions above the ceiling. He could easily crawl along it safely with the Wraith who had been hunting him unable to get him as he was now beneath the floor. An excellent plan. But which direction? After a moment to get his bearings, Radek started off down the duct.

He was alone, deep in the superstructure in chambers he'd never seen before. Of course he could look for a terminal and activate it, which would involve finding some sort of control facility with power. Or he could turn on his radio, which would be tantamount to telling the Wraith where he was. This did not seem like a good idea. Better, he thought, to look for a terminal or a turning that would lead him to a familiar part of the city. There were literally a hundred kilometers of corridors beneath the surface, and he had only begun to learn the least of the city's secrets in the year he had lived here.

Radek crawled along the ducts until he came to another vertical shaft. At the bottom there was a grate in the wall, an outlet into the room below. Carefully he slid down and looked out.

The room was mostly dark, a sole emergency light illuminating what had probably once been office space judging by the built in surfaces at desk height along one wall. There was no sound except the faint whisper of the ventilation, the city breathing. Excellent. The grate stuck and he had to kick it out, but he told himself the sound would not carry far coming from inside a closed room.

Radek got to his feet. Yes, some kind of office. There was a closed door which probably led to the corridor he had just paralleled in the ceiling. The door stuck. No power, but the manual override was just inside. He opened the door very quietly.

Indeed it was a major corridor. It had the barred lighting fixtures in the walls, which even dimmed gave off enough light to see clearly. Turned on full, they would be bright as daylight. Wide and unobstructed, this corridor went somewhere important. Perhaps it was one of the main access corridors that crisscrossed the city. If so, he would soon reach a transport chamber. Yes, they were deactivated, but they had maps…

A noise ahead caused him to dash into the nearest cross corridor. It was narrower and darker, only illuminated by the light bleeding in from the main hall. Radek hurried down it a little way, stopping behind one of the pillars that jutted out into it containing things that looked like fishtanks that may once have been decorative. He stopped, his breathing sounding very loud to himself.

Slow footfalls. Long, slow footfalls like a man in boots walking cautiously. Wraith.

Radek froze. Perhaps he had gotten far enough down. If he moved now, the Wraith would hear him. If he ran, the Wraith would stun him and then feed at leisure. And he was unarmed. No, his best hope was to be as quiet as possible.

The footsteps stopped. Was the Wraith scanning? Listening? Radek didn't move.

There was an explosion of sound in the main corridor, a P90 opening up with a spray of bullets, the horrible sounds of impacts. A two second burst, and then it stopped. Radek looked around the pillar, ready to thank the Marines. Ah, not Marines.

The young man who bent over the Wraith's body to check him for signs of life was Athosian, small and lean and dark haired, his hair pulled back in a long tail with a twisted steel clasp. Another Athosian stood behind him, a P90 in his hands, tall and broad-shouldered and vaguely familiar. The two women with them wore Atlantis scientists' uniforms, one South Asian and the other with short red hair, a P90 slung across her chest like she was used to it.

The red haired one asked in clipped British tones, "Dead?"

"Dead," the Athosian who bent over the body said. He looked up. "Dr. Chandrapura, anything on the life signs detector?"

The South Asian woman glanced down at the white box in her hand. "No more Wraith. But there is a human. There." She looked up, her eyes meeting Radek's as he stepped from behind the pillar.

"You have a life signs detector," he said. "You have the ATA gene."

"Yes."

The big Athosian was staring at him. "Dr. Zelenka?"

"Yes." Radek drew himself up. "Who did you expect?"

"We need to go," the British woman said quickly.

The young Athosian who had checked the body met her eyes. "Do we?"

Radek looked at him, at the big Athosian who seemed familiar. "You are Athosians who wanted to stay and fight and who the Colonel gave weapons."

The big man's hands relaxed out of fists, and he swallowed. "Absolutely," he said. "Teyla said we could help find the Wraith who were in the city."

Which was absolutely true. Teyla had recruited some of the Athosians to help guard the city, and Colonel Everett had armed them. The younger Athosian was unfamiliar, but Radek did not know all the Athosians. But the big man was lying. He was staring at Radek like he'd seen a ghost, and his unease was palpable.

"And you." Radek looked at the two women. "I know every single scientist in the city. I supervise every scientist in the city. I do not know you. And we do not have a Dr. Chandrapura with the ATA gene. There is no such person."

"We came with Colonel Everett," the British woman said quickly.

Radek's eyebrows rose. "I did not see any civilians come with him. In fact, we have evacuated most of our civilian scientists to the Alpha site. Who are you really?"

"She's a Marine," the tall Athosian said.

"Then why is her accent British rather than American?" Something was very, very wrong here.

"I'm a British Marine," she said crisply. "Lt. Jillian Draper, Royal Marines."

"A female Commando?"

Her eyes widened slightly. "We have them now," she said. "It's not 1940."

Radek shook his head. "You're lying," he said. "If this is a trick of the Wraith, it's very, very good. But not quite good enough." If it was, he was trapped, but being trapped made him bold. "I do not know who you are, but you are all lying."

The young Athosian with the long dark hair stood up abruptly. "There's no point in deceiving Dr. Zelenka," he said. "Remember? He has to know."

"T.J.," the other Athosian began.

"He has to know," the Athosian named T.J. continued. "Because he already does. Otherwise he couldn't have told General Carter."

"You can't say that in front of him," Lt. Draper said.

"Why not? There might be lots of General Carters. Dr. Zelenka has to know."

The tall Athosian let out a long breath. "T.J. has a point."

"Know what?" Radek demanded. Not a trick of the Wraith, but something far stranger. "Who are you?"

Draper looked at T.J. and then Radek, then nodded slowly. "If we must. Go on."

T.J. took a step toward Radek, his hands held away from his sides. "Dr. Zelenka, have you ever seen me before?"

He was small and dark, lean muscled arms beneath a brown leather vest that laced over loose black pants, his only ornament the oddly scrolled steel clasp in his hair. He looked like a martial artist. He was a stranger, and yet there was something about him that reminded Radek of someone, something that teased at the edge of his thoughts. "I do not think I have," he said.

The young man's eyes did not leave his. "What would you say if I told you that you will see me for the first time four years from now upstairs in the infirmary, when I lie in my mother's arms as a day old baby? You will come to see me and you will bring me a stuffed giraffe and you will tell my mother that you had never lost hope that she would be saved. And you will say no more because you cannot. You cannot say that you knew I would be born and that she would be rescued."

"What?" Radek said.

He lifted his chin. "My name is Torren John Emmagen. We are here from the future."

Radek took a deep breath. He should say it was impossible, but he knew it was not. There had been accidents with the Stargate at the SGC, accidents that had created temporal paradoxes, that oft-written about and theoretically impossible thing—time travel. It could happen. An accident with the gate… But no. They had not spoken like people who were lost, the victims of a random conjunction of a solar flare and an outgoing wormhole. They were exactly where they were meant to be. They had learned to control the phenomenon that Lt. Colonel Carter had described. General Carter. Of course.

All this went through Radek's mind in the moments that they waited, looking at him. He put his hands in his pockets. "So General Samantha Carter sent you into the past?" he asked calmly. "From what year?"

Dr. Chandrapura looked nonplussed. The tall Athosian started laughing. "I told you Dr. Zelenka was the smartest man in Atlantis," he said to her. "Didn't I tell you so, Saroj?"

Another piece fit into place. "Jinto?" Radek looked at the big man over the top of his glasses? "Is that you?"

"It's me." Jinto grinned. "It's Dr. Hallingson now. I have a PhD from a university on Earth."

"In what?"

"Mechanical engineering," he replied. "Thanks to you, Dr. Z. If you hadn't…"

"You shouldn't tell him that," Dr. Chandrapura said. "Remember, if it's not about the mission…"

"Quite right," Radek said briskly, though he itched to know. "You should not tell me more than is necessary. But Jinto, I presume Lt. Draper and Dr. Chandrapura were on Earth, and T.J. was not born yet — but is not your presence here a paradox?"

Jinto shifted from one foot to the other. "I think it would be if I ran into myself. But as General Carter discovered when she visited 1969, it's possible to be in the same time twice if you're not in close proximity. She traveled from Colorado to New York in 1969 when she was also a baby at Pope Air Force Base. General O'Neill was a teenager in Minnesota and Dr. Jackson was a young child in Seattle. All three of them were already on Earth in that same time, but they were careful not to go anywhere they might encounter themselves. In this time…" he glanced around the walls of the corridor, "I'm already at the Alpha site. Eleven year old me, that is. As long as I'm gone before I get back, it shouldn't be a problem."

Radek frowned. "So why are you here?"

"To help you," Jinto said simply.

Lt. Draper cleared her throat. "Rather, to make certain that the command chair is functional before the Wraith fleet arrives. If it is not, Atlantis will fall to the Wraith before the *Daedalus* brings the ZPM that will allow you to power the shield. And the only way for the chair to be functional is for you to reach it alive. Currently you're cut off from the chair and from the nearby transport chambers by at least ten Wraith. It is highly likely that without assistance you will never reach it."

"And then our world will never exist," T.J. said solemnly. "I will never exist. My mother will be killed in the last defense of Atlantis."

"Teyla's son." Now that he knew, he could see it. T.J.'s hair was darker, but he had the same lithe, compact form, the same shape to his face. His voice sharpened. "Ten Wraith between here and the chair room? How do you propose to get there? Even with four armed people we are seriously outnumbered."

"We're not going to go through them," Draper said. "We're going to go around them."

"How?" Radek gestured upward. "Fly? We are deep in the city's infrastructure, probably below the waterline by several stories. The transport chambers are not working and in any case you say we are also cut off from them. If you do not mean to shoot your way through…"

"We're going to go under the city," Draper said. "Underwater."

"What, in wet suits?"

"We have a better idea," Dr. Chandrapura said with a smile. "And that's why I'm here. I have the ATA gene naturally expressed." She shifted her weapon. "Did you think we came in through the Stargate without anyone seeing? How could we have done that?"

"Then how did you get here?" Radek asked.

"By puddlejumper," T.J. said.

"A rather special puddlejumper," Dr. Chandrapura said. "It's a long story." She looked at Draper. "Now that we've found Dr. Zelenka, perhaps we should go back to it as quickly as we can?"

Jinto nodded. "It's this way. Come on, Dr. Z." He led the way with Radek and Lt. Draper. Dr. Chandrapura was just behind them while T.J. dropped back to take six, his steps so light that Radek could barely hear him. They hurried down the main corridor and then a second one without consulting any map or device.

"You know your way around," Radek observed to Jinto.

He smiled. "I explored the city for years as a boy, and I know it as a man. That's one reason I came on this mission. Lots of people know Atlantis today, but I explored it in this period, before…" He broke off.

"Yes, yes, before something happened you can't tell me about,"

Radek said, but his curiosity was piqued. "So you know Atlantis, and Dr. Chandrapura has a strong ATA gene. Lt. Draper is obviously in charge of your team. Why is T.J. here?"

"He has some skills that are useful," Jinto evaded.

He was spared from saying more because T.J. said calmly, "There are Wraith ahead. Two."

They halted and Draper looked back. "Work around?"

"They're in the chamber beyond the next bulkhead," T.J. said.

"Then we can go down this way," Jinto said, "if we backtrack one section." He turned to go back.

"Wait," Radek said. "There are only two. Can't you take them on?"

"We could," Draper said.

"If you leave them, who knows what they will do?" Radek said. "What sabotage, or who they might kill."

"We know exactly who they might kill or what they might do," Lt. Draper said evenly. "We know who died. And we know what sabotage happened and what didn't. If we engage these Wraith, we don't know what will happen as a consequence. They could go a different way and kill someone different, or blow up something critical that they never reached before."

"You don't know that," Radek said. "You might spare the lives of people who they killed."

"Or they might kill you, and the Wraith might take Atlantis," Draper said. "Or find the puddlejumper and change the course of the war." She shook her head. "We can't change random things. We're not supposed to interact with anyone except you. If we start changing a load of other things we might lose this siege. In war you never know exactly what small thing is going to be critical." She turned to follow Jinto, shepherding him along. "We're going to leave the Wraith alone. If we can do this without a firefight, we will."

They hurried along the connecting corridor and then through a large, open empty room. Radek wondered what it had once been. A warehouse? A ballroom? There was nothing to tell him, just empty space that they skirted from one door to another, their footsteps echoing.

Once more T.J. stopped them. "Wait," he said quietly, and they halted by the door for some minutes, their breath seeming loud in the silence, until he said it was safe to go on.

"What is he doing?" Radek asked Jinto in a low voice. "Dr. Chandrapura has the life signs detector."

Jinto looked uncomfortable. "T.J. senses the Wraith," he said. "Like Teyla."

Jinto opened his mouth and shut it again.

"It's ok," Radek said. "We found that out while you were at the Alpha site. We already know that. You are not telling me something I do not know."

"It's just that the Gift is a touchy subject among Athosians, especially now that we understand its origins…"

Jinto was interrupted by the door ahead opening into yet another chamber. If the last one had been bare, this one was breathtaking. Floor to ceiling, there was a window that looked out into the sea. They were perhaps ten or fifteen meters below the surface, the water only slightly clouded. It was full day, and the sun filtered down through shoals of pink and yellow fish, some the size of his hand and others much larger. They had six fins each, and the largest spread them like umbrellas stretched to catch the light coming down.

"Oh wow," Dr. Chandrapura said, stopping short. "Any aquarium on Earth would envy this view."

"Absolutely," Draper said.

It was magnificent. "Where are we exactly?" Radek asked. He had lost track of the turnings.

"Directly between the city's main sublight engines," Jinto said. He gave Radek a sideways grin. "This is one of your favorite places."

"It is now," Radek said.

T.J. went to the window and pointed. "And that's where we're going," he said.

Radek looked out. The city's superstructure protruded, a long stretch reaching out that was probably the underside of one of the piers. Not far along, just around the corner really, was a familiar stubby shape. It looked like the front of a puddlejumper docked with the rear hatch against the city. "They go underwater?"

T.J. looked surprised. "You don't know that?"

"Not yet, apparently," Radek said. "But I suppose it makes sense. They are air tight in vacuum, and they must withstand unusual pressure. So a few tens of meters like this could not be a problem to them, if their propulsion works…"

"You can take it apart later," Jinto said. "But right now let's go."

"I do not like being underwater," Radek said.

"All we're going to do is take the puddlejumper from one docking port to another," Lt. Draper said. "That way we don't have to go through the halls or use the transport chambers. Just from one pier to another."

"Ah. Well. If that is all."

Jinto grinned. "Think of it as a glass bottomed boat tour, Dr. Z."

"You have spent too much time on Earth," Radek said.

It wasn't far to the puddlejumper, docked at what was clearly an airlock meant for it. "I suppose the Ancients also used them to explore the seas," he said thoughtfully as Dr. Chandrapura opened the rear hatch.

"Or just for general transport," Jinto said. "Remember, Atlantis wasn't the only installation that was submerged."

"Jinto," T.J. said warningly.

"Right." Jinto shook his head. "It's hard to keep track of what you already know and what you don't. I was here for all of this, but I don't recall exactly what happened which year, just before and after certain important things. But I guess memory is always that way."

"I think so," Radek said. His life was divided into periods by main events, before the Velvet Revolution and after, graduate school in Britain, his time at the SGC, and then Atlantis. He could not tell you, 'Oh, this happened in 98 rather than 97!' Memory did not work that way. No wonder that Jinto was always on the verge of saying something he should not.

Dr. Chandrapura and Lt. Draper entered the puddlejumper and he followed, frowning. Right in the middle of the back cargo bay was a strange device. Bulbous and smooth, the size of a medium crate, it looked Ancient. Other than that…

"What does it do?" Radek asked.

Draper and Jinto exchanged a glance. "It causes the jumper to travel in time," Draper said reluctantly. "That's how we got here. Don't ask us how it works. And don't touch it."

"I wouldn't dream of it," Radek said. "I am not Rodney. I do not have to just crack it open and see what makes it tick."

"That's why he's…" Jinto stopped abruptly.

Radek looked up. "Dead?"

"Noooo," Jinto said. "That's not…"

"Jinto!" T.J. snapped. "Stop! Just stop telling him things. You can't tell him who's alive or dead in 2029. Or anything else!"

"I didn't want him to think Rodney was dead," Jinto said.

"So now you've told him Rodney's alive." T.J. shook his head. "Which is just as bad."

"Am I alive?"

"If you weren't you couldn't have told us…" Jinto began.

"Jinto!"

Jinto looked around sheepishly at the other three members of his team. "Ok. Fine."

"Not another word," Lt. Draper said. "I mean it. Jinto, you have to refrain."

"I will."

"Then why don't you come up and sit with me and Saroj and let T.J. sit with Dr. Zelenka?"

"I see how it is," Jinto said. "Fine." He went forward and sat in the passenger seat next to Dr. Chandrapura while Lt. Draper sat in the seat behind him. Radek sat down on one of the back benches, T.J. across from him.

The back gate rose, and there were the soft and familiar sounds of the jumper's systems coming online. T.J. was very quiet. Possibly the better part of not saying anything wrong was to say nothing. Or maybe, like Teyla, he wasn't a chatterbox. Radek had always appreciated that about Teyla. She was a very restful friend to have.

The jumper slowly detached from the dock, moving forward through the blue waters cautiously, schools of fish parting in front of it without alarm.

"It's just over there," Draper said, pointing at something Radek couldn't see.

"I know," Dr. Chandrapura replied.

"Under that strut."

"I know," she said again. "Jillian, you don't have to back-seat drive."

"Sorry." Draper took a deep breath and sat back against the seat.

"Wishing we had Frankie along?" Jinto asked.

"Are you kidding?" Dr. Chandrapura glanced over at him. "She's got more jumper hours but she'd be blowing the place up."

T.J. snorted, and Radek asked quietly, "Someone you are not fond of?"

"My little sister," T.J. said.

"T.J!" Lt. Draper snapped. "What did I say about not telling him things?"

"I'm not the one who brought up Frankie," T.J. observed.

"Your sister's name is Frankie?" Radek asked.

"Frances Tegan."

"T.J!"

"Ok. Got it. Don't say anything. Though I don't know what deep, dark secret my sister's name is. I think you're being a little bit paranoid."

Lt. Draper turned around in her seat. "Look, we like our future. It's good. So let's try to keep it, all right? Don't tell anyone anything that isn't strictly necessary. Everyone, let's focus on the mission."

Radek started laughing.

Draper stared at him. "Why is that funny?"

"Because obviously nothing has changed," Radek said. "I have heard the gate team bicker like this so many times!"

"We never said we were a gate team," Dr. Chandrapura said from the pilot's chair.

"It is obvious," Radek said. "Along with some other things. Like that the command team in Atlantis is more international. Dr. Chandrapura's English is perfect, but her accent is not British, so I do not think she's a British citizen."

"I'm Indian," Dr. Chandrapura said. "After the *Asoka*..." She stopped. "Sorry. I can't confirm or deny anything. Dr. Zelenka, you must know how it is."

"I do," he said. "But also be aware that I can draw my own conclusions from what you do not say and from who you are." And that was a heady power. An hour ago Radek had been certain they were all going to die. It was only a matter of time before the Wraith overwhelmed the defenders and it was too late. He might be killed in the corridors. He might be killed in the final defense. If he was lucky, he might be killed a few days from now, hunted out of the city's ventilation system like a rat from a sewer. Now he knew he would live. They would survive, many of his friends who were becoming family, and they would build something beautiful and unique. The joy of it was almost overwhelming.

"But I will not tell," he said quietly. "I will not tell anyone what has happened."

"Except General Carter," Jinto said. "You'll tell her."

"And us when the time comes," Lt. Draper said.

It was only a minute before the jumper turned carefully, backing into a different docking port on the South Pier. It was not far from the Chair room, Radek thought. Mainly it was a good many levels down. Stairs, so many stairs.

Dr. Chandrapura looked at T.J. as they slid into the dock. "Clear?"

He nodded, an abstracted expression on his face. "In the immediate area."

"How far away are they?" Lt. Draper asked.

"There are two Wraith several levels up and further down the pier," T.J. said. "They're not anywhere they can hear or see us dock. So we should be clear for now."

"Moving or stationary?"

T.J. closed his eyes. "Moving slowly, I think. We can probably go around them."

"What about human parties?" Draper asked.

Dr. Chandrapura pulled out the life signs detector, wincing at what she saw. "Two parties of five each nearby. All human."

"Athosian?" Jinto asked.

Dr. Chandrapura gave him a look. "How would I know that?"

"They're probably Colonel Everett's Marine patrols," Radek said. "Which is an excellent thing, as I can join them and they will escort me to the Chair room, and your mission will be done!" It was all very neat and tidy.

Lt. Draper shook her head. "We don't know that. We don't know that the Wraith won't ambush them. We need to take you to the Chair room. Then we'll be sure you get there."

Jinto frowned. "I think Saroj should stay with the jumper."

"Why?"

"Because that's a lot of different parties running around. If one of them finds the jumper, either our people or the Wraith, it's going to be a big problem for the timeline. If you stay, you can cast off and cloak if any of the parties get too close and then duck back to pick us up after we've taken Dr. Zelenka to the Chair room," he replied.

"He has a point," T.J. said.

"Who's going to use the life signs detector if she stays?" Lt. Draper asked.

"I can sense the Wraith. And surely we can dodge the human parties."

Dr. Chandrapura nodded slowly. "That makes sense. And

I'm the only one who can fly the jumper. So if somebody's staying it has to be me." She gave Lt. Draper a firm smile. "Ok. I'm staying. Good luck, everyone."

They let the gate down and exited carefully into another darkened corridor, this one quite small and confined with only one door at the far end.

"Nice trap," Lt. Draper said.

"I was just thinking it was really defensible," Jinto said.

"The Chair room?" Radek prompted.

Lt. Draper put one hand on the door release. "Clear?" she asked T.J.

"Clear," he said.

She punched it. Nothing happened. She punched it again.

"The power must be out," Radek said. "The city has taken multiple hits from Darts and there has been a firefight in and out of the buildings. We haven't even had time to check for damage in uninhabited parts of the city."

"Fantastic," Lt. Draper said.

Radek pushed past her. "I can probably open it manually. Let me get to the panel." He knelt down beside the door, reaching for the ever-present multitool in his pocket.

"You're the best, doc," Jinto said. He grinned at Lt. Draper. "Always has been."

"Yes, well. Thank me when I have opened it."

Fortunately it was a standard door, the kind that seemed most prevalent throughout the city, though there were at least eight designs in use in different areas. As of course one might expect of a city rather than a military installation. There were different kinds of doors and different kinds of locks for public and private areas, and they seemed to have been installed over a long period of time, with old ones only being replaced when they malfunctioned. This was an ordinary one used for public areas that weren't high security. It only took a few minutes to release the lock manually.

"There," Radek said. "Now put your shoulder to it and it should open."

T.J. did just that, and the door slid jerkily open wide enough for them to pass through.

"Excellent," Lt. Draper said. "Jinto, which way?"

"Down to the left," Jinto said. "And then when we reach the first stairwell we need to go up two levels."

They hurried along the corridor, Jinto in front followed by Lt. Draper, then Radek and T.J. bringing up the rear. The stairwell was right before them, and they started up, Radek more slowly than the ones in front of him.

He was one turning behind them when he heard a familiar voice above. "Halt! Who are you?"

T.J. grabbed his arm, pulling him back into the shadow of the flight above. They could hear but not be seen yet. T.J.'s mouth was at his ear as he whispered, "Who?"

"Lt. Ford," Radek whispered back.

He could hear Ford on the stairs above, the footsteps of the Marine team. "Who are you?"

"Usten of Athos," Jinto said. "We got separated from our party who were hunting Wraith. You know Dr. Draper, of course?"

Radek held his breath. Ford had never seen Jillian Draper before in his life. But would he admit that? Or would he think she was one of the scientists he'd never paid any attention to?"

"Right," Ford said. "Ok, you guys had better come with us. There are Wraith in this sector."

"We just came up from the lowest level," Jinto said. "And we didn't see anything. I'm glad we ran into you, Lieutenant."

"Cool. Just stick with us." Ford raised his voice a little. "Ok, people. Let's head up the pier on this level and see if we can get this Wraith between us and Major Sheppard's unit." The sounds of their footsteps receded into the distance.

"This is not good," Radek said.

"Jinto will talk his way around," T.J. replied. "Remember, he was already here in this period. He knows everybody. The only problem will be if he runs into other Athosians, because they'll know there's no such person as Usten. We'll go on to the Chair room. If they don't get loose after I've dropped you off, I'll go find them. But I expect Jinto and Jillian can figure out how to get separated. We just have to do our jobs and trust them to do theirs."

Radek smiled.

"What?" T.J. asked.

"You sound like your mother, is all." Radek shook his head. "I will truly see you for the first time four years from now as a newborn baby?"

"You will," T.J. said. "And you'll insist that you don't like children and you won't watch me for any money. And then you will."

Radek looked at him, a young man like and unlike his friend, familiar and strange at once, dark eyes on a level with his own. "I expect I will," he said.

They waited in silence until the last sounds of Lt. Ford's patrol were gone and then waited two minutes more for good measure.

"Up two levels," Radek said. "That was what Jinto said. And then down the pier?"

"Which should be a left, I think," T.J. replied quietly. "If we find a window I can orient us to the rest of the city."

"I think we are still several levels below the windows," Radek said. "This is still substructure lighting rather than living area lighting. As well as we can tell, these levels were storage and manufacturing when the Ancients lived here. The areas that people lived in, and spent time in for pleasure, were above sea level and incorporated natural light."

"Makes sense," T.J. said.

"The Chair room is on the first level below the surface," Radek said. "So I think we need to go a little further. I do not see any useful markings on the walls. Sometimes the Ancients had signs just as we do, especially in public areas, and some of them have survived."

"You mean like how it says 'Welcome to Atlantis Watch Your Step' in the gateroom?" T.J. asked with a small smile.

"Like that," Radek said. It was on the tip of his tongue to ask if the young man read Ancient, but he might have grown up in the city. And that was a new thought — Atlantis not as a distant military outpost, but as a city again, a place where people were born and grew up and went to school. "Have you lived here your whole life?" Radek asked instead.

"Mostly. Here and Athos. I've never lived on Earth, if that's what you mean, though I've visited a few times." T.J. was scanning the walls as they went along, a slightly distracted expression on his face as though he were also listening to another conversation somewhere else.

"There." Radek pointed at a group of symbols at a corridor conjunction. "That says exit. So the way we are going will take us up onto the pier. We want the cross corridor then."

"There's a Wraith that way," T.J. said. "He's far down, but he's coming this way. We could backtrack and go upstairs and try to cross above him."

"And run into Lt. Ford?"

T.J. winced. "Ok. We could get into a room somewhere ahead and wait for him to go by."

"I am with you on that," Radek said. "And I can jam the doors from the inside since the power is out. Even if he wanted to check a room he would not be able to."

"Sounds good. Let's go."

There were a number of rooms off the corridor. Radek glanced up and down, considering. The power was still out in this section, and most of them were sealed shut with heavier duty locks. He swore to himself. He should have thought of that. There was one that was only a palm lock, probably a storage closet or something. He could crack that one fairly quickly.

"You'd better hurry," T.J. said. "He's getting closer."

"I shall," Radek said, making himself not hurry at all. The surest way to make mistakes that would take twice as much time would be to hurry.

"Dr. Zelenka," T.J. said more urgently.

"Almost." With a twist, he released the wire that engaged the locking mechanism. "There." He got to his feet. "It's probably a storage closet..." he began as they shoved the door back.

It wasn't. It was an equipment closet full of some part of the city's HVAC system, probably a dehumidifier. Given that these passages were below sea level and couldn't be vented, it was entirely logical. It also took up nearly the entire closet. There was room for one person if he squeezed.

"That is not good," Radek said.

"Get in," T.J. said. "He's nearly here."

"But..."

"Get in!" He shoved Radek into the tiny space and put his shoulder to the door, nearly closing it with one push.

The Wraith came around the corner. Through the two inch gap between the door and frame, Radek saw him stop and smile, his teeth showing in a feral grin.

T.J. stood in the middle of the corridor, his hands at his side, perfectly placid and calm for all that he had no weapon except a knife at his belt. But then the Wraith was unarmed too. If he'd had a stunner, it was gone. He would not need it, Radek thought. Not against one man. He had the advantage of strength and he would simply close and feed.

And he, Radek, would what? Watch? Cower in the closet while the Wraith killed Teyla's son? If he pushed the door open, if he ran, the Wraith might pursue him instead...

With a snarl the Wraith stepped forward, feeding hand outstretched as he reached for T.J.

Who wasn't there. He was actually six feet away, knife in hand, turning to slash at the Wraith's leg, the point scoring a long gash that would have hamstrung a human.

Radek blinked. He was certain he had seen T.J. in the middle of the corridor. He couldn't possibly have moved that fast.

The Wraith looked equally bewildered, whirling on its wounded leg with a roar.

And T.J. was gone again. He was standing twenty feet

down the corridor watching calmly.

The Wraith charged toward him. He grabbed the front of his shirt with his feeding hand, lifting him off his feet…

… as T.J. sunk the knife almost to the hilt in his back, twisting it free brutally as he jumped back from the Wraith who clutched at nothing. Blood spurted for a moment, then ceased as the Wraith healed.

T.J. backed away, his profile to Radek as he stood his ground.

"How did you do that?" the Wraith demanded. "Speak, human!"

"You could answer your own riddle if you would," T.J. said. A white mist began to rise about him, smoke filling the corridor, dense and almost opaque.

Radek took a breath before he thought better, but it did not burn in his lungs. It had no smell. Almost as if it were not there.

"What are you?" the Wraith bellowed again somewhere in the mist.

T.J.'s voice came from far down the corridor. "A Wraith named Michael killed to find that out. What makes you think you can guess?"

The Wraith screamed, fury and pain intermingled, and Radek guessed that T.J. had stabbed him again.

"What's your lineage, Wraith?" T.J.'s voice was almost beside him, just outside the door. "Not Osprey, or you would see through the mist. Illusions are the Gift of her children."

There were scuffling sounds, another grunt as though the Wraith had taken a body blow. Radek could see nothing except vague shapes moving in the smoke. Perhaps they were fighting? Perhaps T.J. had struck and moved away again.

"What are you?" the Wraith shouted.

"I am an impossible thing. I am a blade of Atlantis."

"There is no… such… thing…" The Wraith's words came in gasps. Another grunt, another scuffle in the smoke.

"There is." T.J.'s voice was far off to the right, echoing in the corridors. Or was it? Perhaps it was to the left. "The son of a human Queen, inheritor of the Gift from both parents alike. I am what Michael wanted. I am what the Ancients sought — a human with all the gifts of a Wraith save longevity — who never has to feed."

Another blow, a scream, the sound of someone falling. Radek strained to see, pressing the door a little further open.

The Wraith's voice was thready. "You… are… not… possible."

"I am." T.J.'s voice was serene. "Mercy."

And then there was silence.

Radek shoved at the door, tumbling out into the corridor.

The mist cleared suddenly as if it had never been. The Wraith lay dead on the floor, T.J. kneeling beside him, head bent.

"Are you…" Radek began.

"I am uninjured." T.J. got to his feet heavily, looking down at the dead Wraith by his feet. "I don't like to kill."

"He's Wraith!" Radek said.

"And I am not?"

Radek took a sudden, uncertain breath. T.J. held a bloody knife in his hand, his long, dark hair straight as the Wraith's, pulled back in a clasp of steel flowers, his dark eyes shadowed.

"He was a brave man, and he would have killed me if he could have, so it had to be done. But there are fine lines between us and our enemies." T.J. met his eyes. "You told me that again and again, Dr. Zelenka. You told me there are lines on a map, lines like curtains of steel that divide us, but when we look into the heart of the Other what we will see is ourselves." T.J. glanced back at the body on the floor. "We are more alike than different, this scout, this blade of Night who took this mission behind enemy lines. It had to be done. And I have done what I had to do." He wiped his knife on the hem of his shirt and sheathed it. "So let us go on and do what we came to do."

"Yes," Radek said, and turned away to follow him.

They came to the Chair room a few minutes later, Radek entering the code cautiously to open the door, just as he'd set the code before the last time he'd left. It was empty as he had hoped, the naquadah generator and the rest of the equipment clustered near the open floor panels. Radek took a deep, relieved breath.

"Everything in order?" T.J. asked. He was looking down the corridor outside, that listening expression on his face again.

"Yes," Radek said. "And now I may turn my radio back on and get to work." He paused. "Are there Wraith near?"

"No. But I hear footsteps." He backed into the room, letting the door close and lock automatically behind them. "If it is your people, I am simply one of the Athosians."

"Of course," Radek said.

The door did not open. No one knocked.

Radek looked at T.J. "Wraith?" he asked.

T.J. shook his head. "No."

"Then I will open it." Radek keyed the door open.

Jinto and Lt. Draper were standing just outside, apparently conversing in furious whispers.

"Hi," T.J. said.

They scurried inside. "We hoped you'd made it," Draper said. "If not, we were going to backtrack."

"We are here and quite alright. You have accomplished your mission," Radek said.

"What mission?" Rodney McKay popped out of a side door to the Chair room wiping his hands on his pants.

Jinto boggled.

Rodney looked at Lt. Draper, and Radek gulped. Any second now Rodney was going to realize that he didn't know her and he should know all the science personnel. Any second now Rodney was going to guess there was something wrong. The best defense was a good offense.

"Getting me here to help you with the Chair since you are obviously not capable of doing it yourself," Radek said. "Also I thought you were handling the jumper. What are you doing here?"

"You didn't answer your radio and the Chair was still offline so I thought you were dead or something," Rodney said. "It took you long enough to get here. Did you get lost?"

"I did not get lost," Radek snapped. "I was pursued by the Wraith. Fortunately I ran into some Athosians who escorted me here. And where have you been?"

Rodney knelt down beside the naquadah generator. "I was in the rest room."

"Well, that is obviously so important," Radek retorted, doing his best to needle Rodney and thereby keep his attention. "While I was being pursued by Wraith, you have been loafing around." He caught T.J.'s eye over Rodney's head, a gesture he hoped conveyed everything he could not say in front of Rodney. "Thank you for the assistance. It is greatly appreciated."

"Sure thing, doc," Jinto said, edging Lt. Draper back into the hallway, since she was the one most likely to attract Rodney's attention in her science jacket.

T.J. followed, meeting his eyes and nodding as formally as Teyla. Everything Radek wanted to ask him must remain unsaid, every question that begged for attention. He would never know — no, yes he would. It would take many years for all of his questions to be answered, but he knew now that they would be. He would survive this siege. And he would have decades to learn Atlantis' secrets.

"I'll see you around," he said with a smile, and put his trust in the future.

OUR AUTHORS

Sabine C. Bauer

Sabine C. Bauer started writing Stargate SG-1 fan fiction in 1999. Her first professional novel, STARGATE SG-1: *Trial By Fire*, was published by Fandemonium in 2004. Since then she has written a second SG-1 novel, STARGATE SG-1: *Survival of the Fittest*, took a field trip into the Atlantis universe with STARGATE ATLANTIS: *Mirror Mirror*, and most recently published the SG-1/Atlantis crossover STARGATE SG-1: *Transitions*. She also edited several novels for Fandemonium and other publishers and wrote a number of short stories, including of course 'When On Earth'. She lives on the Canadian west coast and works as a writer, translator and editor.

Diana Dru Botsford

Diana Dru Botsford writes for television, novels, web series, the stage, and graphic novels. Author of the Stargate novels STARGATE SG-1: *The Drift* and STARGATE SG-1: *Four Dragons*, she also created and executive produced the award-winning science fiction web series, "Epilogue." Her television credits include "Rascals" for *Star Trek: The Next Generation*. Botsford has crossed the globe from Japan to Africa to Antarctica — always in pursuit of great stories. Find out more at dianabotsford.com

Geonn Cannon

Geonn Cannon is the author of over twenty novels, including STARGATE SG-1: *Two Roads*, as well as numerous short stories which can be found for free at his website (geonncannon.com). The first time he traveled out of his home state was to attend the 2004 Stargate convention in Vancouver. He lives in Oklahoma.

Keith R.A. DeCandido

Keith R.A. DeCandido is the author of a metric buttload of fiction. A large percentage of it is in various licensed universes, though he's got plenty in worlds of his own making as well. His recent work includes the *Star Trek* coffee-table book *The Klingon Art of War*; the *Sleepy Hollow* novel *Children of the Revolution*, based on the TV series; the *Farscape* comics trade paperback *The War for the Uncharted Territories*; the *Firefly: Echoes of War* role-playing game module "Merciless"; the novel *Mermaid Precinct*, the latest in his high fantasy/police procedural series of novels and short stories; the short-story collections *Ragnarok and Roll: Tales of Cassie Zukav, Weirdness Magnet* and *Without a License: The Fantastic Worlds of Keith R.A. DeCandido*; and short fiction in the anthologies *V-Wars* Volumes 1 and 3, *Bad-Ass Faeries: It's Elemental, Tales from the House Band* Volumes 1 and 2, *Out of Tune, Defending the Future: Best Laid Plans*, and an upcoming *X-Files* anthology. In addition to fiction writing, Keith is a freelance editor, a contributor to Tor.com, a second-degree black belt in karate, a prolific podcaster (most notably *The Chronic Rift* and his own monthly 'cast *Dead Kitchen Radio*), and probably some other things he's forgotten due to the lack of sleep. Find out less at his web site at <u>DeCandido.net</u>, which links to his entire online footprint, thus simplifying the tasks of cyberstalkers everywhere.

Peter J. Evans

Peter J Evans was born in southern England and has been there ever since, although not entirely by choice. He wrote his first novel in 1999, and since then has completed nine more that the world knows about, including STARGATE SG-1: *Oceans of Dust* and STARGATE ATLANTIS: *Angelus*, plus an undisclosed number that must never be seen or mentioned again. During daylight hours Evans does something terribly complicated involving navigational radar, while at night he listens to Japanese pop songs and writes horror stories. He has heard of sleep, but only as an abstract concept.

Jo Graham

Jo Graham is one of the authors of the STARGATE ATLANTIS: *Legacy* series, as well as STARGATE ATLANTIS: *Death Game* and STARGATE SG-1: *Moebius Squared*. With Melissa Scott, she is the author of the historical fantasy series *The Order of the Air*, a team adventure set in the 1930s. She is also the author of seven other fantasy and science fiction novels. She lives in North Carolina with her partner and their daughter.

Amy Griswold

Amy Griswold is the author of STARGATE SG-1: *Heart's Desire* and the co-author of STARGATE ATLANTIS *Legacy* series novels *The Lost*, *Allegiance*, *Inheritors*, and *Unascended*. She has also written two gaslamp fantasy/mystery novels with Melissa Scott, *Death by Silver* and *A Death at the Dionysus Club* (Lethe Press). Find her online at amygriswold.livejournal.com or follow her on Twitter at @amygris.

Sally Malcolm

Sally Malcolm has written prolifically within the Stargate universe, penning novels, short stories, audio dramas, and video game scripts. Her Stargate novels include STARGATE SG-1: *A Matter of Honor*, STARGATE SG-1: *The Cost of Honor*, STARGATE ATLANTIS: *Rising* (novelization), and STARGATE SG-1: *Sunrise* (writing with Laura Harper, as J.F. Crane). Sally and Laura's most recent title, STARGATE SG-1: *Hostile Ground*, was published in August 2014 and is the first in the STARGATE SG-1: *Apocalypse* trilogy. They are currently working on book two, due for publication in summer 2015. Follow her on twitter @Sally_Malcolm.

Melissa Scott

Melissa Scott was born and raised in Little Rock, Arkansas, and studied history at Harvard College. She earned her PhD from Brandeis University in the comparative history program with a dissertation titled "The Victory of the Ancients: Tactics, Technology, and the Use of Classical Precedent." She also sold her first novel, *The Game Beyond*, and quickly became a part-time graduate student and an — almost — full-time writer.

Over the next twenty-nine years, she published more than thirty novels and a handful of short stories, most with queer themes and characters. She won the John W. Campbell Award for Best New Writer in 1986, and won Lambda Literary Awards for *Trouble and Her Friends*, *Shadow Man*, *Point of Dreams* (written with her late partner and collaborator, Lisa A. Barnett), and for *Death By Silver*, written with Amy Griswold. She has also been shortlisted for the Tiptree Award. She won a Spectrum Award for *Shadow Man* and again in 2010 for the short story "The Rocky Side of the Sky". Her short story, "Finders," has been selected for Year's Best SF 2013. Her latest novels are *Silver Bullet*, written with Jo Graham, the third volume of *The Order of the Air*, and *Fairs' Point*, the third full-length Points novel. Scott can be found on LiveJournal at <u>mescott.livejournal.com</u> and on Twitter as @blueterraplane.

Her Stargate books are STARGATE SG-1: *Moebius Squared* (with Jo Graham) and STARGATE SG-1: *Ouroboros* and she is co-author with Jo Graham and Amy Griswold of the STARGATE ATLANTIS Legacy series.

Suzanne Wood

In the leafy greenness of the world's most livable city, Melbourne, Australia, Suzanne lives and works surrounded by books. Author of STARGATE SG-1: *The Barque of Heaven* and the first official short story crossover between STARGATE SG-1 and STARGATE ATLANTIS for the *Official Stargate Magazine*, she is currently undertaking a Diploma of Professional Writing and Editing while working on two new original novels. She has long-standing interests in Egyptology, ballet and watching Aussie pro cyclists, a new-found passion for family and Australian history, and occasionally rescues stray dogs. Her website is <u>www.suzannewood.net</u>.